PRAGUE

ARTHUR PHILLIPS

 RANDOM HOUSE NEW YORK

PRAGUE

A NOVEL

Copyright © 2002 by Arthur Phillips

All rights reserved under International and Pan-American Copyright Conventions. Published in the United States by Random House, Inc., New York, and simultaneously in Canada by Random House of Canada Limited, Toronto.

RANDOM HOUSE and colophon are registered trademarks of Random House, Inc.

Library of Congress Cataloging-in-Publication Data
Phillips, Arthur.
Prague : a novel / Arthur Phillips.
p.   cm.
ISBN 0-375-50787-6
1. Budapest (Hungary)—Fiction. 2. Americans—Hungary—
Budapest—Fiction. 3. Young adults—Fiction. I. Title.
PS3616.H45 P73   2002
813'.6—dc21   2001048975

Random House website address: www.atrandom.com

Printed in the United States of America on acid-free paper

9 8 7 6 5 4 3 2

Book design by Barbara M. Bachman

for Jan, of course

The age of arms and épopées is past. . . . We are in for a practical era, you will see: money, brains, business, trade, prosperity. . . . Perpetual peace is on the cards at last. Quite a refreshing idea—nothing whatever against it.

—**THOMAS MANN**, *Lotte in Weimar: The Beloved Returns*

CONTENTS

FIRST
IMPRESSIONS

PART ONE

THE DECEPTIVELY SIMPLE RULES OF THE GAME SINCERITY, AS played late one Friday afternoon in May 1990 on the terrace of the Café Gerbeaud in Budapest, Hungary:

1. Players (in this case, five) arrange themselves around a small café table and impatiently await their order, haphazardly recorded by a sulky and distracted waitress with amusing boots: dollhouse cups of espresso, dense blocks of cake glazed with Art Nouveau swirls of translucent caramel, skimpy sandwiches dusted red-orange with the national spice, glass thimbles of sweet or bitter or smoky liqueurs, tumblers of bubbling water ostensibly hunted and captured from virgin springs high in the Carpathian Mountains.

2. Proceeding circularly, players make apparently sincere statements, one statement per turn. Verifiable statements of fact are inadmissible. Play pro-

ceeds accordingly for four rounds. In this case, the game would therefore con-
sist of twenty apparently sincere statements. Interrupting competition with
discursive or disruptive conversation, or auxiliary lies, is permitted and praise-
worthy.

3.   Of the four statements a player makes during the course of the game,
only one is permitted to be "true" or "sincere." The other three are "lies." Players closely guard the identity of their true statements, the ability to simulate
embarrassment, confusion, anger, shock, or pain being highly prized.

4.   Players attempt to identify which of their opponents' statements were
true. Player A guesses which statements of players B, C, D, and E were true.
Player B then does the same for players A, C, D, and E, et cetera. A scoring grid
is made on a crumb-dusted cocktail napkin with a monogrammed (CMG) fountain pen.

5.   Players reveal their sincere statements. A player receives one point for
each of his or her lies accepted by an opponent as true and one point for each
identification of an opponent's true statement. In today's game of five people, a
perfect score would be eight: four for leading each poor sap by the nose and four
more for seeing through their feeble, transparent efforts at deception.

II.

SINCERITY—A STAPLE AMONG CERTAIN CIRCLES OF YOUNG FOREIGNERS
living in Budapest immediately following 1989–90's hissing, flapping deflation
of Communism—is coincidentally the much-admired invention of one of the
five players in this very match, this very afternoon in May. Charles Gábor, when
with people his own age, seems always to be the host, and at this small café
table on this sunny patio he reigns confidently and serenely. He resembles
an Art Deco picture of a 1920s dandy: long fingers, measured movements,
smooth and gleaming panels of black hair, an audaciously collegiate tie, crisp
pleated slacks of a favorite cotton twill, a humorously pointed nose, a sly half-
smile, one eyebrow engineered for expressivity. Under the green and interlacing
trees surrounding the terrace and nodding over the heads of tourists, resident
foreigners, and the occasional Hungarian, Charles Gábor sits with four other
Westerners, an unlikely group pieced together these past few weeks from parties and family references, friend-of-friend-of-friend happenstance, and (in one
case, just now being introduced) sheer, scarcely tolerable intrusiveness—five

people who, in normal life back home, would have been satisfied never to have known one another.

Five young expatriates hunch around an undersized café table: a moment of total insignificance, and not without a powerful whiff of cliché.

Unless you were one of them. Then this meaningless, overdrawn moment may (then or later) seem to be somehow the summation of both an era and your own youth, your undeniably defining afternoon (though you can hardly say that aloud without making a joke of it). Somehow this one game of Sincerity becomes the distilled recollection of a much longer series of events. It persistently rises to the surface of your memory—that afternoon when you fell in love with a person or a place or a mood, when you savored the power of fooling everyone, when you discovered some great truth about the world, when (like a baby duck glimpsing your quacking mother's waddling rear for the first time) an indelible brand was seared into your heart, which is, of course, a finite space with limited room for searing.

Despite its insignificance, there was this moment, this hour or two, this spring afternoon blurring into evening on a café patio in a Central European capital in the opening weeks of its post-Communist era. The glasses of liqueur. The diamond dapples of light between oval, leaf-shaped shadows, like optical illusions. The trellised curve of the cast-iron fence separating the patio from its surrounding city square. The uncomfortable chair. Someday this too will represent someone's receding, cruelly unattainable golden age.

To Charles Gábor's right sits Mark Payton, who will eventually think of this very moment as one of the glowing, unequaled triumphs of his life. Retrospection will polish from this ambiguous, complicated afternoon all its rough edges, until Mark will be able to see nearly to its crystalline center, to its discernible seedpod of future events, to the (extremely unlikely) refraction of himself as a young and happy man, sniffing love and welcome in the spring air.

He sits at peace, a state he is lately finding harder and harder to achieve. When these five met at the Gerbeaud this afternoon, before Charles pulled out Emily Oliver's chair for her, Mark was already discreetly securing the seat he wanted, as he always does at the half-dozen places he's come to love in his two months in Budapest. He knows that his view, and with it his afternoon, perhaps even several days, would have been damaged if his secret wishes had been thwarted by a misseating of even forty-five degrees.

Safely placed, he can turn his head to the left and see the Café Gerbeaud itself, into its antique interior, into the very past: pastry cases, walls of mirrors and dark wood panels, red velvet seat cushions on gold-painted chairs. In daylight, the cushions are threadbare and the paint flakes, but Mark Payton doesn't mind. A reupholsterer would steal a certain something in exchange for his handiwork. Atmospheric decay and faded glory reassure Mark, prove something. Much of Budapest—unpainted, uncleaned, unrepaired during forty-five years of Communist rule immediately following a brutal war—provides similar pleasures. For now.

Straight ahead and past his friends, Mark's New World eye is treated to the grand, intentionally overwhelming European architecture of the nineteenth century (though it has long since lost the ability to overwhelm its native audience). For years Mark has longed to stare at such architecture, to inhale it, ingest it somehow. Unfortunately, he cannot forget that down Harmincad utca to the left, a Kempinski Hotel is slated to inflict its glass-and-steel corporate modernity on the odd, neglected asymmetry of neighboring Deák Square. But at least he can't see the site's unspeakable stretch marks and scars from where he sits.

Just to the right of tiny (hardly mappable) Harmincad utca stands an office building in his beloved typical-nineteenth-century Haussmann style, the sort of giant mansard-roofed beauty sprinkled all over Pest and Paris, Madrid and Milan. That its ground-floor, window-front space is occupied by the dusty and only sporadically open sales office of a second-string airline does not offend Mark's aesthetics, because the décor of the office, plainly visible from his seat, is so absurdly 1960s East Bloc, so unintentionally and yet bittersweetly hilarious, that it evokes a golden age all its own: a sun-faded epoch of boxy-suited apparatchiks and black-and-white Ivy League diplomats in round metal glasses, of stewardesses in pillbox hats, of Bulgarian assassins and Oxbridge traitors, of this amusingly foreign and irrelevant airline acquiring such prime real estate due to ideological compatibility rather than free-market wherewithal.

That office building defines most of the east side, and the Gerbeaud the entirety of the north side, of Vörösmarty Square, the touristic (if not geographic) center of Budapest: artists and easels scattered around the towering bronze perch of Vörösmarty, a poet Mark intends to research eventually, if he can find translations. And the plaza's southern side: nineteenth-century buildings parting to reveal Váci utca, a pedestrian shopping street, curving away and out of sight. From its mouth echoes the anachoristic sound of an Andean band, piping and thumping love songs of the Bolivian highlands. The musicians serve a welcome purpose for Mark: The throbbing serape-clad romantics screen the unsightly view of a blocks-long line of Hungarians, some in finery for the occasion, eager to sample Hungary's first McDonald's.

Of course, the rest of the group has not been spared the square's west side, from which Mark has protected himself. But even with his back to it, he can sense the building jeering at him, the concrete slabs and offensive edges of its 1970s façade (too old to be new, too young to claim the aesthetic privileges of antiquity) painfully visible from the Gerbeaud unless one is farsighted enough to claim the westernmost seat under the gentle green branches, next to the graceful ironwork, with the view into the café's dark interior, into the sparkling past.

Fast losing his red hair and fast gaining weight, his pouched and sagging face always looking vaguely exhausted even when his conversation motors hyperactively on matters of history and culture, Mark Payton comes from Canada, where (barring some quasi-French enclaves) it doesn't look like this. He has just emerged from nearly twenty-two years of education. Having acquired his Ph.D. in cultural studies a few months ago, he is now three weeks into a projected eleven-month European trip, researching the book that he intends to be a popularized expansion of his doctoral thesis: a history of nostalgia.

Next to him sits Emily Oliver, a Nebraskan, though she passed her first, mostly forgotten, five years in Washington, D.C. She too has recently arrived, landing in March to serve as the new special assistant to the United States ambassador, a post she secured on her own merits but also with the assistance of peculiar family connections. Answering the noticeably keen inquiries of the newest arrival at the table, she has just described her job as "neat" but also "a little, you know, menial, not that I'd ever complain," complaining being a crime her widowed father punished with tickling (until Emily was seven), pithy aphorism (seven through twelve), and thereafter with stark descriptions of *real* suffering he had witnessed—in Vietnam or in a local thresher accident or in her mother's last weeks. End of complaints.

Emily looks very American; even Americans say so. ("She smells like corn on the cob," Charles Gábor will say, shuddering, when discreetly asked later this evening about her availability.) She wears her light brown hair pulled into a ponytail, entirely revealing what Nebraska society politely termed a square jaw but which in fact is much closer to a broad isosceles triangle hanging parallel to the ground, suspended from her ears. Imposing as it is, she has always laughingly resisted the well-meaning roommates and hairstylists who devise methods to "soften" her features or "accentuate her eyes."

She embodies and publicly extols straightforwardness, a quality her history-battered Hungarian acquaintances find simultaneously charming and a little inexplicable, a flat-earth approach to the world. Embassy elders and their wives cite her listening skills, her aura of certainty and solidity, her similarity to their younger selves, and she cannot argue with any of that, though she wouldn't mind hearing the last comparison a bit less often. Roommates invariably declare her to be just the sweetest, most trustable woman in the world, not the boring girl you'd expect when you first meet her.

Here at the Gerbeaud this afternoon, as on most days, she wears khakis, white oxford shirt, blue blazer, standard dress for young nondiplomatic employees of the U.S. embassy, but also the unmistakable tribal costume of the world's interns and first-year assistants. Emily appears to be one of those, too, despite her up-beatitude, one of those about to face the disillusionment of boring jobs with glamorous titles, soon to retreat into the warm embrace of another, more marketable degree and a little more time to think.

To her right sits a young man who recently asserted quarter seriously that he will return to school only "when they institute a master's degree in living for the moment." Scott Price's declaration testifies to a diet of self-help books, brief and impassioned love affairs with Eastern philosophies, and a cyclical practice of wading in and out of various regimes of psychotherapy, accredited and otherwise. Scott's repeated requests, however, each sharper than the last, that Charles ask the elusive waitress whether the Carpathian mineral water contains any sodium, and his evident frustration at Charles's unwillingness to comply or even take the question seriously, belie Scott's recent public claim to "have achieved a new, better relationship with anger."

Seven months ago Scott swayed very close to a heaving stage-front amplifier in a Seattle nightclub, and he bathed in a long-overdue and honey-sweet epiphany. "Look at Me, I'm Above It All"—an early hit during Seattle's dominance of American pop—roared over and through him, and though he knew the song's title was meant ironically, he chose not to take it that way; from that moment, he would be above strife, out of reach of another recently fumbled relationship, yet another unhappy work situation, and, most of all, his family's long-distance constrictions and chills and cruelties. He knew he would not return the next day to the small athletic woman who had been guiding his failed six-week effort to tweeze out and incinerate any repressed memories of his parents doing something even more sinister than what he could naturally recall. He stood between the amp and the crowd, and the sound peeled from him years of resentment, which he knew he would never need again.

He left the U.S. a week later, not informing his family in Los Angeles, punctuating nearly two years during which contact with his parents and his brother was already infrequent. He surfaced, breathing easily, in Budapest. There he put his college degree to use as Assistant Head of Programs at the Institute for the Study of Foreign Tongues, a privately held chain of schools—first Prague, then Budapest, Warsaw, Sofia, plans afoot for Bucharest, Moscow, Tirana— hawking that most valuable commodity: English.

It is not only at that school or at this table that Scott's ash-blond hair, nearly Scandinavian features, svelte muscularity (tank top), and patently Californian health stand out. In any corner of Budapest he looks positively exotic, an obvious foreigner even before he confidently mispronounces one of his few words of Hungarian, or, in slow, pedagogic English, pesters underpaid waiters in state-owned restaurants that haven't changed their pork-predominant menu offerings since the birth of Stalin to make him something vegetarian. Not so different after all, Scott has joked, from his L.A. childhood spent among three foreigners claiming to be his parents and younger brother. (Though Scott neglects to mention that he was then the tremendously—cartoonishly—obese blond Jew in a family of more traditional models: short, slim, curly-haired, olive-skinned.)

After four months in Hungary, Scott blundered into his predictable but somehow always surprising moment of sentimental weakness. Late one night, bothered that his mother might suffer even more regret than he would wish for her, he sent to California a postcard with a picture of Castle Hill in Buda and the text *Am here for a while teaching. Hope you are all okay. S.* He regretted it as soon as the card schussed into the little red mailbox, but he consoled himself that he had given no address, and surely even *they* would be able to read between the lines. His carefully constructed world was still safe.

Except that two months later, to Scott's right sits today's fifth competitor, his newly arrived and disproportionately loathed younger brother, John.

ROUND ONE

"WELL, LET'S SEE WHAT'S WHAT THEN," SAID THE INVENTOR AND UNDIS-
puted master of Sincerity. John Price watched Charles stretch his arms around
the back of his chair, lace his fingers together, and lean back slightly to permit
the lowering sun to touch his face. A symbolic opening of the game, John
noted, as if Gábor were holding himself up to the light, an illustration of candor. And yet, it was an *intentionally* symbolic action. Indeed, John thought he
could see that Charles liked the idea of his competitors/friends noticing the symbolism but then being smart enough to reject it as not only a mere symbol but
also an *inaccurate* one, a silent trick, since he surely did *not* believe that turning
his face to the sun demonstrated any *actual* candor. And, John thought further,
perhaps this was a small compliment as well, since Charles trusted that you
were clever enough *not* to take the gesture at face value but to know that the act
of intentionally symbolically revealing himself was meant to show that he was
not revealing himself. Alternately, Charles might have been stretching.

Charles changed directions, leaned into the cluttered table, placed an
elbow on its marble. He looked sideways at Mark and his brown eyes relaxed
into a misty warmth. "To be perfectly honest, Mark," Charles said, "I sometimes envy your passion for your research." His gaze rested on Payton a few seconds longer, the desire to say more wrestling with the regret of having said so
much. A wistful half-smile pulled up one side of his elegant mouth. His eyebrows climbed one carefully calibrated step toward the stark-white parting of
his jet-black hair. "Your turn, Mark."

John had only been in Budapest two days, sleeping on his brother's floor,
meandering alone through the city with a new and already out-of-date map,
occasionally being introduced halfheartedly to Scott's friends. John had only
just met this group, but even he suspected that Charles had no envy of Mark's
research. Gábor had essentially just told the Canadian that he had zero interest
in his life's work, had just allowed himself the luxury of saying the obvious: To
a venture capitalist, Mark's scholarly, slobbery obsessions with the past were
laughable. And Mark had even begun to laugh.

Mark grew distracted by a waitress passing close to the table. Scott reminded him, "It's your turn. We're going counterclockwise." And Mark made a small gesture of having his attention brought back to the game despite himself, a little play of candor that struck John as amateurish compared to the maestro's opening.

"You know," Mark said in a Canadian-accented singsong, apparently somewhat surprised to hear himself admit it, "I'm actually beginning to warm up to those boots," referring to the knee-high open-toe lace-up white-vinyl go-go boots that graced the feet of all Gerbeaud waitresses, women from eighteen to sixty-five, who were also condemned to yellow miniskirts and white lace aprons. All five of the Westerners were baffled that people a few months into post-Communism wouldn't pull down their mandatory go-go boots with the same liberating fervor they had demonstrated in pulling down their tyrannical government. In any event, even the dullest novice to the game would have realized that a man writing a popular history of nostalgia, who had seen cheerleaders and style-free Canadians wearing boots just like that all his life, was probably not going to "warm up" to the look in this context.

And yet there was Emily Oliver wagging her head back and forth, trying to decide whether to believe him. She trapped her bottom lip between her teeth and was examining Mark with visible mental energy, even said, "Hmmm." Finally, she seemed to realize (quite transparently) that she was being quite transparent, and she went to some effort to compose her features. Everyone watched this transformation, and they all smiled with her in their communal struggle not to laugh.

"You are a master of deception, my girl."

"Stop it, you! You came up with this weirdo game, so excuse me if I need a little practice. Normal people were raised to tell the truth, you know." She set her jaw, inhaled, and prepared herself to lie.

And John Price fell in love, five-fifteen one Friday evening in May 1990.

Emily cocked one eyebrow in an unwitting parody of conspiracy and confessed, "I struggle with serious depression all the time. I mean, very dark periods, where I feel totally hopeless."

After a momentary hush, frank hilarity burst from Mark and Scott. Even Charles smiled broadly, though he tried to show the game more respect. Emily herself was forced to look at her lap. "I'll get the hang of this," she said. "You watch."

John, however, was not laughing. He was watching his life unfold at last. He was watching a woman incapable of lying, and he told himself this was one of life's rare treasures. He saw that Emily—as her lie revealed—had never known neurotic depression and therefore lived close to the surface of life, found the soggy and eternally multiplying layers of self-consciousness and identity an easy burden to strip away. He felt a strange contraction of the muscles around his eyes, and he scraped his lower teeth against his upper lip.

John did not savor the moment for long as, with a winning smile, Scott took his turn: "I'm really glad John tracked me down here in Budapest." Emily nodded happily at the warm fraternal sentiment. Mark and Charles looked at their hands. "Really. Like a dream come true."

A gloomy waitress passed tantalizingly close to the table, and John made a hopeful wave and managed to snag her flickering attention, but he spoke not a word of Hungarian. Scott, having spent five and a half months teaching English, spoke almost as little. Mark had been submitting to private Hungarian lessons for a month, to no avail. Emily admitted that she was only able to sound out written words and carry on excruciatingly simple conversations, thanks to her daily classes at the embassy, so John turned for help to Charles Gábor, the bilingual son of Hungarians who had fled to the U.S. in 1956.

"*Ő kér egy rumkólát,*" Gábor said to the stone-faced waitress. Unresponsive, she walked off.

"Jesus. What did you say to her?"

"Nothing." Gábor shrugged. "I said you wanted another rum-and-Coke."

"Well, she looks pissed off," John said with a sigh. "It's probably because I'm so obviously a Jew."

While physically his self-assessment was undeniably true, his grim assessment of anti-Semitism in Hungarian waitresses killed the mood at the table. His blond, blue-eyed, pug-nosed brother grudgingly consoled him, "No, waiters and waitresses here are all like that. They do it to me, too."

"Well, one way or the other, that's my turn," said John, and Gábor let out a small and condescending whistle of appreciation at an excellent play, for a beginner.

Sincerity seemed to have sprung fully formed from Charles Gábor's head, and among the younger Americans, Canadians, and Britons first trickling then flooding into Budapest in 1989–90, the game's popularity was one of the few common interests of an otherwise unlikely society. Charles had explained the rules in October '89, the very evening of his arrival in the city his parents had always told him was his real home. He played it late that jet-lagged night with a group of Americans in a bar near the University of Budapest, and the game spread throughout the anglophones "like a mild but incurable social disease," in Scott's words. The virus left the sticky table and was carried to English-as-a-Second-Language-school faculties, folk and jazz bandmates, law-firm junior partners. It was laughingly explained and daily played by embassy interns and backpacking tourists, artists and poets and screenwriters and other new (and often well-endowed) bohemians, and by the young Hungarians who befriended these invaders, voyeurs, naïfs, social refugees. Each day, Sincerity proliferated as Budapest began squeaking with new people eager to see History in the making or to cash in on a market in turmoil or to draw artistic inspiration from the untapped source of a Cold War–torn city or merely to enjoy a rare and fleeting conjunction of place and era when being American, British, Canadian could be exotic, though one sensed such a potent license would expire far too soon.

ROUND TWO

CHARLES LOOKED STERNLY AT JOHN WITH AN EXPRESSION MEANT TO CON-vey a sense of "you're not going to like this, but I have to speak the truth" and said, "There will come a point, after this initial post-Communist exuberance wears off, when the Hungarians will realize that you can have too much democracy. They'll realize they need a slightly stronger hand at the helm, and they'll make the right choice: a strong Hungary with a real national-corporatist philosophy." He paused, gazed hard at John and Scott, and concluded, "Like they had in the early forties."

Mark: "As my dad always said, one's pain should always be held in perspective. There is always someone worse off than yourself. That's a perennial comfort."

Emily: "The world contains more nice people than mean people. I really believe that." John could see she plainly did believe that, and he knew that this basic faith, rare and extraordinary, was precisely what he lacked and needed in order to live a full and important life. He also loved that the duress of telling two lies right off the bat had been too much for Emily, and now she faced the daunting prospect of producing two in a row to finish.

Scott, not really up for the game at its highest levels, turned to bland possibilities: "I like Pest better than Buda." He lived and worked in the Buda hills, across the Danube from Pest's flat urban rings and grids.

"Boring," muttered Gábor. "Beneath the dignity of the game. You suck."

"Fuck you, fucker," riposted the English teacher.

John (whose rum-and-cola had since arrived, placed for no good reason in front of Mark by a similarly sullen but altogether different waitress): "Fifteen years from now people will talk about all the amazing American artists and thinkers who lived in Prague in the 1990s. That's where real life is going on right now, not here." He reached across the table to gather his drink but knocked Gábor's liqueur onto Scott's lap. Scott jumped, accepted Emily's speedy offer of a napkin, and applied fizzing, high-sodium Carpathian water to the brown herbal goop spreading over the crotch of his running shorts.

"Blot, don't rub," advised Emily with real concern.

ROUND THREE

"I HAVE TO ADMIT," GÁBOR SAID SLOWLY WHEN SCOTT WAS SEATED AGAIN, "I was briefly jealous just there when Emily took such an interest in you, Scott." Charles raised his eyes to her, then looked away, letting his breath stream out in a flutter of the lips before adding, "And the matter of blotting your shorts," as if the smutty coda to his comment might disguise its embarrassing inner truth.

John stopped breathing, stunned at the sudden barriers to the life plan he had been formulating for the last half an hour. Forced to admit that there was personal history at the table of which he was unaware, he finally consoled himself with the likelihood (75 percent) that Charles had been lying. On the other hand, he recalled that while explaining the rules, Charles had cited "one of the game's most beautiful aspects: Players sometimes don't know themselves precisely how much truth they're telling."

"You're a bad person, aren't you, Charlie?" Emily wagged a finger.

Charles looked away, hoping to disguise something he had revealed, or to reveal something he only wanted to appear to disguise, and so he tricked another waitress into coming to the table, and before she was able to realize the trap, she found herself taking orders for replacement drinks and food. "Poor woman," he said as she wound her sour way back into the café. "She'll never survive the new economy. This whole country needs its ass kicked."

"You can't take two turns, Charles."

"No, I know. That was just my opinion."

Mark was nodding. "I guarantee there was never sullen service in this café when it was founded. You're up, Em."

"Oh, jeez. Do we have to go on with this? This isn't the way normal people should spend their time. Okay, okay, gimme a sec. . . . I think I could live in Hungary forever. I don't ever want to move back to the States."

John smiled at the idea of this most American of girls slowing and settling into a Central European permanence, raising her Hungarian children to be the first trusting and cheerful nonsmokers in the nation's history.

Scott's third-round offering: "English is harder than Hungarian."

And John's: "Scott is our parents' favorite."

One could always feel the same sense of malaise creep over games of Sincerity near round four, a peculiar discomfort just out of range of consciousness, a wave of sleepiness or spaciness. Nongame conversation would proliferate, but also grow testy, as players were commonly exerting a great deal of energy trying to remember what they had already said and what of that had been ostensibly true. That evening in May, it looked as if only Charles Gábor and, perhaps, Emily had not lost their sparkle. As it edged toward six o'clock, everyone but Scott, an avid nutritionist, had consumed too much sugar, caffeine, or alcohol. Scott was leaning back in his wrought-iron chair to stare at the softening sky filtered through overhanging branches. John was feeling that dull disappointment and heaviness in the legs of stepping up onto an immobile escalator. Mark had gotten drunk off Unicum, the rough herbal liqueur beloved of the Hungarian nation, and, as he tended to grow maudlin under the influence, was massaging a tendril of red hair and gazing at the dusty airline office with a wistful pucker of the lips and a sorrowful tilt of his brow.

ROUND FOUR

CHARLES SWIRLED AN ESPRESSO BETWEEN THUMB AND MIDDLE FINGER, peered for inspiration at the brown arcs he made on the white cup's inside surface. "I think raising children is probably the single highest-return investment on offer, to reap the profit of self-awareness and self-expression, that would be the essence of existence."

"I suppose it's not entirely out of the question there are MBAs who believe that," Mark said. Wasting a turn but enjoying himself greatly, he added, "Financial jobs are profoundly creative and are vitally important to the well-being of culture and human happiness. Particularly venture capital."

Emily: "Dishonesty comes so easily to me that it sometimes worries me."

Scott Price: "I was adopted. Or John was."

"That's better, Scottie," Charles said. "Though technically a verifiable statement of fact. We'll let it stand for amusement's sake."

John offered, "I can certainly see why everyone here are such good friends."

"*Is* such good friends," corrected the English teacher, leaning back with closed eyes, his two swaying chair legs a tempting target.

Over a round of Unicums, the players revealed their truths and tallied the score. Charles Gábor scored a very solid seven out of eight, though he was visibly disgusted at his poor showing. Each of his first three statements was picked as true by a competitor: Emily believed he envied Mark's research, Mark believed he envied Emily's attentions to Scott, and John believed (and not without an edge to his voice) his endorsement of a refreshed fascist Hungary. But it was his fourth statement—the glories of child rearing couched in financial terminology—that he declared to be sincere. Scott, having suspected that Charles would at least *claim* its sincerity, scored a hit.

Charles also received four points for correctly identifying truth in each of the others. Mark was certain that moody service was an invention of the late twentieth century. Emily did indeed believe that the world's nice people outnumbered its nasty ones. Charles knew that Scott, despite not yet having learned Hungarian, did not believe it to be as difficult as his native tongue. And John, in his two days in Budapest, had already pegged the city as being less epochally and culturally promising than Prague, where he had spent sixteen formative hours on his way into town.

Scott pulled off a six. He received Emily's vote that he must be happy to have John in Budapest, a vote which so tickled John that he did not brood for long over the implications of the original lie. Scott also won two votes in favor of his provocative adoption play. Yes, two: Even John thought it fit too many observable facts not to be true, and would perhaps explain his inability to jump-start a permanent adult relationship with his elder brother. Scott also easily identified John's Prague envy and Emily's chipper worldview but stumbled with Mark, believing his drivel about keeping one's pain in perspective.

Mark placed third, with a very respectable four: He called Emily's truth and culled three points for his boot-strappy theory of pain. "My dad is just the same," Emily had consoled him. "Actually, no," Mark admitted. "My dad began complaining about his life back in about 1973 and hasn't yet stopped." However, Mark voted for John's anti-Semitic waitress ploy and Scott's adoption.

John, therefore, scored a three. Emily, telling him not to feel bad about it, said that it's hard to be the favorite child, too, sometimes even harder. ("To be honest," John replied, "ours is a scientifically unique family in that neither child is the favorite.") He in turn spotted Emily's faith in mankind, not without a quiet intake of breath and happy recognition of fate's turning wheels.

Special Assistant Emily Oliver, displaying a congenital inability to lie or sense dishonesty, therefore scored zero. She sipped her second Unicum, unconsciously grimacing after every taste. Her cheeks began to flush in the cool evening air and from the hot tickle of the herbal liqueur. "This game is sick, Charlie."

Of course, the game is fundamentally flawed. One never actually knows if players tell the truth at the end, or if they even know the truth ("one of the game's most beautiful aspects").

IV.

JOHN PRICE'S DECISION TO EMIGRATE FROM LOS ANGELES TO HUNGARY had required eight minutes. He reread his big brother's postcard and sensed their time had finally come. He recalled a newspaper article praising Hungary's nascent "potential." He savored his approaching resignation from the Committee to Bring the 2008 Olympics to L.A., for which he had been mistyping press releases and making Xerox copies of his butt.

He admitted that Scott would be of two minds, at most, about their reunion. He had tracked Scott down before to solder an essential brotherly bond, appearing hopeful and eager at his college dorms twice. And at Scott's first tiny apartment in San Francisco. On the fishing boat just before Scott set off for Alaska. Again in Portland. And Seattle. And each time, Scott ironically, even amusingly, rebuffed him, deflated him (even as Scott had begun his own steady physical deflation).

Scott had persistently believed, to John's repeated amazement, that their tritely unpleasant childhood had mattered, that it somehow mattered still, and, most of all—never spoken but quite clear—that John himself was not a victim of their family (as Scott was) but one of the oppressive ruling junta itself, a belief John could neither dislodge nor comprehend. After each defeated, angry return to L.A., some months were necessary before John would convince himself again that this time would be different, that enough healing had occurred for a fraternal future to begin.

And now Budapest. After so many false starts, the two brothers would shed everything old and ugly and shine upon each other. In that unimaginable city, far from everything familiar, they would dig past the past, burst through to the essential something that would render John whole and strong, untouchable and wise. Old barriers would crumble to reveal manicured gardens.

Wanting to give some—but not too much—warning of his arrival, John planned to appear in Budapest about a week after an eloquent and nuanced explanatory letter. He had, however, overestimated post-Communist postal commitment. One Wednesday night, displaying the brittle optimism of the frequently disappointed, he had knocked on Scott's door in Buda and confronted surprise and rage, uneasily battling for dominance. "Huh," Scott managed to say, looking at the matching suitcase and hanging bag floating in the May moonlight. "So where are you staying?" Conversation that night fractured and seeped, no one being in the mood to produce the necessary caulking jokes. Scott made John repeat the story of how he had found his address.

And now, eight days later, left to his own devices for yet another afternoon, John stood on top of his brother's hill and watched the haze distort Pest, then returned to lie on the floor of yet another of Scott's nondescript, barely furnished apartments. He considered retreating home to beg for his old job; still eighteen years until those Olympics. But he also thought of Emily Oliver's laugh, and though he knew he hardly knew her, he admired how (unlike his dismal brother) she hid nothing, faced everything, and approached the world as a place roiling with possibility, as he himself did. She was reason enough to be here. And then Scott's mail slithered through the door and slapped onto the floor. John opened his own letter from L.A., read his good intentions and embarrassing, delicately couched hopes. He stuffed it in his luggage.

The phone rang and the voice asked for John, then introduced itself as Zsolt, "of Scott class."

"That's an ambiguous claim."

"Excuse me what?"

Zsolt had news, reported with the sporadic accompaniment of a riffling dictionary: His mother's boyfriend's friend knew an old man with a room down in Pest, on Andrássy út. John hastily consulted his plastic-coated map and traced his finger along one of the broad boulevards through the center of the city. "Scott ask us of his class to keep our ear open for you, because he wants you have a place alone very soon as possible, he say many times, 'Find my brother a home! In Pest!' he say, so I am happy to finded you this flat. The man is an old and is wanting to be with his son and his law-daughter on the countryside." He gave John a phone number and spelled, twice and haltingly, the name Szabó Dezső, explaining for the foreigner that Hungarian family names come first, trivia irrelevant to the goulash of dissonant consonants splashing across John's notebook. "But you must not tell to the city council what he does this, else they will take the place out from him."

"He's subletting a rent-control deal or something?"

"Excuse me what?"

John called Charles Gábor at his office for help, and early that evening—having followed his map to Andrássy, formerly Népköztársaság, formerly Sztálin, formerly Andrássy—the two of them sat on the pullout sofa bed in a very old man's room, sipping pear brandy from paper cups. John complained that Charles's suit would inflate the old man's asking price. Charles, whose venture-capital firm had bought him a lush bungalow in the Buda hills, told him to stop whining.

Dezső Szabó wore a sleeveless T-shirt, baggy checked pants, and plastic flip-flops stamped liberally with the logo of a German sporting goods company. He was extraordinarily thin; his parts fell together and splayed apart like the last few straws in the jar on a hot dog stand. His gray hair stood up, then fell to each side, a field of wheat parting for inspection. He knew two words of English (*New*, *York*) and a smattering of German.

The three men sat, silent as rain filled the air with a staticky buzz. Through the French windows opening onto a balcony, John could see dark branches waving over the wash of Andrássy's white streetlights. The yellow chair under Szabó, a wooden wardrobe, an alcove kitchen, a bedside table with a small green lamp, and a cheap metal cart straining under a new and enormous television with a complex cable hookup completed the furnishings.

Licking brandy from his papery lips, Szabó emitted a few words in the deep monotone of the Hungarian male. Much closed-mouth lip motion ensued, an adjustment of dentures or a savoring of pear brandy that John found unpleasant to watch and hear. Charles responded concisely in the same low voice. The Hungarian continued, brief outbursts on each side. John expected a translation, but none came. His eyes lagged behind the words, back and forth between the two incomprehensible men: Gábor still stiffly creased and pleated and gelled, Szabó a loose and spindly sack of wrinkled flesh, his stiff fingers pinching and scraping at a dry and hairy nose.

"*Igen . . . igen . . . igen . . . jó.*" Charles was nodding, rhythmically repeating "yes" and "good" as Szabó took monologous command. "*Igen. Igen. Jó. Jó. Igen.*" Charles kept his eyes on Szabó but leaned toward John, as if preparing at any moment to interpret. He raised a finger to Szabó, nodding quickly, asking for a pause, but the old man would not or could not (at any rate did not) stop speaking. "*Igen.*" Charles kept trying. "He says he's lived here for thirty-eight years . . . *igen* . . . *jó.* He says . . . *igen* . . . *nem* . . . *igen.*" And finally Charles sat up straight again and the old man rumbled on without a break.

After some time, John decided that whatever was being discussed must not pertain to him. The noise droned on behind him, and he opened the French windows to the balcony, three stories above Andrássy út. The rain drowned out the one-sided conversation.

The balcony was a stone square large enough to hold two or three standing people, and even in the rain it provided a wondrous view: Andrássy stretched itself from Deák Square, on the left, toward Heroes' Square, invisible in the distance to the right. The balcony's floor was cracked in a map of meandering rivers, demarcating flakes, and slabs of concrete loose enough to lift. It seemed evident that eventually the balcony would collapse under its own, or someone else's, weight. The building's exterior walls bore decades-old scars and bullet holes. On the building across the street, the new ANDRÁSSY ÚT plaque shone silvery-white above the faded, dust- and rain-streaked NÉPKÖZTÁRSASÁG ÚT plaque, still legible despite the bright red *X* of paint that covered it from corner to corner.

John imagined himself leaning back on a chair on this balcony, his legs crossed and propped up on the rusty curves of its iron rail, the setting sun gilding the city's most cosmopolitan boulevard. He saw a glorious life beginning on this balcony. He saw himself savoring harsh local cigarettes, his first nibbling notion that he was going to take up smoking. He was engaged in some professional exploit—the nature of which was hazy—that would win him tastefully lavish renown. In his new home, the center of concentric, electric social circles, he would wittily, intriguingly host artists, society figures, spies, stage actors, statesmen, the dissipated scions of ancient or fraudulent noble families, and Emily Oliver. She would stay after the other guests had left. "Come out to the balcony," he would say. "Come in from the balcony," she would say.

"He wants to know if you'll pay in dollars or pengő." Charles leaned against the wall just inside the French doors.

"Pengő?" John stepped inside. "Which are . . . ?"

"Hungarian currency before the forint, until about 1945, I think." Charles smiled as if at a common question, a natural topic of apartment rental negotiations.

"And I would have pengő why?"

"Excellent point. You seem to have a real head for business." Charles raised his flowered paper cup at the old man, then generously refilled all three drinks. He returned to John. "Okay, first the bad news. Mr. Szabó is looking forward to returning to the countryside with me. He's missed me. Doesn't have many people to talk to anymore. Also, he's very glad you and the army have finally arrived. He always knew the Americans would come to kill the Russians and he thanks you. This puts us in about 1956, I'd say, when the Americans most definitely did not turn up. Let's see, what else . . ." Charles straightened his shirt cuffs. "Oh yes, he *was* a Communist Party member, but he wants you to know that everyone was, and now that the fighting is over, he's looking forward to the Americans installing a democratic government. And he wants to cooperate as much as possible. As you'll be influential in this."

"From this studio apartment."

"Right. The good news is the TV has cable, though mostly German channels and two versions of CNN. He also says the apartment's plumbing is very good and that the sofa bed is pretty new."

Szabó interrupted with another croaking soliloquy. Charles translated: "And some more good news. He has no problem at all with Jews living here."

"That's a great relief," John said. "Can you just get him to think about rent in a current currency?"

After just one more minute of foreign dialogue, Szabó rose, shook John's hand, and embraced Charles warmly, kissing both cheeks several times. "Very good news, John. Your landlord has offered marvelous terms and you've just accepted after haggling only briefly." He named a figure in forints.

"Per week?"

"Of course not. Per month."

"That's ridiculous. That's nothing. Offer him more."

Szabó was refilling the paper cups to seal the contract, but Charles's expression was dissolving quickly toward disgust. "Offer him more? Oh, Christ. Please don't be silly. That's twice what he's paying the city to live here. He's obviously happy with the deal. Don't be condescend—"

"Happy with the deal? He thinks I'm Eisenhower's aide-de-camp."

"That's your competitive advantage," Charles explained with a grueling effort to be patient. "That's not something you just throw away."

"I don't think it's condes—"

The old man spoke, his expression troubled. He looked at Charles but pointed at John.

"*Nem, nem. Nagyon jól van. Nagyon,*" Charles reassured him. "Look happy, John. He's worried he's offended you."

John smiled reflexively, not wishing to be rude. They touched cups and drank.

Szabó collected the empty paper cups and put them in the sink, ran some water over them for his new tenant, and replaced the brandy under the TV cart. He rubbed his hands together and began to recite in a businesslike tone. Charles's simultaneous translation was much improved: John was free to move in the following day, this was how the heat worked, this was how you paid your gas bill, and would the U.S. Army be shooting people against walls? They agreed to a two-year lease, the rent payable every three months to a friend of Szabó's who lived two apartments over, this was how you worked the TV, this was how the bath/shower unit heated up, and if there was any information about Russian or Hungarian prisoners that Szabó could provide, he'd be happy to help. He had never been interested in the Communist Party, but as a worker, he had truly had no choice. This was a good apartment, and he was lucky to have gotten it. It was thanks to the Party that he and his wife had been brought into the city from the countryside, had gotten a factory job and this flat, had been able to raise their son here. He lives near Pécs now with his wife and daughter. It has been a good life in Pest. Andrássy is a good street, this is a good district. This is how to light the stove. The Party seems to be doing a good job. It's hard not to think things are better now that they're in charge. Szabó and his wife moved in just last year, and they hope to have a child soon; Szabó wants a girl, but Magda wants a boy. The Party has been a great help in getting them started. This is the key to the building's front door, this is the key to the apartment door, this is how to get an outside line on the telephone, this is a picture of my wife, Magda, she died in 1988. Here is my son's telephone number in the country. Good luck with everything. Thank you for coming. See you tomorrow at three.

"*Viszontlátásra,*" said the old man.

"*Viszontlátásra,*" said Charles.

John nodded, smiled his mute good wishes, and the Americans left to find dinner.

V.

THE NEXT DAY AT THREE, CHARLES WAS AT WORK, SO MOVING IN WAS A matter primarily of sign language. John felt no trepidation, however, at being alone with the old man, who proudly welcomed Jews: Gábor had admitted the previous evening that he had invented that comment because the negotiations had grown boring. Szabó had in fact been marveling at the opportunities in America, considering that a man of John's age had risen to such power.

John found the old man's son, nearly fifty, helping pack for the move to the countryside. He spoke a few words of English and, to John's relief, seemed pleased at the bargain his mentally incapacitated father had struck. "Good business okay" was his repeated validation of the contract. "Good business okay." He added, "Dezső the name me."

"John. Juan. Jan. Johann. Jean." John produced his name, accelerating, in as many languages as he could muster.

"János." Dezső the younger provided the Hungarian. "János the name you," he said, and tapped John twice on the sternum.

"Exactly. Thank you. János the name me."

John's luggage (college graduation) was quickly installed. He mimed an offer to come back later, after they had corralled the old man's proliferating, scattering belongings, but the son refused. "House yours," he said. He took John's arm and walked him to the yellow chair. "House yours. Rest." For twenty-five minutes John straddled the chair's obtrusive springs, watched the son pack suitcases and cardboard boxes and then haul them down to a waiting car, each time refusing John's wordless offers of help.

And at last the apartment was objectless and lifeless, merely furnished. When the son was downstairs on his final trip, the father stood in front of his starkly empty armoire and simply stared at it. His head rolled slowly to his shoulder, then he lowered himself slowly onto the floor, ending up cross-legged. John too felt the undeniable force of the gaping, emptied closet, its doors flung open in melodramatic pleading. Its emptiness gave the room a different light, even a different smell. Szabó, his back to John, stared up at the open wardrobe, the crack in its wood lightning-bolting down its back panel, the hanger-bar sagging under the mere memory of shirts, coats, dresses.

The old man rose and turned. Hair grew from his ears, and he hadn't shaved that day; whiskers lodged in deep diagonal furrows. He nodded and moved his lips in the way that had seemed so unpleasant the night before but was now somehow different; the action no longer disgusted John. It now seemed to reflect something other than a need to adjust dentures or savor brandy. John imagined words caught behind the lips; he felt certain Szabó was trying or hoping to say something. He stared with an expression John took to be one of longing, but after a moment the old man just went to the sofa and lay down on his stomach, his head tucked under his arm, turned away from the room.

The son found the new subtenant on the balcony, leaning against the rail, facing into the apartment, watching the old man apparently asleep. "Okay, János! Good," the younger Dezső pronounced. He shook John's hand, then re-entered to poke his father in the ribs. The old man mumbled in Hungarian and sat up sluggishly but did not stand. The son spoke briskly, gestured to John and the door, obviously time to go. The father responded angrily: He stared at the floor but now shouted his responses. The tone changed rapidly to an argument, which swelled and darkened into a storm front with a speed that surprised John. He remained leaning backward out over traffic, as far as he could be from the squall without leaving the apartment. He did consider leaving, but that would have required passing right by the raging Magyars on the way to the door, making a show of his departure while they argued, which they might read as an effort to make them feel bad for impinging on the "wealthy" American's time, so he stayed where he was, leaned against the balustrade, stared at the men in uncomprehending embarrassment.

The son raised his arms in exasperation and made the sound of air being let out of a tire. He half turned toward the balcony and yelled, "Okay. 'Bye-bye, János. Phone if needs," and tossed John the keys: a small apartment key and a two-and-a-half-pound skeleton key for the building's converted carriage door. The old man did not move as his son left. John heard the enormous front door of the building open beneath him. Over his railing he saw the man stride to his green Trabant, lean against its hood, and light a cigarette.

Behind John, the old man was up and off the sofa, pulling something off the wardrobe's top shelf. He yelled, *"Amerikai, für Sie,"* and then some Hungarian. John stood on the threshold of the French doors, shrugging the apologetic shrug he had mastered whenever someone insisted on speaking to him in Hungarian. The old man held two framed pictures. After a deliberation, he placed one on top of the cable box and the other on the bedside table next to the lamp. He stretched his arms out to the two pictures, his fingers spread wide and his palms facing the frames, clearly to say: *Leave them like that.* "*Igen? Igen? Ja? Ja?*"

"*Ja. Igen.*"

He shook John's hand without looking at him and left. John retreated from the closing door back to the railing, even more uncomfortable in the empty apartment than during the packing or the fighting. The echo of the front door rose again from the street. The old man shuffled down the sidewalk and folded himself into his son's passenger seat. The Trabant burped and choked, slowly joined the boulevard's traffic. Cartoon clouds of black smoke marked its path from curbside to disappearance.

John examined the decorations he had agreed to maintain. On the cable box, a black-and-white photograph in a size format he had never seen before: a baby, no more than two or three weeks old, in a bundle of blankets, photographed from above, crying, its eyes shut tight, tiny fists flailing. Next to the sofa, again in an odd size and in black and white, a gold-painted wooden frame embracing a young woman in a white dress. No great beauty, no aura of magic or romance. Just a woman standing in front of a tree, her hands behind her back, her dress probably not fashionable at any period or in any country.

VI.

THE PARTY HAD STARTED AT THE GERBEAUD AND THEN ROLLED INTO A restaurant, the Hungarian name of which was slippery now, burrowing slickly under the surface of John's memory as he lay on the still-folded sofa bed.

Emily had sat squeezed between two of Scott's students, at the far splinters of the long wooden table. Hungarian folk musicians careened in and away, so John could rarely hear her, but a visionary director had framed her with Hungarian diners and wandering waiters and posters of caped horsemen and garlands of smoke and the noise of foreign talk and foreign music, and every time he raised his eyes, she had just discovered some never-before-seen and heartbreakingly charming gesture or facial expression. She leaned back laughing, caught him watching her, and waved, the first of many times.

"So what was our Scott like when he was boy?" a student asked John.

"I was six hundred pounds," Scott replied before the same answer could be given seriously, and the crowd laughed at the impossibility. John would have protected him, resented the unnecessary maneuver.

"He was like a god to me," John said, watching Emily. "Like a god of war, unfortunately."

"Right after I was born, I urged my mother to have her tubes tied, but to no avail."

Charles explained to Scott's Hungarians why their country was doomed to eternal poverty, conquest, betrayal, and the students nodded and mashed out their cigarettes and rolled new ones and absolutely agreed, liked Charles for understanding how things really were, despite being American. "Oh come on, *no*," Emily insisted, and John's heart spun on its axis. "Don't you listen to that kind of talk." Hungary had an opportunity it had never had before, a totally new and unique moment in human history. John seconded her, happy to share with her Charles's and the Hungarians' condescension.

There had been a peculiar salad, lettuce tossed with a mixture of unlikely or unrecognizable components, then the ubiquitous paprikás and vineyards of Hungarian wine. Gábor simply kept ordering more. It wasn't bad, and only 118 forints a bottle, somewhere under two dollars, a price John found more and more hilarious as the evening progressed. He discoursed on the uncanny symbolism of Americans taking advantage of post-Communist exchange rates to drink too much Hungarian wine. The significant details of that symbolism, insightful and amusing to his drinking audience, subsequently grew wings and escaped, could not be recaptured. Later, at A Házam, a nightclub, Mark had called John a genius, but it was not clear why.

Now, in his new apartment, as he lay for the first time on the old man's sofa bed, and horns and motors vibrated the air from three stories down, John had no recollection whatsoever of the dance club, could only recall that Emily was with them for a while and then was not. He had a vague notion that Mark had walked him home, had made him take two aspirin and drink an entire glass of water in a single go. John had slept fitfully, spinning a few revolutions on his way in and out of slumber, to which he now returned.

He dreamed of the woman on his bedside table. She stood in front of her tree, and Hungarian folk musicians were visible off in the distance, in an open field. She rocked a bundle of blankets in her arms and smiled at John with infinite tenderness and love. He knew that all was well in his life, knew his life would be happy and satisfying forever now that it was beginning at last, and he walked to her, each step marking an irrevocable commitment and commencement. She inclined her head to the blankets. *"Amerikai. Für sie,"* she said. *"Igen,"* John said. *"Ja."* She handed him the bundle. Carefully cradling it, he parted the blankets at the head, but found he was holding only the photo of the crying baby. He was surprised that he was not greatly surprised. He tickled the chin of the child in the photo and rocked the bundle lovingly, though he wondered if his actions would make the woman love him less or more. He was nervous to look at her lest he discover that all was not still well in his life, but finally he could not put off the moment any longer. He looked up, ready to kiss her, but she had left.

VII.

WHATEVER SAFETY PRECAUTIONS MARK PAYTON HAD TAKEN IN GRADUATE school while clinically investigating the toxins of nostalgia, they had been insufficient.

"Extraordinary creativity in research methodology" was a professor's assessment of Payton's doctoral work. The excitable professor had been referring to Mark's scholarly visits to museum gift shops, art-house and revival movie theaters, travel agencies, postcard and poster manufacturers, the airless and depressing conventions of collectors of sundry valuable and valueless oddities, and antique stores, among other outlets of nostalgia. There was not an antique shop in Toronto or Montreal that had not received the peculiar letter, requesting highly specific information: ". . . categorized records of old orders and sales, organized by year . . . shifts in popularity of certain items/eras as listed below . . . sudden spikes in demand for particular styles . . . paintings organized by subject, rather than artist . . . the enclosed checklist comparing sales of specified items in ten-year intervals . . ." The letters were followed by visits from a pale, overweight, jarringly eager red-haired student with a slight tic in his left eyelid.

In this fieldwork, Mark had grown familiar with all the major Canadian species of antiquarian: rude, barely literate pawnbrokers who seemed to hate their buyers, their sellers, and their business but who wore old-fashioned visors and vests that were marks of nostalgia in themselves; reflexively, calibratedly untruthful jewelers with wrinkles around only one eye, a professional hazard from hours and weeks and years of squinting through loupes; furniture refinishers, as chummy as used-car salesmen, who spoke in broad accents about the Second Umpire and Louie Cans; matrons with two hundred years of regal and fanciful china patterns archived in their memories, driving from their heads the names of their own husbands, children, grandchildren; buxom, middle-aged divorcées who had invested their savings and alimony payments in a long-held dream but a bad idea and so ended up running discomfortingly clean but bizarrely stocked shops with names like The Den of Antiquity, Ancient Chinese Secret, Bea's Hive, and Mother's Attic; dust-covered booksellers, their skin like vellum paper, their eyes compensating for the aridity of their shops with excessive wetness; statue specialists, little round men distinguishable from the plaster Cupids that made up their stock only by their waistcoats and their ability to walk and speak.

The questions Mark asked of this core sampling of history merchants brought him overflowing data, which filled notebooks and computer diskettes by the hogshead, by the peck, by the avoirdupois ounce.

To quantify nostalgia, to graph it backward into the misty and sweet-smelling past, to enumerate its causes and its expressions and its costs, to determine the nature of societies and personalities most affected by the disorder—these were Mark Payton's obsessions, and he wove academic laurels from their leaves. He strained to establish laws as measurable and irrefutable as the laws of physics or meteorology. He strove, for example, to determine whether there was, within a given population, a ratio, p/c, that could predict the relationship between individuals with a "strong" or "very strong" leaning to Personal Nostalgia (i.e., nostalgia for events within one's own past) and those with a commensurate leaning to Collective Nostalgia (i.e., nostalgia for eras or styles or places that were outside of one's personal experience). In other words, if you were likely to be affected by recollections of your Hungarian grandmother's sour cherry soup served in the Herend bowl with the ladybug at the bottom, were you more or less likely to feel fondness for movies that treated with tender, nearly eroticized affection the life of English aristocrats in their country houses prior to the First World War? Payton felt certain he could arrive at a predictable ratio p/m, the relationship between a strong tendency to Personal Nostalgia and the possession of an objectively good Memory. Either hypothesis (that the relationship was direct, or that it was inverse) seemed feasible to him. Finally, the ratio c/h, the relationship of an individual's propensity to Collective Nostalgia and his or her actual Historical Knowledge of the place-era for which he or she felt this nostalgia, was theoretically determinable, and here the scholar strongly suspected an inverse proportion: The less you knew about life in those country houses, the more you wished you had lived there.

His research produced more questions than answers, but he had been forced by finicky academia to restrain his noisy and intrusive curiosity for the sake of a degree; his dissertation was necessarily limited to issues of methodology and quantifiable measurement in *Vacillations of Collective Popular Retrospective Urges in Urban Anglophone Canada, 1980–1988*. But now he was free to answer everything. The work that had brought him to Europe would sate the ravenous *why* that lurked behind his tangible discoveries.

Why, according to one of Mark's surveys, did fully 48 percent of the entering freshman girls at McGill University bring with them from home a framed copy of Robert Doisneau's photograph *The Kiss at the Hôtel de Ville*, an icon of interwar Paris (cataloged Nostalgipathic Place-Era #163). Another 29 percent of the girls bought the print within six months of matriculation.

Why, according to publicly available sales data from the publishers, did prints of that beloved poster vastly outsell Alfred Eisenstadt's thematically indistinguishable *VJ Day Kiss, Times Square*, even in Paris, where a measurable level of cross-cultural envy should have hoisted the American past Doisneau? Or, conversely, if you didn't buy that, then why didn't familiarity and ethnic pride nudge Eisenstadt's numbers over the Frenchman's in New York sales?

Why was there a sudden upsurge from 1984 to 1986 in orders placed with Ontario's specialty furniture manufacturers for Victorian daybeds, a popularity far too large to be attributed solely to the period films that appeared in a crinkly crinoline rush from 1982 to 1985?

Why did the years immediately following World War One show a drop-off in all manner of antique sales in Toronto except for military equipment and pictures?

Why was the videocassette of the film *Casablanca* rented three times more often in Quebecois video stores than in Ontarian outlets, even after statistical corrections for VCR-owning populations and the number of available dubbed copies were made?

Why did the past (and, more often than not in Canada's case, someone else's past) do this to us?

Like a dying man railing against an unfair God, Mark kept asking, *"Why?"* And every academic question was merely a restatement of a more pressing personal one, one he had been asking nearly as long as he could remember thinking, one he was embarrassed to ask even as he kept asking it despite himself, one he would only share with a friend while drunk or laughing: Why am I unhappy in the era and the place I was given?

It did not take a very long acquaintanceship before Charles labeled Mark "sad beyond help, unfit even for commodities trading." Scott, in turn, had identified the Canadian as "prematurely elderly."

VIII.

MARK WAS VAGUELY EXPECTING SOME HUNGARIANIZED VERSION OF ONE OF his familiar Canadian antiquarians the morning he walked between the two matching cannons that guarded the entrance of the Gellért Hill shop. Having thus far spent his European research time in libraries, this was his return to fieldwork and he was prepared to meet, in this city of renamed and re-renamed streets, another odd soul making a fair to poor living selling off the histories of others.

The door closed behind him with the predictable tinkling of a bell, the shape and placement of which he knew without looking. After the bright sun, he stood for a blind moment, allowing his eyes to adjust to the shop's intentionally dim light and, he knew, allowing the still invisible owner to inspect him and assess his likelihood to buy.

"American? *Deutsch? Français?*"

The voice was the Hungarian male drone, and Mark answered before he could locate its owner. *"Kanadai. Beszél angolul?"* He rashly used all three of his Hungarian words at once.

"Yes, yes, of course. But you talk very good Hungarian. We should do that." And the voice behind a desk, behind a gold floor lamp, had a face: thick black hair, thick and drooping black mustache, pale, bags under the eyes, the head tilted slightly back, polo shirt and a gold-link bracelet.

"Oh no, no," Mark said politely, still at the door, the bell just fading away. *"Nem,* I mean," he said, now truly exhausting his Magyar vocabulary. "I only know how to ask *Beszél angolul.*"

"Canada, you say? Your mama and papa are Hungarian, of course."

"No, actually. Irish. And English. Some French and German. Cherokee, claims one grandmother. I'm a mongrel."

"So how do you talk Hungarian so nice? You have the Hungarian girlfriend, I think."

"Actually, ah, no. I just came last month."

"Plenty of time."

"Yes, but actually, no."

"You find them pretty, though, yes? Our Hungarian girls? The most pretty anywhere? Like French girls?"

"Yes, sure. Very pretty."

"Well, you know what is true. The best place to learn a language is in the bed."

"Yes, I've heard it said." The Hungarian looked down at some papers on his desk and Mark looked away, ready for the inevitable shaving mugs, the incomplete sets of silverware, the refuse of dead people's mantels.

Instead, his eye snagged on a photograph on the man's desk, a small framed picture of a group of soldiers, vintage World War II. Payton could not identify the uniforms, but he did recognize almost instantly the pale soldier squatting in the front row, second from the right, staring at the camera with sleepy eyes and a droopy black mustache. "You were a soldier?" As soon as he spoke, Mark knew the question was foolish; this man would not have been more than a child.

"Yes, how do you know this of me? Oh, I see. No, that is my father. Many say we have similar looks. It was with friends who joined together, this picture. Right when they start. He had to shave his mustache soon after this. This was a farewell-to-mustaches picture." Mark picked up the photograph and stared at the antiquer's absolute double (but for the fatigues), the soldier's head thrown back, allowing him to look down his nose with ironic martial bravado. "Come to look here." He led Payton to a corner of the store, where oil paintings in golden frames lined the walls and leaned against each other on the floor. "My grandfather."

High on a yellow wall hung the same man's face again. Here, his mustache was slightly longer and his hair swept back. He wore a blue cavalry uniform with golden braiding on the shoulders, and he stared, in three-quarters view, from out of the dark background tones. The haughty officer's eyes, from a head thrown slightly back, followed Mark's with military frankness as the scholar walked back and forth in front of the painting.

"He wears the uniform of the emperor's guard. We have it still, there." The man waved across the shop at a headless cloth mannequin in a braided blue jacket, matching tight trousers, and spurred black leather boots. "I do not sell these, of course. For now." The shopkeeper returned to the desk and riffled through more paintings leaning against the back wall. "Here, we find it," he exclaimed, and turned to face Mark with another golden frame, this one smaller. Two Hungarian hunting dogs, vizslas, lay awake on a floor of chessboard black-and-white tiles. A young boy knelt beside them and rested one hand on the head of each dog. He wore short pants, a velvet shirt, and a lace collar. A woman, presumably his mother, wore her dark hair loose, and it fell over her shoulders and blood-red dress. She smiled slightly from within the embrace of a large ornate chair. She held a baby in flowing baptismal clothes. Standing beside her, his hand on her shoulder, in front of half-open French doors revealing a green park, stood—yet again, to Mark's delight—a man with the shop owner's face. Now he wore an expression of serene, paternal pride, his head again tilted slightly back. His uniform featured long tails over tight white trousers. An eyebrow was slightly cocked. He wore no mustache and his long black hair was held in a short ponytail, but the resemblance was otherwise total.

"This," the owner said as his finger hovered near the baby in the baptismal gown, "is my great-grandfather, the father of him." He gestured toward the headless mannequin. "This boy, soon after this"—he pointed to the elder child with the dogs—"died. This is lucky, I think. For my line. The picture is done in 1822. The boy with the dogs, who is dead, is five here. His father, my great-great-grand, I think is born in 1794. He was a nobleman, you can see."

"All the men in your family serve in the military?" The antique dealer clicked his tasseled-loafer heels, and Mark asked if there was a picture of the man himself in uniform.

"Of course, of course," he replied, and his English began to grow oddly worse: "But is not of pride. It only, you must know, tradition one way and desire another." Mark nodded encouragingly. "I have a picture, but I find it very little." He brought out a small plastic photo album, turned a few of its pages, and pointed to a black-and-white snapshot glued under a cellophane sheet. "This is when I am twenty. I am in a base near Győr and we train against Austrian invasion. A ridiculous idea, you know, to think we fight Austrians in 1970."

The photograph showed a young crew-cut soldier in green fatigues, staring at the camera, holding his floppy cap. His head was angled slightly downward, and his broad smile appeared almost shy as a result. His eyes wrinkled up tightly as if he were facing bright sunlight. His face was tanned and clean-shaven. "This one here is you?"

"Yes, yes, of course. But it is not like my father or grandfather, is it?" The man was not referring to any physical dissimilarity. "I am not a free man here who fights for his people, am I? No. I am here a boy who has no choices. To fight in that Hungarian army was like to be a slave for Russia. It was like the Hungarian Legion of the Russian Soviet Imperial Army. My father fought for Hungary. My grandfather fought for his emperor. My great-grandfather and his father—these were proud men. And they carry arms for their people and their families and their land, for Magyarország, for Hungary. And I?" He stared hard at Mark, his resemblance to his painted ancestors growing. "In 1970 I must join a conqueror's army. I should be an officer, a cavalry officer to be commanding, but I am instead a slave, or a trophy, like when my family's land becomes a collective farm. And I can never be a high officer, because my family history make me a class criminal, you understand. What must I do? Hey? What?"

"I don't know."

"A soldier fights, but a Hungarian cannot accept this lie of an empire, this Russian shit. What do I do? Do I fight like a brave man or do I say no like a brave man?"

"I don't know."

"I do what my grandfather would do. I train and I work with a gun and running and digging. If an enemy attack Hungary, I would fight. But they don't attack. You know why?"

"I don't know."

"Because the enemy already here. They never leave after the World War Second. So I am a bad soldier. I make mistakes. I lose equipment. I take my troop into the woods and we have wine and food and we talk all day instead of doing what the Communist idiots tell to do. I have honor by fighting the enemy by not fighting. But I have no honor as they had." He waved at his ancestors on the walls, at the headless cloth mannequin. "No honor as a true, open defender of the fatherland."

Disgusted at the rape of tradition by corrupt ideology, Mark sought the words to express his groaning empathy (and mild envy), unaware that he had simply been hooked by a sales pitch he had never seen in Canada and now appeared as naïve as some American tourist ready to buy an Elizabeth II Jubilee commemorative shaving mug. "And what do you shop for today? I can show you maybe a nice jewelry for your girlfriend?"

IX.

UNTIL THE DAY HE LEFT, NEWLY WED AND HEADED FARTHER EAST, SCOTT Price never looked quite at home in Budapest, and he liked it that way. He was, for a start, legitimately tan and shimmeringly blond. He smiled often, easily, and, in the eyes of the average Hungarian, excessively. He favored conversation about nutrition and digestion and the politico-economic implications of both. He daily braved the toxic fumes of Trabants, Dacias, Skodas, Wartburgs, and the occasional madly stampeding Mercedes to jog over the guidebook bridges and along the parapets and paths that run alongside the Blue Danube, which was this morning, as always, the deep cerulean Matisse blue of caramel or mahogany.

In his college shorts, running shoes, tank top, and a bandanna to hold back the white-gold sheaves of his hair, he irritated the Hungarian pedestrians, who, smoking more often than not, stared at him in his froth as he stamped by. It was one thing to run with your athletic teammates, all in matching track suits, or in the countryside as part of military training, but to wear almost nothing and sweat up and down the Corsó marked one as aggressively foreign. More than one old woman, conditioned in her own way, scolded Scott as he passed. "Don't run fast near people!" she would bluster, unable to find the words to express her dismay. Not that it mattered, since Scott only had enough Hungarian to smile and puff out *"Kezét csókolom,"* the standard polite greeting of men to women. "You are going to kill someone!" they hissed. "I kiss your hand!" he would say, running backward. "This is not right to do, your running!" they yell. "I kiss your hand!" he says. "No running! No running!" "I kiss your hand!" Scott told his students he found their elderly compatriots to be charmingly loquacious and delightfully supportive of young men seeking to maintain good cardiovascular health.

Scott Price, happiest when arriving or departing (in or from cities, groups, relationships), discovered a very surprising continual joy living in one place as a perfect foreigner, living without language and outside of language. For the English teacher in a Hungarian world, every day was an arrival and refreshing departures were easy to execute. This was explicable: Scott knew that hostility was a language-borne virus. If only a few people could speak your language, then the vast majority of toxins were denied access to your system. To live here knowing only English, poor Spanish, and a few phrases of melodious, biblical Hebrew was to be almost completely vaccinated. Then, to have a few Anglophone friends and a nice job, a steady stream of pretty girls eager to pay to learn a few words of your valuable language (and, as he had heard it frequently said, the best place to learn a new language was in bed), well, you couldn't help but be happy today, and tomorrow would probably not be too different, and anything unpleasant was now all the way across a continent and an ocean and a continent again. Of course, vegetarian cooking was elusive, and the air quality left a lot to be desired, but the city was good-looking, and you could breathe fine if you stayed in shape, avoided hostility and fat, ate three garlic cloves each morning, absorbed plenty of antioxidants, avoided yeast bread within three hours of a scheduled elimination, lived up in the Buda hills, and avoided rigidity in your attitudes.

Across the river and through the morning haze, Castle Hill shone, its dome and spire floating high over their rippling twins on the Danube's surface, floating just above where Charles, John, and Mark were tossing a very foreign looking ball back and forth, laughingly discussing the antique store proprietor's eloquent nationalism and unintentional ironies, and definitively determining the future of European politics and economics. Scott turned off the riverfront and onto the narrow streets that ran between and behind the three hotels lining the Danube, past the Hyatt and the Forum, past the John Bull English Pub and the Intercontinental, past the little grocery where fruit cost twice as much as anywhere else but where you could buy American toothpastes rather than the local brands (or the West German one with the unnerving label that sported cavorting devils and yellow-toothed ogres dancing around an ultra white–toothed maiden tied to a tree). Realizing he would be late to the football game if he didn't head back in the direction he had come, Scott turned into the middle of Váci utca, dodged the velvet ropes corralling the line of people awaiting admission to McDonald's, ran past the similar line at the store that sold one Western-brand athletic shoe and the mysteriously empty and lineless store that sold a different Western brand of athletic shoe. The sweat fell from his face and hair as he jogged past the pastry shops that daily tempted his once-obese self; past old peasant women who sat and stood on the pavement, displaying scarves and blankets to the tourists; past young Syrian men offering to sell forints for hard currency at some magic number higher than the bank rate; past "folklore" stores (with no lines crowding their entrances) where one could buy costumes of the Hungarian countryside, traditional dolls, china, crystal, paprika. German businessmen, their dress white socks flashing from under the cuffs of their shiny suits, entered hard currency banks and hard currency stores off-limits to the gooey-currency natives. Scott passed a young American in an expensive suit telling his younger, bald colleague, "—fully serviced offices.

All top-of-the-line. I know people on the city council so finagling—" Hungarian teenagers in leather jackets smoked hand-rolled cigarettes and stood like James Dean. The Andean band sang of the Paraguayan highlands and love lost under the starry skies and the condor's wings over the hut where . . . and so on, just like the Andean bands he had heard in Palo Alto and Portland and Prague, Harvard Square and Halifax and The Hague. But this time would be different, Scott decided; he was in Budapest to stay. A little patience would be necessary before John gave up and went back, but it shouldn't be long now, and when he finally did break, he would take with him his contagious restlessness and dissatisfaction and guilt, his little gestures and phrases and attitudes that stank of their parents and the past, and Scott would relax again and prove to himself that he had settled all that, left it far below him.

Scott arrived on the playing field on Margaret Island, the giant green trowel set face-up in the cloud-smudged river. His brother and friends were already there, and—dismissing as ironic John's unironic awe at Scott's outstanding physical condition—happily joined the opposing team, wishing only that it were tackle, not touch.

X.

FRAMED MAPS OF BUDAPEST AND THE COUNTRYSIDE; PHOTOS OF THE EDItor shaking hands with presumably famous people (each with that nimbus of celebrity, but none of the faces familiar to John); an old advertising poster for a Hungarian liqueur showing a man on a scaffold, a rope around his neck, licking his smiling lips in appreciation of his last-wish cordial; a doctored photograph of kangaroos and koalas frolicking onstage at the Sydney opera house; the first issue (2-18-89) of *BudapesToday* under glass; dunes and bluffs of paper eroding everywhere, on the desk, on chairs, on cabinets, on the floors, trembling as if sound might knock them over, yellowing into obsolescence while John waited for the man's intimidatingly withheld attention.

"These words weren't placed here at random, by God." The editor's Australian mutter had emerged at last, though he did not look up from the pages he was ferociously marking. "No sir, an intelligence, an almost human intelligence, placed these words in this order to achieve some kind of sense." He examined John. "Though what fucking kind of sense it was certainly escapes me, I must say."

"No good?" John asked, but the editor was scrabbling in one of his desk drawers.

"Where the fuck did I put that fucker, Mistah Proyce?" he asked, stooped, invisible behind piled papers.

"Which fucker, sir?"

"Don't call me sir, Proyce. I'm only thirty. Call me chief. Ha! *There's* the fucker!" The editor, bearing a rubber stamp at least three inches long, hove into view from behind the cresting tides. He pounded the stamp into the moist red embrace of an open ink pad and slammed it down twice on what he had been reading. "*That's* the fucker I wanted, John boy!" He held up the sheet, stamped twice with the words WASTE OF MY INK & MY TIME. "And, olé, *that's* the fucker, isn't it, Proyce?"

"Yes, chief. That is evidently the fucker."

The editor opened another drawer with nearly enough force to pull it clear of the desk. "Look at this one. I just got this one. People fax me inane shit all the time now, John-o, so look at this." Another rubber stamp. The editor pushed a button on his fax machine, and a broad tongue of blank white emerged from between its lips. "Okay, okay, so let's say that this is some unsolicited piece of shit faxed to me by some tosser, right? Right. Okay, here it comes: piece of shit, piece of shit, piece of shit." He tore the paper from the machine's maw and gave the black device a little pat of gratitude on its top panel. "Okay then, I read it and it's some, let's say, junior exec at a local branch of an investment bank who wishes he were a journalist instead, so he's going to try to get his start by getting published on my pages, right? Right, Proyce?"

"Right, chief."

"Wrong, you little bastard. No sir. I read it, this wanker's best efforts"—the editor mimed reading the blank sheet of fax paper— "and he's got, 'blahblahblahblahblah' and *lovely*, absolutely *marvelous*, it turns out that he has submitted his wisdom about—what a shocker—American investment bankers and Hungarian girls, and he even tells us the best place to learn Hungarian is in bed, isn't he a great wit, and of course his piece sucks, mate, as I think you Yanks say. It sucks, right, Proyce, right? Right?"

"Sucks, chief."

"So what do I do, John? I take this" —the new stamp—"and whammo!"— into the ink—"and blammo!" —onto the sad investment banker's stumbling first efforts at prose—"and *voilà*, John boy, *voi*-fucking-*là*." The editor held up the fax paper, blank but for the bright red words YOU ARE WASTING MY TONER. PLEASE RE-IMBURSE.

The editor looked John in the eye and breathed very deeply three or four times. "All right then, Mistah Proyce. You aren't going to waste my time or my ink or my toner, are you, mate?"

"No, chief."

"Where'd I put your fucking résumé, John-o?" He burrowed again into the shifting tectonic surfaces of his desk. "*Voilà*, my child. We have your life here." As John waited, the editor read, moving his lips furiously but in no apparent relation to the text. He dropped the résumé onto the desk, from where it glided to the floor. "Give it to me straight, John. What do you really want to be doing?"

"Doing? This job? I was hired. Already. That's why I'm here." Pause for understanding response. "In this country."

"Yes, Proyce, I know. Now, answer. What do you *really* want to be doing?"

"I suppose whatever needs, you know, doing."

"No, fuck a sheep, John. I mean what is *it*? Are you a poet? Scripting a movie about a journalist at an English-language daily in an unnamed Central European capital, are we? Planning a hip documentary video about the crazy ways American kids are getting laid in Hungary? Secret business scheme? What's the plan, kiddo?"

John wondered if the correct answer was to deny any interests outside of the newspaper or to confess to some deep but unachievable goal. The latter. "Yes, I chisel—"

"Fine. We've got that out in the open then, don't we? No sin. Wish you all the best. Hemingway settles abroad, tired and cynical but ambitious, writes dispatches and jots down *The Sun Also Rises* in his spare time. Lovely. Wonderful career path. Hope things pan out for you and the rest of your lost generation here in Paris on the Danube. You heard that one yet, John-o? BP is Paris on the Danube? Reliving Paris in the twenties, all that?"

"No, chief."

"Good. Ear to the ground. I like that in a cub reporter. Listen here, you don't have any Hungarian, do you, mate?"

"No, I didn't claim in my letter that—"

"John. Please. Shut up. I'm just confirming the situation. You don't need Hungarian to do the job I've got in mind for you. You're going to love this job. No worries, mate, you'll soon have screenplays pouring out your arse."

"Great. That sounds nice."

"*BudapesToday* is my baby, and while I admit she's no *Prague Post*, I'm going to let you play with her. You write me a column twice a week on just about whatever the hell you feel like as long as it's about Budapest. Learn Hungarian—it can't hurt, though in five years there won't be a human soul outside the distant fucking Hungarian hinterlands who will speak it and nothing else. As they say in Latin, English is going to be the French language around here, and we are going to be the French-language daily, get me?" The editor had stepped from behind the desk and was walking in circles around John, punctuating his well-practiced speech with barks of "right?" and "get me?" and occasionally kneading John's shoulders fiercely. "Now then, mate, when you're done writing your poetry that will make you no money, you'll wish you had worked harder for me so that you could cash in with me and go live in the fucking Greek islands instead of this God-forsaken paprika-stained Austrian test market. Get me? Write me expatriate and local color. Make it punchy, snide, modern. Do that long enough and well enough and we'll find other tasks for you to perform and then you'll get rich with me, yes?"

John asked about reporting, had thought he was hired as a reporter.

"Mistah Proyce, I have bilingual Hungarians. I have a wire service. Don't go loitering around the prime minister's office looking for a scoop. Just give my paper some style and I'll be content." He sat again and fondled his rubber stamps, red ink invading the crevices of his fingers. "One other thing. Don't write screenplays in this building or on my time or on my word processors. Don't piss off our advertisers. Don't lie in print—not that anyone would sue us, not that this country even has libel laws right now as best as my lawyer can unearth them. Don't forget you don't speak Hungarian and you probably cannot get any other job that pays even the pittance I'm going to. Don't forget that if you went into real journalism at home, perhaps after thirty years you'd get an opportunity this good. Never forget that would-be Hemingways and Fitzgeralds are being airlifted into this country on C-141 transport planes and are night-parachuting into all the good cafés by the lost generation–load. So." The seated editor offered John his red-blotched hand. "Don't fuck up, mate. You are highly replaceable. First column for Thursday, please. G'day."

And John was back in the "newsroom," a tiny office space filled with writing and design equipment spanning sixty years of manufacture, with ten employees of three different nationalities, each with a desk, and every other desk's bottom drawer containing an unfinished screenplay about life on an English-language daily in an unnamed Central European capital under the command of a colorful Australian editor-proprietor.

XI.

WHEN THE MONDAY SUN HOISTED ITS FIRST YOLK-YELLOW ARC OVER AN eastern hill of Buda, Emily Oliver was already waiting for it on the broad balcony of the newly built bungalow she shared with two other ambassa-babes (as one of the marine guards had dubbed Emily, Julie, and Julie). She was in the third part of a five-part high-impact-aerobics workout that she had done every morning since her first day at the University of Nebraska. No matter how late the night preceding, no matter the latitude or the longitude, no matter daylight savings or the season, she began the routine before sunrise and at the first glimpse of the sun, she would say, "Boo!" just as her father had done every morning in Nebraska, holding little Emily on his lap on a porch swing or at the kitchen table. "Quiet now, Emmy. This time we'll surprise it and we'll scare it and it'll go back down and we can all go back to bed and get some sleep until tomorrow, when it'll try to sneak up in the west."

"Boo!" she still said every morning, as a gift to her dad. "Boo!" she said this Monday morning while the Julies still slumbered. Emily had had about five hours of sleep the night before, but she reminded herself that she was working hard at her new job and she was still getting used to new food, new air, new words, new people, not to make excuses. She hoped all of this would explain her body's excessive appetite for rest and other uncharacteristic lapses. Certainly it was temporary.

The day of her high school graduation, a friend grimly warned Emily about the "freshman fifteen," the inevitable weight all young women gain in their first year of college. Emily had never heard the phrase before, and realized that if it hadn't been for her friend's stray comment, she might never have been prepared. She was furious with herself for being ignorant of such a well-known, avoidable danger.

Emily gained six pounds her freshman year at Nebraska, six pounds in muscle tone she kept to this day, this Monday morning when she made another futile effort to scare the sun back under the earth, not because she wanted to go back to bed, but because she was pretty sure her dad, whom she missed terribly just now, could use the rest, and—seven time zones to his east—she was his first line of defense.

"*Kezét csókolom, kisasszony.*" The old Hungarian security guard at the embassy's front door always greeted Emily with the same words: "I kiss your hand, miss." He would smile as broadly as he could without revealing the teeth he had never known were bad until he started working for the Americans.

"Then I will never wash it again, Péter," Emily would say, and he would wheezily bow, not having precisely understood her as she bounded through the security gate and into the lobby manned by two U.S. marines in a bulletproof enclosure. "Good morning, marines."

"Miss Oliver, good morning," the crew-cuts would reply in unison.

"Todd," she said this Monday, pointing to the black soldier's sleeve insignia. "When did you get that second rocker?"

"Confirmed on Friday, sewn on Saturday. Thank you for noticing, Miss Oliver."

"Congratulations, marine. Are you going to lord it over Danny now?" she asked, referring to the white corporal in the booth.

"He does need discipline, Miss Oliver." He smiled at her, as people everywhere tended to do.

She admonished the new promotee to be firm but fair and made a point to call him gunnery sergeant. She walked through the metal detector, regathered her change and keys from the soldiers on the far side, where her smile triggered yet more grinning. She walked behind sliding glass doors into areas of the embassy with lead-lined walls and microphone detectors and communications scrambling systems, in which secure environment she would make the ambassador's coffee, smile at the Hungarian finance minister, pick up the ambassador's shirts, and lunch at a table with the wives (and one shy professorial husband) of French diplomats while the widowed ambassador met in a separate room with the diplomats themselves.

She was working hard. She appreciated the opportunity and the importance of her work. She admired her boss and her colleagues; they were about what she had expected. She was exceptionally well prepared for this experience, she reminded herself. Everything was fine. Her father had told her how well-suited she was for this. He was enormously proud of her. She reminded him of her mother, he had told her at the airport, and of a South Vietnamese colleague of his, killed in the Laotian highlands just before Christmas 1971. These were his two highest compliments. Everything was going fine, and just as she had expected.

And yet, how to explain certain aberrations?

Yesterday, Sunday, she had been reading under a tree on Margaret Island. Bells chimed eleven o'clock, she was reading and watching a group of American and Canadian guys play a shabby sort of touch football. None of the boys would have passed muster in even the most relaxed Nebraska game, except for Todd and Danny, of course. And then she was opening her eyes and the sun was well behind her and she was staring at the underside of the treetop and the players were all gone except for one, sitting next to her, leaning against the tree, reading her book. "Good morning, sleepyhead."

"What time is it?"

"Four-thirty." She made him say it twice; she thought he was kidding. She was still drowsy, even fell asleep again for a few more minutes. A five-and-a-half-hour nap in public.

And yet she stayed under the tree, felt no need or desire even to stand. She lay with her hands behind her head, her knapsack serving as a pillow, and she talked with John because she couldn't think of anything else to do or anywhere else to be, a strange sensation. She talked about her family, simply because he asked. She talked more about her family than she ever did, showed almost no reflexive discretion or loyalty, because those did not seem to apply to this situation, for which she felt herself unprepared but with none of the adrenaline rush and careful analysis that unpreparedness usually triggered.

"Tell me about your dad," he had asked, somehow sniffing out the central issue immediately.

Where to begin? A farmer, a widower . . . no, she decided to begin with the circles. Ken Oliver had inculcated in his children the value of the circles. We live in the center of five concentric circles—each of us does—and the circles define our place in the world and anchor us against danger, and also magnify our own strength like waves coming off us. At the center, there is the individual with his or her individual God-given gifts; then the circle of education, which is the ability to develop those gifts; then the circle of family; then the circle of community; then of country; then of God. Duty flows outward from the center; strength flows inward toward the center.

"Whoa. Do you believe that?"

Of course. Although no one had ever asked with that tone before. She didn't usually talk about it with anyone who didn't already know about it. Beth, her elder sister, married and with two kids on another farm about forty miles closer to Lincoln, did say once that the circles were maybe not that helpful, even to Dad. (Beth remembered their mother most clearly and said her death affected Dad just by "making him even more like him.") Emily had repeated Beth's heresy to Robert, her younger brother, a marine now at Twentynine Palms. Robert disagreed, said Beth just hadn't thought hard enough about it yet. No one could ask her older brother, Ken Jr., of course, since he just took off one day and that was the last of Ken Jr. "Drugs," her father explained, and never mentioned him again, though he did do some volunteer work with a local church group that helped recovering addicts.

"So you pretty much come from arranged-marriage country," John said.

"Oh absolutely. I'm promised to a farmer seven counties over, and I come with three nice cows, but I have to pass a purity test after I come home from Hungary."

She didn't tell John all of the rest of this, but she told him enough that she later wondered what was happening to her in this country.

From 1961 to 1967, Ken Oliver's tours in Vietnam and the surrounding countries were reasonably rare and of reasonable length. After Tet, however, he had no choice but to leave his wife and four kids in Georgetown and spend more than three leave-free years in Saigon, making frequent trips up north and into Laos. The last of these expeditions occurred just after Christmas 1971, during which he witnessed the death of "the noblest man I ever knew, Emmy." He made it back to Saigon "by the grace of God" only to receive word that his wife, Martha, had gotten quite suddenly ill and that he had immediate leave to go back to Georgetown to see her. He never returned to Vietnam, resigning from the service after Martha's rapid death and taking the kids to Nebraska, where his own parents lived in a vast agricultural expanse better suited to raising children than Georgetown's diplomatic parties and cancer wards.

John must have been sitting there watching her sleep for a couple of hours, she realized, even after his friends and brother had left the island. Men who thought and spoke like lesser versions of her dad were all around the embassy, but people like John were not. He was so aimless. He enjoyed this sort of aimless talk, seemed to have no need to be busy. He was not like the Julies, who were just party girls, not serious at all, just biding time until they found men. Nor was he like Charles, who resembled nothing so much as certain money-grasping (and Emily-groping) agribusiness majors at Nebraska. Scott was angry, like a smart-aleck teenager. But John . . . and Mark was a new type, too. The strangest thought came to her as she stared up at the birds on the lowest branches and John talked about what sounded like a miserable childhood, though he was laughing about it: There was probably a range of people she had never experienced in this world and for which she had no preparation.

He asked about her mom, and she simply answered him. "I was only five. I remember my dad cried at the funeral. But never again, Beth says. It was hard, I think, for him. I missed her for the longest time, but that wasn't really the sort of thing you could talk about. It wasn't fair to him to bring her up or make him think he wasn't enough for us. Not that I'm complaining."

"Jesus, Special Assistant. I think you're allowed to complain about that. You had two great parents and you lost one. What else is complaining for?"

She lay on her back in the silence, watched the branches and the softest blue sky. What indeed *was* it for? There was an answer to that. It was just bubbling up in her memory, something about—and she recognized the look in John's eye, had seen it cloud up boys' faces, just before they leaned in to kiss her. " 'Complaining,' " she quoted with a smile, shoving her book into her knapsack, standing up, and slapping the dirt off her legs, " 'is for people who don't know how to make things better.' "

Monday at the embassy, she checked her to-do lists, read the Monday Memos. She would be accompanying the ambassador to a reception at the Saudi embassy this evening. She also had a note from her supervisor, asking for a moment of her time, which he used to chide her for a relatively minor lapse in judgment on her part that he had witnessed last week—not a major incident, but if she was going to learn, then it should be brought to her attention. "Thank you," she said. "It won't happen again."

"How's your famous father?" he asked.

Complaining was certainly not for being justifiably corrected at work, she reminded herself as she went downstairs to confirm schedules with the ambassador's driver. And yet she hated the schoolmarmish, uptight scolding over virtually nothing, and then she was ashamed, not just of not taking correction well (for which you should be ashamed) but of her original honest mistake, for which you should never be ashamed. And that—to be ashamed of making an honest mistake—revealed nothing nobler than dirty pride, which of course was shameful.

XII.

JUST FOUR STREETS AWAY FROM THE AMERICAN EMBASSY'S IMPOSING façade sat an even more impressive villa, rented for a ninety-nine-year term by Charles Gábor's employers, a New York venture capital firm whose 130-year-old name would literally, several months after the events described here, fall from its perch on Wall Street and crash into the pavement, disintegrating into marble dust and pebbles, only a few days before its executive board—with bluster and denials—would itself, due to similar structural errors, disintegrate into convicts, parolees, state's witnesses, memoirists, and consultants.

But in 1990, in a piece of symbolic topography destined to find its way into one of John Price's columns, Charles Gábor, a venture capitalist one year out of business school, worked in a riverfront office that was larger and more luxurious and with a better view than the U.S. ambassador's.

Charles Gábor was a grandchild of '56, one of those Americans and Canadians whose parents had left Hungary after the failed anti-Communist uprising of that year. In Toronto, Cleveland, and New York, this younger generation had tried to explain to their primary school chums that the S in Sándor was pronounced Sh before bowing to superior numbers and thereafter answering to Sandy or Alexander or just Alex. Then they would patiently explain to their middle school friends that no matter what President Carter says, the Communists are bad, they stole my country, until, at last, in tenth grade, they grudgingly accepted the idea of the Soviets as threatened or misunderstood and the Cold War as an inexplicable mutual aggression with plenty of blame to go around. Later they would tell their high school history teachers that the Versailles Treaty was properly called Trianon and was a vindictive and ill-conceived act that mercilessly and unwisely stole land from defeated governments struggling to rebuild, uprooted innocent families, incited more warfare, and led to generations of tyranny . . . before they finally stopped beating their heads against the curriculum and admitted that, yes, the winners had done what they had to do. At Versailles.

Those who went to college would major in East Asian studies, communications, finance.

On summer break, though, one might be at home and listen with amazement as one's father, slightly drunk for the first time in memory, would let slip that he had not just escaped in 1956 but had fought, had run up the back of a tank, dropped a Molotov cocktail in its hatch, and shot the emerging panicked blond, crew-cut Russian boy through the eye with a generations-old revolver, shot him just underneath a mole sprouting two long hairs, and then had run as the body slumped back into the tank, blocking the only exit for its choking, burning comrades.

Charles Gábor's parents met in Cleveland, though they had both escaped from Hungary at the same time. Family legend grew around the amazing coincidences of their love: They had been at the same marches, then some of the same street battles of the uprising, had left the country within a day of each other, had killed time in refugee-holding areas in Austria within a kilometer of each other, had reached Cleveland within a month of each other, but still did not meet for another two years, until New Year's Eve of 1959–60, when, at a party, Charles's father was kissing another girl ("If I remember her name, it will be a miracle—Jane, Judy, Jennifer, Julie, something very American") and, with closed eyes and one hand full of angora-sweatered breast and the other stroking plaid kilt–draped rump, heard his future wife shout at someone, "Happy New Year when they still sit at my Gerbeaud with their fat, stupid Russian faces? When those Russian animals are defecating on my streets? It is not happy. Not happy at all." Charles's father often told his son he had fallen in love with her voice, views, and unwilling English even as his tongue was in the other girl's mouth.

Charles, né Károly, was not born to a couple eager to experience the wonders of American assimilation, and his first language was Hungarian.

"In your hometown, there is an island in the river where you can play football and then have ice cream and a bath and a massage."

"I am too small for football."

"Nonsense! You would be very good as goalkeeper. You will be tall enough someday. I should begin teaching you to play, where to look when their offense breaks through your defenders, how to bend your knees so you can jump in either direction."

"They do not have goalkeepers in football, Father."

"What are you saying? Ildikó, what is he saying? What are they doing with him at that school?"

"Your father is right, Károly. You would be an excellent goalkeeper. That ice cream," she squeezed his father's hand. "My God. Sour cherry."

"But this ice cream is good, isn't it?"

"Yes, it is okay, but the ice cream on that island is like nothing they make in Cleveland."

"I think I am right about football."

His parents often tried to reconstruct for each other the lives they had led in parallel before they met, their reminiscences often triggered by Charles's current age, as in: "I tried to walk across Lake Balaton when I was a little girl, not much older than that." She gestured at her son. "I thought I was tall enough."

"Then that was the age I kissed a girl for the first time. Dohány utca. I kissed her on the cheek." He stroked his wife's cheek with the back of his hand. "She was a Jew, and even though I did not know what the term meant, I knew something about it was dangerous and I thought I was very brave, because my father would have found it quite alarming."

"I was kissed the first time right next to the Vajdahunyad. I miss that stupid castle."

"Whenever I think of the Corvin I cannot believe you were there and you could have been hurt and we would never have met. There was a great battle at this movie theater, Károly. Not a movie about a battle, but a battle at the movies! Have you ever heard of such a thing?"

His parents spoke often of real estate in mysterious hands, and struggled to re-create for each other (and for their heir) the homes they had known.

"You have an apartment, Károly, smaller than this house but much more beautiful, in the fifth district of your hometown. It is yours and someday you will be able to reclaim it and live there."

"You have another apartment in the first district, my boy. Also very beautiful!"

"I have two apartments and this house? How will I know where to live?"

"This house is nothing special. It is those apartments you will like."

"I like this house. Clark lives next door. And Chad lives on the corner. I don't want to live anywhere else."

"Don't be silly. No one is going to make you leave this house, but someday you will want to, because they will give your apartments back to you and you will be very proud to have such lovely homes in your hometown."

While the little boy sat on the floor with his toy soldiers and dreaded being forced out of his house, his parents described his two apartments, and as they did, they left the places they had been standing (near the fire, near the cocktail cart), came across the room to each other, and lay down on the couch, his father's arm around his mother's neck. They stared at the ceiling and whispered details of their apartments to each other in quieter and quieter tones until Charles could not hear them at all, and he was relieved to be left alone to play on the floor of his house, in the company of his friend the cat, Imre Nagy (Big Jim, as he introduced him to friends). The cat had lived in that house longer than Charles himself, and would, nightly, pounce on and bat from paw to paw one of Charles's soldiers, a shiny silver knight with a sword. The glint of it attracted the cat, and though he ignored the rest of the tiny military forces, that knight was nip.

"Four flights of stairs, sixty-four steps top to bottom, and in the courtyard an elm tree. The boy would be climbing it today. You hear, Károly? A tree in your—oh never mind, he's lost in his soldiers . . ."

"The tiles meant to look like a Byzantine mosaic . . . I'm sure some Red bastard has smashed . . ."

As he grew up, however, none of his parents' dictates or practices could protect him from the flood of English words and American habits. Friends, movies, school, books, television: Cleveland and Hollywood occupied far more of the known world than did that unknown faraway city, the black-and-white stories of long ago, the confusing, urgent, parochial politics, and the language none of his friends could speak but which several of them compared to a slimy alien's gurgling in *Star Wars*.

The boy handed down the sentence of banishment three years prior to its execution: At age nine he announced to his parents that he was tired of people calling him Ca-RO-lee rather than KAR-oy and therefore he would henceforth be called Charles, a dictate happily accepted by everyone he knew except his parents; but he was twelve when Hungarian words finally grew less familiar than English ones. Twelve-year-old Károly the Hungarian lived dormant inside Charles the Ohioan throughout high school, college, and business school, unnecessary, unnoticed, unwelcome.

His Hungarian stopped developing when he was twelve but clung to him like a vestigial appendage. He spoke Hungarian only in occasional private conversations with his parents in front of third parties. And with this linguistic divide came an inevitable cultural one. His father in particular began to see Charles as a foreigner who needed education to be restored to his heritage.

"Admiral Horthy was misunderstood," his father lectured him after disgustedly tossing aside Charles's eleventh-grade history textbook and its single mention of Hungary's appearance in the Second World War, included in a sidebar list of Other Fascist Countries. "Americans have no appetite for anything other than black or white. There were more than merely bad guys and good guys. It wasn't a cowboys-and-Indians John Wayne movie, you understand? Tell that to your ridiculous teacher. Horthy kept the Nazis out as long as he could *and* fought the Russians. Who else does your little school think could do that? Churchill? Incidentally, you might inform your teacher of what passes for history in this country that the proper term for that act of rape on page 465 is Trianon."

But having bided his time, Károly the Hungarian awoke one day. The 1989 revolutions in Central Europe and Charles's omnipresent belief that he was destined for something better than his classmates led him to tell the recruiter, "Yes, I speak fluent Hungarian and would welcome the challenge of helping open the firm's Budapest offices." Suddenly Károly was again a valued and welcome member of Charles's psychic cast and crew. Unfortunately, Károly was still twelve. As a result, the investment professional who arrived in Budapest in October 1989, after three months of peculiarly infantilizing training in New York, was a cocky, opinionated young venture capitalist of style, intelligence, and intuition who, in Hungarian, unbeknownst to his employers, spoke to the managers of potential investments very much like a twelve-year-old boy in a well-dressed man's body.

One morning, John sat on Charles's office couch and photographed Charles, looking important at his desk, the picture window behind him comprising one-third Danube, one-third Castle Hill, one-third cirrus-smeared heavens. The photo, which Charles sent home to his parents, showed five stacks of files in front of him. Each stack was of a different height, and Charles explained to the semi-interested John what he did all day, most days.

Every morning, Zsuzsa, the firm's Hungarian office manager, nestled new files into leather covers embossed with the firm's logo (a knight holding high a sword, looking forward into the gloom while sheltering behind him a disheveled, nearly nude maiden). This stack of files on the left—Charles tapped the tower of booklets—represented IQs, Incoming Queries: letters and materials that argued hopelessly on behalf of old state-owned Communist enterprises seeking private investors, inventors requesting seed funding, groups of young entrepreneurs wishing to form a casino, et cetera.

Every afternoon, Zsuzsa would remove the stack on the far right, nearly equal in teetering altitude: SRs—Summary Rejections. Here were yesterday's state-owned companies, too inefficient to merit resuscitation and with little value even as scrap; inventors too implausible to earn even an interview; and young managers whose inexperience made Charles shake his head in wonder. He had quickly concluded that virtually the entire managerial class of the country was either without experience or burdened by years of the wrong experience courtesy of Communism's inefficiencies, irrelevancies, immoralities.

Between the pillar of Hungarian hopes and its near twin of despair lay three significantly smaller stacks. The first—Investigation Requests—was composed of those offers interesting enough to warrant further interviews, on-site visits, requests for financial data, and so forth. Charles passed these files with a strictly enforced four-line summary of his findings to the office's managing partner, a forty-four-year-old VP from New York, burdened with not a single word of Hungarian but with nineteen years of Wall Street experience. This leader leaned inordinately on Zsuzsa and the bilingual junior members of the team. Resenting his sudden neediness, however, he would frequently and with strident machismo lecture them about "how it's done Stateside."

With some excitement at first, Charles followed up on those few cases approved by the VP for further investigation—Under Reviews. But this long-awaited action usually disappointed. Charles laughed through interviews with talented young entrepreneurs willing to surrender too little control or hypothetical profit for the American dollars they sought; nerve-racking exhibitions of prototype inventions unable to perform their hypothetical tasks as despairing inventors grew first chatty then weepy; and tours of state-run factories every bit as laughable as their American P.R. agency–penned descriptions had been arousing.

"Usually," said Charles, sighing.

But for every 5 percent of Investigation Requests that the VP approved and elevated to Under Reviews, perhaps 5 percent of those stood up to some scrutiny. These became the tiny little stack of HPs—Hot Prospects. These files then went back to the VP with Charles's second report, now allowed to bloat to five lines, as a single line of Analyst Recommendations was permitted. And after nearly seven months on the job, Charles had seen exactly none of his HPs return. Some had been rejected out of hand by the VP, who expertly discovered some minute flaw in the material Gábor had naïvely collected. Others had received the VP's endorsement only to be vetoed by the New York office for being insufficiently flashy or potentially lucrative to be the firm's first Hungarian venture.

"First?" John smirked.

"Our first," Charles repeated with disgust, "while they pour money into

Prague." Eight months after Charles's arrival, nine to eleven months after ador-
ing articles in *The Wall Street Journal, The Economist*, and the Hungarian press
declared a brave new world, eight months after historic meetings with the finance minister and receptions with the prime minister, eight months after the
ninety-nine-year lease had been signed, handing over the former headquarters
of an obscure and extravagantly nasty division of the secret police, seven
months after Charles had read his first nervous and badly phrased request for
money, nothing had been accomplished. "And nobody cares," Charles said as
he slumped back into his chair. The cost of running the office was a small expense for the firm; they could afford to take their time and get their P.R. just
right.

But Gábor was not going to be a junior member of the team forever, or
even for very long. Eventually the Very Pathetic, the Presiding Vice, would tire
of being essentially illiterate, his ache for the good old lunches at the Box Tree
and the Quilted Giraffe would overwhelm him, and he would relax back to New
York with tales of the quaint Hungarians (of whom, Charles said, the man
knew perhaps two, including his office manager). By that point, Charles's value
to the firm would be so evident that his promotion to head of the office, or at
least to a job where decisions were made, would be a given.

Alternately, he told John, Budapest being what it was right now, he would
have no problem finding investors of his own even that very day. Raising money
in Hungary was beautifully easy, he explained. The hotel lobbies were sloshing
with it. You just needed a suit and a bucket. Bored rich men and the hungry,
beady-eyed representatives of bored rich men occupied nearly every room of
the major hotels, boldly executing "fact-finding missions," proudly reminding
one another that "since democracy requires free markets, a high-return investment is nothing less than a blow struck for liberty." "You'd love these guys,
John. You can't swing a dead cat in the Forum lobby without knocking them
down and watching money fall out of their pockets." Charles had met a few of
these capitalist pilgrims in his office, at embassy parties, in the lobbies. His con-
servative assessment was that in six months or less, he could raise whatever
backing he needed to make a fortune on the Hot Prospect of his choice.

XIII.

WHO WON THE COLD WAR? WE DID. OUR GENERATION. OUR SACRIFICES
broke the Communist behemoth. Yes, granted, okay: Our parents lived through the

flickering black-and-white-footage days of the Cuban missile crisis and Vietnam. But those of us born under Johnson, Nixon, and Ford—we are the triumphant generation. We faced Armageddon from birth; we never knew any other way but mutually assured destruction, and we never blinked. We came of age staring down Brezhnev, Andropov, Chernenko, Ustinov. We were inured to their stony silences, wrinkly faces, and short reigns. When Gorbachev peered out from his Kremlin bunker, what did he see? He saw us entering college, pretty much willing to make do with slightly smaller student loans in order to fund Star Wars, doing what had to be done, voting for Reagan.

We were the Soviet studies majors; we skimmed all our reading on Communism and we never once doubted that dreary doctrine's worthlessness. No Cambridge spy rings, no pink fellow travelers in our ranks. Those who went to farm stuff for the Sandinistas were laughed at, and they came home chastened. We read the CIA techno-thriller novels—all of them. We laughingly registered for a theoretical draft and in such numbers as to make the Kremlin quake. And never forget that we were the generation that inspired MTV and CNN; no Berlin Wall could keep them out and no red-blooded East German could look at the choice of Madonna or Erich Honecker, Miami Vice or the Stasi, and not think it was time for a change.

My God, that was a time, that was a feeling then. You knew where you stood. You stood arm in arm with your friends, in summer internships in Washington, D.C., or backpacking through France, arguing with snot-nosed Danish kids who were certain that the Cold War was all about American imperial stubbornness.

"Where were you when they let the satellite nations go, Grampa? Where were you on VCW Day?" These are the questions our grandchildren will ask us, and I for one will be damn proud to answer, "Me and my buddies were there, Timmy—the whole time. We were in our dorm room and we watched the whole thing, on a screen so big and with Surround Sound speakers so powerful you could practically feel the sledgehammers hitting the stone. That was freedom, Timmy. We did that for you."

Who brought down the Berlin Wall? You and me, Jack, you and me.

And yet, and yet, at what cost? Who among us can say we came through it unscathed? Who among us doesn't look back on a youth largely stolen from us? Sunny days, but not for those of us on the front. Yes, we forged friendships tested by fire. And we are men, though perhaps too soon. Our souls have seen the abyss. A blessing? A curse? Simply a fact, my friends.

And now we are the occupying army, benevolent, offering our vanquished erstwhile foe an open hand and a fresh start: smart investment opportunities, top-notch language instruction, and a whole generation of neo-retro-hippies, bad artists, and club kids. Just like MacArthur in Japan.

A fresh start for them, but for us? I'm afraid of the answer to that question. We must simply nurse our wounds and hope that our children and our children's children and our former foes' children and our former foes' children's children will fully bloom in this new Arcadia, paid for by our sacrifices. We must cultivate our garden.

See you Friday night at A Házam!

Scott put the newspaper on the desk, admitting to himself that John was at least good for a laugh if nothing else, and looked at his class. "Okay. Vocabulary questions first. Yes, Zsolt?"

"*Arcadia?*" asked the young engineer.

"Arcadia. Like paradise. Eden. A mythological reference to a green place, free of worry. Kati?"

The woman from the travel agency moved her lips for a silent sentence before recalling the sound, "*Snot-nose?*"

"*Snot-nosed.* A slang word. Literally, their noses are wet and running. Snot is a vulgar term for nasal fluid. Figuratively, the term means immature and arrogant simultaneously, childish in a negative way."

"And this word, this *snot-nose—*"

"*Snot-nosed,*" accentuated Scott. "It's adjectival." Over the previous forty-five minutes Scott's handwriting had materialized in different colors on the white board: *Your hair color changes as often as my wife's/Your hair color changes as often as my wives. Dafter law/daughter laugh. Cough. Rough. Plough. Thorough. Through.* (Good luck, Magyars!) And now he added: *snot-nosed.*

"Yes, okay, this snot-noseduh, it is only for the Danish?"

"Are only the Danish snot-nosed? No, but a good question. The writer *does* refer to Danes here, but perhaps not literally. Perhaps he refers to a *generic* type of mid-eighties, reflexively leftist Western European youth. I think the writer could just as easily have used *Norwegian.* I'd say this is a good example of synecdoche as we discussed yesterday."

"Who is this writer?" asked Ferenc, a lawyer working for one of the large new Western firms.

Scott answered that the piece was drawn from the previous day's *BudapesToday* and labeled as the first of a new column, "Notes from the New World Order."

Ferenc asked, "Is this a view that—I do not know the word. Do Americans believe like this? What he is writing here?"

"Do Americans believe it? I don't know. I suppose some might."

"Do you?" asked Zsófi from the medical school. There was a sharpness in

her question that irritated Scott; he recognized with distaste her usual ambiva-
lence to ambiguity.

"Do I?" Scott walked around to the front of his desk, hoisted himself up,
and let his heels bounce a few times off its dented steel apron. "Well, how about
this. Do you think the *writer* believes it?"

Scott Price's Advanced Conversation, Comprehension, and Analysis
Class, students aged twenty-eight to forty-six, did not immediately respond. The
class's discomfort grew palpable—something more than the Beginners' shy-
ness or the Intermediates' struggle for vocabulary—a feeling Scott took as a
good sign, hard thinking.

"Why does he write it down on the newspaper—"

"*In* the newspaper, Ildikó."

"Yes. Why does he write it down in the newspaper if he is not believing—"

"To believe is a state of mind verb, Ildi, remember."

"Okay. Yes. Why does he write it down *in* the newspaper if he *does not believe* it?" Ildikó, her grammar in order, looked at Scott as if she deserved an answer.

"Why does he write it in the paper if he doesn't believe it? I'm not saying
he doesn't believe it, Ildi. I don't know if he does or not. What clues are there in
the *text*? What's under the words? That's really the only thing that matters. Pull
it apart. What can you find? That's my question to you guys."

"I am thinking maybe it is not a good question, Scott," said Zsófi, the medical researcher.

"To think: state-of-mind verb," he replied. "In the world of science you
may be right, Zsófi. But what do I say about English? Tibor?"

Tibor spoke very slowly and with a trace of the British accent imprinted
on him by his first English teacher. He stroked his unruly black beard as he
talked. "English is a matter of attitude as much as vocabulary, you say, Scott. I
know you say this. It does seem to be more true than of Hungarian or German.
Your slang changes more rapid, and your culture style has encouraged more,
mmmmph, more shattering? Shattering of the tongue into groups of speakers?"

A few attempts were necessary to untangle the linguistic wiring of Tibor's
thought, but he and Scott finally succeeded, and Tibor continued as Scott
printed the new vocabulary on the white board. "Yes, to splinter into subcul-
tures, each with their own language. Yes. Exactly."

Tibor had a Ph.D. in Hungarian literature, spoke fluent German, read
Latin and Greek, was a published author on the work of the nineteenth-

century Hungarian revolutionary poets Sándor Petőfi and Boldizsár Kis, and was expecting a university appointment for the approaching term. Scott, as he told the students the first day, "spoke flawless English vernacular, a product of twenty-seven-odd years of rigorously enforced linguistic immersion in an Anglophone culture."

His pupil proceeded: "It is my belief that irony is the tool of culture between creative high periods. It is the necessary fertilizer of the culture when it is, how does one—*mi az angolul, hogy parlagon hever?*"

Zsófi, though entirely at a loss as to what Tibor was getting at, was the fastest with the *Magyar-Angol* dictionary. "To lie fallow," she reported proudly.

And Scott was back at the white board writing in red erasable marker: *To lie fallow. Fallow (adj. agr.)* Tibor continued to massage the mass of twisted black hair falling from his chin. "Fallow. Yes," he began again. "American culture lies fallow now. There is nothing living, only things waiting. And the earth gives off only a smell. This smell, not pleasant, is irony. Like this newspaper writer. Very self-knowing." *Self-conscious (adj. psych.)* "Yes. This is the self-conscious newspaperman's place in the world, I am thinking. It is the role now of your writers and thinkers in your culture to absorb what have come before, to filter the last good harvest, and to throw off the—the bad wheat." *Chaff (n. agr.)* "To throw off the chaff. To clear the land. Put in fertilizer. Put the good grain in the tall barn." *Silo (n. agr.)* "In the sheelo. To throw off the chaff, put good grain in the sheelo, put the bad-smell irony everywhere, and wait for new seasons." Tibor stroked his beard. The rest of the class looked to Scott as the day's curriculum had unexpectedly delved deeply into agricultural questions.

"Well. Who agrees with—"

"Oh, also, Scott, I am sorry."

"Yes, Tibor?"

"Arcadia is not a mythological paradise as Eden. It is a real part of the Greekland." *Greece (country)* "A real part of the Greece. It symbolized first, as you say, a green and perfect country life, but then we learn that Arcadians were very uneducated and violence and cruel. For smart people then after, Arcadia is a symbol of intellectual's wrong effort to see happiness in savages."

Silence.

"Okay, great. Thank you, Tibor."

"This is not good," insisted Zsófi. "It is a simple question, yes? Does he think it is true, he saved us from Russians by liking to watch MTV?"

István, a young politician from one of the new parties, who would six years hence become minister of the interior, responded, "It is Marx upside down, and I think, yes, he may be right. Capitalism provided for people better than Communism, and with strong TV signals everybody knowed it."

"Knew. Simple past. Know, knew, known."

"We all knew it."

XIV.

"YOU WANT COME HOME WITH ME?"

Mark, who had been staring at the young man from across the nearly empty bar, answered yes in a lurch. "No," he corrected himself. "You come home with me."

And so it was that Mark Payton slept with his first Hungarian and later, when the need to make conversation returned, found himself in the cliché role of the spent adventurer who seeks to feel human again with the stranger in his bed.

Early summer moonlight spilled over the bedside windowsill and onto Mark and László, both stretched out nude. László smoked a hand-rolled post-coital cigarette, a nostalgic affectation Mark found charming and atmospheric, and he read the gesture as a sign that this Hungarian stranger felt as the Canadian did about the world. The smell of the cigarette rising in the old apartment brought the building to life, made Mark's Buda home more real to him. Such cigarettes had been rolled and smoked here during wars and revolutions, under tyrants, at moments of hope, during peaceful stretches of simple domesticity. Mark thought of his own childhood homes, of dormitories and first apartments, all modern, bare of history and therefore of peace. Here, though, was a bridge to the better past, smelling of tobacco from a plastic pouch.

"They say the best place to learn a language is in bed." Mark delivered this ridiculous proverb in a plausibly deniable tone but still hoped to provoke the offer of an intimate, collegial tutorial. The Hungarian made a quietly dismissive noise.

Mark tried again; rolled over and propped his chin on his stacked fists. "*Elnézést, uram, megtudná mondani mennyi az idő?*"

László laughed low. "You learn in a class?"

"Yes. *Igen.* And on my own. Why are you laughing? Did I say it wrong?"

The man blew a stream of smoke at an angle just slightly away from Mark's face. "You speak anything besides English or you like all Americans?"

"Okay, one: *Kanadai* is different than *amerikai*. And two, yes. I read classical and church Latin and ancient Greek. I speak pretty good Quebecois. I have functional Cornish and I can speak Manx."

"Don't get angry on me," said László, flicking ash into a bedside glass of water. "I just am wanting to say that in these languages—"

"I'm not angry."

"Fine, okay, you not angry. But look. In English you say, 'Hey, man, what time it is?' Right? So where did you learn *Megtudná mondani mennyi az idő?*"

The scorn surprised Mark. He had learned it from a Hungarian textbook. Didn't it mean *What time is it?*

"No. It means, 'Excuse me for bothering you, very high up sir, I am nothing, you are a big important person, we are from different classes, I am like an animal. I am guilty to bother you and you are ashameful to talk to me, but I am too poor to own a watch and too scared to go into store to look at a clock, I am dirt, but can you please, please, be good and tell me what time is it and then maybe spit on me if you like, since I am only a little faggot to you?' " László took one last drag, then dropped the butt into the water glass, where it made the sound of fading expectations.

"I said all that, actually? Hungarian is awfully efficient."

"Man, what time it is? *Mennyi az idő?* That's it. Simple."

Mark rose from the bed and walked to the bookshelf to find his textbook and notes. "But what about being polite?"

The naked Hungarian lay on his back, looking at the ceiling. "What I say was polite. But yours, yours was like British shit. We are not British, man. We have chance to be new now, with the Communist shit finished. What will be us now? We start from nothing, so why be British? These are rare chance now, you know?"

The intellectual point—the idea of developing a new culture based on free elections—struck Mark as laughably ahistorical, but, relieved at least that the nude man was interested in subjects like this, Mark grasped at the chance for connection. "You can't make new people, László. You still speak the same language. Besides, it was only the government. You still have your culture and the country and the buildings and people's habits." Mark disappeared into the kitchen and struck a match to light the stove, an Old World necessity he found beautiful and comforting. He put on a kettle and called into the next room, offering tea.

László sat cross-legged on the bed and rolled another cigarette, then put on his briefs and rose to examine Mark's shelves. He turned his head sideways to read the spines. The authors' names nearly all ended with Ph.D. and M.Phil. The covers were colorless and the titles bisected with colons: *The Devil You Know: State, Society, and Angst in Berlin, 1899–1901. Mapless, Flapless, and Hapless: Early Popular Images of Aviation. Mistakenly Thought: A Compendium of Discredited Science. You Had to Be There: Approaches to Humor, 1415–1914. Piqued in Darien: Expressions of Emotion in WASP Culture, 1973–1979,* by Lisa R. Pruth, M.Phil.

Mark returned to his bedroom holding two cups of tea. He found László wearing underwear. Two lamps were now on, and the foreigner was messing up the order of Mark's books. The curtains were still open, and Mark was at a loss as to what to do first. Put on his own underwear? Close the curtains? Protect his belongings? He felt himself suddenly sweating, and his chest and stomach hurt. He sloshed the tea on the TV table, grabbed his own underwear and jeans, tugged them on hurriedly, and sat in the apartment's only chair.

"Hey, relax, man," said László without looking up from the title page of *You Had to Be There.* "You read all these books?" László asked in the present tense. Mark thought the stranger's voice carried some scorn or doubt. Only later would he wonder if it had just been the untranslatable intonations of a foreigner, the inevitable cross-cultural misunderstandings lurking in tones and glances and assumptions.

"All of most of them, most of the rest of them." Mark's stock answer spilled out of his mouth in one sullen, toneless word—*allofmostofthemmostoftherestofthem*—and he watched it fall into the linguistic cracks between the two of them. A syllable or two splintered off and lodged in the Hungarian's ear. Mark saw him wrestle with the words and was pleased he had confused this arrogant foreigner, had forced him to acknowledge his lack of what he probably valued most: English fluency.

"All or most of the rest?"

"Yeah. That's right," Mark replied. "Mostly all of rest or not within."

The Hungarian nodded and looked back at the book he was balancing open. He sipped his tea. "What else you learn from your book of Hungarian?"

And as quickly as it had come, it left. Mark softened and answered with a proud smile, *"Legyen szíves, uram, kérek szépen egy kávét."*

"Man, you go and do it again, fuck Jesus. You want a coffee, just ask it. You say please fifteen times first the waiter gonna be asleep. *Kávét kérek.* That's it, man." He examined the author's biography on the inside back cover of *Piqued in Darien.*

"Yeah, but why should I trust you, László? What if everyone in Hungary thinks you're the rudest guy in the country and I learn how to speak Hungarian from you and then I'm the second rudest guy in the country, even though actually I was polite at home, even for a Canadian? Suddenly polite Mark becomes rude Mark and I never even know it."

"Big fuck. Who's cared?"

"I'm not scared. I'm just saying—"

"Nobody's cared."

"Okay, some people are scared, but so what?"

"So, fine, one guy's cared, but just be different and new. Be rude, man, if that's what life and Hungary make you."

"You're not Hungary, László. You're just you. You're just—"

"Yes, nice working. You catch me. I trick you. The secret police pay me to make foreign men act rude. You're a genius from reading all your books." He tossed the book on the bed, kicked his jeans up off the floor and into his hands.

Mark saw in the collection of the jeans the clear first step to the door. Thinking only slightly, he stood up, placed his tea on the table, took off his own jeans, and lay back down on the sofa bed. "Hey, don't go. Tell me about the new, about what the new Hungarians will be like. Tell me about that." The words crowded their way out of Mark's mouth, but László kept dressing.

The Hungarian pulled on his Rolling Stones concert tour T-shirt and slumped into the chair to put on his socks and Nikes. "What the hell, man? What is that—a question for some study book? I just say we aren't British or German or old Communists. We will just be people now. You are not understanding what I mean, but"— he stood and put on his varsity-style letter jacket as Mark lifted his own hips and slid off his boxer shorts—"but that's your thing, I think. Ciao."

"Ciao," said Mark quietly, naked. László turned away: 1972 FREE MY VALUE TIGERS it said in English on the back of his jacket in the swooping sewn-on typeface of American high school sports teams. The door closed and Mark listened to László walk past the window, alongside the courtyard, down the steps.

Mark Payton lay on his back, and though he cried until the pillow collected two wet spots on either side of his head, he also had to admit that he found the whole thing very, very funny. He struggled to remember the exact wording of the ludicrous jacket; that would be essential for retelling.

XV.

BY THE END OF JUNE, HIS PRIMARY REASON FOR HAVING MOVED TO BUDA-pest growing increasingly unattainable and more and more ridiculous to him anyhow, John Price had developed a habit of saying good night to his wife and child before bed. Sober or drunk, he would stop to visit with them at their permanent positions atop the cable box and on the bedside table. He would kiss his fingers and place them on their lips or brows. When he was sober, the entire ritual was, of course, a comedy. "Sleep well and dream of me, doll face," he would say to the woman in the dress. "Tomorrow is another day, tiger," he told the incurably unhappy baby.

When he was drunk, however, the ritual was more complicated. To an observer (of which there were none) it would not have been absolutely clear that John understood these photographs were not truly of his family. There would be no irony in his tone as he described his day to the black-and-white photograph of the woman in front of the tree. He might sit in the chair across from her and lean forward with his legs apart in an effort to stay awake. He might doze for a minute, then half open his eyes with a muttered apology. He might say he had made a mistake in moving to this foreign city—it had seemed like a good idea in California, but now where else could he go? He would explain in grim detail how Scott had been an intolerable and intolerant figure for much of his youth, how Scott was disappointing him every day now and seemed to be enjoying it, then quickly laugh and do imitations of his editor or other people at the paper, trying to make her laugh, knowing it was only a photograph and yet still speaking to her as if a relationship existed, or perhaps just practicing for Emily. Hours might pass in which he slept in the chair and then he might awaken, some degree closer to sober, and as his eyes opened slowly and painfully, he would see her picture spotlit under the bedside lamp, just a few feet away from him in the darkness, like the end of a long journey just now in view, just a little farther on, and he would smile. "Are you still awake?" he might ask in the intimate whisper of 3 A.M. lovers who half arise, warm and happy, to find they have been in someone's company during all those lost hours of sleep. And he would stumble to the still folded sofa bed.

The next mornings, none of this remained, no memory, no idea, no anger toward Scott, no warmth of having slept in another's company, only the tired ache and sour stomach, the dry gums and eyes and balled-up tissues, the warm and suspect spring water in plastic bottles, the cracked porcelain of the ancient sink, the fruitless search for an interesting cable channel, the first cigarette on the balcony and the accompanying first thought about Emily.

JOHN HELD NOT ONE religious belief, was not a painfully closeted homosexual, boasted no particular physical deformities. Intelligent enough, interested in the world around him, not raised under any particular regime of antisexuality, not matrimony-mad, attracted to women in general and some women in particular, John Price was a virgin.

A healthy American male, born in 1966, navigated adolescence and co-educational college and reached July 1, 1990, age twenty-four, a virgin?

From well before puberty, from well before the first time he noticed a girl's distinctive shape and perfume, from well before his first horrifying playground misinformation about the pertinent mechanics, from well before his first pounding, merciless erection, which threatened to drain the blood from his brain until he passed out, John Price had liked to read.

An avid and precocious reader like his brother before him, from books he extracted pithy life lessons, which he kept in a small notebook, whose cover bore a picture of Willie Stargell, the charismatic captain and first baseman of the Pittsburgh Pirates. Opening in the sloppy printing of an eight-year-old, advancing to the cautious cursive of a ten-year-old, developing into the reckless swoops of a twelve-year-old trying to mimic his father's hand, and then arriving at the sloppy printing of a college freshman, John inscribed lessons such as:

age 8: avoid sea travel (*Treasure Island*)

age 9: as you get older, it's harder to have any fun (*The Lion, the Witch and the Wardrobe*)

age 9: don't go looking for trouble (*The Hobbit*)

age 10: it takes a lot of money to get out of trouble (*The Count of Monte Cristo*)

age 11: sometimes it's better to just leave well enough alone (*Dr. Jekyll and Mr. Hyde*)

age 12: if you're not really, really careful, you'll grow up bitter (*Moby-Dick*)

age 13: always know where your escape routes are and what you can use as a weapon in case of trouble (*Heart of Darkness*) age 13: don't read too much (*Don Quixote*)

age 15: it's better to die, even to die slowly, than to get married (*War and Peace*)

age 15: a lot of people feel like I do, but they've learned to hide it (*The Stranger*), because they're phonies (*The Catcher in the Rye*)

age 16: I want to live inside a glowing circle of love and romance (*title never included; entry violently scratched out with black ink shortly after being written*)

age 17: once it's past, forget it; it won't help to think about it (*The Great Gatsby*)

age 19, *last entry, freshman year of college:* No one cares. And why should they? (*No Exit, Nausea*)

Some of these lessons were forgotten, consciously rejected, quietly outgrown, or modified for later use. But some weren't. In his tattered notebook, among more than two hundred entries, one maintained vigorous control of John's behavior for many years.

It was written at age eleven, just about the same time he was forced to share Scott's bed, because their father had been exiled to John's on his way out the door for the first of many times: "Sex makes men behave how it wants, not how they want. Sex turns men into idiots and should be avoided, though this seems to be difficult." (The supporting examples were entered over several years, in all those different handwriting styles: *Mike Steele and the Cleanest Killer, The Three Musketeers,* Sherlock Holmes' *A Scandal in Bohemia, Ivanhoe,* Genesis, *Lolita, Exodus, Tess of the D'Urbervilles,* Deuteronomy, *Swann's Way,* and so on, through his freshman year of college.)

There was something about that creepy Mike Steele thriller, something about the betrayals, fumblings, and uncertainties of d'Artagnan and Athos a year later, something about Sherlock (trusted, solid Sherlock!) mooning around after that ridiculous Irene Adler, not to mention Mr. Price. Somehow, at age eleven, and with some real pride, John Price had perceived, entirely on his own, what he took to be his first observed law of human nature. In book after book, story after story, sex corrupted principles, derailed careers, intruded into peace, tempted heroes into idleness and silliness. For a while, reading became literally sickening to him as hero after hero turned into buffoon, as nearly every book mapped the same tragic terrain. The eleven-year-old boy knew willpower would have to be engaged and sacrifices made, but he was ready: He would not have any of this sex.

He had derived a very comprehensive plan by the time he was fourteen: Despite countless efforts to protect themselves with little "moralities" and "guidelines," people (not least his parents and, lately, gargantuan Scott) continued to make fools of themselves; therefore, the only safely dignified sexual behavior, the only *moral* behavior—if you insisted on that word—was complete, uncompromising, lifelong no-sex-at-all.

John adopted this view as an expression of his truest self. He shaped it into a coherent, publicly held policy that, even into high school, he would propose to and defend from his friends, first flabbergasting then exasperating then just impressing and frightening them with his extreme and unpopular position. By the time he entered college, he was unsurprisingly tired of being the sole defender of human dignity. The transition from a Southern California high school to a Northern California university seemed an optimal time for personality overhauls, so John consciously decided never to discuss his position again. But if his evangelical urges were curbed, his dumb, head-shaking wonder at other people's behavior was not; the array of foolish semi-ethics still surprised him in this new world, where bunk beds and thin walls made sex an audible and ubiquitous reality. People still spoke loudly and frequently of their ideals, their philosophies, their rock-solid (until later that night) dividing lines between right and wrong. Even as they rejected their parents' sexual rules as the naïve products of an imaginary 1950s, they insisted on declaiming their own, and John knew he alone was calm and happy while everyone around him went mad with lust, love, or loneliness.

But for this one quirk, John led a normal life at school. He did drink rather more than his friends, but that was hardly frowned upon. He achieved sexual release in the time-honored, private fashion his philosophy grudgingly tolerated, often concluding the practice with a half-serious, half-spoken "There. That ought to hold the bastard for a while." He went to parties, danced, and even dated slightly. And of course he did think less often of his theories. Unlike in high school, weeks would pass without even one thought of avoiding sex and, slightly drunk at a party, he might find himself kissing a girl with whom he had just danced. But years of theorizing had hardwired him: Without a thought for human dignity or heroic natures, and despite his attraction to the girl, he would blink as if coming out of a trance and murmur the words every woman longs to hear: "I should probably go." His principles were in place without his ever having to think about them. Alcohol made the mechanism work more smoothly: He would feel hot, flushed, and unsteady (a common side effect of mixing alcohol and someone else's saliva) and would need air and solitude at once. A cool and sober kiss outside would have been fatal, but somehow John was never exposed to that variety.

XVI.

A MURAL COVERED THE BLUE JAZZ CLUB'S SKY BLUE WALLS AND CEILING. Painted by two students of the Hungarian National Academy of Fine Arts, deceased legends of jazz chatted, smoked, drank, and played in heaven. The departed musicians, dressed as they had been in life, also wore angel wings of varying styles. Billie Holiday—restored to the fresh beauty of her youth, in a silver evening gown, the trademark hibiscus in her hair—sang into a crystal microphone atop the ridges and rolls of a golden-white cloudscape. To her side, peeking out from under his porkpie hat, Lester Young played, his tenor sax twisted high off to one side like a giant's flute. Duke Ellington hunched over a transparent grand piano while Billy Strayhorn penciled changes to the score in front of him. Off to their left, Ben Webster and Coleman Hawkins swirled their amber lowballs and laughed as two dimple-buttocked cherubim—their faces copied from Raphael's *Sistine Madonna*—attempted to produce sound from the men's saxophones, though the horns were too large for the tottering *putti* to hold. Just to the side of the stage, Chet Baker lay on a cloud, on his back, his unobtrusive wings discreetly attached to a lightweight blue canvas jacket, zipped halfway. The afterlife had been kind to him, too, and his youth had returned without grudge. The marks of abuse and suffering had been erased and he looked again as he had in the 1950s, like a native of these clouds. He wore khakis and white shoes without socks, and he was playing his trumpet and staring straight upward, as if heaven were okay but there might be a better place just a little farther up. Behind and beneath him, on a bank of clouds sculpted as cumulal thrones, the Virgin Mary and a half-dozen female saints (recognizable by their traditional emblems) sat or stood in a group, enraptured by the sight of Chet and the sound of his trumpet: Saint Elizabeth of Hungary, her basket of roses on her lap; Saints Gisella and Petronilla half swooning against their brooms; and matronly Saint Anastasia—her double chin in her fleshy palm, her moist, swollen eyes fixed on Chet, her huge legs plodding heavily even here (straining the cumulo-ottoman they rested on)—briefly paused at her loom, leaving unfinished a tapestry of (almost) this exact moment: Chet on a cloud, on his back, his unobtrusive wings discreetly attached to a lightweight blue canvas jacket, but his trumpet floating unused next to him while he passionately kissed a not at all matronly Saint Anastasia.

At the back of the room, Mingus, Monk, and Parker chatted just over the round table where John Price and Emily Oliver sat side by side listening to a peculiar band finish "I Cover the Waterfront." Pool balls clicked from the club's other room just to John's right, and from the bar, at his left, came the love calls of glasses and bottles and charged hoses. He wore his one blazer and drank Unicum from a glass labeled with the name of an American rum and flicked the ash from his Mockba Red cigarette into a plastic ashtray that advertised the Western smokes preferred by obsessive lovers and tough-minded individualists.

A few days earlier (after another game of Sincerity in which Emily had performed dismally or enchantingly, depending on one's point of view), John had mustered the nerve to propose this date, which opened at the Tabán Rooster: chicken paprikás, rice, cheap red wine. John spent his few new words of Hungarian to order the meal, and an elderly busboy chipped in his handful of English to make up the difference. Emily apologized for not being much assistance, but she explained she hadn't been paying the closest attention in her class and had been relying pretty heavily on the ambassador's driver and cook for help in performing those of her tasks that required fluency.

She laughed easily, was somehow different from the woman waking under the tree; the word *shinier* occurred to John. Conversation wandered effortlessly from the paper to the embassy, through expatriate existence, the pleasures and lunacies of Budapest life. She held her wine in both hands and laughed when the Gypsy violinist in a spangled black vest accepted John's forints in exchange for playing farther from their table. John played up the complications of the deal (the exact price stated in feet from the table per forint) to keep her laughing. She complimented him on his first few columns, and he thanked her, quietly pleased that she had read them at all. She described her days—errands and calendars, hostessing and apologizing—with a sort of quiet sincerity that John took for intimacy. The widowed ambassador was a good man, she said, but lonely, and he needed a woman's advice on certain matters. He tended to ask a lot of social-protocol questions, surprisingly, and lately he was starting to trust Emily about his wardrobe, "specifically the troubling mysteries of necktie selection," she reported. He was a career diplomat, not a political appointee. His name—so rich with old money—did not seem to her a very accurate guide to his personality or his style; his confidence flagged at funny moments, and he even stuttered when unprepared for conversation. She had been expecting a cold boss, but she was fond of him, enjoyed having him rely on her more and more. "Lucky ambassador," John allowed himself, and she rolled her eyes and said, "Oh please."

How John sees them after dinner: They are walking across the Chain Bridge—the city's postcard superstar—crossing the Danube toward the new jazz club he has recently discovered and instantly dedicated to their first date. He's walking backward a few feet in front of her and leaning slightly toward her. His hands gesture in support of a funny story he's telling, and she walks with her hands in her jacket pockets. Her head tilts back when she laughs, and John remembers her like that (even as it's happening): walking toward him forever, forever laughing. The Chain Bridge's lights have painted its pocked stone bricks a soft yellow and Emily's hair a dark gold, and the river stops flowing for John to memorize it, to count the blue and white lights sprinkled over the roll of its immobile waves, and the passing cars go silent and emit no exhaust, so that the only sound is her laugh and the only scent, her perfume.

They played pool, then sat under Mingus, Monk, and Parker, drank Unicum, and listened to the music. A white American woman about twenty-five, billed as Billie Fitzgerald, wore a hibiscus in her hair and sat spotlit on a stool with a microphone in one hand and a lowball of Scotch in the other. Her band was a nineteen-year-old Hungarian pianist in a T-shirt and an old tuxedo jacket, corduroy cutoff shorts, and blue plastic flip-flops stamped with the logo of a German sporting goods company; and fifteen-year-old Russian twin brothers, one massaging an ancient upright bass with albinic patches of fading stain, the other swishing brushes over a minimalist drum kit pieced together from several donor kits: a red snare, a few cymbals of different makes, and a blue glittering bass drum with the name of some rock 'n' roll band written in Cyrillic lettering across the head.

"I Cover the Waterfront" came to a quiet bass-and-piano close. The singer cleared her throat with an amplified crack and swigged her drink. Emily checked her watch and excused herself to call her roommates. "They'll want to know what time I'll be home. Back in a flash! This group is good, aren't they?" She moved away to the phone on the far side of the bar.

"That's the last time we're going to do that tune, though it is pretty," the singer said to the crowd in English, in a smoke-sanded alto. "It's another one of those tunes that make women seem pathetic, always waiting for their man to pay attention to them. I don't like how often those Tin Pan Alley guys showed women waiting for love, waiting for their man to treat them right. So we don't do those tunes anymore." She took another hit of Scotch, crunched a piece of ice, and spit half of it back into the glass. The audience, mostly Hungarian, seemed to be listening politely, and John was trying to gauge if she was serious or not, but he was distracted by watching Emily pick up the receiver, examine and deposit coins, dial, talk. Her back was to him now. Her neck arched out of her collar as she cradled the phone against her shoulder. She took something out of her bag. John imagined walking up behind her and touching his lips to her unoccupied ear or to the curving, throbbing cords in her neck. "Individuals have to make a stand in the workplace. This is my workplace. This is where I make my stand, and all my backup musicians agree with me or I wouldn't hire them. Right, guys?" Her Eastern European musicians nodded and she counted off the next tune.

As the sung chorus to "Love for Sale" gave way to a piano solo, John watched Emily, still on the phone, her back to him, about thirty feet away, inaudible over the music and the bar noise, facing the phone's antiquated gray-metal wall attachment. He approached her back, and began to hear just the slightest sounds of her conversation, not yet words, just the faintest murmuring cadences under the music, cadences just vaguely foreign. The drum solo started with a cymbalic crash, causing Emily to look back over her shoulder, where she saw John approaching. "I will," she was saying. "The band's pretty neat. Old stuff, like jazz music and stuff, but it's a neat bar. We should hang here sometime. Yeah, okay, I will. See ya, crazy!" She hung up. "The Julies say hi. Okay, it's a school night, guy," she continued, "so let's have one more drink, but then I gotta get home."

When they approached the bar, the bartender—who had been watching the band from his post near the phone—turned first to Emily and said something quick and unintelligible in Hungarian. She made the face of noncomprehension, shrugged the shrug. *"Nem beszélek magyarul,"* she laughingly, laughably managed to produce in her strong Midwestern American accent. The bartender laughed and again expounded in rapid Hungarian. Emily shrugged again, said, "Sorry," with a smile, and returned to the table.

"She is Hungarian, yeah?" the bartender asked John in English, his face a mixture of puzzlement and offense.

John returned to the table with drinks as the singer was accepting applause and introducing her bandmates. "The bartender thinks he knows you or some—"

"We should buy the band a round, shouldn't we? That's like traditional, and it would be so fun, wouldn't it?"

Men on first dates generally do what they are told; a few minutes later, Billie graciously accepted another lowball of brand name Scotch; Kálmán, the pianist, joined John and Emily in an Unicum; and Boris and Yuri, the Russian rhythm section, had colas. "Real Coke! Not Pepsi, yes? Real Coke. Please," Boris insisted, while Yuri pleaded for Pepsi.

He returned again from the bar, pressing the bouquet of glassware together for his strange companions. Two cola-addicted Russian children, a freakily dressed piano player, and a showily politically conscious jazz singer surrounded his date, and it required an act of will not to throw the glasses to the floor and ask what in the name of holy hell she was doing entertaining the Misfit Symphony when the two of them could be out in the night air, kissing under the stars, dancing on the riverfront, planning a life and a future where they—. There she sits, though, listening to that madwoman talk about misogynistic jazz. She listened to me like that at dinner, and now she's escaped me. She can just move in and out like that. And there she is, easily being with the band. How to jump across whatever this is and arrive, on the far side, sitting next to her without a thought but that? This is my fault. I lack something or else I would be here without a thought, like her, on the other side of whatever this is. And then it's over, we're done, yes, nice to meet you, too, we really enjoyed your music, absolutely, yeah, great. Shall we? A walk to the door, a mouthful of summer night, and, at the mere sight of her, a taxi sprouts from the ground and opens to embrace her. Yeah, I had a nice time, too, good. So I'll see you at the July Fourth party, I understand you'll be working, but we'll get a chance to talk there, great, no problem, no, please, I had fun, too, so don't thank me, the hesitation and then the cheek. And done. Still on the wrong side of whatever this is.

He leaned against the lamppost in front of the noisy club and lit a cigarette as her cab entered the stream of light and fume toward Buda.

A moment sticky with clichés: a young man leans against a lamppost, blowing cigarette smoke into the night. Music spills out with a wedge of light from the open door of a jazz club and it creeps into the circle of yellow that he occupies under the lamp, and he watches the cab drive off with the woman who has wedged her way under his skin, the woman whose heart is a mystery to him.

Self-consciousness arrives in fast and merciless stages: First he assumes that clichéd position under the light without giving it a thought, the natural physical expression of his ache and hunger and thwarted efforts, but hardly has he struck the match before he notices what he's doing, how he looks. As the first vine of smoke winds up the pole toward the light, John's very stance—the bend of his knee—belongs to a private eye fed up with it all or a heartbroken crooner on the cover of *Music for Lonely Nights*. John is a supremely, expertly cynical adman's most masterly condensation of fifty years of images of love, loss, solitude, and self-disgust. Even his grunt of disgust at this discovery—he knows before it has faded—sounded just like a gumshoe's disgust at the treachery of broads or Bogey's hard-won knowledge that this war is making fools of us all or the crooner's amazement that he's lost at love again, oh, oh, oh, he's lost at love again. And then, at last, John is anointed with the soothing balm of irony: When even his spontaneous grunts are impossibly and automatically insincere, he can only laugh. As in front of a tailor's triple mirrors, he sees the silliness of seeing the silliness of it, feels the pleasantly dry, infinitely regressing amusement he can feel at his own expense. It is only now that he finally loses sight of her cab as it blends into traffic. (Part of him is stunned that it can blend at all, that it isn't marked with some sort of phosphorescence.)

And as she vanished, a little seesaw that John had unknowingly been constructing in his heart over the last month tipped to the other side: He was in a cab giving his brother's address before he knew why. He crossed the bridge, watched the lights of the next bridge upriver, inhaled the warm wind, and realized that he could now provide Scott what they both needed: a matter of deep personal importance without any tie to the past, to their mutual grievances, griefs, resentments. He would meet his brother in the present, looking straight ahead, humbly coming for help and candor. He would describe what he had found in their friend Emily, would even plot romantic strategy and tactics with his brother, since Scott always seemed to have girlfriends, even back when he was grotesque and embarrassing and the girls were, too.

Scott opened the door barefoot, in jeans and a T-shirt, holding upright a margarine-shiny spatula. "Hey, good. Listen, I really want to talk to you about—"

"Bro!" Scott bellowed. "Enter! My pleasure at seeing you chokes me with emotion!" John followed him to the kitchen, and the smell of something strange drove from his brain all his reasons for coming. A beautiful young brunette, also barefoot, sat on a tall stool. She wore an oversize white shirt that hung low over gray sweatpants emblazoned with the name of Scott and John's high school (only the last syllable of which was visible under her shirttails). She had rolled the sleeves several times to reveal her small hands, and the sweats were bunched at her naked ankles.

"Johnny, Mária. Mária finished the school's Beginners Two course today, so we're having a celebratory meal." Scott stood at the stove and scraped at something. "Mária, this would be John, my birth brother."

"I am very happy to knowing you."

"And since it's kind of a private celebration," Scott said, smiling broadly and intentionally talking too rapidly for his date to understand, "I really look forward to catching up with you soon. That would be fantastic. I really look forward to that. And be sure to call first, as a rule." The door closed behind John, who considered calling Charles Gábor to have a drink but then thought better of it before hiking down the dark, suburban, cab-free hill toward the distant river.

XVII.

IN THE PRECEDING FIVE OR SIX DECADES, PEST'S NINETEENTH-CENTURY town houses—unlike the stylistically similar homes built by the nineteenth-century rich of Paris, Boston, or Brooklyn—had been left to erode under the tide of years, unbarricaded by money, exposed to the ferocity of the relentlessly crashing surf. A walk along any one of the city's dark, narrow side streets, late in the evening of the Fourth of July, 1990, would have provided a natural history museum display of the resulting striations and accretions.

The ornate iron grille in front of the leaded glass of the heavy, curved front door at number 4, for example, was only slightly touched: The black paint was scrubbed entirely away—not a single flake of it remained—and rust barnacles had sprouted in spots, but the plump iron leaves, the graceful metal ivy, even the brittle metal twigs were still solid. The frosted-glass panels behind the ironwork, though, had long since turned to wood and nails under the rhythmic lappings.

To the right, at number 6, inside the unlocked front door, one could still see the old square tiling of the entryway floor. Time had repainted the tiles, stubbornly insisting on two shades of dull brown streaked with gray rather than a forgotten human's choice of pearl and ebony, and had then cracked almost every one and swallowed some of them whole, leaving here and there a small square of soft, gray dust recessed below the level of the floor, cunningly camouflaged traps where high heels and cane tips were lured and devoured.

A noisy crowd milled in front of number 16, at the corner where the street opened onto a small square. The building's façade had been worn until the stone garlands under the windows appeared to be paradoxically both smooth and crumbling. The balconies, like John's on Andrássy út, were invitations to gamble. Bullet holes, administered in two doses, still drilled the front of the building, like the work of massive, lithovoric termites. One of these cavities— much to the amusement of generations of neighborhood children—penetrated the plump stone bottom of a floating cherub, who supported one end of a disintegrating garland. He had been looking over his right shoulder at the time of the shooting and now was trying to glimpse his wound. One could imagine a young Russian or German invader avoiding certain crucial details and reporting this incident as a confirmed kill or, in 1956, a Hungarian rebel sniper across the street, shooting perhaps from his own bedroom window, bored in a lull in the action and testing his skill on a promising target that he had looked at every day and night for nineteen years.

Number 16 had been a gift when it was completed in 1874. Its birthdate was carved next to a Latinized version of the Hungarian architect's name in the ornamental stonework over the front door, but by 1990 the entire 7 and the right half of the 8 had turned to dust (one lazy grain of rock at a time, like an aesthete preacher's illustration of eternity) until only a mysterious hieroglyphic remained, a date without a decade and almost without a century, 1ε 4.

BUT IN 1874 the building is in the very latest (French) style. It is the gift of a decliningly rich man to his second son on the occasion of that son's wedding. The son and his new bride take possession of the house in June of that year, one month after the date appears above the door. Man and wife arrive from Budapest's Nyugati rail station in their carriage, directly from a wedding trip that had taken them to Vienna, Italy, and Greece. The husband helps his wife down, takes her arm, walks her the ten yards from road to front stairs, past hedges and flowers, past welcoming staff (a cook and two maids come with the residence). At the threshold, husband smiles at bride, whispers something in her ear that makes her blush, kisses her hand. "Welcome to your home, my dear," he says, and a maid opens their door.

BY 1990, THE HEDGES and flowers were gone. The road had been expanded, and a sidewalk only a few feet wide separated the six thin concrete steps to the front door from the daily parade of fuming tailpipes and balding tires. A side door for tenants led into the courtyard and from there to the crowded upper-floor apartments. Next to the front door, however, hung a hand-painted sign, red and black letters on wood: ISTEN HOZOTT A HÁZAMBAN [Welcome to my house].

LATE ONE AFTERNOON, after the house is settled, the furnishings arranged, and a social life as a couple is embarked upon, the new husband is made to understand by his father that there is not enough money to support three sons without careers. The bulk of the father's fortune will naturally pass to the eldest son and a small annual sum—enough to pay for certain essentials, such as the house, for example, but far insufficient to rely on for everything—will accrue to the two younger brothers. In a small study off the main hall the father delivers this news to the young man in a tone of jovial inevitability, nothing surprising in the matter at all; nothing else could ever have been expected or supposed. The house, his father explains, was meant to provide a fair beginning and should serve that purpose in the family for generations. The father, feigning not to notice his son's expression, lists several possibilities that can be arranged for him, none terribly taxing or at all unbecoming, good opportunities to think over, no hurry, of course, but do let me know your preferences: a seat on the stock exchange, participation in some commercial ventures, a position in the government. The son is silent, his wrath overcoming his initial astonishment at the betrayal. The father, still avoiding his son's glance, concludes his practiced remarks, says he understands the boy will want some time to think about it, and offers to show himself out. The owner of the house waits until the sounds of his father's exit have faded before he hurls his coffee cup at the wall, where it shatters with an explosion muffled only by his obscene expression of fury.

THE SIGN—ISTEN HOZOTT A HÁZAMBAN—was hung in 1989 by Tamás Fehér when the legal standing of his new project was still unsettled. The sign was a joke, a feeble disguise expected to fool no one. And even when the club's legal status was secure, nothing more official or easy to use replaced the old sign. Instead, the institution grew in popularity without any name at all and was widely known simply as A Házam [My House]. The building's interior layout had changed substantially in its 116 years; by 1990 the small study (where the first of the wedding china had broken) corresponded only approximately to "Backroom 2," where several cartons of liquor lay stacked next to Tamás's desk. The small study off the main hall had been larger than Backroom 2, however, and if the china cup had exploded just over where a framed photo of a Hungarian fashion model now sat on Tamás's desk, it had actually been thrown from a spot located on the far side of the curtain that separated Backroom 2 from the bar.

THE NOISE WILL SOON conjure his curious wife. The thought of her seeing him like this, humiliated by his father and elder brother, is unbearable. He strides out of the room, passing a frightened maid coming to clear up the remnants of the cup, and turns away from the main stairs, pretending not to hear his wife calling him. Still unfamiliar with parts of his new home, he finds himself in the kitchen, walking rapidly past the baffled (and territorially offended) cook, who is in conversation with the faceless second maid, both of whom jump to standing and bow their heads as their fuming master passes. He opens first one door, which he finds full of pots and pans, then a second, and walks down the brick stairs in front of him. The staircase is impossibly dark, and in a rage he turns back up the stairs. "*Gyertyát!*" he demands, and the maid quickly complies. Armed now with a candle, he closes the door behind him and heads downstairs again. He stands on the new brick floor of a cellar he did not know he owned, whitewashed and clean, larger than what his candle can illuminate all at once.

IN 1990, THE CELLAR was lit by metal lamps, plain round stainless-steel hoods, enclosing extremely bright single bulbs, attached to plastic claws that gripped heat and water pipes. They were pointed at the corners, where the dirty white walls met the stained and cracking ceiling. The reflected light was sufficient, even atmospheric. Tamás had been pleased when his fashion model girlfriend had brought him fifteen lights as a gift, prouder still when she described stealing them one or two at a time from the studio of a West German fashion photographer based in Pest. The windowless, unventilated cellar held about 250 people on the night of the Fourth of July, 1990.

———

HE WALKS THE ROOM'S perimeter while he thinks what to tell his wife. He drags his left hand lightly along the white plaster. Ledges that are cut into the wall support sacks of potatoes, flour, other staples. Realizing the room's shape, he crosses it diagonally. In the center of this cool rectangle, bottles of French and Tokaj wine recline in tall wooden racks. The cellar must stretch all the way underneath the courtyard. He tries to recall the layout of the floors above him and walks aimlessly, carrying his small circle of yellow light with him, guessing which pieces of furniture float over his head. Directly above him, he decides, sits the long chair next to the fireplace, and above that is the bed, and above that, the maid's basin, then the roof with birds' nests, then open sky. Through all of this furniture, weightless over his head, on invisible floors, stroll staff and wife, layered over each other, amid floating and carefully arranged décor. Then the unbidden thought comes, soothes him, solves everything: If he were to arrange the death of his elder brother, all would be well again. He stands straight, turns to face the wall, looks up again, and wonders how it could be accomplished. He knows he will never do it, even as he hopes that he might. He says aloud that he will never do it, thus permitting himself to plan.

AGAINST ONE SHORT WALL, Tamás had built a small wooden stage, about four and a half feet off the floor. On the Fourth of July, 1990, the stage supported Cash Ass, a band composed of three men and a woman. She wore a black cocktail dress and high-heeled black shoes. Her platinum-blond hair was cut in the smooth, curving Hollywood style of the late 1950s. While she waited in the background during an instrumental passage, her face expressed a fleeting interest in her bandmates and calm indifference to the hundreds of eyes watching her. The three men were playing the instrumental opening, the sixth and final song in the third of the night's three-set contract. The men, too, wore black cocktail dresses and high-heeled shoes to match hers, and their platinum-blond hair aped hers so perfectly, it seemed likely that she too was wearing a wig. One musician played an assortment of children's instruments—ukuleles, banjos, cowboy guitars—all heavily amplified and blasted through the several large speakers slung around the basement. The second man played a bass guitar with incredible facility, maintaining a funk groove interlaced with thirty-second and sixty-fourth note trills, machine-gun patters, like bandoliers worn as fashion accessories. His thumps and pops caused dancers to twitch and jump in the steamy heat. The third musician sat at an array of cassette players wired to a single control panel. Brushing his platinum-blond bangs away from his eyes, he brought up the volume of one cassette while he lowered another. During this song, he orchestrated:

- a baby crying and an elderly male voice attempting soothing Hungarian.
- a Soviet-era speech in Russian. (All of the Hungarians in the room had, at one point or another in their academic lives, been required to learn Russian, but it was a point of pride to assert forgetfulness, the highest achievement being lack of any Russian vocabulary whatsoever, a common claim belied by the number of dancers who now laughed and made faces.)
- the theme song from an American children's television program, sung in a happy major key by a man, a woman, and several gifted children.
- a Hungarian couple exerting themselves, moans and bed squeaks.
- cut-and-spliced British cricket commentary: "The South Africans have rather a steep hill to scale steep hill to scale have rather a steepsteepsteep hill steepsteep hill to scale the South Africans have rather a steep hill to scale this afternoon, Trevor, Trevor, Trevor, Trevor."
- the Hungarian national anthem, recited atonally by three friends of the band. They imitated distracted schoolchildren until, after about ten seconds, the three voices were at three entirely different places in the anthem, and the crowd's applause and shouting grew deafening as the nation's hymn scrambled toward incomprehensibility.

HE WALKS SLOWLY down the center of the empty room, toward the wine rack, and his thoughts come quickly. Easiest matter in the world to loosen this wine rack, for example, so it falls on someone reaching for a bottle in a high nook. There would be blood and broken bone, and if it were late at night and the victim had already drunk a large quantity, the explanation for the accident would glow in the very red face of the deceased. I will express to my father how pleased I am to take his suggestion, how fine an arrangement that stock-jobbing position is, and then I will invite my good brother over for a brotherly dinner. How late we could dine, how happily I would see my wife off to bed, how pleasantly I would send the servants away, how joyful I would be to sit up late, chatting and drinking with my beloved brother. And then I would take him down to show him the cellar. How horrified I will be! How heartbroken! It is like the loss of the sun—no, that is too much.

———

HALFWAY DOWN THE ROOM, at the very center of the throng, a wooden platform stood high enough that people could dance beneath it. Perched with his
head just under the ceiling, an army buddy of Tamás's operated the sound
board. Just behind his aerie, next to its splintered and graffitied wooden ladder,
Charles Gábor, wearing khakis and a black polo shirt, buffeted by the twist of
the crowd, was kissing a very short girl he had never seen before but who moments earlier had bumped into him and plunged her hands into his pants.

HOW DIFFICULT CAN IT be to poison a potato, he wonders as he stands in front
of the ledges cut into the back wall. No, the risk of the wrong person eating it,
or . . . of course. It's a new house. Surely the balconies might have been installed badly, a balustrade may be loose, a person could easily fall. The wine
rack seems the best plan.

AT THE BACK of the room, on a ledge cut into the wall, Scott and Mária held
hands, yelled things to each other, but as they sat directly beneath one of the
club's speakers, they soon gave up, hoarse, and settled for kissing and watching
the band. The volume of the guitar and the bass suddenly dropped, the tape
jockey brought up a scratchy recording of a funk drumbeat, and the blond
woman approached the microphone. She closed her eyes, crossed her arms,
placed her hands over her breasts, and sang in Hungarian-accented English,
with a well-trained operatic voice:

We all live underneath the hammer
Wielded by Vogue, Mademoiselle, *and* Glamour.

The crowd, with variable English fluency, joined in a repetitive chant of
the couplet while the woman's singing slid slowly but definitively away from
her operatic training into a hard-rock voice, then to a raw scream. She snarled,
more and more angry, and the sound of the crying baby grew louder, the
ukulele more piercing, the bass groove ever more complicated, and the Hungarian national anthem more and more confused. People jumped up and down
and screamed the lyrics, couples danced, and young men shoved other young
men they did not know. Hungarian and foreign men smoked near the front of
the stage, trying to look moderately interested, shaking their brains, almost to
the man, in search of the right thing to do or say in order to win even the
slimmest chance of sleeping with the singer.

HIS ANGER HAS PASSED, and with it his more baroque plots. He completes another circle of his basement, his free hand dusted with white from dragging it along the cool walls. He arrives at the staircase again, still hoping for his brother's death, but now only in a vain effort to forestall thinking about what he must tell his wife, what he must agree to do. He will never kill his brother. Far more horrible solutions will be necessary.

ON THE LEFT SIDE of the room beckoned the dance hall's only exit, an opening to a brick staircase that rose from the poured-concrete floor, lit by the same clamped, hooded spotlights. This sole artery was stenotic with descending prospective dancers and ascending drinkers hopeful for fresh air. Everyone smoked.

JUNE HAS BECOME MARCH and he sits on his basement stairs again, crumbles bits of the mortar between his fingers, and tries not to listen to the screams. He tries instead to think about some detail from his government job. He is not unhappy with the post. All the nonsense he caused, the broken cup . . . It turned out to be the simplest thing in the world. Rather pleasant, even. He told his wife of his father's announcement that very night, of course, said he had expected it, had known about it for months, he said, simply hadn't wanted to bother her with the details on their honeymoon and wouldn't she be proud to say to her friends that her husband held a post on the stock exchange and . . . But by then the damn tears were coming again, and even though he tried to stand up and go to the other room before she saw them, he allowed himself to fall back into her arms when she pulled his hand, and he simply wept there, ashamed, while she stroked his head and brushed the white dust from his hair and began to kiss him.

The screams stopped, but he doesn't know when, doesn't know how long he's been sitting in silence as well as darkness. He climbs up to the kitchen. He stops to listen. The screams are definitely over. She must certainly be out of danger, but he does not move from his position near the cold kitchen stove. Then screams return, but now they are the first protests of a baby. And still he does not move.

THE STAIRS LED from A Házam's dance cellar to its ground-floor bar and lounge. Behind the bar, Tamás and two other men ministered to the crowd's needs. On the walls behind them hung framed photographs of various Soviet and East Bloc leaders, all autographed to Tamás, though in Hungarian and with the same thick black pen and the same hand. "Big Tamás," read the Hungarian inscription on Stalin's photograph, "I will never forget that time with the three Polish girls! You are the best! Joe." "Tamás, your house, my house: There is always a party. Rákosi." "Tamás, mistakes were made, excesses committed, but never by you, cool baby [these last two words in English]. Nikita K." "You come to my house, T. I'll show you what the girls like! VN Lenin." "Best wishes to our dear young Tamás from Mr. and Mrs. Ceauşescu."

HE STILL OCCASIONALLY RECALLS plotting his brother's death so many years ago and, that very same night, conceiving the child whose vicious arrival killed his wife, and in an instant of extreme pain, he still cannot deny that the two events are connected, and he is pricked by a barb of the perfumed religion he never otherwise touches: The child was conceived in the shadow of his sin, and he essentially murdered his wife that night nine months before her death, by taking her when murder was still throbbing in his head. And in these moments, the guilt of his crime is so physically painful that he will close his eyes to defend himself. This wince, much less common ten years on, is still immediately followed not by relief but by an almost equally painful feeling that he is a fool. Tonight, though, in front of a fire that is not quite sufficient to warm the room, the boy has noticed his father's face and for the first time musters the courage to ask what pain his father suffers to cause such an expression. "You are almost too big to sit in my lap," his father replies, pulling the boy up from his toy soldiers to join him on the long chair. He looks at a son and summons up a favorite thought, one that has soothed him many times in the past: Most men would consider the boy the murderer of his mother, but I do not; he is an innocent in my eyes. I will never make him pay for what he did to me.

THE LOUNGE'S FURNITURE consisted of wooden cubes, some stools, a couple of mismatched, salvaged booths, and several dilapidated couches flung randomly around the room. On every available surface someone smoked, drank, kissed, laughed, stared. A giant placenta of smoke obscured the ceiling and attached to a hundred smoking fetuses through a hundred smoky umbilical threads.

HE LIVES ONLY to the spring of his forty-second year, dying on an unusually warm night. His son, now a nineteen-year-old soldier in the army of the Empire, finds the body, but not until the next morning, as he has spent the night away from the house, first on patrol, and then in a brothel with two of his comrades. The disposition of the house falls to his uncles and the lawyers, and doesn't, at first, much interest him one way or the other. Never much light or amusement there, if you ask him. And with those rousing words he turns his back on his father's funeral and marches to barracks, arm in arm with his comrades, all of them eager to "shake life by the heels and see what comes out of her pockets."

AS EARLY AS JULY 1990, A Házam danced on the precipice of overpopularity; everyone felt that their secret had slipped out of their control. The very hippest Hungarians felt there were too many foreigners. The very hippest foreigners had the impression there were too many uncool foreigners. The rest of the foreigners, unaware they were uncool, were noticing too many obvious tourists. By September, it would become a favorite bar from the past that you couldn't really go to anymore without aching for the good old days when it was yours alone. But for a few weeks in July of that year, before it won praise in a college-published budget travel guide for its authenticity as a locals' hangout, A Házam was everyone's first choice.

SOME MONTHS LATER, over the lawyers' and his uncles' occasionally strident advice, he stands firm and orders the house and all of its furnishings sold at the best possible price and the money deposited in his account. That and his father's legacy will provide him with an ample cushion to support his military career. His defeated uncles have not seen the boy more than once or twice a year for his entire life, their brother having kept increasingly to himself over time. They remember a quiet boy willing to do what his father instructed, and they are somewhat surprised at his sudden decisiveness, offended that their counsel is so flippantly and brusquely ignored. The younger uncle takes the soldier to lunch at the Casino, however, and finds the boy really quite amusing, though with nothing more serious on his mind than women, the new comic opera, military advancement. The house is sold at an excellent price within five weeks and the uncles do not hear from him again.

Twenty years later, October 1915, the one who took him to lunch notices his name in the fallen heroes list in *Awakening Nation*.

THE FRONT DOORS, which let in the July heat, opened onto six concrete steps that led down to the narrow sidewalk and road. On the fourth step from the bottom sat Mark Payton and John Price. Across the little square from them, a few old women leaned out of their upper-story apartment windows and angrily or curiously watched the crowd of young people milling below them.

Emily Oliver sat with the two men from time to time, appearing on one side or the other of Mark, reflected streetlight curved over her dark eyes. When she laughed at John's jokes, when he watched her listen to Mark talk about his latest research (and when she and John had danced in the steaming basement and had drunk at the smoky bar), John's senses sharpened, not only in the quantity of aromas he could distinguish, for example, but in the meanings he could perceive beneath them: The final time she sat on the stairs, an element in her perfume reacted with the fragrance of the trees on this particular street, and the little cars' diesel fumes turned in the summer air with the competing brands of cigarette smoke, until it all smelled of significance and beginnings, real life and permanently memorable moments.

"Because there isn't anything new of any value," Mark answered her sorrowfully, "In science, I suppose there is, but even that never really has any effect on you or me. We only benefit from scientific discoveries years after the fact. You actually should be nostalgic for really old medical researchers." John flicked his cigarette butt onto the street and leaned to one side to allow a crowd of Americans to pass between him and Emily. When he re-elevated to conversation position, she was disappearing upstairs among a flock of hilarious Julies.

And later, when the Julies swept her downstairs and down the street, waving at him and Mark indistinguishably, John cursed his ineptitude and their intrusion and her inaccessibility in quick succession. That same mixture of aromas now curdled with a faint tang of probably permanent despair. She was locked behind some barrier, and he could not say whether she wanted him to break through or not, and, if she did, why she wouldn't or couldn't help him. His theories multiplied and contradicted one another: He was not effortlessly openhearted enough to match her, and so she could only disapprove of him; she had some knowledge that, like breathing, could not be taught, but which she unconsciously waited for him to prove he understood. Perhaps he should be more forward. Or less.

"It is, is it really, is you?" someone asked him. Two Hungarian girls, about seventeen or eighteen, had stopped at the bottom of the stairs and turned back to look at John with eager amazement and happy doubt. One whispered something, they both giggled, then the thinner girl pushed the fatter one toward him. "Is it you, it is?"

"I suppose so," said John. Handling this situation smoothly would amuse Emily, he thought, before recalling that she was no longer there.

"We are very big fans of you," said the pushed girl.

"Every movie!" The thinner one stepped forward, regretted having allowed her friend such easy conversational prominence. "We have seen every of your movies!"

"Really?" said John. "Which one's your favorite?"

The girls laughed uproariously. "I do not know the name in English," said one, slightly panting. "It was showed last month at the Corvin. Where you are lost in the outer spaces with the blond girl and the two funny little dogs."

"Of course, of course," said John. "That's my favorite, too."

"She is not really with you in the real life is she, this blond hair in the cinema?" asked the thinner girl, ignoring Mark's laughter.

"She is not the right one for you," said the fatter girl seriously, and her friend berated her in Hungarian.

"Okay, we leave you alone now, but thank you. We love every of your movies. But wait, we want to say this, too," said the thinner. She looked at the ground, then at her friend for support, then at John from under a wrinkled brow. She spoke quickly and seriously. "We read this in the paper. Please, because we are loving your movies we say this. Stay off of the drugs, please. You are so good a cinema actor and a very beautiful boy, even in the real life. Please no more, the drugs. We know they will kill you if you do not stop them. We know it is hard."

"We know it is hard," agreed her friend, "but they will put you back in the prisons if you do not stop. Please."

John was moved by their concern, had never had young women nearly in tears over his well-being. He knew he couldn't make any promises; that would be unrealistic with a problem of this scope. He thanked them again, said only that he would do his best. They stood shyly one moment more, until one asked if she could kiss his cheek and the other quickly applied for the same favor. John hoped Mark would report this to Emily without being instructed. He waved back each time the girls looked over their shoulders as they walked arm in arm down the dark street.

Laughing, neither Mark nor John could guess what actor he had been, but for a tick or two of alcohol time, he still felt warmed by his fans' attention, until the next wave of migrating club-folk herded onto the street and slowly melted away, revealing Charles Gábor, kissing the tiny woman who had groped him in the basement. His head and neck drooped low to meet her upturned face. She stood on the tips of her toes and kept her balance by clutching his ass with both hands. He bent his knees slightly and helped stabilize her by pressing one hand against her back and massaging her chest with the other. John and Mark silently watched their friend lick the short girl's neck and speak Hungarian with her. Spring-loaded by lust, the girl leaped up, wrapped her legs around Charles's stomach and her arms around his neck. They kissed again, his head now stretching up to meet hers, and Charles stumbled down the street like that, blindly, toward a boulevard and a cab.

"You hate to see something like that," Mark said, standing and heading across the square. "Come here, I want to show you something."

The road quickly quieted, as if a door had been closed, as they left the club behind. John followed Mark onto a small side street, where Hungarian drifted out from open ground-floor windows. Under Trabant and Skoda tailpipes, puddles trembled, overlaid with gasoline rainbow spirals like tiny stray galaxies.

"I love your columns, you know," Mark said. "They feel like the subject of a future legend about some lost, glamorous time. 'Remember those columns back in the early nineties?' "

"Thanks," John said distractedly, not in the mood at all. "What did you want to show me?"

"A lot of things. I want to show you a lot of things. I'm curious if you—this street, to start." Mark ran his fingers through the red hair at his temples, pulled it until it stood straight out to the sides, like feathery tufts on a sickly bird. "That's what got me into this research, since you ask. Actually, I guess it was Emily who asked, but I'm drunk enough not to distinguish. I love everything about this little street. The lives that used to be lived here. The way people felt here. What it felt like to stand here and be in love. Can you imagine standing right here and being in love and seeing the world how it looked before movies existed, before movies made you see everything a certain way?"

Mark walked backward down the middle of the street, his head tilted back to examine the buildings he was passing. He pointed out architectural details to his semi-willing tour group, described in equally zealous tones the planned and unplanned features; neither was superior for him: delicate cornices and bullet holes, carved dates and crumbling stonework, once elegant upper-story stone balustrades now missing one or two urn-shaped pillars, gaping like sparsely toothed old crones whose charms only Mark could detect. "Please, please tell me you know what I mean."

"Oh yeah, yeah. Buildings."

"I love that this little street is so perfectly run-down, but you can still see what it looked like when it was a new development, probably the 1890s or so. Look how the street is laid out so it delivers the opera house for maximum surprise and drama." He stopped just where the street began to reveal Andrássy and the opera. "Alternately, you come this way, after a romantic night at the opera, and just a few feet away from the lights and the carriages, you have an intimate setting for a lovers' stroll. You'd walk down this street and feel perfectly happy, perfectly alive, and you'd never wonder why. But the city planners did it on purpose. You know, there are very few places in the world where I am at home. Isn't that pathetic? And there are actually fewer of them every day, too. And they're shrinking. Does this happen to you? There is going to come a time when there will only be a very small space. And that's all I'll have. I'll have to remain very still and only look in one direction, but then I'll be okay, actually." He laughed. "You know what I mean, John?"

And John laughed, as he assumed Mark meant him to.

They turned onto Andrássy, away from John's apartment, onto the long stretch of tree-lined boulevard leading to Heroes' Square. Mark's face glowed briefly green under a neon sign hanging in a ground-floor shop window: 24 ÓRA NON-STOP announced a grocery store and snack bar, and John followed him into the fluorescent dazzle and onto a tall counter stool.

"*Egy meleg szendvicset, kérek szépen,*" the Canadian said to the fifty-year-old woman who materialized behind the counter. John ordered the same and an Unicum. His shirt stank of other people's cigarettes and his eyes hurt; he wondered what time it was. The woman turned to a small toaster oven on the shelf and began cooking two pieces of rye bread with melted cheese and slices of pink ham. She poured John his black digestif. They watched her in silence, looked at their own half reflections in the window. John ordered a second.

"Do you ever wonder why artists hung around cafés?" Mark asked in a quiet voice, staring at the woman's apron as she licked a bit of melted cheese from the back of her thumb. "This is what I did all day today, and I kept thinking of you for some reason, that you in particular would like this. Really. So why did poor artists originally hang around in cafés?" He waited for an answer, and when none came, he said this was serious, that the answer mattered.

"I don't know. Inspiration from the atmosphere."

"Ha! No, you've been tricked, too, just like the rest of us. Cafés didn't have inspirational atmosphere at first. That only came later, when you knew artists had been hanging around in them. First they were just rooms with coffee in them. No more atmosphere than this place."

"*Amerikai?*" asked the counterwoman. Her hair was the color of much-turned brass doorknobs, and her breasts hung against their faux angora restraint like overweight sloths.

"*Nem, kanadai,*" responded Mark. She nodded, satisfied with the conversation, and turned to straighten items on the shelves: liqueurs, packaged cakes from Norway, German breakfast cereals with German cartoon mascots, French contraceptives bearing explicit instructional and marketing photographs.

"All the way back, I can follow them," Mark said. He rattled off dates and names and events with an expert's ease, starting slowly, then building in excitement: 1945—Lenoir hopes café life will be just like it was before the war and even organizes a group to assure that the best cafés stay open, with the same hours and menus and tables; 1936—Now, before that war, Fleury sadly decries how much the cafés have changed since before the *last* war. He is too young to know this as an observed fact, but he writes it in his journal nevertheless. He also writes, with childish delight, about actually *seeing* Valmorin one day at his café. He's amazed to see his idol standing there, in the flesh. "He thought Valmorin would never come to the café anymore because of its supposed decline," said Mark. "After that day, he never wrote a word of complaint until Valmorin died. Then, of course, he declared the cafés well and truly dead, though he still went all the time. That was 1939."

Nineteen twenty: Valmorin himself, in a letter to Picasso, writes that perhaps cafés aren't as important to the art world as they were in Cézanne's day. Eighteen eighty-nine: Cézanne writes in his journal that he feels unwelcome in the café because of his break with someone whose name escaped Mark just then, despite hitting his forehead repeatedly in an effort to dislodge it. But Cézanne has to make his appearance at the café nevertheless. He writes that the whole café scene is a professional necessity, but an embarrassment, a farce played out by monkeys. "That was his word, John," Mark said with admiration. "Monkeys. And back it goes," he continued. "It's a perfect chain. Everybody cites some dead guy for why he has to go to the café. Everyone says the cafés worked well at some point just before their own birth. But go back to *that* date, and someone else is saying the heyday was a few years earlier. And then I actually found it. My discovery. Mine. You will be amazed by this. I memorized it. I read it over and over again, like, for an hour or two, actually. I could hardly believe it when I found it. It was so . . ." Here he could only shake his head. He described a letter to Jan van den Huygens, dated 1607.

Van den Huygens was an innkeeper and artist, a specialist in painting drunks and prostitutes, since, in his inn, they were plentiful and cheap, often forced to pose to pay off bar tabs. He would dress them in fanciful costumes of ancient Rome so that they could pass for Bacchus and Venus, safely sellable canvases at the time. The finished products, however, lacked that classical something. "They just look like sad, broken-down people in bedsheets," Mark clucked, "with a drunken grin and red cheeks or an exposed tit or two. Van den Huygens didn't sell more than a few of the things his whole life, actually, but he painted acres of them. They turn up now in some of the less choosy Dutch provincial museums and in U.S. and Canadian college collections hungry for anything that can pass as an Old Master."

John signaled for a third Unicum and Mark waited patiently.

"Van den Huygens receives a letter in 1607 that should by all rights have been immediately thrown away. Instead, thank God, it survives for four centuries, because van den Huygens dies less than a week later. He dies, and his widow has a canny realization: A sale of her husband's paintings and papers might bring in some ready money, actually. I think she has a gift for seventeenth-century P.R., because in less than a month she manages to sell *all* the paintings of a man who never managed to sell more than a few during his life. She sweetened the deal with the late artist's 'papers.' His diaries and his letters—including this one from 1607, which happened to be still warm on a table when he keeled over—get sold, and the buyer (an art dealer who always, always, always backed the wrong horse) catalogs every scrap of paper that the widow van den Huygens sells him. The papers are bound in fine leather, with gold embossing. And that's that."

Mark was entirely unaware that he had lost his audience: John was savoring the ringing in his ears, the pleasant scrape in his throat, the flashes of color and shadow behind his eyeballs—all the desirable effects of a third quick-succession Unicum. Technically, he was listening to Mark's rambling story, but minor characters were taking shape in his mind as people he knew. Specifically, Emily Oliver, a seventeenth-century Dutch lady of pleasure, was staring at him from behind a rough, low wooden table in front of the enormous, blazing fireplace, a spitted hog dripping into the chatty, licking flame. Emily wore only a toga and laurel wreath. A still life was spread before her on the table: green glass goblets of golden wine, bumpy half-loaves of bread, sliced lemons with dimpled flesh, mackerels glowing platinum, violins varnished into mirrors, silver scalloped bowls of fire-lit grapes and ridged nuts, a skull or two supporting guttering candles. Emily selected a single red grape and stretched one bare arm skyward. She tipped back her head, bent her arm, took the grape between her teeth. She widened her eyes and bit gently down, pressed her teeth just perceptibly against the grape's skin, just hard enough to make the fruit change shape but not so hard as to burst its delicate coat. John placed his dry palette next to his blank canvas, tossed his floppy hat aside, approached his model. She took two slow steps backward, laughing through the tooth-clenched grape, and let fall her toga.

"Until the letter is included in a biography not of van den Huygens, whose biography *no one* will ever write, I promise you, but of the letter's *writer*, Hendrik Müller, a truly significant artist. That's where I read it, though the biographer completely missed its significance."

Mark smiled and now spoke very slowly and quietly, regaining John's attention briefly. "Müller writes, 'Jan—The winter months are brutal cold. Working in my studio during the day is bearable, but holding discussions there at night is unfeasible. Can you arrange to hold a regular table for me and some friends by your fire? We will buy food and wine, and perhaps you can lower the price for it if we promise to come every night until April or May.' "

Mark recited from memory this poem of unsurpassed eloquence and emotional power. All the world at that moment for Mark Payton was to see John Price understand this letter and, by extension, Mark. He spoke very quietly now, his fingers laced tightly behind his neck. "Understand, John. Müller—an acknowledged genius—is speaking to us. To you and me. He is in the room with us now. He . . . he is touching you on your shoulder like this. He's a friend of ours, Müller. We love his work, of course, but so does everyone, that's not what's important to us. No, I love him because, oh . . . how well he holds his liquor. Or because he's such an open book to us. He dances quite badly, unless he's drunk. Or how he looks up to his asshole brother, or, or—" (Mark took his hand off John's shoulder, faced the counter again) "—anyhow, he says to us, 'Guys—John, Mark—my apartment is cold, y'know?' And we do know, don't we? We're there all the time."

Emily was removing her toga and standing in the slithering, tentacular glow of the seventeenth-century fire. She bit through the skin of the grape and

John tore the loose white shirt from his body with a grunt, managing, however, to ask: "His apartment's cold?"

"Yes. Freezing." Mark stretched the word *freezing* into two elastic syllables. " 'It's so cold in my apartment, actually, that I think I should meet somewhere more comfortable with my friends and students for our daily talk about painting. Why not in my friend Jan's inn, where there's a big fireplace and food and wine?' " Mark spoke in a possibly Dutch accent, and waited for the magnitude of what he was saying to dawn on his audience.

"It would be warmer, I suppose," John offered.

"Yes! He went to van den Huygens's inn—*to a café*—because it would be *warmer!* Only that. *It would be warmer.* You see? John, do you see? All over Europe at that time, painters must have realized that an inn—that is, a *café*—would be warmer. A whole world of people going to cafés because it would be warmer. Their students, perhaps, even continue the practice—not a tradition, no, just a practice—because they would be warmer . . . But *their* students or their students' students . . ." Mark's voice became lower, slow. He blew air out from puffed cheeks. "*They*, they go to cafés because that's what painters *do.* Now do you see?" Mark asked this of John directly, and in his heart, he could not even bear to hope that John or anyone else—friend, lover, or stranger— would ever see Hendrik Müller as a hero, a man who acted without a glance to the oppressive past, to any longed-for golden age. Mark could hardly find the words to express to himself Hendrik Müller's shattering significance. To feel at home. To be at peace. To know one's desires are truly one's own and not inadvertently, unavoidably, just the desires of one's forebears long dead or, worse—worst of all—the manipulations of faceless Habit, Style, Tradition, History. To go somewhere because it would be warmer, to live and just to be. With the right person for the right reason, like this very moment, so that even this place, this historyless little grocery could glow with the importance of the past, right now, tonight. One last try: "You, of everyone I know, John, you should see how amazing this discovery is."

"I can see you're a complete maniac, if that's any consolation."

XVIII.

WHEN JOHN ENTERED THE NEWSROOM THE NEXT DAY, HE SCATTERED HIS hellos and slid in front of his computer to type up his notes from the U.S. embassy's July Fourth party. *They longed for freedom for forty years,* he wrote, then stared at this improbably precise and insightful sentence, and at the screen's blinking cursor. He alternately deplored and savored the frequency with which Emily would storm into his brain, displace something more relevant, taunt him. His jaw slackened and he stared at the unfinished, unbelievable generalization on the computer screen. The cursor blinked more and more slowly, lazy and arhythmic, an occasional sigh. Blink. His hands rested immobile on the keyboard until he recalled Emily in her toga, the night smells on the street, her closed eyes when she danced with him, her rapid escape with the Julies, and his hands typed, of their own accord, *asdfjkl;* and set the cursor panting like a blood-maddened hyena.

"I think you and I should go to lunch today."

The frenetic voice was Karen Whitley's (Arts, Restaurants, Nightlife Listings, Want Ad Sales). She sat at the adjacent computer and was hanging up her telephone. The noise shocked him into typing.

They longed for freedom for forty years, asdfjkl; and yesterday selected members of the recently oppressed watched us celebrate our two centuries of liberty and free markets like the dashing old pros we are. Red, white, and blue cake and small talk, which, of course, are the benefits of freedom. Still, this week you could feel some mutual doubt at the U.S. Embassy's annual July 4th party. VIP Hungarian thoughts were easy to read: "Is this all there is, after our sacrifices? This is what we were taught to fear, but instinctively loved? This is all there is?" And from the other side of the divide, "What have we done lately to deserve this cake? If it demanded a rebellion against tyrants, would we have it in us?" Which side was tired? Which was ready for the future? Who had won? And what came next? Is this a thousand words yet? What about now? asdfjkl;lkjfdsasdfjkl;lkjfdsasdfjkl; I have a great insight coming, I have a great insight coming, here it comes—

"Let's go to lunch when you finish that," repeated Karen, but this time she was not on the phone.

Karen Whitley had introduced herself to John on his first day of work, only moments after he had emerged from his torturous interview with the editor. She toured him through the office and shared her secret discovery (source confidential) that Editor (who shed his definite article for those in the know), despite his Australian accent, was from Minneapolis, a journalism minor and the second son of one of the world's richest office-equipment manufacturers. "Electric staplers are bankrolling this little venture," she disclosed in her high-speed, former-champion-high-school-debater rat-a-tat. The next moment, she slid her arm through John's to introduce him to other staff, like the hostess at a fabulous party. The rest of their conversation then fell into a pattern that, although relatively new to John that day, grew comically familiar as Budapest's spring turned to summer: how they got to this odd place at this odd moment of history, what they hoped for from their obviously temporary jobs, what they dreamed of doing with their lives in this sudden window of possibility—the same intensely personal conversation John came to have with expatriates all the time, often immediately before never seeing them again. And sure enough, since that first day of excited mutual frankness, John saw Karen as little more than a piece of speaking furniture.

After producing a feasible if creakily portentous draft, he found himself with Karen in a restaurant near the office, one of the dozens of old state-run places sleepily serving identical, just tolerable fare. The co-workers sat with command-economy salads and five-year-plan paprikás, and John waded in and out of Karen's peppy monologue. She needed very little conversational fuel to keep her boilers steaming. He listened, mm-hm'd. She described childhood in New York, college in Pennsylvania, sketched a Hungarian boyfriend. No, not a boyfriend precisely, "a brief encounter," she sighed, world-weary, leaving a forkful of red-orange chicken to hover just outside her mouth, "which I'm starting to think is all the Hungarians are good for, you know? You *must* know. I can see it. *You* know. Oh, yes sir, you know. Listen to this example of enlightened Magyar manhood. True story, this: This happened to a girlfriend of mine. Real life. She's with this guy, they're undressing each other, and he goes, 'What's that smell?' And my friend is thinking, Oh cool, okay, he likes this perfume. She was wearing this all-over vanilla body spray, right? Which is, I think, you know, a little sweet but very pretty. So she says, 'Oh, it's vanilla,' or whatever and he says, real life, this guy goes—and remember, okay, this is, like, their second date and only their first time, so you know it's like, hey, guy, be a little sensitive, right? He goes, 'Vanilla?' " Karen adopted a fair Hungarian accent: " 'Vanilla? Listen, I want to fuck a woman, not a piece of candy. Shower.' He says, 'Shower'! Can you believe that?"

"Fuck a piece of *candy?*"

"Ex*act*ly. So my friend kicks him out, but he's, like, lecturing her on the way out the door about Americans' fear of the body and its natural odors and blahblahblah, you know that old tune. So my friend calls me right away, double time, quick-quick, and tells me this story, and we're just laughing our heads off, like, no tomorrow. But I asked her if I could use that line in my movie, and she said I should use his full name."

And she skittered into neighboring territory, a discussion of the screenplay her Hungarian experiences were already producing, the solid, solid stuff she was seeing every single day, her notebooks, how she was careful not to let Editor see her working on it, how she was writing in a café and was going to start a salon, and—

And Emily stood, a single grape between her teeth. She bit it to nearly the bursting point. Fireplace shadows stroked her arms and danced along her neck. She loosened the shoulder knot of her toga—

"Because somebody needs to tell this generation of ours what it's *for*, you know. Do we stand for anything? Or against anything? Well, I tell you, I'm game: I'm starting that conversation right now, in this film. It's all about just that—*us*—our generation, because it's our time now, we can't wait any longer, we have to redefine before someone else—someone older and already corrupt— does it for us. We have to stand up, you know, and say, 'Hey, we don't think *that*, we think *this*—' "

Emily's hand crossed over her chest, toying with the last crossed ends of the slipping sheet's vanishing knot. The sound of the fire grew pronounced, each click and pop filled the room—

"Ask me. Go ahead and ask me. I'll tell you: The last time any generation was in our situation was 1919. That's a *fact*; that's a socio-historical *fact*. You can prove it. With *numbers*. We are as lost as any generation has ever been lost before, and I for one *love* it, mister. Look at our cultural signifiers, how every interaction is framed by—"

And the toga—the tie at the shoulder, the sheet tight across her breasts— fell away, melted away, shimmered backward from her stomach, as though a magician were revealing her with an impossibly gradual flourish of a dissolving cape, her head thrown back, her hair blown by a strong but sourceless wind—

"And besides, this paper is *not* going to be profitable in our lifetime. Free tip, there. Editor's bonkers if he thinks he's going to make his fortune on this rag." She paid the waiter for the meal. "It's abso*lutely* on me. You get the next one." She tapped her teeth with her coffee cup. "Besides, one can't *really* be expected to work for an expat newspaper forever and ever, right? Although there is something amusingly fin-de-siècle in that notion, you know? Which reminds me, I know a guy from home who is living in Prague now, the lucky bastard, and he's trying to start a business making frozen desserts shaped like Proust and Freud, and like velocipedes, and they're called Fin-de-sicles—"

Quite nude now, behind the long, low table, she bit the grape and swallowed it with just the slightest lift to one corner of her mouth. She beckoned him—

They stood from the table. "Thanks for lunch," he said.

Karen smiled, tried not to laugh. She gestured with a downward tilt of her head, and a simultaneous lift of her eyebrows. "I hope that's for me." She widened her eyes. John was wearing boxer shorts under loose-fitting khakis.

XIX.

A CHILD'S MICROSCOPE KIT: A SLIDE AND SLIDE COVER. THE SLIDE: A REC-tangle of glass the size of a Band-Aid and the thickness of a quarter. The slide cover: a square of glass the shape and thickness of a postage stamp. To use the microscope, a child pipettes a drop of fluid onto the slide and then presses the cover on top of it. The cover skates over the surface of the slide, separated from its secure base by the fluid, slipping and gliding as the child tries to press the two pieces of glass firmly enough to make them adhere. The two pieces float as close to each other as possible, without ever, in fact, touching, hovering a cell's depth of fluid apart.

John could not dislodge this memory during his first, brief sexual intercourse, just after lunch on July 5, 1990. He was maddened—with lust, yes, but also frustrated almost to tears. Is this all there is? he thought, even as he spastically clutched handfuls of Karen. This is as close as two bodies can be?

At the same time, he was amazed by how much everyone weighed, that she weighed anything at all. In his imagination, women had been weightless and infinitely malleable. One could lift them, roll them, push them from one sexual tableau to the next, from one gyrating friction to another. Instead, here was this superabundance of gravity—another, denser planet precisely the size of a bed. Parts were pinned, hair was pulled, access was blocked, walls chose to impinge, sheets conspired to interfere, springs squawked to distract and mock him. "I love it when you swear," she said, and swore right back at him.

He lay underneath her standing naked form, a little foot pressing the mattress on either side of him. "You were hungry, John Price. You haven't eaten in a while, have you? We're going to have to work on you. Like, focus that enthusiasm a bit."

She jumped up and down; her feet bounced a tiny inch or two from his hips. "What a delight to get to play with all that enthusiasm, John Price! I have so many lovely things to teach you! Lovely!" Bounce. "Lovely!" Bounce. "Lovely lovely lovely!" Bounce bounce bounce.

Emily stood at the fireplace, quite naked now (with newly focused detail), but she covered her breasts with crossed hands. She smirked at naughty, fickle John. She pouted in mock disappointment, sniffled away a nonexistent tear, then dropped her hands and beckoned again—

"Are you ready again?" Bounce. "You *are*, aren't you!"

Karen lies asleep on her side, her back to him. The sheet clings to and imitates four legs. Work is very far away, and Emily too. He is up on one elbow. He traces the most remarkable discovery of the day: the landscape curve of her side from the bottom of her rib cage to the top of her hip. The afternoon light has turned soft. The room is uniformly laid over with a light gray shadow that he has never seen before, as if an entirely new kind of light has recently been discovered. Through the open window, over her tousled hair and slow breathing, he can see all the way across the street. A street width and half a bedroom away from him, in a recently repainted nineteenth-century apartment building brightly lit by the sun, which hangs somewhere over Karen's building, the stocky top half of a prematurely old Hungarian woman plants her elbows on her windowsill, leans into the glare, into an entirely different kind of light (and world), and watches street life five floors down. She pushes back an errant strand of gray hair and sips from a tall glass. She seems to mean something. New scents pass in the air and mingle with familiar ones—shampoo, deodorants, vanilla. A fly has found its way into the apartment and cannot find its way out, dances with itself on the mirror, then tracks lipstick footprints down the side of a glass to wade in warm lemonade. Do you remember this feeling forever? John wonders, hopes. He's supposed to meet Scott soon. He can't remember where he put his watch.

XX.

THE PRICES WALKED SLOWLY DOWN THE BUDA STREET TRIMMED WITH plane trees. "I need oxygen replenishment," said Scott, and so they set off toward Margaret Island in silence. John spun a cigarette over and under his knuckles from finger to finger, a sleight of hand he had learned in eighth grade with a ballpoint pen. They walked on, past Moscow Square and the market stalls, crossed the trolley rails and the traffic of Mártírok utca. The bus station and subway and tram stops and vegetable markets gave them something to do with their eyes.

"How's Mária?"

"She's good."

"Do you have a light?"

"Are you kidding?"

The afternoon smog nibbled his nose hairs, and Scott sometimes lifted his hand to cover his mouth. John patted his pockets for a truant book of matches. "So what's the story with you guys?"

"Who guys?"

"You and Mária, the lovingest dovingest pigeons in all Pigeontown."

"Story? I don't know. Hard to, hard to say."

"Is she Jewish?"

Scott laughed unpleasantly. "I have no idea. Tip-top question though, bro. I'll get right back to you on that, and you can send home your report to Mom about Scotty's latest crimes, you rotten little shit."

"You really think that?"

"No, of course not, why would I? Water off a duck's back, baby."

Paralysis crept over John's thickening tongue. He had left Karen's and walked across the river to pick up his brother for another of the stilted, tangential, droll, useless weekly dinners he had initiated, all the while spinning and massaging a little statement into shape to present to Scott—a damp and sticky confession of confusion, loneliness, excitement, fear, pride. And yet now he couldn't find the moist clay pot he had so lovingly crafted. No sentence would start. None of his feelings merited the exertion necessary for a single syllable, and everything wafting off Scott told him to keep his mouth shut. If he felt dramatic when he walked out of Karen's building, when he squinted and put on his sunglasses, if he felt pleased with himself on her boulevard as the cars coughed in sympathetic unison and the architecture seemed almost as important as Mark madly insisted, if he felt a mildly funny pang of regret at his vanished and ridiculous principles, if, a block later, he wondered what this meant for him and Emily (did it retroactively downgrade her or prove her relative importance, make her more meaningful or meaningless, was he shallow or manly, had he made himself strong or thrown away something of irreplaceable value and where did he get these antique notions), if, near the new Burger King in the Octagon, he was suddenly swallowing down an actual urge to *cry*, an urge that was finally transmuted into a slightly forced chunk of laughter as he crossed the Chain Bridge, if he stopped twice between the bridge and Scott's school to leave stupid jokes on Emily's answering machine, if he opened the door to the school praying that Scott would explain everything even as he knew Scott would do no such thing, well now, stepping from Margaret Bridge onto Margaret Island, following the footpath to a green opening where a group of young boys was playing soccer, he felt only a growing compulsion to get something, anything, definitive from his brother, even rage: "So are you in love with Mária?"

"That sounds like a song cue from *West Side Story*."

The children tripped and struggled to maintain control of the soccer ball. "Have you met her family?"

"John, are you kidding? We basically just got together, okay? Now, cut it out."

Kick, miss, fall down, grab knee and wince, stand up, run upfield to be in place for potentially heroic goal. Wait there, pick nose. "So how is it? What's it like?"

"How *is* it?" Scott scratched an ear. He watched the game. "It's like a spring rain-shower. It's like Rome under the stars. Box seats for opening day. Your name called from across a crowded room."

"Sounds serious."

"Oh yes, deadly serious. Psychologically complex. Troubling French film stuff. Knock-down, drag-out brawls. Lots of threats. It will all end in tears and yet somehow we can't let go."

"Sounds fun."

"That too. Fun-loving. Kooky. Wacky. Kisses in the rain. Tossing bread crumbs to the pigeons. We've got the world on a string, dontcha know."

"You're pretty happy, then?"

"Excruciatingly. Never knew what the word meant until now. Never glimpsed it, never smelled it, never had a clue, but now I light up from the inside, you know, like I carry a little nightlight in my belly that glows right up inside my happy little head."

"She must be a hell of a woman."

"Salt of the earth. Charms the birds right out of the trees. Can't help loving dat girl. Moxie and spunk, tinsel and Teflon. That's my baby."

"Sex must be pretty extraordinary."

"Oh yes. Kinky. Loving. Communion of souls. Deepest bond. Language without words. Return to Eden." Scott rubbed his eyes. "Body-mind unity. Vulnerable, immutable, you name it. Pfff . . . secrets of the Orient. Techniques from lost scrolls. What exactly do you want from me?"

"Nothing. Forget it."

"Consider it done."

The soccer ball escaped the children's tenuous control and rolled toward the brothers' bench. John kicked it back into play. After another minute or so, it finally rolled between two balled-up windbreakers at the far end of the green, and the small boy whose foot had inadvertently last touched it sprinted on his little legs in a wide, exuberant circle. He pumped his fist and waved his wee index finger while absorbing the intoxicating but inaudible screams and cheers of the World Cup crowd. "*Magyarország! Magyarország!*" the child yelled as he completed his circuit of the stadium. His teammates embraced him and hoisted him precariously on their little shoulders for another lap. The brothers added their four hands to the applause.

"That is precisely how I feel all the time," John said.

"Yeah, it's genetic."

They crossed over to Pest and walked down the riverfront to the Blue Jazz. The club had developed a doorman in the last week, and he asked the brothers something in Hungarian. "*Nem beszélek magyarul,*" the Prices mispronounced their ritual greeting simultaneously.

"Fine. Americans?" the bouncer asked in English. "Dinner and music?" he grumbled, and took their entry fees.

As the rooms slowly filled, the club's new house pianist played. On the handwritten chalk sign propped outside, she was simply NÁDJA. She looked about seventy, a thin and breakable woman in a flowing red gown that, although it fit her well, had done so for many years. As she moved slightly to her music, she resembled an exotic species in an aquarium, a brightly colored swath of tattered material floating and swaying in her own private current. On the cracked and ringed lid of the aging upright piano sat an ashtray, a package of Mockba Reds, and a silver lighter. She played an odd and ceaseless medley that skittered across decades and styles: now a jazz standard recognizable to anyone, "All of Me," played in a very traditional manner with gentle improvisations in the style of the era; then a Scott Joplin rag, memorized and reproduced verbatim; suddenly a bebop tune, Charlie Parker's "Yardbird Suite," with a chorus or two of proficient bop soloing; "Watermelon Man," a jazz-funk tune from the 1960s, with the original album's standard piano groove and Dexter Gordon's saxophone solo transposed for her right hand; "Angel Eyes," "Everything Happens to Me," and "The Night We Called It a Day" in quick succession, a tribute to a forgotten songwriter; a Chopin prelude, only about two minutes long but performed with careless ease; then a Broadway hit and, as it was "Maria" from *West Side Story*, Scott and John put away their pool cues and moved to a table to watch the elderly hands tap and hammer the elderly keys.

As the tune ended, the brothers applauded with about the same spirit as they had the soccer game. This was the first acknowledgment the pianist had received since she'd begun an hour and a half earlier. She turned to her fans and dipped her head, a gesture John found strangely moving; it hit him with inexplicable force and significance; he felt it was the answer to his day, to the questions he had been unable to phrase to his own brother. *A faded old woman bows ironically to joke applause,* he thought with a calming sensation. Emily and Karen were immediately viewed from a far-distant perspective, as if on a sunlit hillside, and they looked fine there. John very much wanted to meet the pianist.

The bartender flipped a switch and filled the club's air with the smoky scratches of an early Louis Armstrong recording. Nádja rose, collected her cigarettes and lighter, and glided toward them. John was unreasonably excited even as he heard Scott mutter, "Oh Jesus."

"I suspect you gentlemen are American," she said in the raspy voice of a golden-age movie star. John stood and lit her cigarette. He shook out the match and offered her a seat, introduced himself and his brother.

She emitted a slow, fine stream of smoke and conversation waited for her. "An intriguing pair," she murmured. "One brother Jewish, the other Danish. How did this come to pass, John Price?"

As a rule, the sound of a European-accented voice merely saying the word *Jewish* was enough to set John on edge, but now he was charmed to acknowledge the disparity that had for some twenty years previous been an instant conversational bore, family reunion tedium. "I make it a practice never to exchange genetic histories with a woman I've just met, at least one whose name I don't know," John replied after taking time to light his own cigarette.

She not only set him at ease, but somehow, with her thin and elderly arms, she was lifting him high up in the air. Her faded elegance and fraying dress, her peculiar employment, her graceful manner and instant mastery of the situation, her glamorous directness: John felt a flutter of fear that she would soon leave the table, and strove to keep her there. Scott watched his brother's transformation and said very little.

"Quite wise, John Price. But what about the melancholic Dane? Will he explain the dissimilarity?"

"I doubt he'll be able to," John replied. "Our parents swear lifelong fidelity. Would you like a drink?"

"A Rob Roy would be a small thrill," she smiled on him. "You are very kind."

Scott, though, rose and seized the excuse to leave her company. Her odd, old-fashioned, upper-class English spiced with the vague accents of Central Europe irritated him. John's clowning irritated him. Her dress irritated him and her drink order irritated him. John liking her irritated him. Anything that would keep John in Budapest one more minute irritated him. Scott would leave the club as soon as possible; he could do without these weekly fraternal tortures anyhow; maybe tonight would mark the end of that forced labor. He returned with his mineral water, John's Unicum, and—after the bartender had angrily consulted a little booklet tied on a chain to the back of the bar—a Rob Roy. He slumped into his seat and managed, "That's a nice ring."

The ancient hand encircling the light orange highball was weighted by a large green-and-silver barnacle. "You are very dear, Scott, to mention it. A gift from a time unspeakably long ago. It has been stolen from me, recovered, used as a bribe, and recovered again. What else? Let's see . . . It was very many years ago at the center of a blackmail situation. And it appears on the hand of a French countess in a terribly mediocre painting from two and a half centuries ago, which you can still see in a very crowded room in the Louvre. This I know sounds a bit of a shaggy dog, but I am told it is true, on an exquisite authority." She held out her hand and gave the ring an appraising look. "It is in horrid taste, isn't it?"

And a strange pause in conversation. She smiled at the two young men, something less of condescension than of invitation, watched them weather her onslaught of improbability. The brothers both laughed—two very different sounds—and she quickly knew from the dissonant tones which of them would provide her more conversational pleasure this evening even before John said, "Why do I suspect you were doing the blackmail?"

"John Price, you are a cheeky young man and I think I am going to like you enormously. Perhaps I will answer your question after we have dined."

"I am very glad you will do us the honor."

"A man of the press," she said over the paprikás and champagne. "Are you a brave foreign correspondent itching to dispatch from the front lines during our next inevitable Soviet invasion?"

"More of a society columnist, to be honest. A historian of the moment."

"Delightful. And Prince Hamlet?"

"I teach English to the local savages."

"And we *are* savages, are we not?" Nádja twirled a strand of gray hair around a long and wrinkled finger, a gesture half the men at the table found grotesque while the other half found it inexplicably enchanting.

She said she was half Hungarian, born in Budapest, in the palace on Castle Hill, in fact, though no more details were forthcoming. "I have lived elsewhere, however, for long stretches, as you Americans say. We have a most unfortunate habit of jollying up to rather the wrong side of world wars, haven't we? And then being invaded by our Russian friends to pay for our sins. I have been forced, from time to time again, to join the sorority of refugees. Yet I come back. And now we are invaded by handsome young men of the West, who come to write in the paper about us and to teach us their guttural, overly complex tongue and sell us better athletic equipment. To our invaders." She lifted a flute of the champagne she had suggested to John.

"To your invaders." One of the invading horde clinked glasses with her.

Scott decided that Nádja was like a hostess in a gentlemen's club, that she received a commission on overpriced drinks and food she charmed guests into ordering. Yet as bait, she seemed so microscopically specific a taste, he wondered how she could possibly earn. He watched his brother's face when she spoke, and vice versa.

"I, with various members of various families, left my country in 1919, returned in 1923, left again in . . . 1944, returned in 1946, left again—yes again, quite an addictive habit, isn't it?—in 1956 and returned only last year. And I think that is more than enough roaming the globe for one life."

"Did you lose everything each time?" John asked with undisguised awe.

"Money could be moved or hidden, even in those dark ages, John Price . . . But once"—she quietly laughed and gently skewered a cube of chicken paprikás—"once, I hoped to save—oh, this is a long and silly story. I must begin a little further back. In 1956, I was living in Budapest for ten years. I was married to a gentleman of great breeding and cultivation, but he had allowed himself to become embroiled in the anti-Soviet violence of that year. When the

Soviets decided to finish us once and for all, my husband and I opted for a hasty departure. We had left it rather late, incurable optimists that we were." She sipped her champagne. "We needed to get to the Austrian border with some speed, but how much speed was not completely clear. The potential loss of money did not worry us; I could always play piano. We hadn't so very much to lose, *quand même*. And I am not a sentimental woman, John Price, so the loss of old photos or mantelpiece gewgaws did not reduce me to sniveling. No, my husband and I had only one regret. We had collected in our years together a sizable library of books and a large set of record albums, neither of which were readily available in those days. Guests had brought us gifts discreetly, knowing our tastes. We had friends who worked in bookstores, one who managed the symphony and traveled with them, others made for us jazz recordings taken from the American radio. We were very proud of our home: books in Hungarian, English, German, French, recordings of classical and jazz musics." A pearl string of bubbles swerved and danced as she tapped on the side of her glass. "We could never, and certainly not at this late date, hope to carry our treasures out of the country with us. Hungary was closing its every border, every gap in its skin, with terrible speed. We had to accept this fate, that our treasure would be stolen from us, and there was terrible regret over this. But my beautiful husband was clever to the very end. He had an idea, you see, because . . . well, I lied about not being sentimental, I'm afraid. I am really an incurable liar, John Price. It is a terrible character flaw and I must correct it. I will soon. You will help me. But in the meantime you must never believe a word I say. So, yes, he saw me weeping—it is ridiculous to say now—over *Alice in Wonderland*. Not the Bible, not Petőfi or Arany or Kis, not even Tolstoy. I could not bear to lose my *Alice*. He saw me on the floor, holding it like a baby—and this is why I was begun to weep—holding it and a record of Charlie Parker called "Blues for Alice." First I was laughing—I had never noticed the two of them together before. I joked to myself that the song was about the book, and then I was crying, and my husband, gathering clothes for our escape, found me, acting a very foolish little girl. He did not scold me for wasting time. He understood at once why I was crying, and he told me what we would do, and we did it. We spent one long night making a catalog of our literature and music. Of our life and pleasures. We took turns with the pen. One of us recited; one of us wrote. You must think of this beautiful scene, John Price, for it was very beautiful. There are tanks rolling up the streets of your home. Where you grew up, where you and our Scott were boys. Where you fell in love and kissed your first little girlfriends.

Now that road is shredded, torn in pieces, because tanks are very heavy, you see, much heavier than regular motors. These tanks are in your road, and there are boys not much older than children, younger by far than you are now, throwing bottles of gasoline at tanks! There are explosions echoing down the streets where you once played—what would you have played? Is it baseball? And behind a blackened window, by candlelight, my husband and I scribble and whisper. Listen to us: I am reciting as fast as he can write, sometimes he is abbreviating and I kiss him and swear I will kill him if he cannot read his little shorthands when we are in our new home. I am reciting and making the piles of books and records as he writes them. I still remember even some of the words I said, titles I will never forget. They still come to me at times for no reason: Bach, Brandenburg Concerti, six discs, 1939, Berlin Philharmonic, von Karajan conducting. Louis Armstrong Hot Sevens, 1927: "Willie the Weeper," "Wild Man Blues," "Alligator Crawl," "Potato Head Blues," "Melancholy," "Weary Blues," "Twelfth Street Rag." Beethoven's *Complete Music for Cello and Piano*, Rudolf Serkin and Pablo Casals in Prades, France, 1953, three discs. What do you think of that, John Price? One hundred and thirty-one record albums, every song noted, conductors, dates, performers, places. Fourteen reel-to-reel tapes of radio broadcasts: *Die Fledermaus*, Metropolitan Opera, 1950, Ormandy—a Hungarian, you know—conducting. Adele sung by Lily Pons; Alfred, by Richard Tucker. *Madame Butterfly*, 1952 at La Scala, Tullio Serafin conducting, Renata Tebaldi singing Cho-Cho-San. Art Tatum at the Esquire Concert in the Metropolitan Opera House in New York City, USA, in 1944 with Oscar Pettiford and Sid Catlett: "Sweet Lorraine," "Cocktails for Two," "Indiana," "Poor Butterfly." Dvořák's "Cello Concerto in B Minor," Pierre Fournier with Vienna Philharmonic, Rafael Kubelik conducts, 1952. My God, they still come to me so easily! And then three hundred and four books. Every author, the title of every story or poem in anthologies. Goethe's *Faustus* in two volumes and *Young Werther*, in German. Chekhov, stories in Hungarian. Every title, publisher, edition, description of covers, each—"

"That's ridiculous. This is completely ridiculous," Scott said, and immediately stood up. "It's impossible. It would have been suicidal. I'm afraid you're mis—" But he just shook his head and walked away from the table before he finished, wisely and healthfully refusing conflict.

Nádja smiled at her remaining listener and accepted a light from him. "Well, you know, I must agree with your brother. Particularly as I listen to myself reciting those records. It *is* impossible. The story is quite absurd. I mustn't spout such fairy stories."

"Not at all, please. Ignore him. We're not even really brothers."

"Tosh! Do not ever be polite to me just because I am as old as an antique vase, John Price. Of course my story is ridiculous. Scott is far cleverer than you, I think. No wonder you dislike him so. Yes, you do. But he is right: What sane person would believe that another sane person, while bombs explode and hours matter, as they rarely ever do, would write down the words"—she closed her eyes—"*The Iliad, Pope's translation into English, cloth cover with golden floral design, 1933.*" She reopened her eyes and patted the back of John's hand. "Your brother is completely correct. Do not believe an old woman who tells such ludicrous stories. She is a menace to your happiness, John Price." She breathed out smoke, and John wished for all the world that Nádja were twenty-four. "Yet there we were, and we did it. We knew there was a risk, of course, we were not fools, we were merely excited and sure that this was worth it and that we would survive and have this tale to tell later, elsewhere, to very impressed admirers like you and that we would have the pleasure of rebuilding this collection. Bombs are exploding down the street and we are writing our catalogue raisonné. We do not know what is the situation in the countryside. We do not know if we have one hour or one week to reach Austria. But we do it. By only candlelight, now my husband—my beautiful husband"—John was sincerely, momentarily jealous—"stands at the bookcase and seizes the books, reads titles as fast as I can write. I do not have his shorthands. He kisses favorite books even as he places them onto the floor for the last time. We are laughing sometimes at what we do. We were laughing when we finished our scribbling. He kissed me. We were laughing, John Price. We had won! We rescued our life—not just our silly bodies like the other refugees would do, but our very life together too. We spoke of when we will remake our home in London or Paris or Amsterdam or even your New York City. Every day we will do this: We will together pass our new, free days in searching in music and bookstores with our list and find our records and buy our books until the list jumps to life. We were laughing because we were escaping with the blue plans, the design for our happiness, and if they exploded our building, if they burned our books, if they melted our records with their flame-shooters, if they fouled my piano, they will still not hurt us.

"We left our home, finally, with the clothes we were wearing and our precious lists. Memory is peculiar: I can remember those descriptions of books and records in details, but I am not at all certain how many pages we carry. I remember a group of papers, perhaps twenty pages. But I sometimes can feel the weight of hundreds of pages. I dreamt for many years of running with a single sheet between us, both of our hands necessary to support its heaviness. I can see that clearly as a memory, but I know this is not true."

The bartender, doubling as an announcer, introduced the evening's headline band. Scott returned with a drink and a refreshed smile, turned to watch five musicians take the stage. Three of them had played behind Billie Fitzgerald; John and Emily had bought them drinks—the Russian twins and the Hungarian pianist. Fitzgerald, though, was replaced now by two young American men in business suits and with shaven heads—a black singer and a white saxophonist. As the band tuned up underneath the blue sky, white clouds, and long-gone heroes, the saxophonist introduced the first number, " 'Beatrice,' a lovely tune written by the saxman Sam Rivers for his wife."

Nádja listened in silence for several minutes. "It is a pretty tune, no? And a time-honored tradition, I think: Write something pretty, name it for your wife or lover, and vow it will make *her* immortal. A familiar lie, yes? You men all do that, John Price."

"Get to the end of the story," Scott prompted her. "I smell a defining tragedy in the offing."

"Is that what's coming?" she mused. John marveled at her ability to disregard the irrelevant Scott, but thought she seemed bored with the story, seemed to debate whether to wrap it up as quickly as possible or just laugh it off. "Yes, there was a motor for a spell, then the petrol goes, so then walking in groups, then just the two of us. And then we were stopped. Not so very far from the border, I know. In an open field, just after we came out of a wood. A very young Russian soldier found us and our list and made us stand while he turned the pages this way and that, waiting, one imagines, to learn Hungarian in a flash of insight. Well, you know, Russian privates are very rarely granted such flashes, so after a bit, he finally calls for his officer. The officer came over from the open military car, the what is it, the, the, the jeep, and he knew enough only Hungarian to talk like a caveman. '*What?*' he yelled, with his head far out in front of his shoulders, like this, and he waves the papers, shaked them at us. My beautiful husband smiled at him, a perfect gentleman ready to help the poor fellow understand what was the situation. He said, 'Friends. Music. Books.' He gently took the sheets from the gorilla's hands and pointed to the Russian names, even though they were not in Cyrillic script. 'Look,' he said. 'Chekhov. Turgenev. Tolstoy. Tchaikovsky. Prokofiev.' He whistled themes from the music. He sang to them. Under the stars, he sang. He sang very well. And I thought, There will be no problem, because his voice does not waver. They will hear he is not nervous and so we are harmless and so there is no problem and they will let us go with our list, and when we tell this story to our new friends in Austria we will tell it as though it was an audition for the Vienna opera. My husband pointed to the paper and said in a funny Russian accent, 'Prokofiev!' and he whistled the theme from *Peter and the Wolf*, and he pretended to be the hunter, pretended to aim his big blunderbuss. And the boy—the private, the first soldier—begins to smile. And he whistles the next part of it! And we know everything will be fine now. '*Da! Da! Kamarad!*' my husband says, because this boy truly is a comrade to know this music. He was ecstatic, my husband, he laughed and they whistled the music from *Peter and the Wolf* together! There we stood, the four of us, on a dirty road in the Hungarian countryside, only a few kilometers from the Austrian border. Only a few kilometers from Broadway, from the Seine. There was half a moon. There were lights from the Russians' car. There was I, trying to not appear tempting to hungry Russian soldiers. I still appear tempting in 1956, gentlemen."

"I don't doubt it for a moment."

The singer stepped to the microphone, unbuttoned his suit coat, and sang over the gentle chords and walking bass:

And now I'm lost without you,
Star-crossed without you,
Tempest-tossed, mildewed and mossed,
And not infrequently sauced without you.

"More champagne?"

"*Köszi*, John Price. That would be delightful."

John lifted the empty bottle and his eyebrows at a waitress.

"So—moonlight and jeep light and amorous, hungry soldiers and big bad wolves and the guns in the distance and wherever will it all end?"

"You embellish a bit, my Danish critic, like a professor, of course, but let's see. Yes. Well, my husband and the soldier acting out *Peter and the Wolf*. The officer all this time is examining our pages, and now he interrupts their game. '*Nyet, nyet.*' Still they whistle and play. '*Nyet!*' And now they stop. 'No. Why?' he demands. He knows this much Hungarian. '*Nem. Miért?*' My husband stopped.

He was pained and he showed it. '*Miért?* Friend, life. Music. Books.' The simplest Hungarian he could manage. The fundamental elements. Then he said the same in German. Then French. English. Neither of us knew any Russian, so he was only just hoping to find a tongue in common with the officer. '*Zene. Musik. Musique. Music. Könyvek. Buecher. Livres. Books.*' I never have forgotten his face, his voice. He was an angel on earth. Eloquent in eight words. He was"—she thought for a moment—"an ambassador for life and beauty and art. He was asking these stupid shit peasants to rise up from their Russian dirt to embrace civilization. And if they looked at him, why shouldn't they want to? He was fearless, so much a man. He pointed to me. '*A feleségem. Meine frau. Mon épouse. My wife.*' What could be clearer? Less threatening?"

She exchanged Hungarian chat with the waitress who cleared their dinner plates, and accepted another flute of champagne from John. She blew her smoke away from Scott and touched his hand, vowed never to light up in his presence again now that she saw his abstinence. "Melancholic Dane, you must forgive an old woman who has endangered your fine pink lungs." The bass thumped out the last notes of a vamp.

"Yuri on the bass, ladies and gentlemen," said the singer to polite applause. "Yuri on the bass."

"Yuri looks to be about fifteen, no? He is very much like that private who whistled with my husband. Now I must finish this long and tedious recollection so that you gentlemen can spend some time with ladies more to your tastes . . ."

" 'What could be clearer and less threatening?' " said John. He twirled his champagne flute's stem between his thumb and index finger.

"Yes. Except to this officer. One must, I suppose, imagine *his* heart, vile as the thought naturally is. He is far from home. He hopes to do his part in putting back this restless corner of empire, a corner not even Slav, after all, that always puts on airs, thinks itself better than the Poles and Czechs and Bulgarians and Russians, and—remember—that fought alongside the Nazis only twelve years ago, the same Nazis, let us imagine, who killed this officer's father, perhaps. In the middle of this little revolt, he must do his duty. On a deserted path quite, quite close to the dangerous border with the West, with those same Nazi people, perhaps he thinks, because, well, *Austrians*, after all. And here, on this path, come a young man and woman who seem to speak everything *but* Russian. And they carry a group of papers, oddly spaced and labeled, sheets of writing, improbable and random lists of names and words, including Russian names. And of course, after some of the record album titles, there are serial numbers. And after every book, words who make a strange kind of sense in his little Hungarian: red cloth, morocco, gold-embossed. What could be clearer? What could be more threatening? I have often thought of this officer, of course. Did he truly suspect our papers were codes of secrets? Or did he simply hate us? Us Hungarians who did not trouble to learn Russian but talk in French and German and English. Hungarians who cause trouble and cause him to be sent away from his family and home in Russia to make us behave ourselves. Did he know people like us and just hate us, us people who talked about Tchaikovsky and Turgenev and Chopin? Or perhaps none of these names sounded even familiar to him, and I make of him an anti-intellectual when he was something much simpler. Maybe his heart held only his orders: Stop everyone, suspect everyone, shoot everyone. I don't know."

The music changed tempo and she started to remove a cigarette from its pack, then stopped, pushed the white tip back into hiding. "I am so very sorry, Scott. Some things I do not remember so easily. Hope beat its wings and flew away the next moment, when I saw him fold the sheets and place them in his jacket's pocket. He barked something in Russian to the private. He looked at us and pointed to the car, to that jeep. 'Budapest,' he said with no tone at all. My husband nodded immediately and laughed, '*Da! Gut. Ja. Igen, nagyon jó. Da!*' as though we were lost on this road and wanted nothing more than a ride home to the blazing capital. My husband laughed loudly and smiled at me and said in English, 'Darling, run when I say!' as if he were saying, 'A happy stroke of luck, what? These jolly lovely gentlemen are going to take us back to Budapest!' "

The singer introduced the next song: "An old tune for those who find love confusing when it comes and even more so once it's gone."

Nádja screwed up her face, as at a smell. "Oh really, one can hardly talk about anything with jazz singers around. Everything becomes quite immediately silly. I'll tell you the rest some other time." The singer began to croon over grudging chords, insinuating bass, and whispering brushes. "Or at least when this sentimental rubbish is over." Scott shoved back from the table and went to the pay phone, shaking his head.

While the saxophonist breathed a mournful, meandering solo, Nádja asked John about his brother, complimented the absent Scott without any evident irony. She asked why a man who could be a movie star or a politician came instead to teach "his unpronounceable and mongrel tongue to us poor Magyars." John had no answer for her, and realized just then—considering all that he had wanted from Scott for years—that he barely knew his brother or his brother's motives. But he loathed admitting ignorance to her on any topic, so he said that English majors had almost no options in the United States after graduation and were forced to become a sort of refugee themselves, deployed to the four corners of the world to teach the only skill they had, which was valuable proportionally to how far from home they wandered. He was pleased when she laughed, loved how she exhaled smoke and amusement simultaneously.

"It is remarkable. He is a Swede in the Congo here," she said. "There is always something interesting in this world." Applause rose from the tables like heartbeats suddenly amplified, and the band announced the end of its set. "Unfortunately, if you will excuse me"—she stood—"I am expected at my piano while the orchestra reposes." She and her flute of champagne sailed toward the stage, the whimsical carved prow of an invisible ship.

Scott returned immediately but did not sit. Nádja began a striding "As Time Goes By," and Scott crumpled and dropped Hungarian bills on the table, one at a time. "That should cover my share in tonight's theatrics. She didn't finish it, did she. Right. Twenty bucks says you never quite hear the end. I'm getting out of here just in time, boy-o. In fact, you know, let's take a little break from these weekly charades, okay?"

"Suits me fine, chief."

"Good."

"Good."

"Good night."

"Right."

XXI.

Some girls need their glass of claret,
Or to be draped head to toe in ferret.
And I know ladies who like lunch time
And there are those inspired by tea
And there are those who want to tussle
Only in chalets après-ski.

And some pretty things like the bal musette
Or to hear bandoleons and a castanet,
But my girl need not leave the kitchenette,
As long as she has plenty flaming crêpes suzette.

Sure, I could make her drink before dinner,
But that would never win 'er.
For an ante-prandial brandy'll
Never make this girl a sinner.

Cocaine makes her nose bleed
And reefers make her sleepy.
For cash and jewels she has no greed
'Tis pastry makes her weepy.

Because she's most spectacular
When she's post-jentacular,
She's my after-breakfast girl!
She's my after-breakfast girl!

Angry faces and loud music greeted John as he entered Mark's apartment building one morning about a week later. Hateful expressions floated behind curtains pulled aside, eyelids narrowed behind windows shut tight despite the July heat. On the dark stairway, two old women bore down on him, stopped his ascent, blocked his way, began absolutely to scold him, though his crime remained necessarily obscured in its Hungarian description and his plea for forgiveness foolishly disguised itself as foreign babbling, a noise that provoked his accusers even more, until they finally continued down the stairs, throwing their arms forward and their infuriated glances backward at the menace.

The building's courtyard and the two tiers of walkway that circled it echoed with strange and scratchy old music, a Charleston-sounding dance tune from the 1920s, something about eating breakfast. Static and noise drifted around the singer's tenor voice like snowflakes drawn to a streetlight. John hardly needed to exert his imagination to know the music's source and why the residents were blaming him for the disturbance: The sound grew, unsurprisingly, louder as he approached Mark's door and it required strenuous pounding before he gained admission. Mark stood in his underwear (boxers, sleeveless T), and his face was red and bloated; John had the impression he had been crying, but now his peculiar friend was smiling broadly and was soon wiggling and dancing around his apartment to the window-rattling noise.

John, newly appointed advocate for the building's alienated population, closed Mark's courtyard windows and began to hunt for the offending stereo. He came instead, in the apartment's bedroom, upon a large gramophone, complete with metal crank and brass horn. His eyes spun as he attempted to read the faded, peeling label on the revolving black disc: *Afr-Bekft Grl*. As his puffy and disheveled host had gone to the kitchen for drinks and John could find no volume control on the elderly box, he gently lifted its enormous tonearm. His skin crawled in anticipation of the excruciating scraping sound to come, but smooth silence flooded the building at mid-verse. In the sudden calm, his touch lingered on the fluted, molluscular ridges and lips of the dull brass horn. He wondered at previous owners, noted a deep scratch in its metal that must have taken great force to create—a bored child with a penknife, a careless mover with a doorjamb, a jilted lover with a grudge.

"My newest treasure!" Mark explained. He carried two sweating glasses of iced tea in his fat, damp hands. "I knew you'd love it, especially. I had you in mind when I bought it, actually: 'This, John will appreciate.' " He had purchased the functioning wind-up antique the day before from a small electrical shop in his neighborhood. It was accompanied by eight thick black discs, strange sounds from a time decades before Mark's birth: coy, archaically smutty lyrics extolling archaic modes of flirtation and sex, flapper dances as ancient and foreign as Etruscan funeral rituals or Aztec virgin sacrifices. Mark's unexplained swollen face left John wondering if he had interrupted a scene with some vanished stranger now hiding in the tub or sneaking out the back or if a tear-stained letter now waited, stuffed half written or half read in a drawer.

But Mark smiled and sweated, complained of no interruption, gave John his drink, and talked rapturously of the records. "I really like that one." He pointed to *After-Breakfast Girl*. "I played it, played it a few times since I got it yesterday, but, ah, listen to this one." Despite John's protests, Mark reverently changed the record, his palms flat against the disc's thick edges. His eyelid tic kicking as he laughed, he cranked the device then delicately placed the tonearm. As the scratches congealed into a voice and a jangling piano, Mark began to dance a slapdash Charleston.

That's the kinda dance that a fella can do
That a fella can do
That a fella can do
That's the sorta dance that a fella can do
With a gal who knows the rules!

The damn toy seemed to have just one volume setting, "because, you know, the past has to scream to be noticed," Mark said in a professorial tone. John peeked through the curtains to see if the neighbors were mounting a lynch mob against the foreign maniacs. When he turned away from the window, Mark was still flapping his fleshy arms like an elephantine competitor in the late hours of a dance marathon, and he was also crying.

Or possibly not. The sweat that flowed and jumped from his hairline and eyebrows could have explained the watery, stung look of his eyes, and his panting and laughter seemed sufficient to justify the red nose and slobber. Unless he was crying.

"Jesus, I'm sorry I came. Please, in the name of God, stop. Take a shower. We're supposed to have lunch. This is horrifying."

"I love this song! Listen to it! This is music! Why *couldn't* I?"

John refused to answer the nonsensical question even on its first and second repetitions, which is when he decided (relieved) that Mark was joking in some obscure, historiographical way—"why couldn't I" most likely being the last words of some nineteenth-century parliamentarian or circus performer. The dancing ended, the noise melted into the consonance of the gramophone's whooping repetitive scratch and Mark's wheezy breathing. John closed the device's lid. "Watch it with this thing. Your neighbors want to kill you."

Mark flopped down onto the couch and chewed ice cubes. He nodded and spoke very quickly (John thought briefly of Karen's patter): "I know and they, they would, because, the thing is, I had a pretty serious breakthrough today in my work. You know, I'm going to have this appendix, a daisy chain of nostalgia. Basically, you start with this year or whenever and you find the cultural wave of collective nostalgia that's happening right now, like, say, a thing for the fifties, which we are *definitely* entering now. I'll have to pinpoint it and back it up with the usual evidence—crew cuts, Chet Baker record sales, capri pants—but then I'll go backwards to the longed-for time in question and I'll find—and I know it's there—that there was actually a nostalgia wave *then* for some even *earlier* time, right, and I'll pinpoint it and go back to *its* source, and sure enough there'll be another one and on and on, all the way back to Charlemagne. The good old days, you know."

"Are you going to shower before lunch?"

"I will, absolutely. But the problem is, it's too broad. Why forty-year chunks, right? What about a decade at a time? Someone in the eighties longed for the seventies, whether that's the 1970s or the 1470s, you know, so I could daisy chain in decades. But then I realized I could actually document it even tighter. What about annually?"

"We could go for paprikás and goulash. I think I found one place that might serve them."

"Exactly. This is my breakthrough. So of course the music makes them mad, that always happens like that, actually. Why not *monthly?* I could do that. I could prove monthly. I could. It's easy-easy if you know how to research, if you know what you're looking for. I could take you back every month to William the Conqueror. But then maybe that's not close enough, is it? To really *matter* to people. To cure them, I mean."

"I met a woman you'd really like last week, this old piano player."

"This is where I make my name, John. You're going to be very proud of me, and that's the whole point. And this is why the neighbors are a little cranky. Daily. I can *prove* daily. Today, somebody longs for yesterday and they are leaving steaming evidence of their sadness and I can prove it, but yesterday there was somebody who was sure happiness ended the day before. I can go all the way to Jesus Christ and keep going. It's going to take research, I admit that, but this is there. And I *will* help people, despite themselves. So, you know, my neighbors had better get used to that and, and stop coming at me about the music or the rest of it."

Inevitably, John was laughing now. "Please, I'm begging you to go shower."

Mark toweled off while John read a *Herald Tribune* in the kitchen, at the small table, underneath a poster promoting Sarah Bernhardt's upcoming tour of America. "I'm glad you came when you came," Mark admitted in a tone the shower had softened, slowed. "The music was actually starting to get to me, I think." He toweled his head and disappeared into the bedroom. "I bought you something." He returned to the kitchen, the towel around his waist now, and placed on John's head a fedora with a laminated PRESS card in the band. He left John, amused, experimenting with jaunty angles.

In the international paper John read an article about "The New Hungary" by a renowned foreign correspondent. It described a nation psychically damaged by years of tyranny, hoping for change, but stifled by economic hardship and entrepreneurial inexperience. The writer detailed a clear Hungarian national character, the shared traits that would have an unavoidable effect on the nation's growth into democracy and free markets, compared their prospects to those of the more promising Czechs. The journalist peppered the piece with anecdotes of ordinary Zsolts, their travails, hopes, fears. John shouted excerpts of the article down the hall to Mark, but disguised the nation in question, as in "Blank is a country that has known more than its fair share of hardship, and if the Blanks are wary of strangers, it is for good reason; if they have a reputation for charming slipperiness and an endearing pessimism, it is hard to blame them. The Blank people look to the future with understandable trepidation." Mark was dressed now and John asked him to identify the Blanks, whom he admired and envied in this context.

After three wrong guesses (Afghanistan, Angola, Argentina), Mark lost interest and admitted he didn't read current newspapers ("Besides, *everybody* looks to the future with understandable trepidation"). He had only bought this particular copy because something was odd about it, right on the front page. The Canadian tapped significantly at the date at the top, smiled, and awaited his friend's dawning realization, but dawn did not arrive. It was the correct date, John pointed out. *"Obviously"* was the sarcastic retort. "Oh, come on! Look at it! You know how in the first couple days or weeks of January the dates on newspapers look strange," Mark explained patiently, as if to a child. "Like they're from science fiction, where someone travels into the future and is stunned to see a paper because the year at the top of the paper is so weird and far into the future? That happens the first few days of every year, right? Like, 1990? Not 1989 anymore? Or you know how for the first few checks you write after New Year's, you have to think about what year to write, and you might even put down the old year by mistake? Well, look at the date on the paper again!" Mark tapped it loudly and whistled. "This is the latest in the year this has ever happened. I mean, it's *July*, but the date has that science-fictiony feel today. When I saw the paper I was amazed, because dates have been mostly fine since, like, the second or third week of January, but then today—it was just before the gramophone called me from the shop window—I saw this paper and I was, like, July 14, 1990? That looks *bizarre*. So I bought it as a souvenir. This is a record: It's *July*, after all. You should buy a copy. Something to show your grandkids."

Over lunch on Castle Hill, the historian talked again of eras and the significance of dates in a way John could almost swear was a joke. He didn't find it at all funny, but it felt like a social duty to laugh at Mark's words, as if Mark were pretending to lose his mind, aggressively demanding from his audience at least a polite laugh of appreciation for the effort.

"Think about the year 2000. That's only ten years away, but the number is ridiculous. It's not a real year, like 1943 or 1862 or, or 1900, if you must have zeroes. Two thousand is nonsense, from movies. Honestly, I—" Mark flipped leaves of lettuce around on his plate. They sat on the patio behind the Hilton Hotel, luxury built around the ruins of a medieval monastery. John listened to his friend speak and wondered what made a man like Mark Payton worry about the things he worried about, wondered if it wasn't all affectation. But to what end? Surely there must be an unaffected first cause, a sincere reason that prods the affected to act that way. Perhaps Mark had cobbled together this strange persona for mating purposes, perhaps a plump but plain Canadian, one of nature's bachelors, would naturally seek a way to differentiate himself from the buffer, sleeker competition, and the Man Obsessed by the Past must have some lurid, offbeat appeal in whatever dark grounds of sexual hunting his type was compelled to stalk in post-Communist Central Europe. Or, maybe Mark was entirely scrubbed free of affectation. Maybe his research work and his natural inclinations had just gotten the better of him and he really couldn't get out the door anymore without thinking how the date didn't feel right or the architecture was criminally violating him. Maybe he had lost the skill (if he had ever had it) of carrying on conversations about anything but lost time; perhaps he subsisted solely on a diet of linden tea and madeleines.

"Honestly, I find it frightening. It's too futuristic a number—it's not for men like me. And you. It's for spacemen or conglomerates." Mark was gripping his silverware until his fingers turned white, but John was staring at two young tourists—a man and a woman—arguing in front of one of the fairy-tale bastions along the promenade. They were out of earshot. The man poked the tip of the woman's nose with a firm index jab, an oddly clear symbolic punch. She turned her back and stomped off.

Mark noticed at last that he was talking only to himself. "I'm really growing tiresome, aren't I? Me and my 'issues.' " He held up four fingers around *issues*, looked for a companionable laugh, which didn't come, and returned to his food. "You met a woman piano player, you said, a piano player?" he said, remembering a scrap of conversation from an hour before. "What about you and Emily?"

"Different sort of relationship." John wondered when and how his non-romance had become public knowledge.

"No great mystery," Mark said, answering the unvoiced question. "If you know how to watch. And before you interrogate me, no, I can't tell you a thing about her. By the way, what's up with you and Scott? What did you *do* to that guy?"

John declined to answer, spoke instead of the nightly visits he had been paying to Nádja at the Blue Jazz. As he recounted the old woman's adventures— her escape from Budapest, her bohemian life in the United States, her affair with a world-renowned concert pianist, her outrageous dealings with lesser European royalty—he kept his tone skeptical, amused, reflexively suspecting that the scholarly Mark would find her implausible, even as he hoped that the nostalgic Mark would find her elegantly incontrovertible. In this tone, he imagined himself in the stories he was retelling. Sometimes he was the supporting character—young Nádja's cultivated and heroic husband or the concert pianist making slow Chopin-accompanied love to a vaguely Emilyesque woman. In other stories, he was the leading character herself: *He* sprinted—frightened, alone, and literally listless—across the Austrian border; *he* dined with the seedy viscount in the dark and freezing dining room there was not money enough to heat; *he* sailed the world and grew slowly bored on a billionaire's yacht.

"A lot of that stuff could be verified. You've got to know most of it's improbable to the point of—" Mark professionally and calmly began explaining research techniques John could use to check Nádja's stories. The topic relaxed him. "Every story has aspects that can be checked." He spouted a catalog of scholar's tricks: address records for given years, boat registries, refugee rosters, the tour schedules of world-renowned musicians.

"Check her? Why? Do you think she's a liar?" John regained his tone of mild noninterest. "I hadn't really taken her too seriously myself. I just thought you'd find her entertaining."

"Hey sure, I'd love that. Bring me to meet her, hey? What about tonight, the two of us?"

They passed from the patio to the Hilton lobby, then back outside, through the revolving doors and into Szentháromság Square. "I gotta do this interview. I'll catch up with you at the Gerbeaud." John turned to the right.

"Call me, hey? We'll visit the pianist." Mark turned left toward the palace and the National Gallery, wondered when they'd catch up with each other, he could go and do his work at the Gerbeaud right now, be sure to be there when John turned up. He pushed through an immobile throng of pathetically indecisive tourists and was suddenly angry at the damage they were doing to the mood of Castle Hill. As he emerged at the herd's far side, his anger quickly transformed into anxiety: He was bothered by the sense that despite his best efforts to hold it tight to himself, his hard-won peace had been stolen from him by conspiring, malignant forces during lunch. John was not an official delegate of the malignant forces, but he was more and more their unwitting instrument, as were all of these unpleasant tourists, as was the young waitress with the dragon-headed-lamb tattoo on her sinewy, starkly hairless forearm. It was a great relief to be away from company now. It was so much work to explain everything to everyone, even to John, whose obtuseness was often incredibly charming but also exasperating and possibly even willful. It was so much easier to be alone, if one could find just the right location. The palace courtyard shone in Mark's memory with an almost palpable, almost edible promise, a promise with a color all its own: a sort of soft golden red. The palace courtyard would do the trick. He bore the five-minute walk through heat and tourists with the knowledge that soon his day would find soft golden-red comfort.

He installed himself near the courtyard fountain and eagerly awaited the peace that should flow from the continually splashing water and the soothing, historic construction on all four sides, the permanently prancing stag, the flagstones and archways, the high windows and the square of eighteenth-century blue sky.

Yet nothing.

His eyes moved slowly, then quickly, from one of these pacifying sights to the next, faster and faster in frustration as he felt less and less at ease, more and more betrayed by the place, by the flagstones and archways in which he had put his faith. Even in the few short months since his arrival, there were fewer amenable places. He closed his eyes and tried to hear only the water fall from the mouth of the fountain with precisely the same noise it had made for centuries.

Rudely imported from the imbecilic vendor just outside the palace and freshly stripped from their chocolate innards, bright yellow-and-blue candy wrappers, like a troupe of supernatural acrobats, tumbled, cartwheeled, took wing, and soared over the brown flagstones of the courtyard. Mark made an effort to look elsewhere but was greeted by fat German tourists in shorts two sizes too small and Americans with video cameras filming each other film each other and a squadron of Japanese photographers and a middle-aged British couple who wore matching plastic waist packs and sunhats topped with plastic-coated pictures of the queen mum. Mark leaned back to stare at the upper stories of the palace, the clouds that sponged the blue sky behind the oxidized eagle's head. But it was too late. The palace felt like another dreary theme park, built to look not like the past, precisely, but the way the past was commonly accepted to look by the dimmest members of the present, a fantasyland with crummy rides, but workers dressed convincingly as sullen Hungarian tour guides.

A day's worth of reading awaited Mark faraway on his kitchen table. The music had prevented him from working last night and this morning, and lunch had dragged on for a heartbreaking eternity. The two piles of books under the poster of Sarah Bernhardt seemed to him forlorn and needy as they grew and teetered and beckoned to him to leave the palace. There was a towering stack of books on millenarian cults of the approaching year 2000. Next to it and in its shadow, there moped a sad, small bump of slim texts on millenarian beliefs around the year 1000. The promise of work did nothing for him, though. He had been working seven days a week for several months now, with breaks only to meet friends and sit at the Gerbeaud or to sit alone in this palace courtyard (now dead and off his list forever), sit on the benches in Kossuth Square near Parliament, sit on the Pest-side riverfront, sit near the opera, sit at the Gellért, swim at the Rácz Fürdő, walk slowly through Pest, avoid the construction sites, imagine old construction sites instead. He slowly stood, taking it on a cracked faith that it would feel good to work by the time he got home, if he could make it home safely. He wondered how John's interview was going, hoped he understood the fedora and would wear it right. It was only two-thirty. He left the palace and, too hot to walk down Castle Hill's winding path to the river, he bought a ticket for the minute-long funicular ride that carted shutterbug tourists up and down the slope. He stood at the little station at the top of the hill and watched the two counterbalancing cable cars, each with about eight passengers, as they glided up and down in opposite motion, passed each other midtrip, and, in between runs, gazed sadly at each other from opposite ends.

JUST OUT OF THE Hilton's revolving doors, John was embraced by the July heat, particularly heavy after the air-conditioning of the lobby. Had it grown hotter since he had lunched on the patio a few minutes earlier? he wondered.

Could climatic fronts be so specific as to start on opposite sides of a hotel? He tried to concentrate on the interview for which he was already half an hour late. He came to the end of little Táncsics Mihály utca without being aware of his surroundings, except for the way the cobblestones bent the thin soles of his shoes into concave embraces. *Why Hungary what investment prospects do you have do you miss the rough-and-tumble of Washington how do you think the Hungarians see your work what bars and restaurants do you prefer is life here what you would have expected and in the future will all of this be noticed as an event why does what you do matter are you proud of yourself is that even the right standard these are ridiculous questions.*

He passed a lamppost, green and stuck with bits of poster for last year's elections and something called THE NEW AMERICANS. And there was a small tan-and-white hound with long, plush ears folded like velvet curtains, a hound that hopped on three legs in an effort to push his fourth leg ever higher, to keep his balance while he dishrag-twisted his torso to urinate higher and higher up the lamppost, arching in a vain effort to seem, retrospectively, a big dog to later sniffers.

John came through the old fortification called the Vienna Gate, picking up his pace, and surprised a couple leaning against a tree, kissing. He lost his breath as he recognized the woman whose back was to him: Emily. He stopped, stared, couldn't believe how quickly it had fallen apart. Her partner's one visible eye opened, saw immobile John, and his tilted, half-hidden face changed, filled with menace and readiness. "*Mi a faszt akarsz?*" he hissed at the stranger.

John fumbled for some Hungarian, decided instead on saying her name, maybe asking why, but she was already turning her head to see who had taken her lover's attention and lips away, and she revealed herself to be a round-faced Hungarian girl with braces on her teeth and far-apart eyes. "Oh, *elnézést kérek*," John managed with a gesture of peaceful misunderstanding, fell back into English. "I thought, wow, I'm sorry, I thought I knew her, but I didn't, I mean . . ."

The man slid from behind the girl, took a step toward John, revealed the oddity of his haircut, demonstrated the depth of his English. "You know her? Who the fuck you are?"

"No, no, my mistake. I *don't* know her. I just thought—"

"You take a big look now, go ahead, now you are looking real careful at her, yeah? You know her?"

"No, I sure don't." A ready smile, still, haha, these things do happen.

The Hungarian seemed unable to understand John's denials. He stayed beside his threatened property. "You don't know her, you had your look, so fuck away now, man."

John resisted correcting the obscene grammar, laughed, and continued walking down sloping Várfok utca. Behind him, he heard the menacing bad English shift into Hungarian rumbling, interrupted occasionally by the complaining song of the unkissed female. Her voice predominated a second or two or three and then John felt a warm nausea in his head, followed by a sharp pain as his knee and left palm hit the ground. When he lifted his right hand, it returned from his scalp wet and red. Still on the ground, he turned—wincing, dizzy—to see the man biting his thumb at him, walking quickly backward toward the ancient fortified Vienna Gate, pushing his woman up the hill behind him, as if counterattacks might still be in the offing. The conquering rock was round enough, John noticed with an interest he knew was out of place, to keep rolling down the hill past where its latest victim still knelt.

MARK'S SENSE OF STOLEN peace dispersed with the first jerk of his funicular car's descent. He placed the corner of his ticket in his mouth, let two eyeeteeth meet in the blue paper slip's punched hole. The east appeared in the front window of the car, unrolling from the bottom up: nineteenth-century Pest, the gloriously antique Chain Bridge, and the slow-moving, brown Danube laid themselves out for him. The sun painted stripes of white and yellow on the river for him. He felt his heart rate slow, and sounds organized themselves for him: the whir of the funicular cables, the invisible bird whose song did not grow more distant as the car descended and so, Mark realized happily, must in fact be sitting on the roof to drink in the same flying joy as Mark himself. He could hover here happily forever, drift and sit in the sky like a child's dream of flight. His morning and his lunch retrospectively swelled with comprehensible importance, he felt fond of John again, trusted and admired him, looked forward to seeing everyone at the Gerbeaud soon, looked forward to the warm bath of work that awaited him.

When, however, the two funicular cars passed each other halfway, Mark felt a small sadness bite at his throat. He hurriedly reminded himself of the Parliament's mass and height, its ridges and curves and spired helmet, the ring roads' arching embrace of Pest's grid, the clouds that trolled their shadows through the streets and dragged them soundlessly over buildings without snagging them on chimneys or antiquated antennae . . . but aching moments later, all of that was being snatched away from him. With shortening seconds, Pest's riverfront buildings rose and blocked everything to their east, the Danube shimmered one last ripple, then evaporated like a summer highway mirage behind the Buda traffic at the bottom of the rail—silent, flattened toy cars just a few seconds earlier, but now inflated and sprung into speed and noise.

At the bottom of the hill, he did manage to leave the station, proud of pulling himself together, ready for work. But then all the cars on the round-about in front of the Chain Bridge stopped him and he looked back up at the cable car resting at the top of the hill. There was actually no decision to be made; it was simply a matter of answering an imperative need. And so he turned back to the funicular's ticket booth.

JOHN MADE THE LAST downhill block with only one or two stumbles, his cold hand glued to his hot, matted head. The shabby office building's elderly concierge guided him to the wooden door with the typewritten paper affixed to it with three strips of transparent tape: HUNGARIAN-AMERICAN CAPITAL DEVELOPMENT GROUP, INC. The young American man with the stubbly shaved head, ill-fitting khakis, and worn blue blazer who answered the door found the alarming sight of John Price's bright red–smeared palm held up in mute explanation of why he could not shake hands quite yet. "Can I use your bathroom?"

The basement washroom's cold water burned a hole in John's head and flung cherry swirls into the caramel-vanilla patterns of the ancient sink. He cautiously dabbed at his scalp with a paper towel and looked at the familiar figure floating over his shoulder's reflection: "You're the sax player from the club, right?" he managed to say before leaning back over to vomit, rattling the brain in his concussed skull. The voice behind him admitted it uneasily and asked John not to mention it "up there." John rinsed his face and mouth. "You dress sharp when you play. What's with this high school graduation outfit?" He leaned over and gagged again. The voice requested again, in a pathetic, pleading tone, not to mention his secret musical life "up there."

"Up there" was a single room with two tables, two chairs, two phones, several boxes of contradictory business cards, and little else. And then a too-loud voice—Harvey Lastnamelost—and hard hair split by a white straight-edge part, and a hand shaking John's violently while John's vision blurred and his head swelled. A proffered glass of tepid, salty club soda. Saxman sent out for coffee. A story about Harvey (check notebook for last name), heavy with post–Cold War symbolism, something about the Soviet ambassador, broad hint that the ambassador would take a job with Harvey, wolf out of a job, empire crumbling, rats, sinking ships, very droll to sit in the office of the Soviet ambassador sipping brandy, once the very control room of his empire's outpost, the room from which this country used to be run, for God's sake, and then to have him virtually begging me for a job, or at least a lead! Beautiful moment. What's your story going to be about? I was profiled before, you probably read in the *FT* and the *Journal*, both right behind us, smart journalism supports the cause. Exciting what we're going to do here, brave new world, a chance for all of us to make money together, and that's exactly what I tell the Hungarians: I want them to get rich, too, because I know I can get rich happier and faster if we all get rich together. All in the same boat. Western-style office buildings, I have a head start on approvals, option for building convention center, minister a close friend of mine, first-class fellow, I admire his poetry, published poet you know, these new artistic governments, so funny, they won't last here or in Prague, of course, it's nice after the Commies, but eventually they'll get back to having businessmen and lawyers in charge and that's how things get done, you can't really have a cabinet full of sculptors, more of a tourist attraction for now. John, I tell you, between you and me, just us right here right now, all I can say is best time for a man of honor and faith to step up, never will there be an opportunity like this, not just for the money men but for this country, will they throw off their shackles, I want to see money make men free, John, I'm the luckiest man alive to be here now, we're planning an opening fund $37 million, I want them to get rich right alongside me. That's right, and it shows a respect, too, the little Hungarians are pleased with. We can't just storm in and start buying up their country at fire-sale prices just 'cause they're down and out, right? Actually, John, we can. No, I'm kidding. I suppose that some of the smarter ones will make money, can hardly help it if they're not entirely as stupid as I sometimes suspect they are. It's all about how you choose to live life, you see, John. A man grabs life by the ankles and shakes her, sees what comes out of her pockets. I like your style, John. You're like me. How old are you? You ever want to get out of writing for the paper, you come talk to me. John, men like you and me deserve certain things, have to bite life on the neck and see if she screams, tickle her tits, you know? You want life? Well, she wants you to show her you can handle her, that you know how to get her wet. She wants to be mastered. The Hungarians used to know that, but they've forgotten how to do it, sad to say, and sad to see: a country of men so busy playing dumb under the Russians, they wake up one day and they can't help it, they're not playing, they're just *dumb*. John, honestly, I would love to teach them how to do it again, but there's no time for that. Opportunity's now. It's a matter of forward motion, you're like me, can't imagine why you don't put down your pen, grab your cock, and come work for me. I recently met with, and I said, "Senator, when you're ready to leave politics and return to the real world, there's a corner office in Budapest with your name on the door, a bright brass nameplate."

THE FIRST RIDE BACK up the hill was almost entirely joyful: the view only improved, grew more panoramic by the second, each moment shaming the last, until suddenly, treacherously, the car jogged to a stop and the tin roof of the up-hill station hung halfway over the front window and then the door clattered open and the whole thing felt like the ridiculous, panting, slightly nauseous anticlimax at the bottom of a roller coaster. A few minutes standing at the walkway at the top, leaning against the railing, enjoying the immobile view, sufficed to send him home to work again.

But of course this next ride down could not possibly have the innocent enjoyment of the first. This second descent was stained with the knowledge of how the end would feel just a minute later, so the joy was both briefer and more precious. When the car stopped with a shudder at its noisy, smoky, crowded lower terminus, Mark—shuddering, too—had the sensation that forty seconds of peace on the first trip down had become, this trip, thirty seconds, but a much more intense thirty seconds. He left the station again, ready to go home, ready to laugh off the unnecessary round-trip, but then wondered if the pattern would continue on the next trip, if it would become twenty seconds of new-found profundity, and if such a pattern didn't have some bearing, actually, on his research.

JOHN COULD SCARCELY BELIEVE how weak he felt when he finally propped himself into a cab's backseat. He grunted as his head scraped along the vinyl. In his pain and polygonal anger (the guy with the rock, Harvey the aesthetically offensive investor, Scott the inaccessible bastard who would never let John make things right), he was inspired: *Grab life by the ankles*. He decided to give the driver Emily's address. He leaned from side to side as the cab's bald tires slid with each turn into the hill. He would let her see him like this, would let her rescue and nurse him. A picture of sacrifice and love: a victim's very last energy spent on a kiss. *This is how it began. I should have gone to a doctor but I went to your mother. I kept hoping the Julies weren't there. And they weren't. Do you remember the first thing you said, Em, when I poured out of that cab? Tell them what you said. You said,*

"John Price? You are not healthful? Scott is being absent." The accent was Hungarian. He looked around, hoped Emily might somehow still appear, though he was at his brother's house and she was hills and hills away. Mária wore his brother's college T-shirt.

THE TRIPS UP, however, grew only finer and finer. By early in the evening, as the sun started to disappear behind the funicular and the view was lit by a fading, westering, indirect light that seemed to lend the buildings a more forceful third dimension, made them jut out from the silver-blue-green sky in shimmering bas relief, the rides became almost too beautiful to bear, and on several of the ascending journeys Mark felt his eyes wet with gratitude. The *motion* conjured the magic, the gradual change in the panorama over the ascending minute, watching this picture paint itself, flatten itself into two dimensions. Yes, it was pleasant to stare at the finished product from the walkway at the top, but it wasn't as potent as the slow ride up to that same walkway.

And as a scholar, he was interested to note that the window of pure peace did close slightly on each descending trip, but those shrinking, sinking moments grew geometrically sweeter and more trembling; the pleasure of the trips up increased only arithmetically. By sunset, with the couple standing next to him in the car kissing loudly and the girl's braces reflecting the light in silver flashes between embraces, the moment lasted only five seconds, perhaps— three seconds before passing the ascending car and another two seconds after—but in those five seconds, there was an annunciation, the feeling of absolute comfort and of loss simultaneously, a flight into the permanence of an antique postcard (he had been in or just out of the frame of some hundred tourist photos in the course of his miles of vertical, back-and-forth travel that afternoon). Permanence and impermanence blended, became momentarily identical—the permanence of his rightful place, and the impermanent view, impermanent buildings, the fading light, fading years, styles shifting so fast, somehow the undeniable but elusive meaning of life. Five seconds is all, but that's more than most people get in a lifetime, he thought, felt smug in that fifth of the five seconds, until the sixth, when it became clear that those cars were going to grow noisy and smelly and large again, and the river, growing black with sparkling stripes, was vanishing yet again, taking its promises and history and permanence with it.

The hundred snapshots that featured Mark would come to life over the next weeks in photo shops all over the world, he realized. The back of his head in shadows or the corner of his face lit by a lowering sparkle of sun or one eye red from the flash or his whole face caught in a moment of perfect peace: He—they—would turn up all over the world, in a hundred bulging paper envelopes, on a hundred translucent negative strips, in a hundred slides bordered in thick white plastic-coated cardboard. Who would develop *the* picture, the one of perfect peace and happiness, the sight of him in his own skin in the right place on earth, at his perfect moment when the beauty of the past and the possibility of his own life were not in grim, relentless opposition? Stockholm, Sweden? A couple just returned from their honeymoon, which years later they would agree comprised the happiest six days of their lives. But now, still young, still looking forward with an infant's faith that life would only grow richer and happier, they flip through the photos that represent the high point of their love, and there in the corner of a shot from day six is the face of a stranger, a face at the precise moment of its deepest satisfaction with its life. Dubuque, Iowa? A group of high school students return from their summer educational trip and must prepare reports on what they learned. One student cannot find the words to explain the significance of the face in the corner of her picture of Pest taken from the moving funicular. She can only pay with her own pocket money (earned from babysitting and paper routes and a little soft-drug dealing) to have the photo blown up to poster size and then silently place it on an easel for the class to gaze upon until (take as long as necessary, ignore the ringing bell) they feel what Mark means to them in their malleable youth. Tyson's Corner, Virginia? An elderly American man—recently widowed, a long-retired spy—returns home from a nostalgic trip to all the Cold War hot spots where his life's meaning was written in invisible ink, and he meant to take a picture of the wooden bench inside the funicular where he once sat and received microfilm from the only woman he ever truly loved, a woman shot for her betrayal of her country, shot on his account, and he hoped for a picture of an empty bench, but who is that young red-haired man in his picture and why does he look so—so . . . What would possibly be the word that could explain the significance of his plump face?

Three trips later, as the tail end of sunset, like a peacock wandering over the lip of a hill, trailed a few final slivers of silver into the west, and the east darkened from teal to navy to plum, after Mark had shared the wooden bench with the elderly photographer who was not a retired spy but in fact a Welsh cardiologist on his way to meet his wife for dinner, Mark stood at the bottom of the funicular and tried to regain the feeling of smugness he had felt on so many descents that day: Some people never even get five seconds when they glimpse life's beauty, he insisted. "Five seconds," he repeated, this time aloud.

Some hours later, Mark stood a few feet to the left of that same spot. He decided now that he could not end this day on the down trip, that the sensation after the descents, standing here in the roundabout of Adam Clark Square, was growing too powerful; this funicular could never carry him home. He bought a ticket from the girl whose shift had started three hours before, and he did not notice the unkind expression on her face or the tone of her question—*A ticket for you today, sir?*—or how she called out to her friend at the turnstile. He did not notice the sarcastic way her friend welcomed him into the car. Instead, he thought about the pleasure of the ascending trip with an anticipation he knew he would hold up to later experience as the very benchmark of good, real life, the first unspeakably delicious tremble as the cables began to move. In later years, perhaps, the very thought of the Budavári Sikló (he noticed on this last trip the wooden sign with the funicular's Hungarian name) would hum and vibrate with happiness for him. Perhaps he would not be able to look at a picture of it or read about it in a guidebook in the travel bookstore next to his Toronto home without feeling a quiver of electricity run along his spine, and he would recall sunsets that used to last all day and those five seconds that had made the other seventy years seem almost worth the bother.

JOHN LAY ON HIS STOMACH. His hands were on the sofa's cushion, under his chin, and her warm washcloth touch parted his hair and lifted away—gently, stingingly—the layers of red and brown. She smelled like a flower. Her hands moved very slowly. She apologized three times for Scott's absence, twice asked if she was hurting him, wrung out the cloth, said it was beautiful that John came here when he was hurt and in need, trusting in his brother first of all. He wondered if she was serious, wondered what she knew and what Scott said of him. She let one hand rest, soothing, on the washcloth on the back of his head and the other gently kneaded his neck. He lost interest in whether she had been joking.

Scott had told her so much about the brothers' life in beautiful, beautiful California, she said, which she would love to see someday, and this was like another time, was it not? John coming to Scott, hurt on his head? She recounted the secondhand story to one of its own lead characters: Several children had made fun of John for being fat, and when he tried to fight them, he was hit on the head, just like this, and he had come to Scott for help, just like this, and Scott had beaten up two of the other children while John watched and bled and cried. John listened to this episode of his childhood—accurate but for the reversal of the brothers' roles—but did not correct her, even wondered by her tone if she did not know she had been told a refracted version and was now daring John to set her straight.

John recalled Scott as he had been. Scott had been fat, so ridiculously fat, John recalled with a keen pleasure, and he still was fat really, lean and muscular physical appearances aside. He closed his eyes and listened to the trickle of the washcloth twisted over its bowl. She spoke of Scott's life from the kitchen as she poured him a cold drink, fondly retold Scott's exploits to his brother without thinking he would have already heard them, an obtuseness John found endearing. She spoke of athletic accomplishments that had never happened, regaled John with acts of adolescent rebellion he recognized as the feats of their childhood friends, but all with Scott in the leading roles—Scott's misaligned fireworks, Scott's outrageous nudity, Scott's spray paint, Scott's guitar. Now quite near him, she offered ice water and healthy food, urged him to eat, asked him what he liked best about California, then (John somehow knew this was coming next, could have finished her next sentence for her) Mária retold the story of the little girl in the swimming pool after dark who had been saved, but in her version, wet, clothed John, gasping for air as he dragged the girl to the deck, metamorphosed into wet, clothed, gasping, dragging Scott. "It was very bravery, was it not?"

"A brave man, our Scott," he agreed, and touched her cheek. John sat up straight, as if a weight had been taken from him, and old wounds scarred up smoothly in time-lapse haste: Scott had nothing to offer, no future potential. John had for years been pursuing a receding back: Now he had caught it, turned it to face him, and found he had the wrong fellow all along. Scott wanted John's past? My God, he could have it; John certainly wasn't using it. John would happily trade it for the present: It was only too bad that Scott didn't take grasping Mária seriously, because that would make this even funnier: the flower scent and her nearness. The licensing smile. Her lips did not move immediately away. A tentative response. Then a soft cheek, perhaps in gentle rejection. But then the lips again. His hand against the outsize T-shirt of his brother's alma mater, the picture of the college mascot, flaky from careless laundry, distorted over her shape, itchy against his palm. Her smiling reference to the clock and the time remaining until Scott's return: "A brave man, our John."

THE HORVÁTH KIADÓ

PART TWO

I.

ASK IMRE HORVÁTH, IN YOUR YOUTHFUL AND TIPSY EXCITE-
ment, something as pretentious as the meaning of life or his purpose on this
earth. Or, thoughtlessly passing the time with your eye on the blonde across the
crowded room, ask him a question as banal as the reason for that glass of milk
he takes at nearly every occasion, even this cocktail party. Concerned about
maintaining your diplomatic wardrobe, ask him how his Italian suits are so
marvelously well tailored and perfectly dry-cleaned, the Hungarian clothing
industry being what it is just now. Pondering a possible book or article (which
will probably never progress past a few scribbled bullets on a damp napkin), ask
him whether Communism will ever return to Hungary, whether democracy
will last. Scour for common ground and ask him what ails the Hungarian national soccer team this year. Strive to understand this little country where you

are passing a few jet-lagged days before hitting the vistas of Vienna and the parties of Prague, and ask him who brought more suffering to his nation, the Nazis or the Russians. Ask Imre Horváth anything, O Westerner, and he will begin his answer in about the same manner.

He will begin with a strangely gentle smile. If you know nothing of the man, this first smile will seem disarmingly profound, vaguely amused, even a little ridiculous, but in ways you cannot quite specify. He seems to know something he cannot bring himself to tell you, and both of you find that funny, though not in the same way.

But if you know more of his life, if your host dropped hints of this or that episode, this prelude is immediately exempt from laughability; Imre Horváth becomes one of those rare and intense people whom you could never even conceive of mocking. You may have heard of his arrest. He lost everything, escaped Hungary to rebuild a family fortune, came back several times despite looming threats and even some threats made good. You have heard he shared prison cells and perhaps torture chambers with men who have now, in the fairy-tale justice of 1989–90, ascended to power in Hungary by free election.

Now in his smile you suspect you witness a struggle, not a joke. He must have suffered terribly at the hands of the Communists, and you imagine his smile surfaces from beneath dense layers of horrible memories, must prove itself strong enough to deserve visible expression, prove itself stronger than the omnipresent memory of tyranny (which, for all you know, is probably as painful as tyranny itself).

He is a tall, broad man, who communicates strength in his posture, his tone of voice, his gestures, his large hands. His thick, steel-colored hair flows straight backward in a waterfall of silver that reaches nearly to his shoulders. He wears it long for a man of his age, but he does not seem to wish he were younger. His eyes are of a translucent blue, the color of shallow water in a swimming pool. They are clear, despite his sixty-eight years, and the whites are veinless. His gaze reminds you that he was often tested, that behind these mournful, amused eyes there are depths beyond your reckoning, and yet he would like to answer your question to the best of his ability, to help you understand a time that must seem to you (his smile implies) like ancient history. Because you are a child and you come from a nation of children.

You are growing overly sensitive, perhaps. You feel something meaningful communicated in the skin and muscles around the squint he narrows at you (despite perfect vision), in the eyebrows that come together and then, upon meeting, rise and part company in mild, mild amusement, heroic in itself, after God knows what efforts by God knows what forces to crush it.

When you ask him your little question—profound or prosaic, about tea or tyranny—he will seem to marvel at the sweet and unlikely triumph of Life and Justice that allows for a world in which you, young person (though you may be nearly as old as Imre himself), can thrive and exert yourself, free of dictators, and have the time and freedom to wrestle with questions such as this one. He appreciates this new world, charmingly represented by you and your curiosity.

Only a second or two have passed and now he speaks: "Ohhh, my friend . . ." The "ohhh" is a sound as rich as a long bow stroke on a cello's open string, full of feeling, history, that mild amusement again: "Ohhh, my friend, you must understand how it was to be here," he will say with an accent that reveals a long habit of imperfect English. "I never, or perhaps I should say first . . . no. That is to dredge seafloors. There is nothing there but an old man's . . . Instead, only this: Not so very long ago, before you came to visit our beautiful country and live here in our humble Budapest, this was a different place. It was on the surfaces, yes, as today, but truly very different from the place you enjoy now. I love the new dancing nightclubs the young people have made come to life. We owe you a great deal for this . . . Ohhh, you see, then there was no room in this nation for the man who would not bend, who would not swallow lies, who would not act the parrot in a room of imbeciles. There was no room at all for such a, such a, shall one say, *fool* as that, except, perhaps, he belonged in dungeons. And yet to *be* such a one as this, this fool, for whom there is no room, a type as impossible as some mythical beast with the body of a lion and the head of a man and yet real. Real yet impossible. Can you imagine being such a one as this, in such a place? I hope you shall never have to. You are very lucky, and have been given great things. And you will do great things, I can see this inside you, oh yes, absolutely. But back then, the poor imbeciles in government, in secret-police chambers and other such game rooms of stunted, cruel children, what can these poor imbeciles do when such a wild beast walks free? They stop. They gawk. They fumble for orders. They consult secret manuals and hold secret meetings. They try to be cruel, for they have not the imagination to do anything other. They whisper awkward to each other. 'We cannot admit he exists,' they say. 'Yet we have nowhere to put him, and he stands there as real as a tree. Can we tell the people not to look? Or say he is not what he appears? Shall we say nothing? Perhaps he will go away. Can we kill such a beast as this, or will he rise from the death?' This is the complexity your fine question grapples with, my friend. Ohhh, it is difficult to know how much to tell you . . ."

Your question is forgotten, by you most of all. Either you were only making small talk when you asked it, thinking it unlikely you would discuss weighty matters with such a man as this and now you are pleasantly surprised, almost intimidated by the confidence; or you were straining to ask something about which, you now realize, you know almost nothing. So now you will learn the essence of this matter, a priceless gift, tonight at this cocktail party, an unhoped-for glimpse of what the *real* world can be, vouchsafed to you, who would otherwise have glided through life exposed only to surfaces. This breathing symbol, who has stood immovable under the rush of History, has now stepped down from his plinth and his granite horse to stand next to you, to nod gravely and suffer you to place your tiny, trembling hand on his beating heart.

And yet he is not without Modesty. "I hope I am not boring you with this silly talk." There is in nearly every gesture and word the unspoken assumption that what he has done and what he has said are precisely, necessarily what *you* would have done and *you* would have said. And with a humble nod and a flush of pleasure at this unlikely and patently unbelievable compliment, you thank Modesty for having taken time from what must be a very busy schedule indeed to pass this message to such an undeserving auditor.

Imre Horváth enters this story today, July 15, 1990—for all his monumental dignity—as a file folder modestly awaiting his turn at the bottom of a stack of file folders on the surface of a desk glowing gold from river-bounced sunlight.

II.

LINGERING OVER THE CITY LONGER THAN ITS APRIL OR FEBRUARY COUSINS, the July sun didn't reach Charles Gábor's west-facing Danube-view window until late in the afternoon. By then he had processed nearly twenty-five of his files for the day. Some demanded very little of his time: balance sheets precariously off balance; cheeky assertions of 1,500 percent return on investment within "maybe at the most perhaps six weeks, we are confidently in projecting conservatively"; insufficiently provocative references to unnamed inventions; warm offers of 49 percent partnership in rickety Communist-era building-material companies in exchange for a "reasonable investment in human re-training, plant and tool re-purchase, manufacturing process re-engineering, marketing re-evaluation, and trade network re-construction. Management decisions, naturally, will remain in the hands of those experts currently experienced in the operation of this factory." Other files opened onto loving, soft-focus vistas of badly stocked shops, elderly shipping containers, weather-beaten vineyards, rows of compulsorily smiling old women in headkerchiefs sewing by hand traditional Hungarian costumes.

Some files merited slightly more attention: portfolios sent from the State Privatization Agency (the unique new bureaucracy charged with selling back to the private sector the same properties stolen from it forty years earlier); not entirely impossible sales projections for not thoroughly undesirable products; management passingly familiar with Western accounting standards; and six different pairs of childhood friends who wished to open sporting goods stores. None of these would lead anywhere, Charles was certain. His whole job was a joke. Nothing the Hungarians could come up with would ever pass muster with New York, which was, of course, too busy cash-lavishing Prague to pay the Magyars any mind. He had come to this backwater, it now appeared, only for a P.R. stunt.

With only two files remaining in his stack and the sun bright behind him, Charles pushed himself back into his chair and stretched his arms over his head until his elbows cracked and his fingertips touched the window. Yawning, he pulled the bottom folder from the stack, a mental game to prod the drudgery along. Later, he would tell a story of prescience, flashes of intuition, canny business savvy.

Dear Sirs and Madams,

The pertaining information under attachment is in regards to the Horváth Press, which publishing house has been held in the family Horváth dating since the year of 1808. The currently sitting head of the family is Mr. Horváth Imre, Director-General of the Press. He is available for discussions as to possible investments, joint ventures, or other conceived natures of relationship. If the pertaining history and financial datas make interest to your firm, Mr. Horváth stands prepared to have discussions at a time to be determined of mutual convenience.

With every best wish for any such talk,

I am your humble servant, *Toldy Krisztina*

HEAD OF SECRETARIAT

A HORVÁTH KIADÓ/HORVÁTH VERLAG/
THE HORVÁTH PRESS

Charles wandered lazily through the dense underbrush of accompanying documents. He blamed poor presentation and his own creeping sleepiness for his confusion as to the exact whereabouts of the Horváth Press. Financial data referred to a plant in Vienna, but the Toldy woman's letter and the Horváth name implied a Hungarian publishing house. The financials and photographs boasted enough professional veneer to win closer inspection later, but nothing about the package could hold his fading interest or prop his heavy lids. He slid the folder toward the day's few other Investigation-worthies and opened the final file of his supply. He soon recognized it as a rewritten application, laughingly rejected a few weeks earlier on grounds of bold managerial incompetence but now sparkling with shiny new adjectives and paradigm shifts, thanks to an American P.R. firm's craftsmanship.

Leaning against the window frame to look down upon the glowing golden Danube, Charles found his thoughts wheeling over familiar late-afternoon terrain: the frustration of obeying gutless superiors, the absurdity of fielding offers for maximum investment and limited control, the horrifying prospect of always manning the engine rooms and never being handed the helm. When he thought of this country and these people as the country and people he had been promised since childhood, he grunted audibly, as if from stomach pain.

He did not doubt that his business school training and his natural acumen qualified him to run something. He should have been allowed to make use of his leadership, charisma, and intuition to make himself (and others, of course) extraordinarily . . . something. Here he was at a loss, and was forced to use the word *wealthy* to fill the space in his internal monologue, though he knew that wasn't quite it.

In a world at war, Charles would have cast himself as a field marshal whose encyclopedic, casually conversational knowledge of traditional tactics and strategy would be surpassed only by his uncanny ability to forsake them, occasionally, in favor of startling bold strokes that would transform theaters of military operations into canvases for his stark, coldly superhuman genius. But in 1989–90 the world was not only not at war; it seemed it might never be at war again. Men of Charles's mettle, he knew, would need other canvases upon which to paint and other traditions to forsake, occasionally, for more shattering victories. A junior job in a frontier branch office of a second-tier venture capital firm was not such a canvas.

And so Imre Horváth and Charles Gábor met on July 15, 1990, though neither of them knew it yet.

III.

ON THE MORNING OF JULY 16, 1947, WHEN HE WAS TWENTY-FIVE, IMRE Horváth buried his father, Károly, age sixty-nine, under bright sun at the Kerepesi Cemetery. The old man had himself, over the previous forty-six years, in Kerepesi's densely populated Horváth-family vault, deposited an only daughter, three sons, and a wife, deceased from, respectively, typhus (1901), flu (1918), American bombardment (1944), Russian bombardment (1945), and intermingled German and Arrow Cross bombardment (1945). The elder Horváth had at last succumbed to chronic, untreated heart trouble.

That afternoon, following a dreary lunch with no one he knew very well or cared about at all, Imre walked, in the middle of a somber procession, to his father's offices, in a building comparatively undamaged despite extensive, jagged evidence of warfare on either side of it. There, in that oasis of commerce, he conferred halfheartedly with the familiar, familial lawyer in a shaggy, patched suit. With ill-concealed boredom and a heart uncertain whether to grieve or not, Imre signed the absurdly formal documents that gave him control of his family's worthless business. He became the sixth Horváth male to guide the Horváth Press since 1818.

IV.

THE PRESS WAS FOUNDED UNDER ANOTHER NAME IN 1808; IN 1818 IT WAS purchased by Imre's great-great-great-grandfather (also Imre).

The press's actual founder—the printer Kálmán Molnár (Molnár Kálmán in Hungarian)—had died as the result of a duel for which he was singularly ill prepared, never having fired a weapon in his life. Though Molnár initially survived the exchange of fire (and received some gossipy credit for having stood up and then fallen over like the gentleman he was not), he finally yielded, two weeks later, to an infection of the wound received in his thigh.

The death left stranded a widow and three and a third orphans. More to the first Imre Horváth's interest, it also left without guardian a printing press, ink, plates, paper, binding equipment, and a storefront. Two hours after her husband's death, the grieving, desperate widow accepted Horváth's inconsiderable bid, and Horváth—who had watched her husband tumble over sideways in the grassy enclosure, having been hired to ferry the combatants to Margaret Island through the morning mist—became the owner of the quickly rechristened Horváth Press.

The first Imre's great contribution to the business that would bear his family's name for six generations was the Unicum-inspired design of its colophon—the logo printed at the bottom of the last page of books, in the corners of posters, and as the company's general identifying trademark. The words *A Horváth Kiadó* encircled a small picture of an ornate dueling pistol. Out of the pistol's barrel emerged a cloud of smoke and a speeding ball. On the ball were inscribed the letters MK, memorializing—to Imre's private chuckle and solemn words of respect in public—Molnár Kálmán, the aimless, unwitting founder of the Horváth Press.

V.

UNDER THE FIRST IMRE'S SON, KÁROLY, THE HORVÁTH PRESS SOON SPE-cialized in Hapsburg imperial announcements and publications (in Hungarian and German), pamphlet collections of poetry, and anti-Hapsburg political manifestos, which in the 1830s and 1840s proliferated with leporine fertility. By 1848, Károly's father's tasteless drawing fired on the bottom of imperial-government edicts pasted to kiosks, at the back of little volumes of János Arany's verses, and on public-education bulletins of reform-minded Hungarian parliamentarians. The little pistol smoked at the end of a concise booklet celebrating the birthday of the simpleminded, epileptic Austrian emperor: *A Volume in Honor of the Birthday of Our King and Emperor, Ferdinand Hapsburg, the Fifth of That Proud Name, Long May He Reign and May His Wisdom Guide Us, with God's Blessings and to the Benefit of All His Loyal Hungarian Subjects Who Prosper Under His Paternal and Munificent Care.* But the MK bullet also sped immobile on the last page of a collection of poems by the Hungarian revolutionary-poet-adventurer-lover Boldizsár Kis, entitled *Birth Songs for My Country*.

When Hungary—inspired in part by men like Arany and Kis—revolted against its Austrian emperor in 1848, Károly Horváth lost all of his contracts with the expelled imperial bureaucracy. He also lost a child. His first son, Viktor, was killed at the battle of Kápolna, an early clash between the squalling, newborn Hungarian Republic and its reflexively disciplinary Austrian parent. Soldiers of Hungarian origin fought on both sides. Viktor Horváth, age twenty-four, was hit with a cannonball, which sheared his head and neck entirely from his shoulders.

All was not necessarily lost for the press, however. The temporary existence of an independent Hungarian government promised ample replacement-business opportunities—announcements, legislation, ever more manifestos, and countless volumes by countless self-styled revolutionary poets. In an effort to win this business and burnish his ambiguous credentials, Károly Horváth inadvertently secured the lasting, glorious reputation of his press. Heroic Boldizsár Kis himself—in debt to Horváth for the sizable sum advanced to him for his *Candid Recollections of a Lover*—sealed this victory for the mourning publisher. At the zenith of the doomed rebellion, when the Hungarians seemed to have won their freedom from Vienna at last, Kis repeatedly (and thus famously) praised Károly Horváth's press, citing it as the "conscience of the people and the memory of a nation." In a letter recommending the press's services to the new Hungarian government (later edited as an essay and published by the Horváth Press), Kis diplomatically ignored Horváth's indiscriminate service to political parties of all stripes as well as to the Hapsburgs. The poet sang instead of the firm's Magyar patriotism. He reminded his newly empowered and nervously overworked colleagues of the man's son, sacrificed for revolution. More lastingly, he explained the hidden meaning of the Horváth Kiadó's bold colophon, which had always clearly called for the freedom—from the barrel of a gun!—of the Hungarian Republic, the Magyar Köztársaság. MK. Of course, Horváth had been forced by commercial necessity to work for all sorts of clients, Kis conceded, but look at his trademark, his burning brand of revolutionary loyalty! The tottering new government—busy with an unfinished and unpredictable war of independence—distractedly awarded the press extensive contracts. A letter of praise and appreciation was even written to Horváth over an ambiguously legible but very possibly highly influential name.

In an 1849 volume of his poetry—published again at Horváth's expense, but with all sales payable directly to the printer until the poet's lingering debt was recouped—Kis included this complimentary verse:

From our brave men of ink and press
Come tidings of a new dawning age
And with the force of a ball from a pistol shot
Cracks loud the news of what can no longer be denied:
Our republic, our republic, our republic!

When, in the fall of 1849, with Russian help, the Hapsburgs reasserted their control over the troublesome Magyars and unleashed a horrific thunderstorm of reprisal executions, imperial government pronouncements and condemnation posters were decorated at the bottom by a familiar symbol. After Boldizsár Kis had vanished into the Levant, the poster that declared him an enemy of the emperor-king bore the Horváth logo, but then again so did the much-cherished copies of Kis's poetry, editions of which sold better than ever since he had become a fugitive, finally recouping (and then some) Horváth's advances to the escaped poet.

VI.

KÁROLY HORVÁTH'S SECOND SON, MIKLÓS, WAS SLIGHTLY TOO YOUNG FOR revolution and warfare and so in 1860 he inherited the press that would have been his late elder brother's. That same year, his own son (and only acknowledged offspring) was born and received the name of his great-grandfather. Miklós delivered a verse for the occasion:

The boy will become the man
The man will become the boy
Sing, Muses, for Imre, the Magyar hero
Who will lead us to a world of light and righteousness!

Under Miklós's administration, the Horváth Press suffered severe setbacks due to inattention; Miklós was more enchanted by his efforts at poetry than by running a business. He allowed his assistants to make nearly all company decisions, deal with customers and writers, and negotiate with the refreshed

Austro-Hungarian monarchy. They were also allowed to manage the firm's financial matters, which many of them did to their personal advantage and the press's slow but steady decline. Even the most honest of his assistants paled when forced to face the inevitable losses inflicted by the compulsory publication of Miklós's poetry, volume after volume hurled upon an indifferent world, in progressively more ornate editions and optimistic quantities.

When Miklós was not halfheartedly dabbling in his family's business, he was to be seen in Budapest's cafés and brothels, wearing his hair long in the Byronic fashion of four decades past, demanding paper, pen, and ink from barmaids or whores. He would disappear from his wife and child for days at a time to roam the countryside on foot and then return with pages stained with paeans to nature and his own untamable spirit.

In 1879, invoking Boldizsár Kis, János Arany, Sándor Petőfi, and the rest of the Hungarian revolutionary-poet pantheon of the generation preceding his, Miklós published his final collection, *Where Are the Heroes of Verse?* Each poem in the book was ostensibly written in the style of one of his poetical masters, each singing the praises of, and predicting immortal greatness for, Miklós Horváth. Sándor Petőfi chimed in from his unmarked grave outside the Siberian prison camp to which the Hapsburgs had dispatched him post-revolution:

> *Sing of brave Miklós whose heart thumps the anthem of*
>   *all Hungary*
> *Who marches over country road and city street leading all the*
> *Laughing children*
> *And women with breasts like Greek melons.*

The poet dedicated the book to his brother, Viktor ("Who fell for his Emperor"), and had it bound—over his manager's confused protests and stuttering monologues about cost—in kid leather with gold inlay nymphs and sirens, three fine parallel strips of black velvet running the length of the spine and the poet's signature stamped across the cover in yet more gold. Thirty-seven copies were sold. Thousands more perished ten months later, when heavy rains swirled through a storage basement.

Miklós's son, Imre, turned twenty in 1880 and, though still living in his parents' home, already had a wife and two-year-old twins, Károly and Klára. Imre hardly knew his father. Raised by his mother, Judit, under limited circumstances, Imre had worked at the press from an early age. He had no illusions about where money came from or what life was like in its absence or how his father's business judgment had fared. At age twenty, he watched his father, the failed and foolish poet of forty-seven and the owner of a rapidly failing company, suffer from late-stage syphilis, which had literally cost him his nose and only a few months later would leave him entirely blind.

Miklós's decline—which proceeded with a gruesome implacability—spurred him to drink heavily and write nearly constantly. It drove the melting man to melancholic gestures, and a shallow but sentimental appreciation of the family he had ignored for years during his fruitless courtship of an unwilling and uninterested muse. Miklós, feeling in his corrupted veins that his imaginative and expressive powers were at their peak precisely because darkness was falling, now wrote odes to his illness, to death and encroaching night. He scrawled his verse in a trembling, wandering, half-blind hand that, lost in the thickening mist, roamed across pages then circled back, leaving knotted tangles of ink stranded in vast white spaces. His wife and son would find these poems outside their bedroom doors in the morning. By then, the poet himself would have left the house again for a favorite brothel, where he paid no longer for pleasure but only for the comfort of familiar voices and blurry faces of those who nursed him with limited skill but professional affection, at the same rates he was accustomed to being charged. His underdressed nursing staff brought him pen and ink, paper and drink.

The twenty-year-old son—husband and father himself—knew that his own economic security demanded certain steps. While Miklós's latest scribbled pages fed the kitchen fire, Imre consulted with his one trusted parent on how best to proceed. Later that day, with the help of his mother and two loyal managers, the second Imre Horváth became the de facto head of the Horváth Press and began straining to right his family's capsized firm. This was still some months before the death of the previous owner, who clung to life until January 1881, though neither his family nor his business heard from him again.

Apologetically but definitively turned out of his previous residence on December 23, 1880, for frightening other customers with his howls of syphilitic suffering (serving as an inadvertent warning label on the establishment's otherwise alluring product), Miklós was taken into the home of an admirer, one of his prostitutes, a woman of thirty-four who had pleasured him the first of several hundred times when she was thirteen, producing along the way two live children, among others. He died in her scarcely furnished, tiny attic cube, on the floor, on a thin mattress, under a splintered shelf that, in his total blindness, he could not see but which supported one copy of every volume of his published work—eleven collections in all. His unearthly wailing brought obscene complaints from the other residents of her building, but for eight days she fed him and cleaned him, though he did not know where he was or who he was or who was with him. She was holding a damp cloth to his scarred and seeping forehead when at last he died. "Finally, light," he said, though his eyes were closed. She remembered his last words for many years.

VII.

THE SECOND IMRE MAJESTICALLY GUIDED THE HORVÁTH PRESS TO ITS golden pinnacle of influence and glory. From his unopposed coup in 1880 until his own death thirty-three years later at the age of fifty-three, the family business grew to occupy a place very near the center of a culture in renaissance, a politics in loquacious reform, and a city in feverish reconstruction. Though several new publishers appeared and offered overdue competition, there were suddenly more than enough Hungarian geniuses in every field to go around and more appetite for newspapers, magazines, and books than ever before. The colophon of the little gun—now encircled by Kis's celebrated words A HORVÁTH KIADÓ—THE MEMORY OF OUR PEOPLE—emblazoned the published plays, novels, poems, histories, political essays, scientific and mathematical treatises, textbooks, and sheet music of a society blooming into a verdant artistic and scholarly springtime. The company's fortunes, like those of its home city, peaked in the early 1900s. The population swelled, education spread, peace reigned. Hungarian translations of Shakespeare, Dickens, Goethe, and Flaubert joined native works under the Horváth aegis.

The press (and Imre) prospered and prospered. His weekly sports newspaper, *Corpus Sanus*, was a profitable venture from its third issue, but he would have had a booming business if one accounted only for his production of brightly colored advertising posters for concerts and cafés, operas and plays, liquors and tobacco, haberdashers and clothiers, sporting events, art exhibits, and travel opportunities. His financial paper, *Our Forint* (later *Our Korona*, *Our Pengő*, and yet later *Our Forint*), was widely read in business circles, but he also happily accepted his large fee, in 1890, to publish the manifesto of the first Hungarian socialist workers' party. And only a fool would turn down government contracts, Emperor-King Franz Josef notwithstanding. The little pistol smoked away. MK! Imre shed the memory of life in his parents' sparsely furnished and gloomy home. He began to understand that he was more than a successful businessman.

Imre—proud of his wardrobe and his apartments, his wealth and his business acumen, the family and national tradition of which he was the embodiment—considered himself and described himself to others as a man of culture, a man of letters. In Budapest's increasingly liberal society, his lack of formal education did not disqualify him from that claim. Imre considered himself a giant straddling two worlds—commerce and art—and he frequented the social clubs of both. While he was heartily welcomed and unaffectedly admired in the company of publishers, printers, and newspaper writers, he was still Miklós's son and he felt more himself, more welcome, and more happily a leader among artists, writers, and actors. He would often say to his wife, "The artists recognize me for what I am; the publishers merely envy me for what I have achieved." He was a member of the KB, a group of writers and artists that met regularly at the Gerbeaud for evenings of drink and recitation, praise and insult. Named for Boldizsár Kis, the clique was also a discussion group about politics, particularly the issue of Hungarian independence. Somewhere in the course of such talks Imre would toast the memory of his uncle Viktor who fell at Kápolna for Hungary's short-lived freedom from Vienna.

But no matter that he thought himself a man of letters, no matter that many members of the KB relied on him for their livelihood, no matter that the artists were polite, even jovially friendly to him at the Gerbeaud: He was not one of them, though the fact escaped him (except in sad, quickly forgotten moments of solitude and clarity).

Endre Horn, the playwright, used Imre as the model for Swindleton, the crooked English businessman in his farce *Under Cold Stars*, going so far as to give the character a twin son and daughter. Imre never noticed the similarity. The poet Mihály Antall penned lines (rhyming in Hungarian) that were passed from hand to hand and referred to obliquely in conversation but which Imre never saw:

> *When the businessmen grow tasteful,*
> *And walk with dainty steps,*
> *And lecture us of Shakespeare,*
> *Then who shall buy the drinks?*

"What has become of the memory of our people?" they would ask if Imre did not appear at the Gerbeaud. "I submit to the memory of our people," they would answer, smiling, when Imre continued to argue a position everyone else at the table silently judged as philistine. "To the memory of our people!" They would raise their glasses when the bill arrived. "It seems the memory of our people is short," quipped the composer János Bálint, passing along the rumor of a child born to Imre by a woman not his wife. "Poor memory," they quietly murmured at the funeral of Klára, the twin daughter, dead from pneumonia. "Memory fades," they said nervously whenever Imre's business stumbled, and again when he began to grow thinner and alarmingly thinner from the long sickness that eventually killed him.

VIII.

THE SECOND KÁROLY, IMRE'S SON, WAS FIRST INTRODUCED TO HIS FU-ture legacy when he was fourteen, but he did not become head of the firm until twenty-one years later, at Imre's death in 1913. His two decades of apprentice-ship thoroughly taught him the workings of the press but also convinced him of his pompous father's incompetence. As years passed and Károly remained a subordinate, it was each quarter clearer to the overdue heir that despite the press's success, the business would have been far more flourishing had *he* been at the helm rather than his gutless, art-struck nineteenth-century father. Imre's victories were irritatingly easy; Károly would have bettered them. Imre's failures were glaring; Károly would never have been so careless, cautious, trust-ing, suspicious, reckless, cowardly. By the time Imre and the press began relying on Károly, press employees knew of the prince's scorn for the king, and even Imre's more obtuse friends in business circles would chuckle and counsel him to have someone taste his food. By 1898, one wag in the KB had taken to call-ing Károly Brutus when speaking to third parties. Imre himself referred instead to "the boy's desire to participate in his family's traditions," to fulfill his destiny in national life. In private, though, he too wondered how he had won his son's ridicule. For as a very young boy Károly had loved his father, revered him, imi-tated his speech and gestures, had told his mother at age six, "Papa and I are alike in every way. We are two men cut from the same fine cloth."

Part of the problem began at the KB. Károly was first granted the privilege of accompanying his father to the Gerbeaud one summer evening when he was twelve, and the boy noticed immediately that the other men dressed differently than his father. They spoke differently. And when they bothered (plainly un-willingly, Károly felt) to talk to the boy himself, he felt their laughter. That first evening, the painter Hanák performed some simple but practiced sleight of hand for the boy. The grubby artist borrowed a banknote from the senior Horváth, showed it to the child, then folded it small and hid it in his huge fist. "Which hand is the filthy lucre in, young Károly?" he asked, to the boy's mounting distaste. Károly pointed at first one then the other of the artist's hands, disliked their hairy knuckles and paint-stained fingers. One then the other of the fists creaked open to reveal nothing but smudges of color on palms of cut leather, textured like the pads on the paws of Károly's beloved pumi dog. "A mystery, is it not, little boy?" asked the artist. The painter returned to drink-ing, chatting, and ignoring the boy, who asked Hanák, though his father did not hear it, "So will you keep Papa's money then?" The artist laughed and raised his glass of beer to the youth: "You understand magic very well, little boy," he said before again turning his back on the demonstratively unhappy child.

Twelve-year-old Károly had taken the invitation to his father's special evenings as a sign that he was now his father's adviser and peer. He took his re-sponsibility to heart. "I did not like these men," Károly told his father very seri-ously as they walked home together past the endless construction of new homes around Deák Square and Andrássy út. "There is something wrong about them. The dirty one stole your money." Károly was angry, not least be-cause he had been used as an accomplice in the theft of his father's (and his own) wealth.

His father struck him quite hard on the mouth. "He did not steal it and he is not dirty," Imre said quietly as the boy brought a hand up to his face. "He is a great artist. He needs the money more than I. Should I embarrass him and ask for it back? Would you like that, my little philistine? Should I shout that I am rich when he is poor? No. I allow this to happen as a favor to him. In return, he produces great things, which I admire—" The father, with an increasingly lighter tone, spoke at some length on the discretion required of patrons of the arts, how these men of the KB were his own superiors (in talent) as well as his equals (in taste) and his inferiors (in wealth and success). But after a while, after trying to understand how he could have been wrong in his actions and his words, the boy no longer listened, simply grew angrier and more confused. He settled at last, with the unshakable certainty of a twelve-year-old, on the concrete violation of objective principle: *These men are criminals. And father is their victim, though he will not admit it, as he is ashamed of it.*

For the rest of the silent walk home, Károly looked forward to discussing the evening's events with his twin sister, whose intelligence he respected above all others'. But when they arrived home, his mother told him Klára felt poorly and had gone to bed early. The pneumonia, which began its oozing assault that evening, ended her short life not long after, and to the end of his own life, Károly was never quite able to shake the irrational, gnawing feeling that the KB had somehow harmed Klára fatally, had stolen her too that night, making of him an accomplice in that evil as well.

But Károly's father did not release him from the gift of attending, from time to time, the meetings of the KB. After a period of banishment for his first reaction (which quickly became a period of mourning for the loss of Klára), the boy, now different in a way his father could not quite specify, was brought again. And though he sat mute every evening he was brought, his father believed him intimidated in the face of the brilliant company. Imre—more than ever addicted to these evenings of culture and gossip after death had rendered his home so dark and his wife so irritatingly distant—intended that his boy grow up in the company of intelligent men and artists. Such men, he told his son on the walk to the Gerbeaud not long after Klára's funeral, were the only ones capable of providing a balm to the brutal wounds life inflicts. Károly pitied his father.

The boy was a few years older when he understood they were laughing at his father, though the men of the KB hid that laughter in ways he could not explain. After more evenings spent in silence, he also felt they were trying to corrupt him against his father, to teach him to laugh at him in their private fashion, just as Hanák had drawn him into theft. "Shall we hear out your old man's views?" the composer János Bálint whispered to him one evening in the middle of a long and mysterious debate when tempers had flared and several voices were trying to drown Imre's quiet, unyielding lecturing. "Or shall we take this opportunity to sneak outside for some much-needed air?" Bálint stood, favoring his good leg, and took the boy's hand, but Károly pulled it back sharply.

"I wish to hear my father," he said clearly and calmly. "He is very smart, and if you cannot see that, then you are very stupid." This retort, hissed out and bitten off with a snap of the head, amused the composer as well as the journalist who sat at Károly's other side. That evening, the walk home began with a blow, but that did not suffice to compel Károly's respect for the exalted membership of the KB, and now after several silent evenings the boy would not be quieted. "He tried to take my hand, Father. There was something wrong with this."

"The man is married with children, you—" Imre began to say, but Károly's insinuation nauseated him. "He is a great composer—" he began again in an effort to compose himself. Finally, he had nothing to say but "Stand up" when the child did not immediately rise from the sidewalk after another light slap. "Get up," he spat, "for God's sake. These men are your *country*."

The next banishment lasted nearly two years. Károly was left in the gray, unhappy home in the company of his mute, daughterless mother until his rarely seen father, assuming the boy had matured, allowed him to return to cultured company. Now Károly laughed with them, not because he agreed with their unspoken, hidden condemnation of his father as unintelligent or under-read or out of his element. Károly laughed with the KB at his father because his father could not see that his heroes despised him, and Károly could, and that was bitterly funny. If one refused to see the truth, then one could hardly expect to be loved for one's blindness.

"It would appear you had rather a better time this evening now that you are older. Am I right, my boy?" came the satisfied question on the peaceful walk home.

"I think they laugh at real men, Father. I think they are rotted. They are hateful. They are not my country." The father thought at first Károly was making an obscure joke in dubious taste. He stopped walking, considered his son, and realized the boy was now too large to strike. "Come along, Father," the son said with just the same smile he had seen on Horn's lips when Imre praised a current play written by a talentless rival.

Károly refused all future invitations to the KB, and his father had no further tools to improve the boy's behavior now that corporal punishment was unfeasible. The matter was never discussed, and when members of the KB came to the press to discuss work, Károly was either noticeably absent from his post or instead displayed a form of impeccable, quasi-military politeness that puzzled his father and "made my flesh crawl," in the words of the historian Balázs Fekete.

The press was superficially successful, Károly would admit to a temporary confidant (usually a low-level employee, starstruck to be warmed by the rising son), but it was fundamentally unhealthy, out of balance. His father, and the health of the firm, relied too heavily on the continued so-called inspiration of these so-called Hungarian so-called geniuses. Besides which, if the Horváth Press was in fact the memory of the *Hungarian* people, it should print *Hungarian* writers, and one need not know much to know that the members of KB were no such thing. For those who cared to look, he told his agreeable if quiet companion, there was a simple, obvious reason they made a profession of laughing at real Hungarians: They were *not* real Hungarians. "Their works are foreign, un-Magyar. They do not address what concerns the Magyar. They tinker with entertainment. They ignore their duty to educate, because they cannot help it: No non-Magyar can express a Magyar soul. This is a question of hard principle," Károly explained as his listener drank, "not fickle opinion or fleeting popularity. Hard principle."

The heir knew, however, that he was not a debater, and could not prove to his father his knowledge, and so he went to great trouble to find the voices that could. Though never well liked at the press, Károly did cultivate some employees who helped him find the newspapers and books that made sense to him. Much to Károly's shame, these newspapers and books were usually printed by other houses. He was ashamed to work for a press that seemed to avoid true Hungarian writers, writers of hard, scientific truth, simply and plainly expressed, men like Bartha and Egán, concerned with the nation's health rather than its cheap titillation, men willing to state and prove the obvious to ostriches: Jews were not Magyars. Liberal liars were not Magyars. Much of corrupt, cosmopolitan Budapest was not Magyar. And all the while the foolish chattering voices of liberals, Jews, and self-proclaimed artists and intellectuals created an intolerable cacophony in the house that was once the memory of the Hungarian people. For business reasons alone, for the family's fortune if not for the sake of the nation, Károly's father had to be made to see reason. He would stress hard numbers; only profits remained to guide his errant father back to rectitude.

One morning, when Károly was just twenty-one, Imre was late coming in to breakfast due to a long evening at the Gerbeaud the night previous. Károly awaited him at the cluttered table. His father settled slowly into his chair and looked with disappointment into an empty coffee pot.

"Exciting evening, old man?" asked his son with unnecessary volume.

"Exciting, no, I wouldn't say. Illuminating."

"Illuminating? With those Jews and scribblers? To each his own, I suppose."

"Jews and scribblers?" Imre responded groggily. "What is this now?"

The young man tapped the newspaper article lying open on the table, slid it toward his father. "Nothing I haven't thought myself, but it's nice to see it in print. Nice to know there is still time enough to save our fortunes. My inheritance, don't forget. Time to consider whether our fortune isn't founded on the wrong stones. The memory of *whose* people, I wonder," the boy concluded with an ironic grin that would hardly have been out of place at the Gerbeaud.

Imre, hungover and permanently unsure what to make of his moody offspring, picked up the newspaper and after a few moments began to laugh. He reached over the table and pinched his son's cheek, a gesture he had almost never performed even when Károly's age would have been appropriate. "You almost fooled me," he said.

Károly had prepared himself for a necessary, cleansing dispute on principles, and now found his father's condescension almost mystifying enough to erase the practiced grin from his face. "Did I?"

"I think this is Horn's best effort so far," his father mused.

It seems to me, began the column that so moved Károly Horváth in 1899, *that the Jews and scribblers who pollute our stages with their little plays, and pollute the city with their little cafés, and turn Budapest into an absolute Sodom and Gomorrah with their unnatural habits are putting us real Magyars at a terrible risk. I for one do not wish to be sitting at the table next to them when God decides to send a bolt of lightning down to destroy this plague once and for all. I for one do not wish to be in the theater watching a sordid little play written by moneylenders when the nation finally rises up in disgust and tears the actors and writers limb from limb, after tolerating yet another display of what feebler minds than my own insist on reviewing as "flashing wit" and "high comedy" and "perhaps Endre Horn's finest work to date." I ask you, good Magyar brethren, how much longer must we wait before some relief will come to us? I suppose we cannot hope that God will strike down these deviants prior to the play's closing on the 18th of next month, since the full houses that it plays to must contain at least some decent, if misguided people. However, if the rapidly approaching century's end is not a good time for the judgment day which will separate the wheat from the filth, then I do not know when a better day would be. Far be it from me to tell God His responsibilities; surely that's the Pope's job, but I for one am looking forward to January 1, 1900. I shall be hiding under my bed and when the flood is passed and the streets are clean and God in His wisdom is ready to receive the worthy up the golden ladder which He will drop down to us, then I will emerge with all my friends and family from under that bed and we will step lightly over the twisting, screaming*

*forms of these so-called playwrights, and rise to heaven where surely there will be bet-
ter entertainment than Endre Horn's* Brutus and Julius, *now playing at the Castle
Theater on Színház utca, and better reading than Mihály Antall's latest collection of
doggerel and so-called love songs,* Season of Lights, *recently published to extensive
foolish acclaim by the Horváth Press, and true celestial music rather than the awful
experiments of János Bálint, whose music leaves good people gagging while the so-
called taste makers pronounce him a genius of the first order and a credit to Hungarian culture. I, for one, do not intend to read or listen to such works when I am
sitting at the left hand of our Lord, after God tells me it is safe to come out from under
my bed, where I will soon go in preparation for the gathering storm.*

It demanded all of Károly's patience to understand why his father
found this tremendous, blistering (and artistically metaphorical) attack on his
squalid, treacherous circle (and even our press, by God) to be funny rather than
revelatory and alarming. In this writer, Pál Magyar, Károly had finally found
someone who put into words all the disgust he felt for his father's false friends,
all the shame of tying the family's fortunes to this un-Magyar filth, and now his
father was laughing, and congratulating Károly for having nearly fooled him.
The explanation came agonizingly slowly.

The vitriolic column condemning the KB as "Jews and scribblers" that had
so captured Károly's attention and distilled his own feelings that morning was
written by none other than Endre Horn, the same leading light of the KB who
had lampooned the senior Horváth in *Under Cold Stars*. Writing under an
assumed name, Horn was at this time contributing (with great and comically
unnecessary subterfuge) columns to the small, struggling, nationalist, anti-
Semitic newspaper *Awakening Nation* (Károly's favorite, introduced to him by a
press employee since fired for drunkenness). In these pieces, under the name
Pál Magyar, Horn espoused extreme nationalist views, but in staggeringly bad
prose. The essays had to be credible enough to slide past the well-blinkered but
purity-mad editors of *Awakening Nation* but still bizarre enough not to be taken
seriously by the average reader, and, most important, serve as self-promotion
for Horn himself, hidden though he was behind his nom de mockery.

Károly remained quiet, was forced by circumstance to be Horn's admirer,
found himself at his own breakfast table gagged and bound at a distance by the
Jew scribbler. He could say nothing. And so Károly laughed. The betrayal of the
press by his own father (Károly later told a colleague) brought hot tears of
shame to his eyes, the ruination of a once great man. "A man can be destroyed,
of course, but a national institution cannot."

But he went himself that day to the offices of *Awakening Nation* and assured himself the editors would not repeat their error. There were still some men of principle in this world, though his father could no longer be counted among them.

"Oh, here's a pity. Horn's game's been discovered by the clowns at *Awakening Nation*," his father reported one hungover morning.

"Has it really? What a *remarkable* turn of events."

IX.

THE SECOND IMRE HORVÁTH DIED IN 1913, TEN YEARS AFTER BLEATING A widely parodied eulogy at Endre Horn's very elaborate, very Catholic state funeral.

At Imre's passing, Károly Horváth was thirty-five, married with three sons and still saddened by the memory of his infant daughter's death twelve years earlier. The girl had been named Klára, for his unlucky twin, and had succumbed in her turn to typhus. But now he shook off the dust and webs of rage and sorrow and climbed at last to the position he had deserved for two thirds of his life.

The day after his father's funeral, he made a list of everything the press should immediately cease printing. This long document began with Endre Horn's plays and proceeded through the works of nearly every member of the long since evaporated KB. Then he made a list of papers and writers he wanted the press to acquire, beginning with *Awakening Nation*, which had steadily grown in popularity in its fifteen years of circulation. The new chief examined his two lists, and re-examined—with the assistance of new and trusted associates—the financial status of the press. Over several weeks, he estimated the cost of acquiring everything he desired and the loss his firm would suffer if he excised all of its disgraceful properties. And then he revised. Some things, unfortunately, would have to stay, even though they were hardly admirable exemplars of the memory of the Hungarian people. Horn, for example, still sold ridiculously well. Antall inexplicably brought in money. But the composer Bálint? No one listened to that garbage, and certainly no one bought the sheet music for the screeching noise. His father had been ridiculously sentimental to publish the work of that ungrateful sodomite. It was with a pleasure almost unmatched in Károly's life that the tip of his pen very, very slowly scratched its way through the letters B-Á-L-I-N-T J-Á-N-O-S, even tore the paper slightly, and

Károly recalled his own precocious words that had stopped the composer pant-ing in his perversely libidinous tracks so many years earlier at the Gerbeaud. "Take your hands off me, you disgusting man. Conduct yourself like a gentle-man or a real gentleman will teach you how." Even at that young age he had known right from wrong and had courageously spoken. Bálint had fallen back a step, grown pale to be so eloquently chastened in front of all his filthy friends, and by a young boy of all people. "And by a boy, by a young boy," Károly whis-pered aloud. On the list of forty-five authors, newspapers, and magazines he hoped to sell off or discontinue, six writers and the magazine *Culture* were in-sufficiently profitable to justify amnesty: seven slow lines, each a joy. The other thirty-five writers and four publications would have to be tolerated and slowly replaced, but surely someone else at the press could be responsible for them. He was guardian of his nation's memory and conscience. If filth temporarily and necessarily brought in money to support this mission, so be it, but he would not dirty his hands with it.

The next year, having purged his company of unprofitable filth, Károly completed the negotiations for his acquisition of *Awakening Nation*, which, as of July 8, 1914, bore the familiar Horváth logo in the upper-right-hand cor-ner of every copy. Károly took particular pleasure composing his monthly "Letter from the Publisher," which he inaugurated on the bottom left of page one, on August 10, 1914, on the topic of the Austro-Hungarian empire's eter-nal and immutable strength. In this debut he used as a symbol his own great-uncle Viktor, a Hungarian who had given his life for the empire at Kápolna. He called on Hungarians to stand firm in the face of current international ten-sions, as strength would certainly prevent war, this crisis would pass, leaving Austria-Hungary more dominant than ever. And though *Awakening Nation* never achieved the circulation of *Corpus Sanus*—with its bicycling results and horse-racing stories—Károly always referred to it as the jewel in the Horváth crown.

X.

MASTER'S IN BUSINESS ADMINISTRATION, FINAL EXAM, CASE-STUDY ESSAY Question, as administered to Károly Horváth between August 11, 1914, and July 16, 1947:

You are the head of a small but highly successful family-owned publishing business. Please outline your corporate decisions after each of the following seventeen events takes place in the country of your operations. Include explanations of how you access materials and labor, gauge the market, determine product range, carry out marketing, and manage an integrated strategic long-term planning function within your senior executive staff.

    i.   Your country fights and loses a world war; labor is scarce; inflation is alarmingly high. You lose your second oldest son to disease, which sinks you into an uncommunicative depression for several weeks. You decide to stop publishing several of your most profitable titles, as their authors are responsible for the flu that claimed your son's life. Revenue earned during the war from publishing government casualty lists, draft notices, maps, and propaganda is almost entirely depleted by the end of your despondency.

    ii.   Your country secedes from the stable political system it has belonged to for centuries; politics are dangerous and the government is weak.

    iii.   A violent Communist dictatorship emerges and nationalizes your press. You lose everything and are arrested. The Communist regime is nearly 70 percent Jewish, a statistic that strikes you as highly significant. Your execution is tentatively included on the Communists' very busy schedule.

    iv.   Your country loses another war (more of an epilogue to the last one) and is invaded by Romanians, who find themselves briefly in control of Budapest before giving it back and going home. You remain in prison throughout, and your execution date is first advanced then indefinitely postponed.

    v.   After only four months of Communism, a right-wing counterrevolution is successfully launched. You are freed from prison, your firm is restored to you (you fire your three staunchly anti-Communist Jewish employees on allegations of crypto-Communist sympathies), and you are personally congratulated for your courage by the new head of state, a regent/vice admiral. (He is a regent, although there is no monarch on whose behalf he administers. He is a vice admiral, although your country no longer has a coastline, having lost it—as well as 70 percent of its land and 60 percent of its population—under the predictably unpopular and embittering Trianon treaty ending the world war.) The regent cites your press as the memory of a people and the conscience of a nation. You receive a medal, which you hang in your office, in a glass case with a small electric light suspended over it. Executions of real and suspected Communists sweep the country. The demand for "national-Christian" newspapers and writers seems a very tempting foundation on which to rebuild your firm's fortunes.

vi.   Civil war is narrowly averted when a pretender to the throne of Hungary briefly appears.

vii.   Peace and prosperity return at last to your country. Demand rises for your back catalog of Hungarian authors and scholars, though you privately associate them with imprisonment, tyranny, murder, and disease. The prosperity they can bring you, though a necessity, seems to you a sulfurous compromise with evil.

viii.   The Depression.

ix.   Elections subsequent to the Depression unsurprisingly favor the fascists. The regent's new government flirts with Mussolini and Hitler and pushes through laws setting quotas on Jews admitted to universities and the professions, then declaring them an alien race. Please detail your firm's extensive opportunities for profit and acquisition.

x.   Another world war. Your country tries very hard to stay out of it, wedged as it is between two very large opposing combatants who don't think yours really counts as an independent nation. Detail your new government and military printing contracts.

xi.   Forced to pick sides, your country wades delicately into the war as a member of the Axis and shyly helps invade the Soviet Union. The government forbids marriages between Jews and non-Jews. Please estimate how many government-edict posters you can produce and paste in Jewish neighborhoods on short notice.

xii.   At the Germans' repeated insistence, the Hungarian government grudgingly, quietly declares war on the United States and Great Britain. New laws force Jews to wear yellow stars and live in a Pest ghetto. After initial efforts to ship Jews to death camps, the government halts deportation when the Budapest police responsible for the roundups threaten to rebel. Please recalculate poster revenues, including both the deportation orders and their revocation.

xiii.   The government implies to its German ally that it would like to pull out of the war now, that it had only gotten involved in order to reclaim a little of the Hungarian land lost in the *last* world war, that it has no serious grievance against the British and Americans anyhow. The regent secretly negotiates with the West, then publicly announces, over national radio, Hungary's separate peace with them. Hungary is instantly overrun by its spurned German ally. The regent's intricate diplomatic ploy was useless: Germany and its Hungarian Arrow Cross quasi-SS allies establish headquarters in the palace on Buda's Castle Hill and bundle the regent off to Berlin. Back in Budapest, some of your countrymen eagerly offer to help load Jews onto trains en route to Auschwitz. Jewish possessions and apartments are free for the taking. The Arrow Cross, some of whose members work or have worked for your press, rival the SS in their spirited brutality. Meanwhile, other members of the government continue to enact the terms of their separate peace with the Allies and declare war on the (occupying) Germans. Your country is at war with everyone. Please be specific as to your business and commercial opportunities.

xiv. The Americans and British bomb you in the mornings. Your eldest son (and trained heir) is killed. The Soviets bomb you in the evenings. Your third son is killed. The Soviets invade. The Germans—having already been driven out of nearly every country they once occupied—decide, for no discernible strategic reason, to hold on to Hungary and, with their Arrow Cross partners, to make a last stand atop Castle Hill. Jews are murdered in the streets and along the lovely Danube riverfront quays, where they are tied together and pushed from the elegant Corsó in front of the bombed Bristol, Carlton, and Hungaria Hotels into the icy river. Tank and artillery battles flatten the city. Your wife is killed. Please explain how to continue profitable press operations despite your crippling grief, thoughts of suicide, and the country's near-total economic collapse.

xv. As the last of the Germans retreat, murdering as they flee (Hungary *is* their enemy), the nation's victorious Russian saviors begin to steal or rape anything worth stealing or raping (Hungary *is* their enemy). Your office is smashed to pieces, and Soviet soldiers defecate on your library, including rare editions dating back to the 1800s, among which are exquisitely produced volumes of your grandfather's poetry. The Soviet Army, needing to meet the deliriously high POW numbers it reported to Stalin during the war, kidnaps Hungarian males to crate back to the USSR whether or not they ever fought and, if they did fight, whether or not they fought for the Axis. Your last remaining child, a strapping boy of twenty-three, hides in a basement for 157 days, then emerges, squinting, ninety-four pounds under his prewar weight. You are not much interested anymore.

xvi. Your country has lost another world war. Hungarian currency is worthless. Ink and paper are scarce. The city boasts no gas, electricity, telephone service, or unbroken glass. Your office building is standing, but your presses are badly damaged. Some surviving Jews begin to return and reclaim their looted apartments, furniture, and other possessions. Please operate your family business in the current chaos, and with scarcely enough energy or desire to get out of your reeking bed.

xvii.   Relative peace, semi-democracy, and rebuilding ensue, though the Communists are organizing in the background, arresting, torturing, murdering their opponents while they take over the police and security apparatus of the country. You have few employees, few capital assets, no appetite to go on. You spend days at a time just sitting in an overstuffed brown chair with a grease-stained antimacassar. The owners of this chair have not yet returned from their wartime residence. The question of whether they will return and then find and claim this chair, which is rightly yours, occupies a disproportionate amount of your thinking. You speak hardly at all. Your remaining son, an accidental child of your middle age, whom you know only slightly, brings you food and cigarettes. You eat little and smoke much. Occasionally, you go to the press and watch silently as some of your employees attempt to rebuild. You are accused of pro-Nazi sympathies for some of your actions and statements during the war, but your son defends you vigorously; rather than being hanged in public, you are largely left alone. You are indifferent. You die of chronic untreated heart trouble and your son buries you at Kerepesi Cemetery in the bright sunshine of July 16, 1947. You are laid to rest in the same vault that contains your numerous ancestors, your wife, your twin sister, and your four eldest children. The owners of the armchair find their way home the next week, and your son does not know what to say or do other than politely hold the door and allow the neighbor he has known and liked since childhood to push her furniture back across the hall, where it belongs.

XI.

THE THIRD IMRE HORVÁTH—NAMED IN A MOMENT OF SENTIMENTAL WEAKness by a middle-aged father who had previously sworn to excise that name from the family history—stood in the partially rebuilt office. His inheritance—stewarded for five generations in preparation for his eldest brother—was worth almost nothing when it was delivered to him, Károly's fifth and only child, that July afternoon in 1947. The press had small cash reserves in a valueless currency. It could scarcely obtain ink, paper, or equipment. It sat in a bombed-out city, where entrepreneurs in private boats ferried joyless passengers from bank to bank, past the semi-sunken, spanless husks of the Danube's great bridges: The Chain Bridge resembled Stonehenge; the golden Elizabeth squatted in the brown water like a society woman gone mad, her fine dresses torn and bunched around her hips while she washed her privates in full public view and sensitive souls wondered what had become of their world.

Imre signed a few unread documents and was handed a set of keys, for most of which he never found a corresponding lock. He had never had any reason, until 1945, to think that he would become the head of the family and then was unimpressed by this nasty honor during his 157-day residence in his building's cellar. By the time of his father's death, he felt equal only to the task of closing the press officially prior to leaving the country. He had never hoped to be at the helm of a business. He wanted to be anywhere but in the smoldering city that had consumed his entire family. He had risen to the leadership of an extinct clan, of an all but dead company. He embodied family traditions and burdens now plainly irrelevant.

Besides which, the Horváth family history had never much mattered to this Imre. He had heard pieces of it from relatives and his father's workers over the years but had never received the concerted education his brothers had enjoyed. He had, for example, been told by his grandmother of a soldier in his family, whom he associated with the toy soldiers that same grandmother had given him on a separate occasion, so that even much later, when he understood that his ancestor had fought and died for an independent Hungary at Kápolna in 1848, he still could not help but dress that distant Viktor in full armor, with a white tunic that matched his squire's pennon.

When he was very young, Imre's mother would take him from time to time to visit his wordless, brusque father at the office. There the little boy saw his elder brothers working and learning the business, and they would stop to tickle him before saying, very importantly, that they were needed down at the machinery or that there was a distribution problem Father wanted them to solve and they couldn't talk longer—the press has to be kept under control after all, Mother—and then the much-admired seventeen-year-old brother and the unpredictably cruel sixteen-year-old brother would stride off, the elder lecturing the younger with professional gestures. Then Imre's mother might take him to the archives, and she might show him the beautiful volumes, covered in gold or soft with velvet, and explain that this one was actually written by his own ancestor, a poet who disappeared mysteriously and was never heard from again, and perhaps Imre might someday write great books. Then Imre's father might appear in the doorway and call for his wife, and she might talk to him in the hall, and Imre might be left alone for a few glorious minutes that swelled to resemble hours, and he would wander through a forest made of books, stacks of books reconstituted into tall trees, behind which lurked enemies Imre would vanquish with lance and mace before composing heroic odes over their bodies.

In 1947, Imre stood amid the tiny remaining stacks that had once formed his enchanted forest and listened to six men who expected him to provide them income. He found it difficult to concentrate as the half-dozen employees who still saw reason to hang around enumerated for him the little that remained of the Horváth Kiadó.

Instead, Imre was distracted by the thought of two fetuses growing frighteningly fast, one on each side of the Danube, the nerve-racking result of a six-month flurry of seduction, which had coincided with the six last miserable months of his father's life. For half a year, Imre had displayed a religious commitment to philandering. A life full of women, he had vaguely decided, was owed to him, repayment for the loss of his family and for his 157 days of fear and boredom. A zesty and fully savored life, full of women, he told friends, was a man's natural embrace of the world, the only noble, human response to the destruction of Budapest. His friends agreed, but none could match Imre's appetite or pace until, in the days afer his father's funeral, his urges subsided as quickly as they had come and snuffed themselves out completely the afternoon of the flabbergasting double annunciation, as one after another barely recalled woman turned up at his apartment to share awful news.

"And that is the sad state of our affairs, Horváth úr." Imre grudgingly offered to come into the office a few more times, at least until some stability was achieved and someone else took control, or circumstances became too obvious to ignore and no one bothered to come at all anymore. While he waited for the others to give up, "a few more times" quickly absorbed a few weeks, and then a month or two, during which Imre was taught by his employees how to work and repair the press's machinery. He learned how messengers sent by newspaper editors brought articles pasted on cardboard for him to print. He learned how books were built and spines stamped (though none were being produced). He learned what the strange little picture of a gun meant. Imre learned about the company's sad finances, about his father's poor—then erratic, then frightened, then abdicated—decisions, about the firm's reliance on clients and partners and writers now overthrown or executed or in prison. Imre gathered opinions from his employees and his friends about what books people might buy if they had any money. He kept lists of these theoretical books, and he searched the ruins of the archives for reprint possibilities, and in the meantime he continued printing two- or four-page newspapers that would go out of business after only a few issues, and modest black-and-white advertising posters that, even in their modesty, were misleading: The shops they sheepishly extolled had pathetically little to sell.

A few months lined up to become six. His skill at scavenging and black marketeering—acquired during a war that felt, until the triple tragedy of 1944–45, like a game he played with undeniable skill—served him and the press well as the primordial economy slowly re-evolved from bartery ooze back to an upright currency. He squeezed enough money from his desiccated legacy to make discreet payments and gifts to two young mothers on opposite sides of the river.

And at last he won his first victories. He commissioned the mothers of a few of his friends to write a cookbook featuring recipes suitable for shortages, and *Enough for Everyone,* the first book to be published by the Horváth Press in four years, sold very respectably. Six worried employees multiplied and became eight occasionally optimistic employees.

Awakening Nation had long since vanished, and any old copies Imre happened to find he promptly combusted, especially those featuring the increasingly raving "Letter from the Publisher." But the financial paper, now *Our Pengő,* began to sell well again. Imre was soon lucky enough to arrange, through a friend, a contract to print ration-book coupons as well. A ninth employee was deemed useful.

Over nine months, the Horváth Press gave birth to four contradictory history books covering the previous thirty-three years. All of the books were financed by new or restored political parties; it was as if, with an uncertain future, the past as well grew hazy and no one could quite agree who had done what to whom or why, who had been wicked and who had been wise, except that everybody agreed Trianon was a crime. Imre read as much as he could of all four volumes, making less and less progress with each. Their proceeds, however, paid for a new truck and repairs to the warehouse and one of the presses.

The reborn Horváth Kiadó's most successful postwar venture was released at the beginning of 1948, just after the final governmental takeover by the Communists. The book was Imre's own inspiration and a work he cherished for many years. He collected photographs from friends and friends of friends and outright strangers all over Budapest. He simply asked people to loan him family portraits, old snapshots, favorite pictures of the city or the countryside—anything they truly loved. He asked for a line or two of written description. Then he edited and combined these donations into an album, which he published under the title *Békében* (*In Peacetime*). He captioned each photograph with its description in the first person, even though the words represented hundreds of different speakers. *This is my brother the day he left to study in England. . . . This is a poor family that lived next to us; they had almost nothing, but they were extremely kind to that little dog, a mutt named Tedi. . . . This is my mother and father on their wedding day, 1913. . . . This is my mother and father on their wedding day, 1919 . . . on their wedding day, 1930. . . . This is a Jew who lived in our building and was very kind to me when I was a girl. I hope he is well, but I fear not. . . . This is me as a little boy on the Elizabeth Bridge with my friends. . . . This is my family at Lake Balaton in 1922. . . . This is a picture of my father riding horses with the regent. . . . This is a meeting of a labor union, and my brother is speaking at the podium. . . . This is how the Corsó looked in 1910. . . . This is the old fish market; it doesn't exist anymore. . . . This is how the Chain Bridge looked before. . . . This is my father in front of his shop; he died at Auschwitz. . . . This is my grandmother as a young girl. . . . This is a party for my name day at the Gerbeaud; I am the one looking at the* krémes *with big eyes . . .*

Among Imre's favorites was the quiet little portrait in the upper-left corner of page 66. It had been presented to him by a total stranger, who had heard about Imre's project through mutual acquaintances. The photo was of a young woman, nineteen or twenty. She sat at a kitchen table, very upright, a serious expression on her face. She was unremarkable. Her hands rested on her lap, and she looked directly at the photographer. *This was the most beautiful girl in the world.*

The popularity of *Békében* was no surprise to Imre, though many of his staff shook their heads in amazement as more and more of the books were printed and bound. There were certainly those critics—professional and private—who called it sentimental, naïve, even misleading, and they may not have been wrong, but Imre felt he had made something good, and sales convinced him he was right. His composite narrator, grafted from four hundred different voices, defied category. Politics were scattershot, a variety of social classes was represented, Catholic ceremonies were presented as family history right alongside Jewish ones: the polyphonic voice of Hungary in peacetime. The words from page to page varied only slightly, and after a while, the parade of strangers described as friends and family seemed, hypnotically, to become just that. This was Hungary, and Imre was its memory. For some, the book acted almost as an opiate: The pleasure of leisurely or impatiently traveling from page to page and seeing lovely Budapest unbombed, undamaged, in black and white, was almost pornographic in its unattainable, voluptuous gorgeousness: Lipótváros, the Elizabeth Bridge, the Corsó, the Castle, the Nyugati Station the day of its inauguration—the day it was the largest, cleanest train station in the world . . .

Imre included three pictures of his own: *This is my mother on her christening day, on my grandmother's lap, and my great-grandmother is standing behind them. . . . This is me when I was ten, with my friend Zoli. We are trying to stand on our skates, but we are not very good, and we will fall just after this picture is taken. . . . This is only two years ago, with my friend Pál on my shoulders. He is four, and even though the Chain Bridge is under water, he thinks now it is peacetime. Look how happy he is.*

By the middle of 1948, despite ominous signs, twenty-six-year-old Imre was operating a business that supported eleven people. He owned a warehouse, offices, a small truck, two fully functioning presses—one producing books, the other, newspapers—a third under repair, and a fourth under consideration. Much to his surprise, he was taking some pleasure in his work. He began to think he might have a knack for legitimate business after all. He toyed with the idea of selling this one, carrying the proceeds to some better place west or south, starting again doing something else.

Still in 1948, all four of Imre's partner newspapers were closed down as enemies of the Party, and the twice-daily deliveries (2 A.M. and 3 P.M.) of pasted-up layouts simply stopped. Imre's back-of-the-mind notion to sell the press and leave the country grew more and more urgent at exactly the same speed that it became completely impossible. The West—once less than two hundred miles away—suddenly retreated infinitely farther: The government was felling trees between here and there and cultivating instead a crop of barbed wire and gun towers. In 1949, the government declared all businesses employing more than ten people to be property of the state. The next day, Imre came to work to find a representative of the Party already in residence, sitting at Imre's desk, examining Imre's papers, firing the hard and soft contents of a plugged nostril onto Imre's floor.

Horváth toured his guest through the offices and showed him the press's reduced archives. "You may find this interesting," Imre said amiably. He pulled from the shelf the 1890 manifesto of the first Hungarian socialist workers' party, complete with MK colophon. "Our ancestors worked together," said Imre with a charming smile, and offered his duly impressed guest a drink.

For six weeks, Imre was kept on as a technical assistant, training new press employees (excess farmers fresh from the countryside). Two of his previous employees had simply disappeared, and a third, György Toldy, was hiding with Imre's assistance in the press's basement. Each morning while the Party commissar sat in Imre's offices trying to understand Imre's papers, Imre stood on the press floor and explained to men who had never operated a device larger or more complicated than a hoe how to turn the daily deliveries of pasted articles on cardboard into copies of the Party newspaper. Three times Imre smuggled home a personal or family item. In a box under his bed, in his apartment, now drawn and quartered to share with three newly urbanized families, he stored a damaged edition of his great-grandfather's poems, a small printer's plate with the MK colophon, and a copy of *Békében*.

At the end of six weeks—the new staff being as well trained as could be expected under the circumstances, and the commissar having no further questions on where anything was kept or what any file represented—Imre was arrested. Two unpleasant members of the AVO secret police came to the press and the Party man, who had been generally gruff but not hostile, called Imre up from the machinery, sat him on the floor of his office, handcuffed him, and explained the accusations against him as the two AVO men took turns kicking him. The commissar recited the charges quietly: Some of the new press employees reported that Imre had called the revolution "a bad harvest," had labeled General Secretary Rákosi "a goat's cock," and had predicted there would soon be a welcome uprising engineered by Hungarian noblemen and British spies. Further, one of his new flat mates reported Imre was himself a spy and used *Enough for Everyone* to code secret messages to the Americans. Imre managed, quite bravely, to laugh at these stories, and, to give them their due, the secret policemen and the commissar laughed with him. Then they kicked him in the testicles. "We understand these people are a bit overzealous in their loyalty to the Party. We are not fools," the Party man said. "But *this* is not a joke." And he waved a copy of *Békében* at the bleeding, crying young man. "This is disgusting." He struck Imre across the face with the hard, heavy book, breaking Imre's nose and two teeth. "Do you have a favorite picture, my lord Horváth?" he demanded, but did not wait for an answer and struck him again with the book, this time against the other side of Imre's face. "Is there a picture from before the Party came to power that you like?" And struck him again. "A picture of your daddy?" And again. "A pretty picture of some rich parties?" And again. "Some of your daddy's Arrow Cross friends?" And again. "Pretty pictures of the pig regent Horthy on a lovely black horse?" And again. Then there was a pause, the end of blows. "Do you like this book very much, great Mr. Horváth? Peacetime without the Party?" And he struck him again. "Now, what does this mean?" Imre remembered being asked as his bleeding, swelling head was held up from behind by hard stranger's hands and a finger with a blood-covered nail angrily tapped the MK colophon on the last page of *Békében* again and again and again, smudging it red-brown. "Now, what does this mean? You are going to shoot us down, great Mr. Horváth?" And the next blow sent him into welcome unconsciousness.

XII.

SENTENCED TO LIFE WHILE HE SLEPT, IMRE HORVÁTH SPENT THREE AND A half years in a work camp.

He did not count his days and nights in bondage because he expected— even two days prior to his release—that his imprisonment would end only with his death. He did not feel some secret part of himself made strong by his hardship. He did not discreetly receive from one prisoner and pass on to the next a tattered translation of the United States Constitution or Montesquieu's essays on the natural rights of man. He was not warmed by a great and unexpected love for his fellow prisoners. He did not organize his companions to assure that the strong protected the weak. He did not hide extra food under his dirty gray pillow and give it to the sick or dying. He did not take responsibility for breaches in discipline that he had not committed in order to save some other prisoner from punishment, and did not win as a result the undying loyalty of a small group. He did not find new solace in his old, untended religion, though the camp did not lack for Catholic priests. He did not mentally rehearse great orations that would soften the hearts of the heartless judges who had condemned him. He did not refuse to participate in education sessions and instead proudly face workmanlike beatings. He did not bait or debate his teachers, did not ask troublesome questions with a delicately ironic voice. He did not scratch detailed schematics in the dust with a bit of stick, squatting amid a circle of admiring cohorts, nodding along, keeping a lookout, chewing on seeds. He did not win the favor of the guards. He did not hold the barbed wire to let others crawl to freedom first, did not shelter a Western spy under his bunk, did not rise under the new moon and tap Morse code on a brilliantly rigged radio that only the finest minds could have produced under such circumstances. He did not look with sympathy on those of his fellow prisoners who were themselves Communists, betrayed, shocked, eaten by the monster they had so lovingly raised. He did not pester those of his block mates who were true democratic dissidents, did not ask for their acceptance, did not look on them as the sainted. He did not gaze amazedly upon his thin, quiet, pale cellmate and realize, yes, yes, this is the man who will lead a free Hungary if we are only patient, and did not, as a result, do all that was in his admittedly limited power to protect that man from abuse, vicious or petty. He did not dream of the day when all of this would be swept away. He did not swear to remember, or to become like a camera. He did not think he would be called to testify, did not expect justice would be done. He did not wonder where his rescuers would come from. He did not know better than his captors, did not fall asleep each night with a sly smile, free despite the illusory appearance of bonds, did not leave them his body while his soul soared. He was not above all this. He did not hide his weeping. He did not ask others to share theirs. He did not watch when someone was taken away or beaten or shot. He did not vow this or that. He made no oaths that someday, and so on. He did not refuse to surrender. He did not die.

And then there came what they called a thaw. It blew from the east, and in its relative warmth he was allowed to melt underneath the barbed-wire walls and flow back to the city whence he had come. And there he was told where to live. And he was told what to do. He was asked his previous work, and he was made again a printer, a low-level printer working the very same machinery he had rebuilt six years before in the very same buildings where his mother had taken him to visit brothers, a father, and ancestors living in the shadows of a forest of books. And he never knew if this re-placement was an oversight, coincidence, apology, tricky test, insult, and he never asked, and he tried to be as he had been in camp but found that he could not, because he was often too angry even to speak. He loaded the ink and manned the spinning drums and tried to be as he had been before the camp, but found that this, too, was impossible, as none of what had come before had brought him here, no logic, no progressive course, not even a game. His actions had determined nothing, and he commanded himself not to think about it.

He spoke little. He would correct the other men who worked the presses, men he did not know but who fed the paper too roughly. They did not take his corrections, nor did they take to him, nor did he find himself suddenly a natural leader of men, seasoned by pain and hard treatment. And this, too, angered him.

The People's Dawn clattered off the spinning drums now, and he did not care that its editorials spoke of much needed reforms. He did not notice that under a new and very different Horváth Kiadó logo, the paper began to report on failures of Communism around Hungary. He neither knew nor would have cared that the paper called for a return to "socialist legality," that it apologized for the wrongful imprisonment of innocent comrades, that it applauded First Secretary Mátyás Rákosi and Prime Minister Imre Nagy for their admirable decision to imprison for life their former chief of the AVO and their simultaneous promise to respect civil liberties from this point on.

Imre Horváth kept to himself, and tried not to think about the past that he thought about constantly. He considered visiting his two children, those products of another time and personality, but he would not recognize them, had no gifts to offer, dreaded conversation with their mothers. After screwing up his courage for one feeble visit to his daughter the first warm day of March, he no longer considered further attempts.

He went quietly to and from his job, spoke little, and wrestled with anger that would reduce him to silence when in company but tears when alone. Twice a day he drank coffee standing up at a coffee bar near his tiny flat. He did not read of the events of early October 1956.

Until the evening of the twenty-third of that month. Because then, everyone in Budapest—even those as devoutly ignorant as Imre—knew something had happened. Imre was sweeping the plant's floor, absorbing if not enjoying the dusk-quiet scratch of his work, when a young man, out of breath, banged on the wall under the open garage door of the loading area. "Who is in charge of this place?" the woman with him asked, also breathless, excited.

"I am," said the man with the broom, since at that moment he was floor foreman, a rotating title that signified little, as only cleaning was in progress.

"Then can you print this?" asked the young man. Now Imre saw the pistol stuffed in the waist of the boy's trousers. Now Imre saw the glow of the beautiful girl's face. Now Imre read the single sheet the boy handed him: a disruptive meeting of writers and poets, then a student demonstration fired on by the AVO, the army called in to crush the students but arming them instead, demands, violence. Two-sided violence at last.

"Yes, we can print this."

For thirteen days Imre slept little, read much, and scarcely left the press floor. Those who had run the press for seven years were suddenly absent, but new faces came and left the plant constantly. News arrived at all hours, typed or handwritten or merely recited, out of breath. Imre began issuing orders: a secretary to type this piece, a messenger to get paper rolls delivered, a driver to distribute single-sheet bulletins all over the city, an art student to draw what I tell you: a dueling pistol, yes, that's right, but a longer barrel, yes, good, now a burst of smoke and a ball, but with the letters . . .

Out into the crackling city they sent sheets that were not even proofread. Spelling errors and smudged ink proved the paper's pressing accuracy and revolutionary authenticity. Copy was merely printed, topped with date and time, and handed to impatient delivery drivers as quickly as possible. (The job of paperboy was suddenly dashing and dangerous, the preserve of swaggering young men.) The headlines of *Facts* made little sense to Imre at first, as if he had forgotten how to distinguish plausible from implausible: Army Backs Students Against AVO; Russians, Go Home!; AVO Shoots 100 Unarmed; Imre Nagy Walks with Us; Freedom Fighters Empty Prison; Nagy Sends Russians out of Budapest; Time for Elections and End of Warsaw Pact; Party HQ Falls to Us; Nagy Pulls Us out of Pact; WE ARE INDEPENDENT! WE ARE NEUTRAL!; Full Soviet Withdrawal Being Arranged; Schools to Reopen—Soviet Troops Back; Soviet Troops Withdrawing; Soviet Troops Promise to Withdraw; Soviet Troops Withdrawing; Soviet Troops Missing; Soviet Troops Circle City; Soviets Attack— Resist! USA Will Back Us!

Imre rode out of Budapest the night of November 7, four days before the establishment of martial law. He said good-bye to no one, invited no one— including his children or their married mothers—to join him except those who were standing closest to him the moment he decided to leave. He drove an orange pickup truck owned by the press. Ten days earlier, the art student had painted the old Horváth colophon on the truck's doors and the press's motto on its back hatch. Now, with the streets torn in tank-tread strips and explosions and gunfire constantly audible, Imre deemed it wise to paint over the speeding MK bullets, so only the words *The Memory of the People* stood out black on the otherwise blank vehicle. Imre chauffeured three former press workers who had returned to help produce *Facts*, together with their wives and children, a cat and a dog, and whatever possessions could fit in the space remaining. They soon merged into the caravan of similarly overstuffed vehicles that crept nose to tail from the west of the city to the Austrian border, flanked on both sides by slightly slower snaking lines of overburdened or underburdened pedestrians.

When they crossed into Austria, Imre had not slept in three days. Safely across, stopped at a holding point, he slept drooling behind the wheel. He dreamed he was carrying a blank white pennon over his head. His arms grew tired and he was about to lower them, but his tiny daughter appeared, looking just as she had during his dismal visit that first warm day in March but now speaking with eerie, urgent maturity: "No, Papa. If you put that pennon down, there will be terrible suffering. All of those people will die. Your failure." She pointed behind Imre, as if great multitudes of supporters awaited his next move, depended on his steadfast arms and the inspirational sight of his snapping pennon. He turned to see just who she meant, but there was no one behind him. He turned back and she was laughing at him until tears rolled down her little cheeks. Nevertheless, unwilling to disappoint her if no one else, he stood with the pennon over his head, and his arms burned, and a wind picked up and blew dust in his eyes and he wanted to lower his arms just for a moment to rub his eyes, and the wind blew harder, and he turned his head from side to side, but the wind blew all the harder from all directions, as if he were the target, the blustery endpoint of all the world's winds, which smelled of potatoes . . .

He awoke because an impatient, amused Austrian immigration worker was blowing in his face.

XIII.

IMRE AWOKE IN AUSTRIA. HE BEGAN TO SEE A PURPOSE, A PROGRESSION from point A to point B, a strict logic underlying the events of his life. Dramatic phrases came to him in Vienna, twirled and whistled for him, in the refugee center and later, alone on a wooden bench in a cold, damp park at twilight. He could not argue with them. They sounded like truth: *I was born for this. My family died for this. I lost the press in 1949 for a reason. They sent me to that camp for a reason. I was floor foreman on the twenty-third for a reason.*

Imre began to feel—very strongly, very often—that he had not only a purpose but an inherited purpose. He stood in a long line, some ahead of him, many behind him. He was expected to hold his place in that line and teach the next generation how to hold theirs. "A permanent institution is composed of impermanent humans, and each of them must contribute their very souls, their impermanent and unimportant lives, if the institution is to preserve its immortality. This is true of a nation as much as a business," Imre wrote in his application to a foundation underwritten by a Hungarian film producer in Hollywood. The wealthy immigrant loaned Imre enough money to start Horváth Verlag in Vienna, a sum the applicant repaid in only three years.

Imre rebuilt. He staffed with refugee Hungarians whenever possible. He began by publishing a series of short pamphlets in eleven languages on the history of the Hungarian Revolution of 1956, and he turned a profit on the sale of several thousand of them to the United Nations. Intending to show the world what was at stake back in Budapest, he hired linguists to translate classics of Hungarian literature, science, mathematics, music, drama, poetry, and history into English, French, Spanish, German, Italian, Greek, and Hebrew, and he shipped this Babel of Hungarian all over Europe and North America. Horváth Verlag also printed language textbooks and local histories for Hungarians trying to adapt to their new homes in Vienna, London, Toronto, Cleveland, Lyon. Imre commissioned new translating dictionaries of the Hungarian language, which enjoyed a brief vogue after 1956 as the West generously and momentarily opened its heart to the freedom-loving refugees, the collective *Time* magazine Man of the Year.

As the 1950s became the 1960s, Hungary's Communist government softened slightly and Imre found opportunities to profit from exile. He hired underemployed émigré Hungarian scientists to translate new Western scientific and medical textbooks, which he then brought back to Budapest himself and sold to the Hungarian government. With each sale, the government ordered its state-owned Horváth Kiadó in Budapest to strip the books and reprint their covers without the provocative MK symbol of Horváth Verlag Vienna.

Imre traveled on his Austrian passport and discreetly met acquaintances from times past. He also brought gifts to two adolescents, who could not quite follow their mothers' explanations as to who he was. On his first visit he came with inappropriately childish gifts, which baffled and irritated their recipients, then returned with joyfully accepted Beatles records. After only these two occasions, though, in a coincidence he tried hard not to dwell on, the two mothers—strangers to each other—within a day of each other both asked him not to come again. Both said his presence was too confusing for the children and their younger siblings. And for the women's gentle, generous husbands.

He returned from these trips to Budapest with manuscripts his old acquaintances had discreetly slipped him, and he would print a few copies despite the expense, and he would store them in the verlag's archive or try to inter-est the Austrian government or universities in subsidizing the loss. He estab-lished the Horváth Verlag Shelves at one of the university libraries, and German translations of the smuggled texts nestled there, almost undisturbed in perpet-ual readiness (alongside other, more popular Horváth publications). Occasion-ally, these secret journals, essays, parables, or histories were cited in works of Soviet-studies research, doctoral dissertations, or scholarly articles. But not often.

After only a few trips, Imre began sending subordinates to Hungary car-rying his compliments. His staff would discreetly meet his old acquaintances and deliver new textbooks to the government in his place. Going back seemed like unnecessary effort, so much discomfort, when, after all, there was plenty of staff to send. Vienna was pleasant enough; it was morbid to return persistently, stubbornly to tragic Budapest.

His sense of mission, so acute in 1957, would falter from time to time. And as it did—as if it had been a temporary vaccine now expiring—he suffered from panic attacks, would fear going into work, without even faintly being able to understand why. He would stand in front of his bathroom mirror or the tele-phone in his hall, would mumble to himself, would say aloud the names of everyone he knew in Vienna, search for someone he could talk to, but he could never think of the right person. And so instead he would scramble to fill the sudden gaping, gasping spaces of his heart. He could not understand why he was suddenly driven to do something, anything, why he would feverishly offer himself to charitable organizations or sit in the pews of a Catholic church every afternoon for weeks or go to the dog track or play chess for hours on end in the cold of a public square or frequent brothels with the burning appetite of a sixteen-year-old boy but the budget and imagination of a forty-two-year-old man of the world.

For a short time at the end of the 1950s (and then again in 1968, when the Czechoslovaks staged a short but critically acclaimed revival of Hungary's drama from a dozen years earlier), Imre became interested in émigré political clubs. He joined organizations with names like the Viennese Society for the Support of a Free Hungary and the World Free Hungary Group. He would sit quietly at meetings as reports were read, detailing the failures of Hungary's planned economy, listing the latest rights violations with improbable precision ("102 arrests, 46 beatings"), and debates were held on the proper role of the Church and the nobility in any future democratic Hungary.

Imre was at times simply unable to go to the press. He might head to the office on foot, as usual, but instead of arriving in ten minutes, he would still be wandering through the city or sitting at a café several hours later. When, by sheer force of will, he did manage to get to the office, he would work with great and speechless intensity until late at night to atone for his lapse. The next morning, however, he might repeat the whole process, sitting at an outdoor table at eleven-thirty, drinking his fourth espresso, puffing his cheeks at the crossword puzzle, bouncing his leg at hummingbird frequency.

From peaks of religious zeal, in which he lectured his employees on the importance of their work to the people of Hungary and the culture of the world, he would fall into depressions, during which he might come to the office but never leave his desk, and his Hungarian assistants would carry on business without consulting him until, after days or even weeks, he would snap out of it and begin asking frenetic, scattershot, detailed questions of them. At the end of this spell, the faith in his calling would return as if from a holiday: refreshed, warm, even-tempered.

When these unscratchable itches had passed, he would sincerely and quickly redouble his commitment to the press. He would tell himself he had momentarily gone mad and forgotten why he existed. Do not forget again and you will never feel so lost again, he would remind himself, confident in his memory's ability to be permanently fixed. He would even write this sentence down and place it in his filing cabinet, the better to assure his future stability and dedication to the press. He knew he would need to teach his successors to plan for their own attacks of panic and doubt. So many things they would need to learn to preserve the press's immortality.

In 1969, he developed a stomach condition that demanded a torrential, nearly constant inflooding of milk, and even long after the condition had healed, he drank almost nothing else.

By the middle of the 1970s, he no longer slept well. He woke several times a night and each time had to wait longer before sleep would return. Having learned that changing positions did not bring relief, he forced himself to resist flipping from side to side in vain hope as the humming digital clock flipped from 2:30 to 2:31, 3:30 to 3:31, 4:30. It was beneath a man of his history and purpose to moan and spin and gnash his teeth simply because sleep no longer came willingly or for long. If the world's most ridiculous tyrants could not break him, then a little lack of sleep would not reduce him to tears. He lay in bed, still but awake, for hours. Soon, mornings turned on him, grew crueler and crueler. A little before five, Horváth would make the first of several trips to the toilet. He would walk, at that hour, with very little of the statuesque majesty that he had acquired in his years of exile. He would wear his pajama bottoms tied under the loose and yellowing skin of his belly, and the strap of yesterday's sleeveless undershirt would fight for shoulder space with the thickets of coarse gray hair the barber arrested weekly as it attempted to creep to the level of the shirt collar. Now, though only in his sixties, he stumbled often and fell occasionally, though never with serious effect.

One morning in 1986, he came out of his apartment in his bathrobe and drank a glass of milk while enjoying the spring sun struggling through the dirty skylight over the building's courtyard. He stood at the railing of the rectangular walkway and wished his neighbors good morning as they emerged for work. A young man, a stranger, appeared, a little out of breath, from the top of the stairs to his left. He looked carefully at Imre's face, and Imre smiled. "Herr . . . Rossmann?" he said after a slight hesitation. Blushing, he explained that he was supposed to meet someone here, someone he had never seen, he only had his description, and he was sorry to bother Imre, but if he was not Herr Karl Rossmann, could he show him which was Herr Karl Rossmann's apartment? Imre pointed to the door on the opposite corner of the courtyard, then entered his own apartment and, after the briefest pause, actually wept a bit, for he had been mistaken for Karl Rossmann, a very, very old man, a tremendously old man.

He grew vain. He began to require as much as ninety minutes to prepare himself in the morning, with exercises designed to tone aging muscle and complicated underclothes that shaped. He groomed and clipped and pared and filed and tweezed and powdered and tweezed again. He wore outfits that had to be composed with care, adjusted, then pressed just so with an intricate machine bought from a French company and shipped at great cost from Grasse.

In the late 1980s, as he slid deeper into his sixties, he did not think about retiring or selling the press; nor, on the other hand, did he vow to continue it at any cost or refuse to sell it under any circumstances. Months could pass without a thought for anything but commercial nuts and bolts: What was selling, can this paper be bought cheaper, why isn't this color registering properly, is Mike Steele still popular, should we increase the production of this or that or cancel this or expand that?

And then came 1989. From the first bulletins, Imre knew exactly what he was seeing, knew what would happen before it happened. Again and again, always the same, history would repeat this gruesome dance of hope and despair: protest marches, a faint and almost funny optimism, a government confused— menacing one day, pleading the next, sputtering promises of reform (practically mispronouncing the unfamiliar word)—then the ominous crackle of the first gunshots, the rumbling, thundering approach of the inevitable, the familiar stench that would again rise from the shredded streets any day, any day now, and then . . . and then . . . nothing? This time an explosion that never came. He squinted through first one eye, then the other; he pulled his hands away from his ears, and there was no explosion. No retribution. No innocents slaughtered. No invasion from the east under cover of flimsy, insulting justifications. No tanks in the streets. No butterfly-fragile attention of the world alighting ever so briefly on the wound of Central Europe. Instead, impossible but true: an almost messianic impossibility come true, an unimaginable realignment of the very stars in the sky—the Wall down, the Iron Curtain down, the Communists down, and elections and freedom and the country free, and can such things be? Has an old man gone as mad as Lear?

And again, reading the latest papers in his café, watching the American cable news on the giant screen in his office, talking to his managers, he received it more strongly than ever, the strongest it had been in thirty-two years: Hurrying home from an irresponsibly long holiday came Imre's burning sense of purpose. That evening he did not pick up his habitual, latest Mike Steele novel from his bedside table. Instead, he laughed out loud. He laughed as he lay down. He put down the glass of milk and he laughed out loud at the latest unbelievable headlines from home.

He laughed because he understood. He had lived in Vienna all these years for a reason. He had maintained the press, despite his doubts, for a reason. He had been careful with his health, his appearance, and his money for a reason. He had not found a family, had not been tied down for a reason. He had found the strength not to quit for a reason—1956–1989: thirty-three years, a Christian number, and he laughed again. And now he was called home. He was called to make the press strong again, back where it belonged, and to let it serve as the memory and conscience of a people, and to make the press live into the next generation and the one after that and the one after that, and on and on, if he could be wise enough, if he could rebuild one more time, if he could find the right people to prepare and teach, people of culture and vision and strength and uncorrupted youth, if he could teach them well enough so that the importance of the press would sing to them as well, if he could write down for them those few diamond rules and principles that would assure the press's permanence. These new faces would provide Hungary with its memory and its conscience, and they would care enough to do important work for an entire nation and would learn, as he had learned, how to use their impermanence to build permanence.

The sharp clarity of this vision was beautiful, and Imre marveled at what had happened of its own accord: A purpose could grow over decades without your ever knowing, until the end, when a garden was laid out for you, a garden you helped plan and build without ever knowing it, and it waits for you.

That night Imre slept soundly and dreamed—not unpleasantly—of his father.

XIV.

"MR. HORVÁTH WILL JOIN US PRESENTLY. HE IS APOLOGIZE FOR HIS DELAY, but ask we begin the coffee of us." Krisztina Toldy sat across from Charles Gábor at the long, blond-wood table of the conference room in the Vienna offices of Horváth Verlag and poured dark black into bone-white Hungarian china. The conference room, with a picture window that looked down on a large hall of silently spinning presses and blue barrels on orange forklifts, was decorated with a framed verse, paintings and photographs of Hungarian history, and engravings of the evolution of printing. Charles skimmed over the German and Hungarian captions with flickering attention: tidings of a new dawning age/And with the force of a ball from a pistol; Mátyás Accepting the Peace of Breslau; Gutenberg Printing a; Kossuth Leading a; a Printing Press Circa; Imre Nagy Standing Tall Despite; a Printing Press Circa; Bánk bán and the; a Printing Press Circa; maps of Budapest and Hungary 1490, 1606, 1848, 1914, 1920, 1945, 1990.

Krisztina Toldy's spectacles hung on a thin golden chain around her neck, and her black-and-white hair was pulled back so tightly into a braid that individual hairs at the top of her forehead could be seen and counted as they emerged from their follicles. Charles counted for a while as they drank. She sipped with her eyes down, silently, and Charles pitied her slightly. There she sat, in charge of softening the money man, little knowing that everything she did amused or irritated him and little knowing that it absolutely didn't matter anyhow what she did because he had sat through enough awkward coffees in his months of venture-capital work, had heard enough slick or humorous or stuttering assistants like Krisztina Toldy work their way through these opening acts, and nothing ever came of it. So he wished she'd get on with her spiel so that the man himself would appear on cue in a flurry of papers and hangers-on and they could talk just a minute or two longer, just long enough for Charles to find the weakness, figure out just why this whole thing was a crock of shit (which it must be if it was run by Hungarians, even Hungarians in Austria), and he could go spend the weekend in Innsbruck on the company's dime before heading back to BP on Monday to report to the Presiding Vice that this particular band of lazy Magyars wanted a billion dollars or the power of invisibility or a nuclear submarine in exchange for a 33 percent share in some paintings of Hungarian history and a big hall of undoubtedly outdated printing presses.

"He is great man, Mr. Gábor. You cannot imagine what he has faced against and achieved nevertheless. It is quite very remarkable." She spoke crap English (despite Charles's offer of either Hungarian or German) and with great earnestness, as if this were the first time she had found the words to say precisely what she had personally witnessed and come to believe. Charles scoffed without moving a muscle or making a sound, a skill of which he was very proud. "He save my father's life, Mr. Gábor," she continued confidently, unaware. "My father work for Mr. Horváth in Hungary. A day come when . . ."

Oh great. A reminiscence. Charles felt he had heard this story before, but with different characters. Somebody had saved somebody else from some horrible disaster, but at terrible personal sacrifice and years of some sort of suffering, and yet no regret because whatever. Was this a movie he'd seen? So familiar . . . Ah yes, an old parental standby: One of Charles's distant cousins had done something not unlike this and, my God, can you even imagine the dilemma, Károly, the sacrifice, the courage, the etcetera and the etcetera.

Charles played a private game to pass the time: He made all the facial expressions appropriate to Toldy's story but tried to do so without hearing a single word of what she was saying. To assure himself that he wasn't cheating, relying on her words to cue his sympathetic faces, he silently ran through German-language pickup lines he might need that coming weekend in Innsbruck. Occasionally, inevitably, her strident words broke through his defensive concentration. Then and only then he would allow himself the crutch of English in his mute seduction rehearsals, but only as long as was necessary to battle her back to inaudibility:

"There was only two doors and the hatch behind the main press. Very quick, Mr. Horváth push my father down into . . ." *I'm not trying to be pushy, but you remind me very much of a painting I saw today at the museum: You have that quick, raw energy and life,* die wichtigste Sache . . .

"And there was Mr. Horváth who merely say, 'Gentlemen, what bring you to . . .' " *What brings you to this place? I've never seen you here before. When you see someone like you, you don't forget it. You just don't.* Eine lange Zeit her ich bin gereist . . .

"Three and a half years! For three and a half years Mr. Horváth is forced to . . ." *Thirty-five schillings seems a fair price for beer this good. Do you know we can't get good Austrian beer in the States?* Amerikanisches Bier ist nicht . . .

"They could have kill him." *It kills me not to be able to explain the effect you have. On me, of course, but on everyone. Look around you. Look at those guys at the bar; they feel it too.* Ich bin nur tapfer genug Dich anzusprechen, und sie waren es nicht.

"My family is Jewish. Who was worst, my father was often ask, the Nazis or the Communists? He always say: The Nazis put me in camp and say they will destroy me; then the Communists put me in camp and say they will teach me be a better man. At least, my father say"—a broad and wisely ironic smile from her at this point, and the hair seemed even more tightly pulled back until Charles expected to see actual popping depilations from the puckered flesh—"at least the Nazis were honest with me."

Charles gave Krisztina a look that he hoped would express: his sympathy; his quiet wonder; his eagerness to speak, work with, and give vast quantities of money to such a man as saintly Imre Horváth; his hope that her father lived and prospered still and was not plagued all his life by terrible guilt for the price his employer paid on his behalf; and finally his polite and understandable desire that she shut up now and bring in the main guy so Charles could find out where and why this particular clown show would hemorrhage any money his firm transfused into it. Then Charles could stage his own daring escape in the nick of time, narrowly making the express train to Innsbruck.

Krisztina Toldy poured more coffee for the American boy and began to sense she was not accomplishing either of her two assignments. How could she relax him *and* make him feel the importance of the press? She realized her two tasks were contradictory: To educate this boy would require verbal force, which would hardly soothe him. Besides, there was something incorrect about this boy. His smile and word of thanks were wrong. He was made of dirty mirrors. She saw he did not care what she said; he was too spoiled to understand what

Horváth had done with his life. She tried her best to entertain the bearer of U.S. dollars, but in midsentence she would find his posture, his expression, his lips and hair so maddening that she would begin teaching and then end by haranguing.

Charles found this exhibition of her predicament increasingly entertaining, savored the sight of her at war with herself, and after his initial impatience, he began to hope Horváth would be infinitely late so that Charles might instead watch this tightly coiled aide-de-camp finally bust a spring. He memorized his favorite example of her confused outpourings and he recited it to Mark and John the next Monday evening at the Gerbeaud: "I am believing you will find Mr. Horváth an extraordinary businessman in your Western style, except that in the fundamentally, he is a man of moralness, and perhaps that is something you have seldomly seen in the West, or perhaps even never, since you are all unfamiliar with how living under the Communists did make some men strong. But perhaps this is impossible for your understanding what I mean."

Charles nodded and smiled sympathetically. "Mr. Horváth certainly was lucky to have been exposed to the Communists' inadvertent influence," he said. She rose and fetched a fresh pot. The coffee was offered and rejected, then accepted on second thought just as she was sitting down again.

"Do you have questions I might to answer?"

"Yes, thank you. This is a family-owned business, I think you wrote in one of your letters to my firm?"

"Since eighteen-eight, yes. Yes, the Horváth family is the business for one hundred and eighty-two years." She was energized again and leaned forward. "He is the sixth to guide this company, this Mr. Horváth. Our Hungarian history has until so far made it impossible for him to bring the most profits to the house—as I know your Western standards must have—but he has kept the press alive and free since forty-three years, like his father did in the wartimes. And we do make profits. We do not lose money here, sir. His father had your name." Pause. "Károly." Her enthusiasm faded as she considered this coincidence, but she continued on. "His father also guide us through danger. We are given leaders that times require for us, Mr. Gábor, and we are blessed to have Mr. Horváth."

"If it's a family business, then who is Mr. Horváth's heir?" Charles interrupted before she could screech another love song. "Which of his children is he preparing to take over the leadership of the company after his death?"

She looked a little shocked to hear reference to her employer's demise, but

Charles made no apology in word or gesture. "No, no, Mr. Gábor. Mr. Horváth will not have a death. He is immortal!" She chirped at her humor in the face of this horrible boy.

Charles replaced his empty cup on its saucer and leaned forward to reward Ms. Toldy a smile commensurate to her witticism. He had enjoyed her struggles to this point, but now he had heard the first piece of information worthy of his trip. Mr. Horváth was old (running the company for forty-three years) and was evidently heirless, as his trusted aide had dutifully not answered Charles's question.

"Heirless," he confirmed to his two friends that Monday evening at the Gerbeaud.

"Can't he use an inhaler?" Mark asked. "I did when I was a kid."

"There's a spray you can rub on your scalp now, I think. It makes it grow back," John offered.

The door to the conference room opened and Charles forced a smile. Imre Horváth, his glasses propped up on his forehead, entered signing papers held by a young man. Two other young men followed them into the room. Papers overflowed, pens scraped, last-minute urgent advice was taken, split-second decisions made, and brilliant, multilayered orders issued in two languages. Charles stood slowly, drawn upward by script and ritual, simultaneously bored and alert, expecting little. "Ohhh, Mr. Gábor" came the English words tinseled in middle-European accents. "You must accept my apologies for being tardy."

"Horváth úr," Charles responded entirely in Hungarian. "Please do not apologize. Ms. Toldy has been excellent and informative company."

The emperor stopped short with exaggerated surprise. His court, too, froze, and the emperor made the recognized face of astonishment, followed by the acknowledged hand gestures of delight. "It is too wonderful," he exclaimed in English. "You speak Hungarian like a genius. These are exciting times when the best young Americans speak Hungarian." The three attendants grinned appreciatively, and Ms. Toldy, standing at the head of the table, smiled and relaxed in her hero's presence.

The older man who wanted the younger man's money shook the hand of the younger man who wanted the older man's position, and they continued their courtly dance. They descended into chairs on opposite sides of the long table. A glass of milk, apparently, materialized in front of Horváth, and Charles watched coffee reappear in his own cup. Ms. Toldy sat at Imre's right, and the three attendants slid themselves, in decreasing height, into three chairs on their master's left; Charles faced the five of them alone.

Imre spoke again in English, a generous gesture in order not to strain the young man's undoubtedly shallow pool of Magyar: "My good Mr. Gábor, we are very honored to welcome you to our press today. We are quite at your disposal. Your trip, I hope, was—" The script was followed precisely (alternating in generous English and generous Hungarian, until the man who reverted first to his native tongue would have admitted the same defeat as the man who lets his business rival pay for the lunch): the names of the three other men, the ritual exchange and tribal inspection of business cards, a joke about the ritual of exchanging and tribally inspecting business cards, Charles's request that the others call him Károly, Horváth noting the coincidence, Charles's travel experience, Vienna, the neighborhood, the building, the sound of the presses clattering behind soundproof glass, questions as to how a young man could speak such flawless (an exaggeration, intentionally crafted to be transparent) Hungarian, brief explanations of family history, a reference to the weather and the inevitability of references to weather, a joke implying great age and wisdom, the teller having seen all the weather there is to see and expecting no more surprises in this life, the prints upon the wall. "This one"—a slow caress over the glass that protected the framed verse—"was written about this very firm, about our Horváth Press, when it was still young and still, of course, in Budapest. A great poet wanted to tell the world about how we . . ." The man's story illuminated nothing; Charles nodded accordingly. ". . . and yet, no doubt ancient history, an old man's nonsense, you come all this way to talk business and here I am—" a mock-humble claim to be uninteresting, a deceptive claim semi-subliminally boasting its own inaccuracy, in fact designed to illuminate an actual, robust appetite for commerce. Conclusion of introductory remarks, shiny delicious early train to Innsbruck not yet an impossibility.

"You are very kind, Horváth úr," continued Charles in Hungarian. "I am here, of course, on behalf of my firm"—the older man nodded at Charles's frank admission that he merely represented other, more powerful, men with money—"to hear more about your company and about the specifics of how we may be able to help you." Charles realized how his words had been taken and so he added, "In that my report decides the firm's next steps."

Charles's questions leaped one at a time from the notebook in which he had lodged them the previous night. As the questions sprang up over the table,

Imre would compliment them, charm them, allow to dance before them visions of history and tyranny, bravery and cunning, place them in a receptive mood before assigning one or another of his assistants the task of filling in details, until the question drifted, exhausted, back down into the notebook, to be replaced by the renewed vigor and insight of its successor. The questions in Hungarian probed cash reserves, capital assets, distribution networks, employee counts, backlists and catalogs, balance sheets and production schedules, income statements and lines of credit, supply chains and unit costs; the answers in English spoke of stories and histories, personalities and ancestors, dramatic events dictating difficult decisions, and dictated decisions yielding surprising results. Each time, Imre in English flattered Charles's Hungarian questions, and Charles in Hungarian flattered Imre's English anecdotes, until an assistant, following his boss by using chunky, metallic English, provided the details that Charles had originally requested. "Your question is insightful, young Károly. Our financial records are entirely at your disposal. The specifics of your question touch on areas we have begun to examine quite closely as we preparing for this great move back to our homeland." And gradually Charles was allowed to understand what precisely Horváth wanted from Charles's firm.

For the last thirty-some years, there had been two Horváth Presses—the larger one in Budapest, nationalized without compensation by the Communists in 1949, and the smaller one in Vienna, reopened by Horváth after his escape from Hungary in 1956. As a victim of the 1949 nationalization, Horváth was now entitled to a reimbursement by the new, democratic Hungarian government: a symbolic restitution for his 1949 losses, a symbolic amount paid in vouchers that could only be used to buy back nationalized property (his own or someone else's) or to invest on the new, wobbly Budapest stock exchange. Horváth was looking for enough outside investment to pool with his feeble vouchers, resulting in a large enough bid to buy back everything that had been stolen from his family in 1949, to refurbish the reclaimed property to 1990 standards, to combine the healthy, profitable enterprise in Vienna with the rebuilt enterprise in Budapest, and to make the Horváth Kiadó once again the vocal memory of the Hungarian people. "Ohhh, Mr. Gábor, this State Privatization Agency, it is charmingly named, no? Perhaps my vouchers will come with an apology? Or a greeting card signed by my jailers? Perhaps I will find they give me my vouchers but have already sold my press to some sad, abused greengrocer? So we must act with speed, you and I. But Balázs"—he nodded to the tallest assistant (though still shorter than the imposing Horváth)—"is wise in matters mathematical. Balázs, what do you say to Károly's clever question?" And the young Hungarian who lived and worked for his hero in Vienna provided the American in English with the accounting data he requested. And the same scorn, the same zealous faith Charles had felt emanating from Krisztina Toldy floated around Balázs's answer as well—no harsh words, nothing in fact but real and projected numbers were discussed, but Charles's rebellion, his unwillingness to bow low to the seated god, seemed to offend everyone in the room but the flesh icon himself.

"We have prospered here in Vienna, you can see. But most important, we have survived and maintained our duty: We are still the memory of our people, and during these dark forty years, this was more important than ever before. We are the publishers in ten languages of all the classic Hungarian authors and poets. The entire catalog of the Horváth Kiadó, gathered over nearly two centuries, and we have assured they have not disappeared from the world's view even as they are banished from their homeland. Surely, Mr. Gábor, you can see the importance of such a feat."

"Indeed. Your books line my parents' shelves in Cleveland, Horváth úr," he replied. "I grew up with your editions."

Horváth smiled broadly and spread his fingers as far as they would reach, allowed the boy to see the strength in his old hands. "Then we have succeeded and I am very filled with pride."

"But is there sustainable, growable profit in selling only classics?"

"Ohhh, Mr. Gábor, do not think me a sentimentalist. You are correct: Something must pay for our mission. When we return to our rightful place, it will be the same as now, but in Hungarian: popular books and magazines, sports papers, a financial paper; *Our Forint* would renew a tradition of my family." Without taking his eyes off the American, he waved vaguely at the middle assistant, who, grateful for the opportunity and with the same fire in his eye as had inflamed Krisztina's and Balázs's, drew Charles's attention to an eclectic catalog that included, among other oddities, the fetishistic but wildly popular series of American "Mike Steele" detective novels translated into German (*Killer in the Bath*; *A Long Hot Shower with Death*; *Suds, Bloody Suds*; *Lathered for Slaughter*, and several others), the Viennese-pastry cookbooks, memoirs of German politicians and spymasters, the investment guides, diet books, pop psychology, inspirational soft-religion books, a soccer newspaper, and the puzzle magazine that had together accounted for 85 percent of the company's revenues for the last several years, while the classics sold with respectable consistency. "We are all great fans of your Mike Steele," Horváth said, raising an ironic eyebrow to the American private detective whose hygiene-obsessed German-language exploits supported the publication of English-language collections of Boldizsár Kis and French-language editions of Endre Horn's plays. And in this comment Charles knew he was meant to hear Europe laughing at the United States, at its philistine tastes and at the clever European ability to use those tastes to pay for more elevated ventures. Charles knew he was being asked to laugh with them and, in so doing, declare himself European, one of their own by their own definition. He smiled, even bowed his head slightly, in acknowledgment of their cultural triumph over shallow America.

All expertise sat in these three managers, Charles decided; the Toldy woman was a gofer, and the importance of the old man was purely symbolic, though, Charles reminded himself, that was not without value for investment and publicity, no matter how unappealing a type he found Imre Horváth. Charles used that very word at the Gerbeaud the following Monday: "He's a type you see all the time. He's exactly like a fat television addict who won't shut up about his high school athletic accomplishments. How can someone live as a shell of their former self?"

An assistant listed the ex-Horváth assets the Hungarian State Privatization Agency had on the block and detailed the likely process of bidding for them before Imre added, "The current Hungarian government, Mr. Gábor, with its former prisoners, its dissidents turned ministers, its poets and its thinkers: Many of them are in our catalog as well. We have published them and other forgotten Hungarians left behind since 1956. This, obviously, involved certain complications in procuring of manuscripts, but such things could be arranged with an Austrian passport and a willingness to, ohhh, extend oneself." The press's catalog of samizdat was patently unprofitable, comprising mostly journals and essays: brutal descriptions of life under Communism, philosophical treatises on living honestly amid dishonesty and betrayal, hopelessly fantastical and irrelevant then retrospectively amazing and prophetic imaginings of a future democratic Hungary's structure and soul. All of it would have been obtained and removed from Hungary at enormous risk. Imre offered no details, merely swung his censer of mysteries and allowed the whiff of secrets to infiltrate the room and tickle the American's nose.

"It's absolutely without commercial value. But good P.R., I'll give the old liar that," Charles said as cakes came. "I might need you, Johnny, to make this deal happen. You ever lobbied? Anyhow, we'll get your little typewriter doing something useful for a change, maybe make you some money." With a quizzical expression, John Price looked up from cracking the caramel top of his Dobos torte. "Yes, my little Hebrew friend," said Charles. "Money."

"It is remarkable, but true, Mr. Gábor: The Communists never changed the name of the Horváth Kiadó. It was the name of class enemies, those wicked Horváths, oppressors of the proletariat, but they also knew the Horváth name was—as I think you would understand—a respected brand. And what did they do with that brand from 1949 until 1989? They told lies with it. Under my name. Under my family's stolen name, for forty years, Mr. Gábor, foolish and wicked men have produced nonsense and lies. Except for thirteen days in 1956 when I was again in charge. Forty years of lies, thirteen days of truth. A bad score, I think." On cue, without looking away from Charles, Horváth accepted a book from his assistant and tapped the spine: *A Horváth Kiadó*. He tapped the cover, the Hungarian words *The U.S. Terrorist Campaigns Against the People of Hungary, by Gyula Hajdú*. He opened the book, still facing Charles, to the back page, with its distinctive colophon: a little drawing of a muscular factory worker holding a stylized shield, and on the shield, surrounded by a cloud of steam or smoke, the letters *MN*. "*A Magyar Népköztársaság*." Imre spoke, at last, three words of Hungarian. "The *People's* Republic of Hungary," he whispered. "But MK," Imre said, and tapped the spine of another book (conjured from a different assistant), where the traditional pistol fired away. "My great-uncle Viktor's design. MK. *A Magyar Köztársaság*. The Republic of Hungary. Since 1808, we have published for a free, independent, democratic Hungary. My ancestor died at Kápolna for this freedom. And now there is such a thing, a real place at last, not a fairy tale or a madman's vision, a true Republic of Hungary, and what do I have? My name and my business, very much one and the same thing, stolen from me to tell forty years of lies. Mr. Gábor, I want your help in restoring truth. This"—he looked straight at the impenetrable boy—"would be a triumph for a young Magyar hero. Not only financial but moral, historical, philosophical. We do need your firm's money, Mr. Gábor. This is obvious. But we can get that, I think, from other sources. We also need men and women of culture who understand the importance of what we represent. We need Hungarians of character, ready to reclaim their heritage. Please tell this to your firm." Horváth rose and four others rose in unison a heartbeat after. "I am needed elsewhere now, unfortunately, Mr. Gábor." He examined the seated Charles. "I am very curious to know what you will do in this situation that faces you, young Károly." He squinted slightly at Charles and spoke in English, low and slow and grave. "You and I shall perhaps tell this story together. This Hungarian story. Your return to Hungary makes our return to Hungary possible. The truth restored by two Hungarians who wish to come home, one young and one old. Are you prepared, Károly, to grapple with such a labor for your people?" He stood over Charles, his arms crossed, his powerful hands hidden in the folds of his Italian suit, his thin oval reading glasses holding back the wash of his silver mane, his blue eyes unblinking under thick lines of forehead, eyes angled sharply down at the American. His voice slowed and deepened further still. "Your Hungarian story. Think on this first, Károly, and on balance sheets second. It is my best advice to you."

The door closed behind him and Imre Horváth stepped slowly and unsteadily down the carpeted hall that led to his office. With great effort, he walked along the corridor and directly to one of the guest chairs facing his desk. He sat heavily under a framed photograph: the current finance minister of the new democratic Hungary, age four, sitting astride the shoulders of Imre Horváth, age twenty-four—a picture used in *Békében*. The two of them squinted into the sunlight on the Danube riverfront on the Buda side, right in front of the bombed and sunken Chain Bridge, its broken connecting cables dipping into and rising out of the river, its main pediments supporting no road at all. The little boy perched high on the young man's shoulders waved and smiled; he had just crossed the river on one of the temporary ferries with his friend Imre, who took care of him from time to time. Imre held the soft dangling ankles in his fists, and pictured sleeping with the photographer, the little boy's oldest sister.

Charles's afternoon ended with a tour of the Horváth Verlag offices, warehouses, and printing equipment, under the leadership of Béla, the shortest of the three assistants, a young man nearly without hair, just a monastic fringe that ran from ear to ear, and a twice-broken nose that resembled one of the lesser-known pastas. Charles again investigated Imre's chain of succession, and Béla replied: "He has only a cousin, I believe in Toronto, but he has no children. By not having the family he was able to go to Hungary and come a little more free, could resist their certain pressures. It was often through family they made you to collaborate, you know, to bend you. He never collaborated, you see. Never. He never bended. But with a family, well—"

"It might have been his Achilles' heel." Charles finished the intolerably slow sentence.

Béla stopped in front of one of the clattering machines, held up his hand with the palm facing his guest and the fingers curving slightly inward, a favorite gesture of medieval saints in flat paintings. "He has no Achilles' heel, Mr. Gábor. He is one of the great men, the real rare men. This you will learn; you will be very lucky to work with him." And Charles saw that this was not a rehearsed part of the day's grand plan to impress the money man, not even really that smart a thing to say to a potential investor—just the absolute truth as far as Béla was concerned. Charles exerted himself to the utmost and did not laugh.

A TEMPORARY DIGESTIVE DISORDER

JOHN PRICE SMOKED A SLOW CIGARETTE ON HIS BALCONY, KISSED the photos of his antique wife and child good night, then lay on his folded bed's covers, unable to file the events of the day, the head injury and fratultery. His brother deserved nothing better. He should apologize to his brother immediately. He was every day better able to appreciate Emily. He was every minute less worthy of Emily. He was a bastard. He was a genius of living.

He was nearly asleep when a mathematical equation glowed behind his closed eyes. In the quick-pulsed, sweaty state between wakefulness and sleep, he watched a well-manicured, graceful female hand move chalk across a blackboard. The equation appeared in clicks and squeaks, the disarmed hand pushing the telltale chalk: *Seriously = not seriously*. As her hand came to the end, the letters began to fade progressively, in the order they had been written, like vapor trails or motorboat wakes. He watched the equation write itself over and over in the same space, at the same pace, fading, reappearing, again and again. *Seriously = not seriously. Seriously = not seriously.* When the word *seriously* began to look misspelled, imaginary, John was escorted into sleep.

The next morning, this equation—unlike great presleep revelations of the past, vast social engineering solutions, mathematical insights, philosophical breakthroughs—had not vanished but sat perched on his shoulder and demanded his immediate and undiluted attention when he opened his eyes: *Seriously = not seriously.* He rose and returned to his balcony, watched the traffic and the foreshortened pedestrians, who, directly beneath him, shrank to mere circles with four telescoping attachments. The equation paraded around, and he couldn't quite think of anything else for several minutes.

On and off during the morning, as he struggled to make sense of the bloodied notes from his interview with Harvey, he would lean back in his chair and chew his lip, considering serious and nonserious until, just before noon, Karen Whitley asked him if he was in the mood for "a special lunch." The equation finally revealed its secret meaning to him as Karen's closed eyes and open mouth swung metronomically in and out of John's range of vision. With each pendulum swing, her torso and head obscured and revealed in rhythmic alternation the ceiling rose, the plaster grapes and garlands encircling her bedroom's light fixture. John tried to see this carving in his mind's eye even when it was blocked by Karen. He tried to make the girl transparent on behalf of Emily, who sat obligingly nude next to him, placed one hand on his forehead, and demanded ferociously, like a martinet drill instructor, that he count the grapes, that he silently describe the garlands and the tiny cupids in complete detail to her. And, as he was following her orders, his equation returned—*Seriously = not seriously*—and John began to smile, and Karen, her eyes open now (vaporizing Emily), smiled back at him, and John smiled more broadly, and Karen, too, smiled more broadly, and John slowly began to understand the vision that had come to him with sleep the night before. After a while, Karen stopped moving and her head fell against John's chest, and the sound of her talking slowed and lowered and became the sound of her breath and then the sound of her sleeping. By then, John understood that some things mattered and some things did not and that the happy people in this world were those who could easily and rapidly distinguish between the two. The term *unhappiness* referred to the feeling of taking the wrong things seriously.

He left Karen asleep and returned to the office to finish his Harvey profile, which now typed itself with nonserious facility: Harvey was not serious; Harvey was amusing. Nothing could possibly be less serious than brother Scott and his Magyar mistress. John tapped at his computer keyboard with a dramatic rising and falling of the hands, like a concert pianist.

II.

"AND YOUR FATHER SAID TO ME, 'BUT THAT'S WHY WE'RE HERE. I'D DO THIS again in a minute.' Think about that. Even in that kind of danger, under fire, with me giving off very unhelpful doubt and fear, he was entirely clear about himself and his purpose. Extraordinary. They don't make a lot of men like Ken Oliver."

"No, that's certainly true."

Ed held her eye until she looked away. "Everything else good for you?" He leaned forward and his chair creaked under the weight. "You liking the work?"

"I love it. I'm honored to do it."

The two sides of her supervisor's personality alternated dominance according to strict scheduling. Outside of secure areas, in the vast surveillable outside world, his ear constantly but discreetly to the ground, Edmund Marshall did not simply appear to be but truly was a round and shaggy-bearded bon vivant, a wheezy jokester, often nearly drunk, loving life and the occasional off-color story, frequently and loudly thanking heaven and his evening's hosts for his diplomatic career, since it kept him near great foreign food. He also kept himself surrounded by a mist of artificial but very credible rumors that his job was in danger, that he had recently been disciplined again for some overindulgence or another. During office hours, however, behind lead doors, he was the most humorless, unsmiling co-worker conceivable, obsessive about the accuracy of paperwork, untiring in constructive self-criticism, with an insatiable appetite for discussing the ambivalences, layers, motivations, and countermotivations of sources and potential sources. He was universally admired by his staff for his sincere, rare, and impassioned vocation for identifying human weakness, doubt, and corruptible ideals. Neither of his two personalities was put on, only perfectly segregated for maximum usefulness, and Emily knew that this ability to put one's entire personality to work was an accomplishment one should aspire to.

"Are you happy here?" he asked her.

She looked up. The question astounded her. "Of course." She left her supervisor's windowless office—swallowing with difficulty the mild rebuke that had then segued into the vaguely illustrative (and self-critical) story of her father in a very different Berlin—and considered the implications of his odd question. No one had ever asked her such a thing before, because no one had ever had to; she had certainly been brought up never to consider such a selfish question, or to put anyone in the position of having to ask her. She didn't know what could have prompted such a question or what conceivable difference the answer could make.

On the other hand, she hadn't heard that story before and couldn't help but feel another flush of admiration for her father, followed closely by an uncharacteristic rage at Ed's probing and prodding, and at his baffling and really completely unfair comment that her Analyses of Human Motivation in the contact reports she filled out after every interaction with any foreign national were still displaying—despite his previous complaints, corrections, and frustrated tutoring—"a callow lack of nuance, tone color, and depth measurement." And so it was with some relief when the marine called from downstairs to say that a John Price was in the lobby to see her. John and Mark lived in some relaxed and rootless parallel universe, where no one inquired after you to make sure you were appropriately happy, holding you up against some mysterious standard of behavior. She wondered how it must feel to float like John must float, all day.

They walked around the block, then sat on one of the old green benches in the middle of Liberty Square, watched the line for visas wind around the side of the embassy. "How did you decide not to join the military?" she asked him after talking about nothing. "What? Why is that funny?"

"Decide? Well, how did you decide not to become a sumo wrestler?"

"Really? It wasn't like a statement or something? You just never thought about serving?" She sat quietly. John's presence confused her just now, his untetheredness, his belief in nothing in particular. He was so unfocused, she felt fuzzy simply being near him. Things she was certain of a few minutes before now seemed questionable. "I've never asked my brother Robert if he's, you know, well, *happy* in the Corps. Do you think that I should have? Is that strange? Cripes, what time is it? I gotta go back in."

John had come to the embassy with an invitation meant to reveal something of himself to her, to open a private space in which they could be alone together. "There's someone I really want you to meet," he finally managed to say as they stood in the lobby under the eyes of two marine guards and several cameras, visible and invisible. "She's amazing. You'll love her."

She agreed to meet him at the Blue Jazz, better than a night catching up on contact reports while wondering if she looked sufficiently happy to pass mysterious muster, better than wasting valuable time with the pointless Julies. She fingered the plastic I.D. card clipped to her lapel, examined John: She wondered if he was happy in a way she was not, wondered if there were some dangerous telltale betrayal of her father or of her principles that showed on her face but not in a mirror. And she retreated through the self-locking double glass doors to do her shy ambassador's bidding.

He watched her disappear. Now fearing he had answered her enlistment question incorrectly (and needing one more column for this week anyhow), John moved across the lobby to the marine guard booth. He salvaged Todd Marcus's name from the touch football game on Margaret Island a thousand years earlier. The marine pushed a button that permitted his voice to squawk distortedly through the Plexiglas wall of the guard station.

III.

SCOTT HAD MADE THIS TRIP BEFORE, WITH NERVOUS GIRLS IN OTHER worlds. He had traveled back in time with them, had entered a childhood home with a college or post-college girlfriend of some maturity or style and then watched in happiness as she split in two: into a girl younger and younger the further they penetrated the house, and into a woman made somehow strange by the experience. He watched in scientific wonder as they grew shy or uneasy or punchy or aroused or irritable. Best of all, when closely watched, these symptoms grew more acute, so that by merely walking very slowly down a hall, turning his head very slowly from a photograph of sweetheart in tears on Daddy's lap, age three, to sweetheart standing right there, looking peculiar, almost nauseous, age twenty-three, he could induce even *more* peculiar nausea without himself ever feeling a thing but scientific splendor and a certain frothy omniscience.

Sweetheart herself—so stylish, sultry, self-contained just this morning—would weaken, diminish ever so slightly, under the glare of swimming trophies, stuffed animals permanently alert in plush formation, dollhouses, ribbons for horseback riding, collages of photos of good times with grade-school pals, pasted with significant one-word clippings from teen magazines: BOYSHEART-SECRET. He would stand behind sweetheart and kiss her neck, catching her eye straight in front of him in the same pink-framed mirror in which she had first learned to braid her nine-year-old hair, in which Mom had floated over her shoulder and stroked her head and reassured the crying thirteen-year-old that she *was* beautiful, so very beautiful no matter what those other silly children (who were just jealous) said.

To see the bedspread she chose when she was twelve, which had served her for all the years before him. Did she exist before they met? How truly strange that she did, and that she looked like that, that she wore that skirt and played with these toys and entertained those friends and imagined this or that future for herself and butterflied her way to third place in the girls under-fourteen 4 x 100 relays, when really, all those years, she was sitting warm in her cocoon becoming a butterfly for him.

With each room they grew more and more uncomfortable, which he found more and more arousing. Sweetheart would slow down and linger to avoid entering the most embarrassing rooms, or speed up and try to pull him away when she saw something in his eye, some laughter or new understanding as he fingered and inspected the little-girl lives trapped in the hardened amber of her bedroom.

After these little history museums, they would approach the central chamber, her parents' room, where there could be no question that something would happen on someone else's conjugal bed, the very soil whence she had blossomed.

Today he received his threshold kiss just outside the door, and then the key turned and the door squeaked open and the hallway awaited him and he already knew what he would find. But he did not find it, and its absence made him light-headed.

There were photos in the hall, but none of her. Here an older brother, an officer in the Hungarian Army. There a black-and-white of (late) Dad, bowing his head as a ribbon was hung around his white neck. And this must be Grandfather here—ah, happy days with army buddies, buddies from different armies, including, ah yes, I suppose that would be the case.

He turned to her, but this time no embarrassment awaited him. She looked up at him with the same smile and affection she always showed, but today, something more, something like an inspection of *him*, some curiosity as she watched him examine her family's photographic residue. A glass case: That same ribbon Dad was bowing his head to accept just over there, a medal stamped with Hungarian words and a bust of, ah yes, I suppose that would be the case.

There were no horseback-riding prizes, no trophies for swimming, just more pictures of a strange-looking family incapable of smiling for photographers. Whenever Scott began to speed up for the next room, she slowed him down, made him linger, slid her arm through his, pulled him close, and watched as he looked.

She made him look at every room. There had been five of them here once. With two elder brothers gone and father dead, now only Mária lived there with her mother and three cats. The apartment was smaller than any place he'd ever known a family to be raised, and he inferred, wrongly, poverty. The brothers' little cube was unchanged since their departures: no rock star posters or college pennants, just stern young soldiers, official portraits in plain picture frames, old dumbbells and elastic bands with handles, a few books in Hungarian and Russian, and a small bulletin board pinned with snapshots of tanks and artillery pieces and jet fighters.

She's just like me, he thought. She comes from nothing, too, a stranger to these people who surrounded her from birth. She had never looked so beautiful as at that very moment, in front of a picture of a Russian attack jet unfurling sharp vapor. He had finally found the only other citizen of his country.

Her room was smaller still, painted a light blue some time ago. The bed, the chair, the desk, the shelves crowded with illegible books, the weird Eastern European crafts and dolls made of un-plush, unlovable substances. On her desk sat the homework he had himself assigned her. On her little bulletin board were stuck two pictures of Miami and one of Venice Beach cut from a magazine; a reproduction of a Manet; a black-and-white picture postcard of a U.S. sailor kissing a woman in Times Square; a picture of a Rodin sculpture, plaster-white and erotic; three photos of her with friends, but none that showed a girl any younger than the woman he knew. On a small table next to the bed was a photo of him taken from a low angle: He was leaping in the air, nothing but blue sky and clouds behind him, flying like a god, his extended arms suspending him from an ascending American football (launched from out of frame by Mark Payton), while two hands (all that was visible of his brother) clutched uselessly at Scott's old college T-shirt, in a vain effort to pull him back to earth. "I wish I could show you my childhood bedroom right now."

"I would like this very much."

"No, you'd hate it, but you'd understand why we're so perfect together."

She smiled and pulled him past the chair and desk her grandmother had taken from a neighboring apartment when the residents moved away (leaving all their belongings behind), pulled him toward her mother's old single bed, its intricately carved headboard a distinct luxury and, to a trained eye, evidence of privilege and unusual buying power.

IV.

LATER, WITH CROWDS STILL MILLING AROUND VÁCI UTCA AS GRATES WERE pulled over windows and as peasant women began gathering off the pavement the scarves and fleece-lined vests they had not sold that day, and with the sun low enough to stretch the ice-cream vendor's shadow all the way to the end of the street, John reported to the first of the two dates he had arranged that morning. He shrank, notebook in hand, into a booth at the New York Amerikai Pizza Place Étterem, and greeted Gunnery Sergeant Todd Marcus and his three comrades, the men he hoped could teach him something elemental (if undeniably foreign) about Emily.

With their identical crew cuts, polo shirts, and Bermuda shorts, the four marines thrilled the new restaurant's young management with the priceless American authenticity they exuded. The five men poured pitchers of Czech beer and pulled apart unwilling slices of pizza decorated with ham, corn, canned pineapple chunks, tiny frozen rock shrimp, whole fried eggs, blood sausage, paprika, and other standbys of New York pizzerias. John, tipping back the press fedora Mark had given him, flipped through his notebook and settled on one of the very few questions he had managed to think of all afternoon.

"Okay, so are you guys all into *Rambo?*"

Through gulps of pilsner and melting cheese, three marines made derisive comments: *pretty cool but unrealistic . . . all about ego . . . totally stupid.* Gunnery Sergeant Marcus added, "I've read some of it, but I prefer Verlaine," and John did not quite see what he meant.

"Okay, look. Here's what I want to write about. You guys are marines, soldiers, trained to kill. I want to write about what that means to you. About, you know, duty and courage and death. All that stuff. That sort of deal." John looked from one to another expectantly. Kurt, a twenty-two-year-old sergeant, very politely excused himself and went to the counter for hot pepper flakes.

"Dude, get napkins," said Luis.

John began again. "So what would you guys fight for?"

The chewing paused to allow for the securing of more slices and disbursement of more beer, and John thought he could see something amused or scornful in Todd's expression. "I gotta tell you," said Kurt, returning from his forage. "I love this place. Craziest pizza I've ever seen, but I do love this place."

"Yeah, okay, but seriously. What would you guys fight for?"

"You mean, like, what are we paid?" asked Danny.

"Not much, dude," said Kurt. "Way below minimum wage."

"No, no, what would you *fight* for? What *causes?* You might die, right, in a war?" He turned from one placid chewing face to another. "So what would get you out of the foxhole?"

The feeding military men said nothing until, at last, Luis—a particularly muscular Latino-Wisconsinite of twenty—wiped his mouth and looked at John as if he had to explain something to a child. "Dude, dude, no. That's not cool. First of all, nobody at this table would die. We take care of each other. And then, so second, it's not like you can choose, you know. It's not, like, *optional.* We don't get to vote on it. We're the *Corps,* man. And I thank God for the privilege." He pulled another slice from the tray and wound the straggling, sagging cheese around his index finger.

Kurt nodded. "Jack, when you sign up, you say, 'I'm yours, man.' And, besides, the officers know what's what."

"Right. Of course," John said. He could not think of another question. The three across the table were all looking high over his head at pop music videos playing mutely on three TV screens behind him. "But maybe an example," John tapped his teeth with his pen. "Okay, Hitler was bad, obviously, but what about—"

"Madonna was better-looking when she did 'Like a Virgin,' " said Kurt.

"If the Russians invaded Latvia, would you give your life to save it?"

"I'd do Madonna to save Edlatvia."

"I'd invade Slovakia, Slovenia, and Slavonia to do Madonna."

Todd spoke quietly: "The world works because people—bad people, John—believe we'd fight for anything the president says we'll fight for. We're the best-equipped, best-trained fighting force in the world, and that about covers that, as my mom used to say."

"Dude!" The soldiers slapped greasy hands. "Yo, yo, write that down!"

"Hey, will your paper pay for another pizza?"

John struggled to rephrase his question, but the more he thought about it, the less he was able to hold on to it. It had seemed obvious—as he sat in the Gerbeaud drowsily preparing for this interview and preplaying the definitive date that would follow it—that the marines would quickly see things as he did, would agree that war was total futile insanity, that (short of defending rape-threatened loved ones or something) *nothing* was worth dying for, that they were gambling their limbs and blood to pay for college or to learn electronics, and the resulting column would be called something like "You Bet Your Life!"

He would go to war for Emily, of course, silently answering his own question as the men obscenely derided the video of a Spanish pop singer dressed as a toreador weeping over the naked dead body of a woman with the head of a bull, a sword stuck between her lovely shoulder blades. Not only to *protect* Emily, but if she just *asked* him to go to war, he would. He would fight and kill if she would watch. What would she want to see him do? He could sit behind a machine gun, grit his teeth, shake as the force of his weapon tore into wave after wave of oncoming men, shredding them, yanking their arms up and their heads back, skewing their bodies into intriguing zigzags. Was she still watching him? Then he could fight close, crack the butt of his rifle against another man's face, crush his nose, rupture his eye, crumple his jaw, and, when the enemy fell and tried to cover his head with his hands, John could shatter the skull at the temple, which, he had once heard, is only the thickness of an eggshell, drive shards of bone into the man's brain and continue pounding still. Would she watch? Would she stand close, stand somehow out of danger but right next to him, close enough so that he could feel her breath in his ear, urging him on, pleading with a soft sigh that he not finish yet? Could he fall on top of an enemy, pull back his head by the hair, drag the blade across the neck, feel the tight skin at the throat give and peel away, uncurl from the blade like paper yielding to flame?

"You got any more questions, guy?"

Three of the marines departed together, but Todd asked John which way he was headed. With an hour to kill before his date, he and the marine walked toward the Corsó. "Don't feel bad. You can't be too surprised you don't get the answers you're looking for. Pacifists don't usually enlist. At least not in the Corps." Todd walked with his hands in his shorts pockets and happily inspected the buildings, the good views, qualifying female pedestrians. "You ever notice I'm the only black man in Budapest?"

John reflexively turned his head to scan the crowds. "Are you? I suppose I hadn't—no, there's a jazz singer, a bald guy. There're two of you. Does it bug you?"

"No. I'm exotic here. That's cool. I was posted at the embassy in the Sudan before this. Down there, I was just another well-armed black guy. So this is all right."

They reached the riverfront. Docked below them, casino boats lit up the July evening haze, and across the river the lights of Castle Hill floated over the tourist funicular creeping up and down the slope.

"Hey, newspaperman, do you know how many men died at Verdun?"

"World War One? No idea."

"Six hundred thousand in four months. About five thousand a day. About three or four guys every second, for four months. The English used to let guys from the same towns stay in the same units together, as a recruitment incentive. You know: 'Sign up with your chums and you can go off together on the great adventure.' " John had no idea what Todd was driving at, and found it difficult to concentrate on the details of World War One while the marine was smiling at every passing woman. Todd said "Hey there" to a blonde. He walked backward to watch her receding figure melt into the crowd, and she looked at him over her shoulder and fluttered her fingers at the huge, dark foreigner. Todd waved and laughed and returned to forward motion. "It kills me," he said. "I can't fraternize with listed nationals, and these sweet little Hungarians are still listed. Can you believe that? Still officially Red. That's a nice view, isn't it?" Todd pointed to the Chain Bridge just as its strung lights illuminated and buzzed white against the lemon-lime and pigeon sky. The wind snapped alive the canvas tarps that—until sandblasters and masons could be paid for—modestly covered the Communist emblems carved into the highest points of the bridge's stone arches.

The two men sat on a wooden bench in front of the modern hotels that had replaced the Hungaria, Carlton, and Bristol (all bombed to pieces), and they watched the passing girls and the antics of a sparsely talented sidewalk caricaturist, all of whose scribbled examples of movie stars seemed about the same: buck teeth, rippling waves of jaw muscle, tiny little legs. Todd smiled at two women strolling arm in arm. "You can tell by their clothes," he said. "The trick is to find Western European or American tourists. *Those* you can fraternize with. And with them you're exotic, because you live here but you're not Hungarian, so you're not *too* exotic." He shifted his weight. "So after a battle like Verdun, you could lose a whole village of English guys—everybody. They signed up together, they trained together, their unit went to the Somme together, they got stuck in the mud together, and—boom. Bad luck. The village now has no men between eighteen and forty. In one second. Every son, boyfriend, brother, you know. Boom."

John was pleased at last to have won, to hear a soldier admit that war was useless. Now he could explain to Emily his principled refusal to enlist. He pulled out his notebook, and Todd continued: "Who thought up that policy? Honestly makes you wonder about the English, you know? Whoa, don't write that." Todd's fingers tapped a martial rhythm against the bench's wooden slats. "But really, it's like they *wanted* to turn people against the war. I'm always amazed there wasn't a big protest thing during the First one. Of course, they were a little queasy about jumping into the Second."

"All right then," John pursued as Todd moved the drumming to his leg. "So how can you not wonder what's worth fighting for? Those guys from the same village. They all die one day for *nothing*. Verdun was basically a draw, right? Six hundred thousand meaningless deaths. How can you know all that history and still enlist in the marines?"

Todd smiled at John serenely, with parental amusement. "They didn't die for nothing. I didn't say that. That's not my point at all. They died in one small action of a draw that tore the hell out of the German Army too. If they hadn't been there and fought, it might not have been a draw."

"Who cares? Dead at twenty-four from, from *mustard gas*? Under a general who waged a trench war because that's what he learned twenty years before? Did you see her? She's definitely not Hungarian. But dead at twenty-four: no wife, no growing old, no kids. And for what? Who cares? World War One is like a history-class joke: *Nobody* knows why it was fought. It's positively medieval."

Todd listened politely but now answered with some heat. "That's not his point of view, the English kid. That's yours and you've got no right to it. You sat at the pizza place and you acted like my guys should make decisions based on what people like you will think of them in seventy-five years. *That's* how people should think? You don't know what those English guys fought for; they were individual people. It's way too easy for you to say World War One was a joke. You're not Belgian. Your farm wasn't overrun by Germans. Your sister wasn't raped by them. Name any war you want. Every single war—somebody had a damn good reason at the time, and they don't owe *you* an explanation for it. Here's what I know, John, and you can print this and you can write one of your smart-ass columns around it, okay? You ready? Here goes: There is no 'grand scheme of things.' That's just a bullshit disguise for cowards. The present has no right to judge the past. Or to act in order to win the future's approval. They're both irrelevant when an enemy's at the door. *That's* why I'm a marine. Whoa, how about that one? Do you think she's Hungarian? Hold on a sec." The marine trotted toward a young blonde smoking a cigarette and leaning against the railing, one leg crossed behind an ankle bare under black capri pants. John watched their conversation, too distant to be audible, saw the girl nod, blow smoke away from Todd, and shift the cigarette to shake his hand. Minutes passed before the marine returned to John, and she waited.

"Good talking to you, man. Check this out: That girl *is* Belgian. How about that? I do enjoy fraternizing with the unlisted." He shook John's hand and returned to his Flemish milkmaid, offered her his arm, rescued her from the invading Krauts, guided her along the riverside, and disappeared into the protective cover of tourists, caricaturists, street performers.

V.

SHE EXTENDED AN ANCIENT HAND, THEN KISSED EMILY ON EACH CHEEK. "The famous Miss Oliver! I have heard so very much of your charms." Nádja's raspy voice carried an archness that bothered John.

He had invited Emily here so she would see the sophisticated (more relevant, more authentic, more European, more engaged, more whatever) life he led when away from their mutual friends. He had invited Emily here so that Nádja could judge her for him and either cure him of his affliction or tell him how to win her. He wanted Emily to sit next to him while Nádja lifted them both high in the air, and they would sit together in the old woman's palm and let their heads brush, side by side, against the ceiling, and from the same high vantage point she would see what he had seen and all manner of things would be clear.

Instead, after a few minutes of sterile, sputtering small talk, John despaired: The decrepit old pianist was not strong enough to hoist them both; she was too feeble tonight to lift even him alone. He grew grouchy to find himself in a rotten jazz bar between a tiresome old woman and a girl who tolerated his presence only out of some Midwestern politeness. Waiting for Nádja to find Emily ideal, waiting for Emily to find Nádja significant, he found them both insufferable. He offered to go for drinks and, as he emptied his first two Unicums standing out of sight at the bar, he was slow in returning.

When he did, the two women were discussing his recent column about Nádja herself. "Dear John Price," she said, and patted his hand in exchange for her Rob Roy. "You made me sound rather too intriguing, I think, but that is a very petty complaint, isn't it? Far better to be too grand than too dull, yes?" She smiled at Emily. "Your friend was just claiming that she is some sort of servant to your ambassador."

"Well, not a servant precisely."

"Then what, precisely?" Nádja clinked Emily's glass with her own and her lips turned up so sharply, she seemed about to burst out laughing.

"Well, I manage his schedules, and I do run a few errands, of course."

"My dear, why would they have a lovely girl like you do such things?"

"I'm a very detail-orientated person . . . I—"

"Oh, let me just speculate for an instant: You meet all sorts of fascinating people, and they are amazed that the ambassador's servant is such a charming and well-informed girl. And these fascinating people open their hearts to you all the time."

"I think I am a good listener. I really do. And I do meet some interesting people, but really it's more like arranging luncheon place-settings."

"Are you hearing this, John Price?" And Nádja did begin to laugh, leaning in to touch his hand as if they were in on the same joke. "This is too delicious." John didn't recognize any of this dialogue from his visions for the evening, suspected Nádja might already be drunk.

Emily asked Nádja about her piano training.

"We can talk about me if you want, my dear, but it won't help. Fine: I am mostly self-taught, from records, from listening to others. But"—John leaned imperceptibly closer, hoped that but was the sound of Nádja gaining strength— "but I did have one teacher when I was a girl here in Budapest, and he was an interesting man . . ." John breathed deeply, recognized the majestic opening of an ancient gate, the slow revelation of great gardens within. He looked expectantly from Nádja to Emily and back again, somehow feeling that he was the indirect subject of conversation and was about to be vindicated in everyone's estimation. "He was a remarkable man, Konrád. I was ten and he was perhaps thirty-three when he began to teach to me my scales and positions and how to read the notes. He was an elegant man who came into difficult money time in the years following the First War. This would be about, I suppose, 1925. He was a spy, you see, in the First War." She smiled at Emily, paused for interruptions, but none came. "As a young piano student, he was living in France when the war began. He offered his services as a teacher of children, described himself to their parents as a refugee of the wicked Hapsburgs, dreamed up some story of confiscated family land, mistreatment at the hands of jealous rivals, refused to return until his family's holdings are released, and such forth. And by the sheerest coincidence, as you can imagine, Miss Oliver, these children's papas did tend to be French military and government men. A dapper young Hungarian, slightly bohemian, a Chopin type, but still, it would seem, of good breeding and money. They took to him quickly, the parents. And, of course, one does tend to recommend good servants to friends, also military and government, of course."

Emily sipped her spritzer and listened with her charming and flattering intensity. John heard other noise in the room yield and dissipate into a faint rumble far below him.

"Konrád would keep his eyes and ears open. He peeked into desks and rubbish bins when opportunity presented. And he was able to shape allies of his little students, of course. Oh yes, the children hear things, too, and think nothing of sharing it with their friend the piano teacher. Secrets have different qualities to different people, as I'm sure you know." John was glad Nádja was making such an effort to impress Emily, felt she was granting him her approval and pulling out all her best stuff to deliver the girl's heart to him. "And so revealing a secret has different qualities, too. Two people might reveal the same secret: For one, the revelation is a betrayal; for the other, a game. A child's game. Of course, when a child has someone *else's* secret, well, that is merely the currency of conversation, a few guineas to buy her some attention and respect. Konrád knew this, and he was very generous and serious in granting of attention and respect. That was his greatest gift, really, not piano playing or teaching. He was the perfect spy of children, could take the dullest child seriously, delicately. Do you know the type?" She sipped her Rob Roy and flushed a cigarette from its pack. John moved quickly to light it for her.

"Oh, I think we all know that type," John replied to the absurd question, and he was pleased that Emily laughed with him. Nádja breathed out smoke, and John watched it curl and weave itself into a net of blue-gray wisps around his circle, watched it filter and softly blur every other person in the club until they became mere color and background.

"He made the child feel important, all grown up. When little Sophie or Geneviève told Konrád that Papa—who was, say, a colonel in a particular regiment—was going to take a trip to Marseilles in a week, Konrád told her he was duly impressed at the maturity of her conversation. And the wives! Oh yes, of course, the wives. They too found something in the handsome young *artiste*, the *amateur* of music, the disinherited and dashing nobleman. Here, again, secrecy is a variable quality. To these wives the piano instructor was a figure of great glamour, but more important, their nearly final opportunity to enjoy life in the *open*. For these women, married to secretive men, the idea of carrying on a secret affair was an act of candor, not secrecy. With Konrád in their beds, they could speak of anything they wished; he was just the piano teacher, what difference could it make? They did not have to maintain the boring, boring caution and discretion that made up their daily lives and drove them nearly mad with tedium and isolation, you see. These women ached to be whimsical, spontaneous, and, as I am quite sure you know, this is not at all possible if you must watch your every word, screen your every thought." She paused and tasted her Rob Roy. "Dear girl, I hope I am not boring you with things you already know?"

"Not at *all*," said Emily with great and surprised enthusiasm. "This is amazingly interesting. Go on, *please*."

Nádja laughed. "These women lived under this terrible burden of their silly husbands' state secrets, and secret burdens, you know, of course, make you old very quickly. These women were reaching that terrible point where youth is harder and harder to see in the mirror. It requires special lights and long coaxing to draw it out from its ever more numerous hiding places. Those are very bad years. You will not like them, Miss Oliver. You know the French words *Un secret, c'est une ride?* Every secret is a wrinkle. With Konrád, they would cast them all off and they would feel young again. They wished to hold the attention of this young man who could have his choice of women. And they think to themselves, Why should he bother with me, an aging wife of a bureaucrat in the naval ministry? Because she could interest him with funny stories about her husband's colleagues or cynical stories about their incompetent projects and stubborn superiors or disgusted stories of how badly certain elements of the fleet were equipped. Of course, these women were not really disgusted with such things; they merely repeated their husbands' talk. Husbands' secrets became wives' coin for conversation became secrets again for Konrád to dispatch to Vienna, to become coin for him."

Nádja apologized for not doing so earlier and offered Emily a cigarette. The girl shook her head and asked, "So Konrád"—her Midwestern accent produced a decidedly un-Magyar *Conrad*—"told you all this sexy psychology when you were *ten?*"

"No, no, my dear. I learned all of this over quite a spell. We were friends for many years, and more than friends for a brief and very happy period."

"Of course, of course," murmured John, happy to have returned to Nádja's world, where things *happened*. Nothing (at least nothing serious) happened in his world. He listened to Nádja's past and wished he could reach Emily's hand from where he sat. The lightest touch of her fingers in this air, at this altitude, would burn him and leave a mark forever.

"Did he help the war effort?"

"Your question is a good one, my girl, but only if, as I suspect, you already know the answer: He was of very little use, I would think. Not much accomplished. He always felt his information should have been put to better use, but the empire that paid him was already crumbling, even before the war. His little tidbits snatched from talentless children and unhappy wives could not begin to change that. He certainly didn't change the outcome of the war, did he? I don't know if his carefully coded messages ever saved a Hungarian life, or won a battle, or even improved those ghastly terms of surrender. That is always the plight of the spy: How clever they can be, but how little they can do," she added with a sharp gust of laughter. "They are always surrounded by lovers, though, interestingly. It is only natural, but a terrible cock-up of nature. They are like some infertile animal with beautiful coloring. They attract only because they seem to have a purpose, but they are really the most *useless* species. It is a terribly silly way to waste one's good years."

John watched Emily's eyes fill with sympathy. "That's kind of terrible. Was he sad when you knew him? Not to have helped more with the war?"

"Sad?" Nádja granted the question a moment's silent attention. "For being a failed spy? No, I shouldn't think so. Dear, the smartest of them grow to realize it is hardly worth bothering with, and he was rather smart. He was sad, I suppose, for some things. He was always unhappy about money. I know he feared growing old. He feared losing piano dexterity and his good looks, which I must say he never did do. He hated the French to the end of his days. People used to call Pest the Paris of the East, you know, and whenever he heard this, he would scowl and bellow, 'Paris should be so lucky!' But to be sad because he did not save his world from destruction by sleeping with middle-aged women and digging in the trash and giving candy to children? Really, Miss Oliver, do you find this sad?"

"Oh, *please* call me Emily."

The band that evening was entirely Hungarian, older men, professors of the music academy. The trumpeter wore a long beard, like a Russian Orthodox monk; from the nose to the chest, he resembled a hand puppet. He murmured something Hungarian into the microphone, and some of the crowd laughed. John—feeling abnormally alert to every vibration around him, awake to every nuance in the room—swirled his Unicum; the twirled liqueur painted melting Romanesque arches on the inside of the glass. The bandleader counted off a tune. It was jazz, but distinctly Hungarian; its rhythm sparkled with shards of something foreign, kicks of Hungarian folk music, the sound of caped horsemen. The melody was in a minor key, with the strange intervals and mournful feel of Eastern European dances, but with the rapid swinging bursts and twisting lines of bebop jazz. John watched the obese pianist perspire to produce this strange new music. He felt that his connection to other people, even to objects, had become, if only temporarily, close but beautiful, not at all constricting. Even his understanding that this feeling was temporary felt like heightened clarity.

"Oh, of course, yes, I've known several spies over the years. They don't have to tell me, though some did. They are not usually difficult to spot, paradoxically. I have always found them—Konrád too—to be rather . . . well, it is difficult work, I suppose, but it is not for people who wish to live a full life, with closeness to others and to experience. I think they are all a little strange. A little *sad*, to use your word."

"I suppose so," said Emily. "I suppose that must be true."

John, his eyes on the ceiling, blew a column of smoke directly upward and nodded: true, true, difficult work, strange and sad. Emily sipped her drink and listened to the band, then asked Nádja if she had ever visited the United States. "Oh yes. I lived for many years in San Francisco, playing piano and—very much like I am to believe you do for your ambassador—I was organizing the social calendar of a South Vietnamese general who was living there in a strangely giddy exile after your war. He threw so many, many parties. I remember once . . ." John grinned at Emily: Nádja was off again, in rare and wondrous form, bewitching her audience with another recollection, exquisitely told, satisfying in its construction, lyrical and glamorous, slightly improbable but nowhere near impossible. And John did not doubt its probability. Lives like Nádja's must exist; he had read enough to know this was true.

And so, having wished Nádja good night and complimented her interlude playing, accepted her thanks for the drinks and the column, having been enclosed by the thick and sticky July midnight, John was surprised and saddened to hear Emily express her amused disbelief. He was walking her home, crossing the Margaret Bridge toward Buda, and she thanked him warmly for introducing her to his friend. She had never met such a charming and entertaining "old woman." The term—*old woman*—set John on edge. He said a little testily, "That's not really a relevant description. The least relevant thing about her, don't you see that?"

"Okay, sorry. Jeez. How about *amazing liar?*" she offered with a laugh. "Come on, you're better than me at Sincerity, so don't tell me you don't see through this woman. She's a piano player who makes up stories. Good ones, okay. I can see why you like her. I liked her, too, she's very fun. I meant it when I thanked you for introducing me. But really, I mean, she's neat, but . . ." Emily stopped walking and looked John in the eye. "John, you cannot believe anything that woman tells you. Anything. She'd say anything to be good company. Or to test her skills or whatever. Anything." She watched him. "That's the thing with liars, I mean." She turned away and continued walking, left John standing perplexed for a moment behind her, watching her march on without him to the bridge's halfway point, where its gentle ascent subtly exhaled into a gentle descent.

His pain was out of proportion; he knew that right away. It made no real difference what these women thought of each other. But that she hadn't seen what John was in Nádja's company, and what Emily herself could be, that she hadn't been as he thought she had been just ten minutes earlier: This was a jabbing, breath-stealing pain. He ran, caught up with her, took her arm, turned her toward him. "Let me ask you something. Don't you *want* her to be telling the truth?" The traffic went silent and brushed soft lights across half of Emily's face, from cheek to nose, over and over again in irregular rhythm.

"What does that have to do with any—?"

"Everything. It has everything to do with everything. Don't you *want* that to be the world?" He was proud to be agitated, in defense not of Nádja but of the whole world she had given him.

Emily's face changed, relaxed into a kind of sympathy. "Oh, sweetheart, I don't want the world to *be* anything." John felt himself fighting to remain himself, fighting to take the word *sweetheart* as a lover, not as a nephew. "The world *is* and grown-ups react to it as best they can. It isn't made of funny stories."

He took Emily's hand. "Yes, but it's where you find—the world isn't just—doesn't it matter—" Finally, he just emitted a grunt, maddened frustration that smoked through his clenched teeth. "I was interviewing these soldiers tonight, your friends the marines. Nádja is the other side, the opposite of that. You can see that, can't you?"

"The marines? I'm not sure I follow you, no."

"Look there. Look!" John grabbed her shoulders and rotated her, faced her toward the Danube, stood next to her and pointed downriver where the Chain Bridge's lights had just switched off—the very moment Emily was speaking—and now left that monument lingering against the dark sky and water like an afterimage projected behind closed eyelids. "And that!" he said, gathering sureness, almost shoving her to look up at the gray-black silhouette of the extinguished palace set against the blue-black sky, almost nothing more than a palace-shaped absence of stars. "Those are real, Em. Those are the world right now. Our world. And so is Nádja. Her life is—that's how it ought—" His voice softened, shifted from excited to soothing. "And you're here with me in it." And his head inclined, and his hands held her face, and his lips found hers for a moment and another and another and one half a moment more, and he was inarguably right, right about all of it.

"No." She leaned away. "John." She pulled away from his hands. "That's not for us." She smiled and laughed, her standard technique to help boys gracefully escape their embarrassment or anger at this moment. "We're both an Unicum or two over the limit, young man, and it's a school night. I'll walk myself home and you get some sleep. I'll catch up with you at the Gerbeaud. You can tell me what Nádja thinks up to say about me."

She's gone. John Price stands at the center, the highest point in the gently sighing arch of the Margaret Bridge, and he leans against the parapet, tries to focus his eyes on the stones of the Chain Bridge. He wishes they had been on that bridge, a few hundred yards downstream. That's where he would feel complete, where he belongs. There, she would have understood; that kiss would have made inevitable sense. After a while, he bites his lips, considers and rejects in turn going to visit his brother or Mark Payton or Charles Gábor. He pushes himself away from the steel railing, his hands gritty from the bolt heads they rested on. He walks back toward Pest, spits into the Danube.

VI.

A WEEK LATER, A FEW HOURS BEFORE GETTING LUXURIOUSLY DRUNK AT the Old Student with John, Charles submitted his rebelliously wordy report on the Horváth Press to the Presiding Vice, who read most of the first sentence of every paragraph, then had Zsuzsa fax it to New York: *My strongest recommen . . . As an opening maneuver in the Hungarian thea . . . With clear synergies with our . . . The attached data leads me to confidently predict more profitable sectors than current management env . . . Likely exits include: grow to suitable threshold for public offer on BP exchange, 18–24 months. Alternately, an industry consolidation is rated a "highly likely" in 6 analyst reports (attached), implying a highly probable M&A opp . . . Due to a historic alignment of rare circum . . . CM Gabor, Budapest Office.*

Charles then disappeared from view for nearly nine days, Saturday morning to Sunday evening. His secretary declared him out of town. His home answering machine spoke and claimed to listen but was unable to produce the man himself. He was absent from evenings at the Gerbeaud, nights at A Házam, and everywhere else. On Thursday night, John, desperate for a heterosexual man's view on Emily, took a tram and bus out to Charles's place in the hills and rang the bell. There were lights behind the curtains, but no one came to the door. On the seventh day of Charles's absence, John's answering machine coughed up this impersonation of the missing man: "There is never an end to it, God help me." Charles was noticeably slurring. "Is there an end to it, Johnny? God help me, I don't think there is." The next evening, Sunday, Charles rematerialized, dapper and reposeful on the Gerbeaud patio, smiling, stubbornly refusing to discuss the past week or the gray-haired couple with whom he had spent that endless week and then just dropped at Ferihegy Airport to catch their plane to Zurich, connecting to New York, connecting to Cleveland, thank sweet Jesus.

Early the next morning, he sat on the note from the Very Pathetic that had been waiting on his chair since Tuesday, four days after his report had made its own trip to New York:

Charlie—NYHQ fast on the pub q. Ixnay, puppy. No way, Hosay. The guy's not even Hungarian. He's an Austrian. It's an Austrian company, Charlie. No good having the first deal be about a bunch of Austrians, right? Gotta say: I think you should have caught this.

Charles leaned his forehead against the still-cool window and passed ten minutes in disgusted consideration of the VP's belief-beggaring stupidity. He then made a few notes on a yellow pad, drew a flurry of straight arrows with big, filled triangular heads that flew from one scribbled, abbreviated idea to the next, twice ending in ornately doodled question marks. It was half a plan, anyhow. He placed one call to a lawyer friend and another to the State Privatization Agency. Finally, after four more minutes of forced meditation while furiously waiting for an international dial tone, he was connected to Imre Horváth in Vienna. *"Jó napot, Horváth úr,"* he began brightly. *"Gábor Károly beszél. Jó hírem van* [I have some good news]."

"It's a little complicated, deal-structure-wise," Charles told John twelve hours later as the journalist lay on the office couch watching sunset change the colors of the glass sky behind Charles's head.

"The word you're struggling for is *lie.* You are *lying.* It's a *lie."*

"This is an ugly and overused term." Golden, heavenly sunbeams shot through silver clouds and lent his silhouette a spiky halo that forced John to squint. "Just loan me the credibility I am credibly entitled to, and everything will be fine. Check this out: I hired a cleaning lady, a cook, and a gardener this weekend," he said. "I have a *staff.* Is that not the funniest thing you have ever heard? A staff. The point is, just help me convince Horváth I'm the guy, and we'll explain the firm's sad position later. When the humor of it will be more readily comprehensible."

"I UNDERSTAND FROM our mutual friend you are a rising and a respected journalist," Imre Horváth said as John sat, three days later, to join Charles and the publisher for the last half of their meeting over the Gerbeaud's coffee and milk, respectively. "My family has been in your newspaper business for six generations," the Hungarian continued. "I expect we shall return to this line of work in Budapest before long." As he sat in the heat of the patio, John's very first response to Imre—less than thirty seconds after meeting him—was awe, an uncontrollable emotional and physical response that John felt in his spine and his tailbone, his palms and forearms, his cheeks and his kidneys. He was taken by surprise after Charles's mocking descriptions of Imre; in person, the Hungarian was an imposing figure, and the gossipy snippets of history and suffering Charles had mentioned placed Imre in a different category of humanity altogether.

Of course, Imre certainly took *himself* seriously, John realized a minute later in an effort to break free of this stifling, unacceptable awe, this sharp envy. Imre was talking about something very prosaic—old newspaper-production methods—but John's mind strolled through a prairie landscape of jealousy of those who proved themselves in the ultimate test of their era and came up worthy. "There was a moment of surprise, yes, when the AVO burst through the door," Imre was saying, and John's envy quickly disguised itself for its owner's benefit as something much more dignified and palatable: scorn: John resented Imre's failed and transparent efforts to coax envy and admiration. He began noticing with satisfaction the holes in Imre's stories, the richness of his suit, his monumental will to impress.

And so now John undertook with pleasure the mission Charles had assigned him. The lies blossomed effortlessly. He pushed the conversation as far and as fast as he could, dared Charles to keep up. "Who's that playwright you are always quoting, Károly?" John asked him. "The fellow with the biting satires? Horn, isn't it? What was the one you read aloud to us here last week?"

"Marvelous!" exclaimed Horváth. "His works are printed by our family since their first editions, all of the plays."

"Whatever happened to your plan to finance a theater, Károly?" John asked Charles. "Károly has often told me, Imre, that it was a love of culture, an aspiration to civility, that brought him into venture finance in the first place," John heard himself saying as Charles bit into a pastry. "Quixotic but true. I want my profile of his work to show how he's always hoped to use capital to promote culture. So far he's been disappointed at the common thinking of those who surround him. I think he doesn't realize how rare is the clarity of his vision."

"We are relying upon it," Imre intoned, "and I am glad to hear I am not the only one who sees this strength and promise in our Károly. Your readers, Mr. Price, should be interested in the successes that can come to a man of youth, energy, and culture as Mr. Gábor is. Particularly now. Particularly in Hungary."

"Precisely. What I find striking"—John decided to use Charles's nom de guerre as often as possible—"is Károly's literacy in a profession that too often stresses the bottom line. Károly is an old-fashioned type, a European type, but a remarkable amalgamation of his Hungarian culture and his American upbringing." He paused to light a cigarette and pretended to search for the right words, though he felt tremendously articulate; he could have produced great chunks of this stuff without stopping for breath. "A gentleman first, a businessman second, our Károly. I am fascinated to see if there is room for such a specimen as Károly in the world today. One can hope, but dare not be certain."

"Take it easy, killer," Charles said when Imre excused himself. "Let's play it a hair slower. You sound like his Hungarian sycophants back in Vienna."

"Károly tells me you are returning to Hungary with quite extensive plans," said John when Imre had returned.

"We do indeed have projects in mind, sir. He and I were discussing different possibilities prior to your arrival." He crossed his arms and leaned slightly toward John. "I suspect our firm's history and future would be of great interest to your readership," he said with a serious expression, and John silently swore not to break eye contact first, though it became almost impossible not to flinch from the blue stare. The three men left the Gerbeaud, walked up Andrássy út, and pursued their crisscrossing agendas: Imre attempted to tell his firm's newsworthy story to the American reporter; John attempted to sell a burnished, partnership-worthy version of his newly Hungarianized friend to the old businessman while keeping himself amused; Charles helped them both.

Soon, to his relief, John could feel his tenacious awe of Horváth entirely swept away by a refreshing, astringent breeze of unadulterated disgust, though John called it clarity. He cleared his mind of the disconcerting smoke and dust of Imre's tragic life and smug moral worth and instead began to see through him. The man's stories were egotistical parables, clumsy and garish and self-serving. Horváth had obviously crafted this idea of himself and was now forcing it on everyone: "Ohhh, sir, if one thing was clear to me, it was a responsibility. Since I am a very small boy, I was told of my family's responsibility to our country and the burden I would bear. 'The people's memory,' Boldizsár Kis called our press, and my father repeated this to me often. One day I would be responsible for maintaining this memory, I knew. Do you know Kis? No? A great revolutionary leader for democracy. Kis wrote a poem to say our press told the story of the Hungarian people, to themselves and to the world. We remember for a nation. Like you Jews with your Passover, I believe. But our story is still being written, it is not ancient history about pharaohs."

And, with that, before they had even passed the Opera House in their stroll up Andrássy, John had the old man cut and dried and pasted in a notebook, just as Charles had described him: pompous, self-important, proud of the badge of righteousness that history's lottery had randomly granted him, and (Charles had neglected to mention) probably a rank anti-Semite.

But two nights later, John sat to Imre's left at a dinner arranged by Charles and his thoughts were much more difficult to corral. "Mr. Horváth, this is my friend Mark Payton, the famed Canadian social theorist and historian" was how Gábor had introduced the last arrival, and from the moment the four of them sat down in a private dining room at a Swiss restaurant in the City Park, John noted the great speed at which his disgust for Horváth alternated with fascination and then quiet stretches of pure respect, noted his inability to assign

Imre to definitive nonseriousness. "If you pay attention, you can discover much about yourself in a work camp," Horváth was saying to Mark at one moment, and John felt small and useless in the presence of a man who had lived such a life. "My press was at the very center of the revolution in 1956," Imre said to the gloomy Canadian only minutes later, and John rolled his eyes.

The restaurant sat in the shadow of Vajdahunyad, the park's nineteenth-century castle, and the private dining room had windows on two sides: The castle's turret loomed out one, and out the other the moon had just begun with a wide smile its slow, monthly yawn. Charles dealt with the wait staff in a peremptory and impressive manner, every gesture a demonstration of his executive skill. He had selected the wines carefully the day before and now raised his first glass of Meursault in a toast to the future of the Horváth Press and to the memory of the Hungarian people. Four glasses met and sang under the shimmering prisms and electric hum of the chandelier.

Despite John's doubts about the Canadian's stability under pressure, Mark had been assigned the role of Charles's trusted cultural adviser. He interpreted this role practically as a mime; he spoke little, just pursued Imre's own history with a predictable, gulping avidity. "An author came to me after the war." Imre crossed his arms and leaned toward Mark but looked off over his head in search of the past. "He had been published by the press in my *grandfather's* day, if you can believe such a thing. My father was forced to cancel his contract, though, because his works really did not sell at all, though I know my father would have wanted to keep him, despite the losses. This fellow kept very impressive company in his life, belonged to clubs of writers and artists, you know, was of a very influential, important generation . . ." Mark lightly touched the tips of his right-hand fingers to his left palm and nodded slowly.

Four waiters brought the first course, Balaton fogas filleted and braised *en pipérade,* as Charles had dictated the day before in consultation with the chef. The staff placed the domed dishes simultaneously in front of all four men and on a signal removed the covers with a flourish. Over the next three and a half hours, the wine changed color again and again, grew heavy, then smoky, then viscous and sweet. Course followed course until the fish starter was as far distant as the memory of a childhood picnic lunch, a whiff of sauce and a remembered snippet of talk, an instant of passing light on a companion's face. From fish to greens to soup to meat to tart to cheese and fruit, John tried to stand straight against Imre's great gusts until the lectures and the monumental histories, the provocative rhetorical questions all spun into one long monologue, which seemed to John the next day to have swallowed weeks rather than hours, and been addressed to him alone, a long immersion in Imre that John could not conceivably have resisted:

"A work of art, Mr. Price. That is our life, everyone's life can be this. I think you are perhaps like this, too. I think we are not so very different, you and I." John silently hoped this might be true. "A life must make sense, it must have a beginning where its purpose is revealed, a middle where its purpose is achieved, and an end where its purpose is made clear to another, to the next generation, who can maintain that purpose, transmit it." John suspected the man had said this before, knew he was talking like this now only for his press coverage, but at the same time he could not drive away the unwelcome and embarrassing, silly sensation that Imre was revealing something of the greatest importance, a moment John swore he would remember forever. "Great powers have been used to muddy my purpose. But I could not be diverted. I say this not as pride. I do not boast," he boasted, "but I say this as wonder: Such is life that I simply followed what I knew to be true and strength came to me." Courses had come and gone, but the re-education flowed uninterrupted, John now leaning close, his thumbnail propping his teeth apart. "I am telling my own story. They tried to take it from me, to tell their story instead, but they were beaten. That is the worst violence one man can do another, young sir. Do you see this? There is torture, but one can withstand that. There is prison, but that is not too much, either. But to steal another man's story is to steal his life, his purpose." He was going in circles, John noted, struggling to get out of Imre's grip and feel like an adult again.

"Youth can tolerate such meals," Imre was saying. "Mr. Payton here can drink four different wines and his expressions remain as calm and serious as when he begin. I have a very distant relation who entered a monkeyhouse, and he—no, this is not the word, is it?" he asked, and with the others laughed loudly, wiping his eyes. "Thank you, Károly. He went into a monastery," he said the word in three syllables, "and he taken vows to be a moderate ascetic. I don't think this would be suiting any of you, except perhaps you, Mr. Payton," and everyone laughed again.

"A moderate ascetic? That's a little extreme, isn't it?" asked John. "If you're into denying yourself things and then you deny yourself even the pleasure of denying yourself things, that's got to hurt." Imre laughed the loudest, and John felt a rush of pride.

"What is the word in English, John—" Charles asked with the hint of a Hungarian accent as the crumb-sprinkled dessert plates floated away and a third round of sweet Tokaj wine appeared in small glasses—"for . . ." Charles waved his hand in the air to capture the word, brush away distractions. *"Mi az angolul, hogy megelégedettség?"* he asked Imre, and Imre nodded and said in English, "Exactly, exactly so, Károly."

"I first drank Tokaj wine at the Gerbeaud with my mother. I remembered this when you and I first met there, Károly. Life was actually very pleasant in the 1930s here in Budapest. I fear I am beginning to speak in ways of my father. He always would say, 'If you did not live before the First World War, you cannot possibly know how pleasant life can be.' To be honest—"

"I'm sorry, but that's horseshit," said Mark, breaking a moody silence nearly half as old as the lengthy meal and knocking over an empty glass without noticing. "Complete horseshit."

"Shut up, Mark," snapped Charles.

"No, really. 'You cannot know how pleasant life could be if you did not live in Belgium before the First World War.' Victor Margaux, 1922. 'If you were not here in Virginia before the War Between the States, you cannot imagine how pleasant life could be.' Josiah Burnham, 1870. Talleyrand twice, if you can stand it. First, 'He who did not live *before* the revolution did not know the sweetness of life,' and then, rethinking things, *'Qui n'a pas vécu* dans *les années voisines de 1789*—he who did not live *during* the revolution cannot know what is meant by the pleasure of life.' 'Sir, you cannot know what is meant by a pleasant life if you did not live in green England before those Germans came here to roost.' The Marquess of Westbroke, 1735. Horseshit, horseshit, horseshit." Mark's voice rose with each example, and a second glass, this one with remnants of an early-evening red wine, tumbled to the floor, sprinkling Horváth's loosened tie as it spun and dove.

"Imre, please excuse me for—" Charles began in Hungarian.

"No, no! Not at all!" Imre was staring at the Canadian in fascination.

"I tried to tell you he's been a little nuts," John laughed at Charles's efforts to remain calm as Mark fumbled to pick up a glass and refill it, horseshit-horseshit-horseshitting all the while.

"No, no." Imre grasped Mark's shoulder. "He is brilliant man and very right, our scholar in our little club. How do we expect to grow up and make a better world if we are all sadly aching for some other?"

"Exactly my point," said Mark, pouring and missing.

Imre grew distracted by a wine spot on his Hermès tie, then pulled himself away from it to stare at Charles with a raised eyebrow. "Fire," he said intently.

"Fire and a stomach to say, 'No more!' This is what youth offers, and I think today's Western youth more than any other. You who grew up with everything are ready now to demand more, to say no more!" He spoke to all three of them, and never had he seemed to John more of a performer and, what's more, a wonderful performer despite outrageously weak material: "I fear this country, our MK, has lost that stomach but we will come home, Károly and I, and we will give it to them. 'Here is your stomach back,' we will say!" He raised the first glass at hand, a water glass with a cigarette butt submarine diving and resurfacing under the command of an indecisive skipper. "To the Hungarian stomach and all you can teach it, men of the youth, men of the energy, men of West!"

Four glasses clinked and slightly spilled.

"Enough," said Imre, more dignified in his cups than the others. "Now we go home." Charles, the host, considered protesting this usurpation of his privileges but let it go as Imre said to him, "Tomorrow you and I must talk again."

They filed precariously down the stairs. The act of standing and moving shook all of them significantly, and they paraded in wobbly single-file silence into the empty main dining room, where, under lowered lighting and the sound of dishwashers both human and automated, tired waiters sat and stood smoking in unbuttoned, stained black vests and undone bow ties, dangling and symmetrical like bat-hide stoles. The restaurant's violinist and accordionist, in black-and-gold traditional costume, had put aside their instruments and now sat at a corner table deep in conversation, a single table lamp illuminating half of each of their faces. They turned their heads only slightly, darkening them, as the four drunks fumbled out the restaurant's door and the lock clicked behind them.

Fresh air and the smell of the park's trees shuffled the sensations in their heads and legs and stomachs. The men swam through the humidity and headed toward the towering gallery of Heroes' Square. For a minute or two longer no one spoke, until Imre bellowed into the night—not a word, just a youthful holler that sounded strange to all of them after the cacophony in the little dining room and the silence since. Charles laughed and yelled a nonsense grunt, too. "Horseshit!" the publisher shouted in response, in an accent that floated between Budapest and London, and he tousled Mark Payton's damp red hair. The Canadian laughed an odd, gasping laugh. "Horseshit!" he concurred at the top of his voice. They came into Heroes' Square, an empty, spotlit semicircle of enormous pillars and statues, arching over the top of Andrássy út.

John leaned against the cool rock of one of the statues' pediments and scratched his back against it. The conversation moved slowly, but he no longer followed it, just broke off pieces at random and held them briefly to his ear.

". . . how many times people want to buy this national memory, this responsibility of us, and it cannot be bought, all of us face this, this temptation, Károly, yes—" Imre bent back and gazed to the top of the horse-bound Magyar king prancing in the center of the square, bit the corner of his lip, and suddenly sneezed with explosive noise.

John walked slowly backward over the labyrinthine tiles of the square until his foot felt the curb behind him and he turned sharply to watch the cars gust right past him, close enough for him to touch their stumpy side-view mirrors as they blurred.

He entered the Blue Jazz alone sometime later, after one last glance: From across the street he saw Imre and Charles and Mark had put their arms around each other's shoulders and were performing an unsynchronized soft-shoe routine behind the traffic.

The interior of the club initially refused to focus. When it surrendered at last, he was relieved to see her at once. It must have been late: It was a Friday, but there were only a few people left: a game of pool, three smokers webbed in their own blue breath, the band—the bald Americans—at the bar taking their payment in food and drink, a couple newly in love in one corner, twisting around each other's lips and bodies like the two snakes on Caduceus's staff and, in another corner, another couple, but this one about to disintegrate permanently, their voices rising high, then crashing to silence every few minutes, like the surf outside a beachfront hotel window late at night.

"Do you think I live a work of art?" he asked, growing slowly sober now in leaps and backsteps, sliding onto the piano bench and gently, kiddingly, bumping his hip against hers. She wore the same dress as on the night he had met her.

"Wicked boy, I am trying to play the piano. No maudlin drunks welcome tonight." She kissed his near cheek, and he smiled with calm relief.

VII.

"THIS IS IT: I AM NEVER COMING TO THIS PLACE AGAIN. END OF AN ERA, baby. Time to just fade away, let it go. Let. It. Go." Scott Price was speaking to none of them in particular as the four men and Emily burrowed their way into

A Házam, the last hot night of an unusually hot July. Cash Ass was performing in the basement to a standard-size mob, but even upstairs there was hardly the necessary space to move or air to breathe. The cigarette cloud hung low tonight, only a few feet over their heads; one could bury a hand in it down to the wrist. "Who *are* all these people?" Scott grumbled. "These are not us, these people. Can they *all* be tourists? This is just sad. You know, Mária says this place was never taken seriously by the Hungarians."

The bar noise was five parts English and three parts Hungarian, strained through mingled accents. Male elbows and female cleavage were equally potent weapons in acquiring bar space, but then only crenellated fistfuls of crispy forints held high could win the bartenders' coolly diffuse attention. Efficiency demanded ordering several drinks at once, so the five of them clutched multiple glasses, stood swiveling their heads, gazed with pioneer squints to find space to sit.

"The worm has turned, boys and girl," Scott sighed. "We are a dying breed, and the foreign devils have invaded our grasslands."

The loudspeakers slathered British and American dance music everywhere, and the effort to move across the room toward a just-abandoned couch (oops, too late) was like passing through an animal's close, moist digestive tract, the thumps of the music like the thumps of its amplified, proximate heart. With every twist and turn through the throng, sufficiently loud bits of conversation were coughed up and strewn in their path: *Hungarian, Hungarian, Hungarian . . . our sound will be the sound . . . Hungarian . . . once I get around to writing it out, then I'll pitch it to studios . . . she's on fucking fire . . . back to Prague ASAP, please . . . Hungarian . . . can I crash with you just for . . . the thing about Hungarians and Hungary that you have to understand . . . no, Fin-de-Sicles: they're like Popsicles but shaped like . . . Hungarian . . . then screw the States . . . do you want to come back and I'll draw you . . . dude, go to Prague; you'll forget this scene in twenty seconds . . . Hungarian . . . two days here, two days in Prague, then the fast train to Venice, I don't know, we talk about way east, like Moscow . . . technically, I billed them twice, but keep it to yourself . . . no way, because the hostel is, like, hostile . . . Hungarian . . . Cash Ass rules, you gotta hear these guys, they're foolish . . . she was a Betty and a tamale with three and a half oil cans . . . how do you say "kiss me" in Hungarian . . . Hungarian . . . I'm a poet, poet vagyok, like Arany János . . . baby, Prague is so far beyond . . . csókolj meg!*

From within the cacophony and squeeze, Mark saw a sofa and table slowly, dubiously abandoned and, with a vault and a splay, he arrived first on the scene to secure them. "Who *are* all these people?" Scott said to Emily in irrepressible ill humor. "Who told them to come here? Our people should not—" Charles told him to shut up.

"No. *You* shut up."

From the sofa, John watched Emily sitting on the table, leaning in to speak to Mark. He debated whether to mention the bridge kiss or pretend it had never happened, tried to calibrate precisely his attentions to her this evening, and then, uncertain himself what had happened on the bridge, strained retrospectively to replay, time, and determine the emotional function of each individual lip-muscle response. He listened to her describe a Julie's suitor to Mark, and he couldn't help but feel her description cryptically reflected her own feelings toward John: "Julie" disguised Emily; "Calvin," John. Julie was frustrated, Calvin was everything she—impossible to hear under Charles's braying to Scott about business. But I think about how Calvin has been—if Horváth, on the other hand. She definitely feels like Calvin is really the only way to secure Horváth's trust to get the deal done if she tells him that where does that leave her? Or should she? Not with the State Privatization Agency being run by monkeys.

Two hands gripped his shoulders from behind, and a voice whispered in his ear, "The great joy in life is the unexpected." With laughter and amazement, Bryon—a dashing Korean-American who had, eight years earlier, been notorious in Scott and John's high school for throwing a Marquis de Sade party—appeared, shrouded in coincidence, shimmering into reality, and John, feeling instantly the diminishment of stature and appeal that befalls the person who introduces someone new to a group, introduced him to the group. Bryon stopped short when John said, "And of course you remember Scott."

John savored the barely concealed look of terror on his brother's face as Bryon tried to reconcile this muscular, handsome jock with the obese, hopeless sap of a dozen years before. "Of course. Man, you look *great*" was all he said, and John felt distinctly ripped off.

In Budapest on a two-week vacation, Bryon sat on the table next to Charles and the rows of waiting drinks. He related his six years since last seeing John in under ninety seconds: After college, he had spent a summer working at the "crappy M. C. Escher House theme park" in his hometown, doing construction work, which mostly meant nailing staircases upside down to ceilings. From there he went back to New York to try acting one more time but could only get modeling jobs, and then only the lowest, most humiliating kind: picture-frame modeling. He spent six months being photographed hugging women under trees, pushing kids in swings, looking off in the misty distance, enjoying a New Year's Eve toast in a spangled, conical hat and even doing period work, in which he would dress up in turn-of-the-century "Chinaman's clothes" and pose in front of a dusty black curtain, looking somber for an old black-and-white camera that took ten seconds to register a photo, all of which work was commissioned by picture-frame companies to fill their frames in photo-supply stores with appealing fantasy suggestions. Bryon claimed, incidentally, to have been invited on a first date, a home-cooked meal in the apartment of "an eerily lonely, very unattractive" woman in New York, and on the shelf over her bed was a square, brushed-silver four- by six-inch frame that still held its factory default picture of *him* (in a cable-knit sweater, kicking through some leaves, a wistful, autumnal scene). "I was on top of her, about to finish up, and I look up and there I am pondering autumn. It was a real high point, I must say. There was something strangely beautiful about it. This woman, for one night, really did have a picture of her boyfriend over her bed, wearing a cable-knit sweater just like boyfriends are supposed to wear, but she never even knew it."

Giving up on acting, Bryon ended up in advertising, and he was still at it, with great success. "If I told you how much money I made, Johnny, you'd start coughing up blood like a consumptive." He described his work in the creative section of one of New York's largest agencies, in a division that targeted "what we categorize in our eleven-group schematic as Lone Wolf Aspirants. Basically, every single person's consumer habits can be identified as belonging to one of eleven types. This is a scientific fact. Everybody on earth. Real lone wolfs, of course, don't respond to advertising, but there aren't more than a dozen of them on the planet. Lone Wolf Aspirants, however, are something else. A very big responsibility, billions in buying power."

John watched Emily's attention stream toward the intruder, and the intruder lean in to lap it up. "The key with LWAs is to exhort rebelliousness, excessive eccentricity, and antisocial or even pathological rudeness. These are what we call the 'internal hallmarks of the LWA's self-assessment.' So, like, for Pepsi, I wrote the ad—well, to be fair, it was a team thing—the one where the guy is leaning against the fence with his arms crossed and you can't see any cola at all on the screen, the guy just looks really irritated, and he says, 'Get off my back with that slick garbage. I'll drink whatever I want, because I drink it for me, not for some Madison Avenue jackass who thinks he knows all about my so-called generation.' And he holds up his fingers, like this, to put quotation marks around *generation.* And then he spits, and the screen goes blank and then you just see the Pepsi logo. Very hot."

Everyone, even Charles, tilted toward Bryon as he spoke, as if he were a newly arrived emissary from the Old World to the New World's tedious, forested swampland, bringing news of loved ones, cities, the court.

"Still a virgin?" Bryon asked him in front of everyone.

"Yeah, pretty much," John replied, horrified, with a species of laughter he hoped would somehow mask the conversation and hypnotize his friends. "You too?"

"Unbelievable!" Scott bellowed when an elbow of the crowd eddying around the couch jostled his drink hand.

Bryon excused himself to go to the bar and returned a few minutes later with a drink and a boy no older than nineteen or twenty. "These are the people you should talk to," he said. "These are your best sources," and he introduced Ned, who was in Budapest for three days to update the Hungarian chapters of the budget travel guide published by the students of his college. Ned had a lazy eye, enervated further by jet lag, smoke, sleeplessness, and road-trip hilarity. He wore an old seersucker jacket over cutoff shorts and a T-shirt with the three Greek letters of a fraternity triangulating around a drawing of three wolves, smoking cigars, licking their lips at the sight of a lamb, who wore a tasseled blue beret with holes for her little black ears. Each of the wolves wore the same T-shirt as Ned, and so on ad infinitum, or at least to the physical limits of silk-screen resolution. John relaxed: Ned was Bryon's lover and Emily was safe. "Hey," Bryon shouted to Emily, apparently just thinking of it. "Do you want to go downstairs and dance?"

The four men remained with Ned, who, as the newcomer, was encouraged by Charles to offer to buy them all a round of drinks, an offer the four men heartily accepted. He came back with the drinks and yelled over the noise that he was in a tough spot because he didn't really know anyone who actually *lived* in Budapest, just other backpackers like himself, and so he had asked that guy Bryon out of the blue just now (*oh no*), because he looked so at home, but he was a tourist too, it turned out, and this was the third of his three days and to-morrow he had to press on to the big attraction (Prague) and would they mind helping him out with his book updates?

Scott shook his head aggressively and yelled, "There's always the weasel,

Ned. He comes to the unspoiled place where people are happy and he pretends to be happy, too, and then he goes off and tells all the other weasels about it, and then they all come back in hordes the next month, and you can't breathe for all the weasel shit all over everything." Ned's good eye skittered away in search of allies or explanation while his bad eye floated aloof above their heads. "I won't participate in this," Scott said angrily, and was immediately sucked backward into the crowd.

"Ignore him," Charles said. "Fire away. We've all lived here for years. We've got you covered, Neddy."

The boy smiled in relieved gratitude. He pulled from his backpack a large notebook and a sheaf of photocopied maps and lists, then eagerly wrote down all of the lies Charles, Mark, and John could produce. "Gay bar," Mark said to fully three quarters of the nightclubs Ned recited from his list. "Gay. Gay and violent. Straight but tipping. Gay. Bi-curious." Ned expressed some astonishment at the proportions. "Every generation has its Sodom." Mark shrugged. "For some reason, Budapest is the queerest city in Europe right now."

"I wouldn't bother giving prices in forints for these hotels anymore," Charles said, looking over Ned's notes. "The country is moving officially to the U.S. dollar in eight months. It's a done deal."

"Did you get a chance to visit the dental museum?" John printed Scott's address on the "Worth-a-Visit" sheet. "The world's largest collection of famous people's dental casts. Plaster models of Stalin's teeth, Napoleon's, stuff like that. Simulations, blowups. You can floss life-size wax models and see what sort of crud would have been caught in Lenin's teeth, for example."

"A lot of it was lost during the war," Mark sighed, shaking his head sadly.

As Charles detailed the fascinating view from the spectators' gallery of the commodities exchange where Hungarian financiers in suits traded (and sometimes slaughtered) actual live farm animals on the trading floor of a downtown office building, exchanging literal pork bellies, and Mark interjected with descriptions of the public sex booths that had been allowed in the Hungarian countryside, once a year from dawn to midday on Saint Zsolt's day, for the last six hundred years, and Ned wrote as fast as he could, sensing an editorship in his junior year, John again felt disembodied hands reach over his shoulders, now running over his chest, now rubbing his stomach. "You are here searching nice pleasures, dear brother?" was hissed into his ear, and John saw Charles looking at him and his invisible but unmistakable masseuse with a certain tilted-head expression of dawning joy.

"Yes, I did," John said loudly enough for Charles. "He just went to get a drink and said he hoped you'd be here tonight." He pointed off in the direction of Scott's last appearance.

"Too sad. We must be planning smarter, favorite brother," came the whisper, this time accompanied briefly by the wet aural incursion of what was most likely a tongue. He leaned forward quickly, to free himself and to hide from Charles, who still stared with open curiosity and amusement. John turned to conduct an overt conversation with the rest of Mária, but she had already been consumed back into the pulsing masses.

Mark was telling Ned about the complicated rivalries and contradictory treaties between Gustave the Unappetizing, Otto of the Laryngians, and Lajos the Crass ("You probably know his famous quote, 'Power is marvelous, and absolute power is abso*lute*ly marvelous' "), but Charles was just sipping his drink and considering John with the same curious entertainment. "What?" John demanded, but Charles just kept on, with half a smile coming and going.

Scott reappeared, and Charles said, "Mária was just here."

"Looking for you," John added. Scott disappeared in search of her. "What?!" John repeated, louder, to find Charles's laughter undiminished. John moved off to the bar.

Sometime later he was back at the table and Ned had been replaced by a tall, long-haired man in jeans, a jean shirt, and a jean jacket. "I in your seat?" he asked John in a Slavic accent, making no movement to leave and something in his tone making it clear that no offer to leave would be forthcoming. The man bent forward with his elbows on his knees and rolled a cigarette at the table. "You American like these two?" He jerked his head toward Charles and Mark, who mumbled, "Canadian."

"Branko's from Yugoslavia," Charles said brightly. "He wanted to sit down. He's *great*."

"Serbia," Branko corrected him with a hard expression.

"What's the difference?" John asked with half a laugh.

"Difference? Difference is Montenegro, Bosnia, Croatia, Slovenia, Macedonia," the man said with disgust, licking and sealing his rolling paper and patting his jacket for a lighter. "It fucking is a big difference."

"Come on," John said, oblivious of Mark's discomfort and Charles's eager attention. "Don't tell me you can even tell one from another. You guys all look the same. Try living somewhere with real racial problems, like New York, where you can tell each other apart at a glance."

"I am a Serb! I am a Serb!" Branko stood up in a lunge, leaned across the table until his nose nearly touched John's, and thumped his fist against his own chest. "I am a Serb!" Spittle gathered at the corner of his lips. "I AM A SERB!"

"Admirable clarity," John managed, and set sail again into the sea of people.

He pushed through toward the staircase, guiding himself by sound. Down the narrow passage of smoke, stepping on feet and keeping elbows out of his eyes, he descended to the throb and moan of Cash Ass. He watched Scott and Mária kiss off to one side. Scott pointed to the ceiling with an irritated expression, said something to her, but then laughed as she tickled him. John drove into the dancing mass, looking for Emily and Bryon, unsure of how he would gracefully decouple them.

Jostled and poked, twisting away from flailing limbs and heads, shoving when shoved, cursing the stupidity of Emily being taken in by Bryon as if he were not the least acceptable mate in the history of male-female relationships, John thought he heard a woman's voice call his name. Looking for a familiar face, he pushed all the way to the far side of the crowd, heard his name again, and was pulled onto one of the niches cut into the wall. She was completely bald, but John found her very beautiful. Her thin, arched eyebrows suggested her hair would have been black. "You're John Price," she yelled over the music. She was American. John could only agree that he was John Price. She laughed at his confused smile and his open examination of her skull. "Go ahead," she yelled, and placed his hand on top of her head. "It's a little stubbly because I haven't shaved since last night. I'm Nicky M. I take pictures for the paper. I saw you there a couple times. I liked your thing on the marines. Very noble. Or mock-noble. Whatever that thing is you do." John recalled a name printed bottom-to-top in small type alongside newsprint photographs of new restaurants, music groups, and Soviet tanks leaving Hungary: the initial *N*, then something starting with an *M*, something generously syllabic and foreign, encrusted with uncommon consonants.

"I've seen your pictures." He inclined toward her every time he shouted. "I always thought you were a man."

"Thanks."

"What's the *M* for again?"

"Forget it. It's Polish. You'll be asking me how to say the goddamn thing all night when we could be talking about something more interesting. Just Nicky M. Hey, how tall are you? What are you, like, five-ten?" She pulled him off the niche and into the crowd. Conversation, straining before, now proved impossible and they danced until they were both sweating profusely, Nicky pulling her black tank top out of her military fatigues to fan air onto her stomach. She looked him in the eye longer than he could stand while they danced, and he often found excuses to slink free, wiping sweat from his eyes, looking at the floor, pointing to someone who was dancing ridiculously or turning to dance with his back to her. But she was always ready to look him in the eye again. She yelled something he couldn't quite catch.

"What?"

"You're all about sex, aren't you," she yelled again, an assertion, not a question.

"What does that mean?"

"There's just something about you. You're just so all about sex."

"No, no," he shouted. "I'm interested in all kinds of things, like, well . . . all kinds of things." He made a display of puzzlement. "Well, maybe you're right. Wow! Say, I am all about sex." Nicky did not laugh at his clowning, just raised her eyebrows and nodded to say, "See?" and now, at last, looked away, turned and danced with her back pressed against him, and laced her fingers through his.

Out in the air, he sat on the stoop and forgot about Emily, drank and talked with Nicky. She shaved her head every day with an ivory-handled straight razor inherited from a grandfather. She honed it on a leather strop emblazoned with her initials and a burnt-black profile of Frida Kahlo. She used her small *BudapesToday* salary to pay for her "real life" as a photographer and a painter. In two weeks, she was going to show in a group exhibition in the lobby/gallery of the Razzia movie theater, and he should come, she really hoped he would come.

They were back at the couch; more drinks were bought. Charles was still exerting himself on Ned's behalf. When the travel writer finally stood to go, he offered profuse thanks. "And tell the blond guy I'm really sorry if I offended him somehow," he said to John, who suddenly felt terrible for the kid, for the lies he was carrying off in his bag. He considered stopping Ned, telling him they had misled him. But then Emily and Bryon were back, and Mark, too, pale and damp, troubled by something, and he remembered the hordes of tourists who would ring Scott's doorbell to see Hitler's teeth, and he felt much better.

"This place *is* getting crowded," Emily said. "It's hard to picnic in locust season."

"Ooh, farm talk! How charmin'!" Nicky drawled at the stranger's comment before flopping down next to her on the couch, taking Emily's hand, and interviewing her as if she came from a distant planet or a chapter in history. John watched Emily's face as she made conversation with the woman least like her on earth, and he compared their opposing appeal. "Are you for real?" Nicky was asking her when Scott and Mária returned, and Scott, holding Mária's hand to his lips, mentioned again to everyone the "very real threat to us," but no one paid him much attention and, as if everyone suddenly being in the same place was too unstable—an artificial, cyclotron-generated atom with an unnaturally swollen number of protons and neutrons—people soon decayed back into the plasma and disappeared for the night: Mark to read ("Call me, JP, hey? I want to meet that old pianist"), then Emily to sleep ("Really neat to meet you, Nicky"), then Bryon ("Great job, Scott, really, you're looking good, keep it up" and a hug for John, who suspected his old schoolmate was leaving to meet Emily discreetly), then Scott and Mária, arms around each other's waist, leaving without a word for anyone. Pleading work the next day and telling John to call him about another possible job "on the Imre thing, which looks like it might end up being very interesting indeed for both you and me," Charles vanished, leaving John and Nicky strewn on the couch.

"Who *were* all those people?" she asked, taking his hand and placing it on top of her head.

"I have no idea." He thrilled to the buzzing tickle of her stubble against his gliding palm.

"I think we'll bump into each other again." She stood up, bent over, and kissed him. Their noses touched and she widened her eyes, poking gentle fun at his surprise. "But I think it's a little overdone to meet in a club and go home together," she said with a winning smile, and disappeared too.

VIII.

"KÁROLY, IF YOUR PLAN IS GOOD AND YOUR SKILLS AS YOU CLAIM, YOU will do what you propose in a month and these terms will apply. This is fair?" More than fair. On a Wednesday-morning handshake, Imre promised Charles thirty days in which to finance the Horváth Kiadó's renaissance. Charles wondered which other VC firms had received the same exclusive promise.

Imre clasped Charles's hand long after it was natural, and peered into his eyes. "I don't want only a bank," he said. "I want the future."

"I very much understand. That's why I'm doing this."

The agreement was simple. Charles, having applied for and been quickly granted a leave of absence from his firm to raise money for the Horváth Press's expansion, repatriation, and renovation, would have August to accomplish his first step. With the full support of his firm (which, Charles explained, was hamstrung by geographic limitations in its charter but was eager to see Charles succeed), he would contact and secure commitments of financing from a group of Western investors. The terms of those agreements were entirely his affair. The minority investors would individually contract with Charles, so that the money he brought to Horváth would represent, in essence, one person (Charles) freeing Horváth from having to negotiate with a group. Charles would then represent this consortium and, on its behalf, acquire 49 percent of a new company, incorporating Charles's new money, the Horváth Verlag in Vienna, and the symbolically insufficient (or insufficiently symbolic) credit vouchers paid by the Hungarian government as compensation for the 1949 confiscation of the original Kiadó. Imre would retain 51 percent of the new company, whose first transaction would be to bid on the rump Kiadó held by the Hungarian state, essentially paying the ransom money necessary to release Imre's past into his control. (The reality was simpler still. Charles, having never mentioned Imre to his firm since they brilliantly rejected the best deal they were going to see this year, had not applied for a leave of absence and would do nothing so loopy— throw away an office, a salary, business cards—until he had secured himself a viable deal with Imre.)

An embarrassed silence invaded the suite. The crumbly and coagulating remnants of a continental breakfast littered a black lacquered tray by the open French window, attracting the traffic noises of Szentháromság Square as well as spastic, motelike mites. On the reflective, swooping cross-section oak of Imre's bedside table, the latest Mike Steele imbroglio—*Lather, Rinse, Murder, Repeat*—lay open and facedown, forming a little protective tent over a pair of horn-rim reading glasses. The open closet door boasted a dozen fine suits, shivering and swaying from time to time in the breeze. Charles silently gathered his notes and business-plan drafts. As the men wordlessly shook hands again at Imre's door, dry-cleaning came to collect his Hilton-emblazoned laundry bag and Ms. Toldy emerged from her room across the hall to prepare Mr. Horváth for his other appointments that day. She nodded frostily to Charles, enjoyed shutting the door on him and the laundry maid simultaneously.

A FEW HOURS LATER, John Price sat in his corner of the *BudapesToday* office almost alone. Karen Whitley was taking four days off to entertain her visiting
parents, and two other employees had just quit, one to return home, the other
to accept a vaulting, gravity-scorning promotion to be the number two in an
international newsmagazine's newly hatched Budapest bureau.

Pondering the two overwhelming personalities in his life, John watched
his cursor, tried to separate Imre's seriousness from Emily's. | | | |

| | | | *Throughout Budapest, all around us, walk the survivors of moral exami-
nation. Tall walk the brave, hunched walk the craven, but we are visibly different from
them, as surely as if we wore decorative scars across our cheeks and discs in our lips.
We of the West have been spared certain tests, and there are those who thank God for
the* | | | |

My God, she went home with Bryon.

| | | | *apparently permanent commutation of that dreadful trial. But some of us,
perhaps, ache for it. We know we might not succeed, as many of those who lurk the
streets of Budapest with downcast eyes did not succeed. We know there is no pleasure
to be found in the yoke of tyrants. But nevertheless, there are those of us from the faraway West, the lucky West, who think of such trials with a certain envy. At least you
would know who you were. You would know what you were made of. You would know
the limits of your potential. And if you succeeded? If you did not break? Can we say
for certain there is no pleasure to be found in that yoke?* | | | |

To live a work of art. Emily would understand what that means. What
Imre is. What Scott will never understand. I am not ready for her, and she
knows it. I'm not serious enough. Not something enough. She is waiting for me
to be something enough. She is trying to teach me how to live like her. She is
waiting for me to see something clearly and to show her that I see it. She could
not kiss me from a position of inequality.

| | | | *And though one sees in many of the Hungarians a natural envy for our
wealth, our ease, our pardon from History, still there is, even in the eyes of the defeated, a certain pride that is justifiable. Even those who were beaten, who compro-
mised, who collaborated, who lost their way, who thought they did right when they
did wrong, or who knew they did wrong but felt they had no choice, or who took advantage of the times and now regret it or merely suffer reprisals in choking anger—
even in the eyes of all of these, I see something very much like condescension: We have
not been tested, and they know it. No one has asked us to collaborate in order to save
a friend, to distinguish between dark gray and dark gray. Even those who failed stand*

somewhat taller when they look upon those of us who were not even tried. They do not only envy us. They also laugh at us. And I cannot say they are wrong. | | | |

Is she with Bryon even now, taking the day off to laze and love under sticky sheets and open windows, slowly, nakedly fetching cold drinks? There's that bald girl.

And, in context, John realized he had in fact seen Nicky a few times in the office, had seen her walk into the newsroom just like this, pinning portfolios to her side, slim and aggressively chic in blazer, T-shirt, beret, sunglasses, jeans.

"Help yourself," she said, and dropped onto his desk a giant scuffed-leather portfolio tied at the corners with thick black string frayed at the ends. "I gotta convince our man from Down Under to take some of these," she said, tapping a second portfolio before knocking once on Editor's door and entering.

You find this, you return this, you hear? she had written alongside her phone number on a mailing label inside the portfolio's cover. He copied the number.

The top photograph in the collection was large, the size of a newspaper front page, black-and-white, a smoothly assembled photo collage: In a large auditorium, an audience of several hundred Soviet government officials—fat and frowning, in identical suits—sit attentively watching a man at a podium that bears an ornate hammer and sickle on its front panel. The speaker is a high Russian military officer, a marshal in a uniform spattered with medals and ribbons at the chest and flowery epaulet blossoms. On the podium rests his hat, one of those oversize Russian military caps like tilted, visored dinner plates. With an expression of great and serious intensity, the officer gestures with a pointer at the enormous screen hanging behind him. Projected there for the hundreds of apparatchiks is an anthropomorphic mouse cartoon character, wearing saddle shoes and a button-down dress shirt. The mouse's short pants, however, are bunched around his ankles, because he is furiously masturbating. Cartoon beads of sweat leap from his forehead and large black ears. His eyes are squeezed shut in violent ecstasy, and while one of his little four-fingered paws vise-clutches his cartoon member, the other holds aloft a photograph of Konstantin Chernenko, one of the late and later secretary-generals of the Soviet Union.

The second picture in her portfolio, smaller, also black-and-white: A young couple sits on a mound of rubble, the dusty bricks and broken furniture from some exploded building. They nuzzle side by side, facing front but turned toward each other for a kiss. His legs dangle in corduroys under a simple white shirt, his feet in untied work boots and a bandanna around his neck. She wears a long dress and black shoes, her ankles crossing. They look very much in love. Their eyes are closed. Just to their left, two soldiers of indistinct nationality fight. The soldier on the right has just plunged his bayonet into the belly of his enemy. His expression is ferocious and convincing, sweat and grime whipped with fear and hatred. The victim is fumbling at the blade burrowing into his stomach. His eyes are open wide in pleading.

"So that's my real life." She had returned unheard.

"I like it. I really like these."

"Do you? Do you really?" She seemed absolutely, sincerely pleased to receive this encouragement, which had gurgled out of his lips as thoughtfully as drool. "That's so great to hear. God, it really is." John couldn't think of anything intelligent to say about her work, but her happiness was contagious and he enjoyed the effect of his praise. She opened the other, her newspaper portfolio, now five pictures lighter, and laid it on his desk. She stood behind him, leaning over his chair, one hand on his shoulder, and she slowly turned the pictures over for him. His hand floated up and onto hers, and he watched the photos pass.

More conventional journalistic shots: leaders orating on this or that fungible topic; storefronts of glitzy new shops; Soviet tanks trundling out of Hungary four decades after arriving, with the top halves of Russians smiling and waving good-bye from open hatches; the members of a popular Hungarian techno-rock band, sweating and screaming under strobes. Artistic soft-news or human-interest photos: a stylized nighttime shot of the animated neon billboards that lit up one of Budapest's boulevards with steaming cups of neon coffee and slowly winking smokers, brands with mere months to live; the dirty faces of Gypsy children stranded in squalor, their tired eyes seemingly aware that they were both the descendants and the forebears of infinite generations of impoverished children who posed, or were still to pose, for infinite generations of compassionate, powerless photojournalists; ironic juxtapositions of Western businessmen and Hungarian peasant women caught in the same frame, standing in line to enter McDonald's.

John tossed more compliments over his shoulder, just to savor her happiness at catching them, a happiness that was so appealing, he started to wonder if it weren't a trick she performed on demand. "If you really like them, I do have more in my studio," she said. "How tall did we decide you were? Five-ten? Five-ten and a half?"

CHARLES SPENT THE AFTERNOON typing and redrafting his notes into investor briefings and Horváth Holdings business plans. He kept his door closed and told Zsuzsa not to disturb him. Toward five, he wandered past the expectedly sleepy Presiding Vice's office and allowed himself to be invited in for inane conversation.

"Five-day weekend for me, Charlie, starting in eighteen minutes. I'll be out of pocket until Tuesday. Vienna. Viennese chickies. The only perk of working in this backwater."

"That and your salary."

"And the press attention," conceded his chief.

The playful sun jumped from cloud to cloud, momentarily illuminating the brass fixtures and glass dome of the man's prized antique, a 1928 ticker tape machine. "Oh, I just remembered I wanted to ask you something," Charles mentioned as he was turning to leave. The vaguer the words now, the more broadly and durably his ass would be covered later if everything went awry: "That publishing deal, do you remember? The Austrian guy? Since we don't want it, I thought I'd suggest some other finance possibilities, maybe introduce him to a few people I know. I sort of like the guy and want to give him a hand, you know. Any objections?"

"Whatever," said his boss, rising sixteen minutes earlier than projected to gather at random a few work papers and folders destined to make a five-day trip to and from Vienna unexamined. "You want to join me in V-town, Big Chuck? We'll bring nylons for the fräuleins."

IN THE LONG, unbroken rectangular room, half a dozen unfinished canvases on easels gestated under tarps while others leaned their foreheads shyly against the walls—punished, contrite, expected to contemplate their errors of composition or color. She turned one or two around for his inspection and bathed in his puzzled praise. She opened another portfolio of photographs. She showed him a darkroom behind curtains, and a clothesline of drying recent developments. She said little except to provide titles. "*Biblical Extrapolation Series,*" she said in front of three small painted panels laid side by side on an old, splintering, paint-flecked table. She walked parallel to him, across from him, and she watched his face respond to each painting in turn, her work reflected and re-fracted off his face for her re-evaluation.

"*John 19:38 and ¹/₂.*" On Mount Golgotha, moonlit and uncanny in chiaroscuro, distant crucifixes dot the silver hills of the sin-stained landscape. A ladder leans against the nearest crucifix, which is empty; Joseph of Ari-mathea and Nicodemus, lit by a sourceless underglow, are removing the body of Jesus. Joseph's hands and lifted knee struggle to control and clutch one clumsy end of the linen-shrouded corpse. The other end already slumps heavily in the dirt, and Nicodemus, his hands outstretched, caught at the exact mo-ment of having let his burden fall to the earth, bunches his shoulders, opens his eyes wide, and winces in shame. Joseph looks over his shoulder, almost directly at the viewer, to see if any prospective Gospelists have witnessed this unholy ac-cident.

"*Genesis 2:25 and ¹/₂.*" Adam, bulging and sinewy with mannerist muscu-lature, leans against a tree. His fingernails grip and tear the bark, his arms locked, veins and tendons swollen, his sculptured legs wide apart, his head thrown back. His long, dark hair falls over his shoulders; his eyes roll up; his mouth is open wide; a filament of saliva connects his lips. Eve stands behind him, her hands invisible as they meet at the point hidden by his outside thigh. Her head turns sharply to one side, revealing her leer. She drags her fully ex-tended tongue over the knobs of his spine.

"*The Gospel According to Matthew 12:50 and ¹/₂.*" Off to the left, a clamor-ing, sycophantic crowd and all their gathered clouds of dust cluster around Jesus, who stands a head taller than his tallest follower. They are moving away, leaving behind a sun-bleached and savior-abandoned square, empty but for his mother, left alone in the heat (visible in distant rippled air). Mary stands un-easily; it seems she has been caught the instant before she can no longer con-tinue. No one attends to her. Her child is walking away, one hand upon a follower's head as he walks; he looks straight ahead in the opposite direction from his collapsing mother. He knows she is there, left behind.

"His last statement was a politico-spiritual necessity. He is a revolutionary. Of the people. He cannot be tied to mere coincidental biology."

"You sure know your Bible." The more her work confused him, the more she seemed to understand something, to have something unnameable that he wanted.

"Lie down." She pointed to the immobile white waves of the unmade single bed. John pressed his head against its pillow. He stretched and closed his eyes and for a delicious instant did not know who was with him; in the self-imposed darkness, he could feel the flaking surface of Scott's T-shirt on Mária's body, the impossibly soft smooth line of Emily's jaw, the slight thousand-faceted scratch of stubble on Karen's calf, the buzz of Nicky's bald head. And he wondered why he had spent so many years worrying about the potentially demoralizing effects of this innocent pastime.

Nicky sat beside the pillow, facing the foot of the bed, which wheezed her a two-note greeting. "I already get you," she said, and brushed her upside-down lips over his. "I see right through you. I know all about what you want." He opened his eyes at the menacing words spoken in erotic tones, and her inverted face floated above him, but she closed his lids again with fingertips he never saw.

"Tell me what you think you know." He imagined all the women who could own the fingertips skimming across his forehead.

She slid the words into his ear: "I know you don't really want *me*." Her right hand hovered just over his belt and shot out crackling bolts of blue lightning.

"Don't I?" he whispered.

"I know your dream girl. Hey, I told you to keep your eyes closed. Close them. *Close* them. Should I tell you about her?" The bed creaked, and he heard her walk across the room.

He moved his head like a blind man who suddenly senses a new presence. "Okay, then tell me all about her."

The bed greeted her return. She sat facing him, kissed him on the mouth, and pressed her hands against his chest. "Keep your eyes closed and I will."

"Tell me who she is if she's not you," he said.

"Don't do that," she frowned in unfeigned disapproval. "First house rule: Don't do that. We both know she isn't me. Close your eyes." Nicky brushed the hair away from his forehead and ran her fingers over his scalp. "Her hair, let's see, is like the woman in Vermeer's *Woman with a Water Jug*." John opened his eyes, started to say he didn't know anything about paintings, maybe she could show him a pic—but Nicky put her finger on his lips. "Shhh. Just shut up and listen." He nodded slowly, his eyes closed as his mouth opened slightly, as if they were on the same pulley system. She put her mouth on his forehead, then whispered, "Her face is just what you've always dreamed." Her lips lightly tugged his eyelashes. "She has the eyes of Munch's *Madonna*." She bit his ear. "And the ears of *La Gioconda*." He tried to speak again, but his mouth was stopped. He tried to imagine this face she described. He imagined faces he knew; he examined but then discarded in turn Karen, Mária, even Emily.

Nicky began to unbutton his shirt. She brushed her knuckles over his lips. "Her mouth is better than mine, much better, like the girl in Doisneau's *Kiss* or *Christina's World*." Her fingers walked behind his neck. "And her neck I see like the girl in Klimt's *Kiss*. Or is she more like Bonnard's *Lazy Nude*? Is she, John?" He nodded slowly. She unbuttoned his shirt and played her lips upon his chest. "Can you see her breasts, John?" She picked up his heavy arm and placed his hand to rest against her T-shirt, and he made a sort of sound. "Like Ingres's *Bather of Valpinçon*?" He nodded, and she pressed his hand hard against her. "Her arms are made for you. To hold you. Like a certain Venus I know."

She pulled his arms from his sleeves, a mother deftly undressing a floppy-limbed infant, and her nails left pale wakes in the triangle of hair on his chest, then schussed over ribs and traversed down his sides. "Do you want to know more?" Again a sort of sound, his eyes tightly shut now. A woman appeared to John in the order Nicky painted her, as if mists were dissipating from in front of her, but slowly, painfully slowly, from the top of her head down, an inch at a time, too slowly to bear, hair, eyes, ears, mouth, neck, breasts, arms. "The stomach"—his hands fanned over Nicky's smooth skull as her tongue slid over the writhing snakes of his abdomen—"of Chardin's *Young Schoolmistress*." John's jeans flew across the room, a striving broad-jumper, and slid to a stop in a tight embrace of a table leg. "Her legs like Manet's waitress at the *Folies-Bergères Bar*." A gust of wind scattered the last strings of fog, and the new woman was revealed to him entirely.

He felt her body lay down next to him. His eyes let in no light; behind closed lids he looked hard at the great love of his life, and as this woman ran her hands over him, as she pulled him on top of her, as she pressed him to the wall, as she yelled and shook underneath him, he was, he knew, for the first time, participating in his real life, a work of art. Bright lights flashed, but he fought and held his eyes tightly shut and would allow nothing to end this, would never again allow the beloved to run away and hide, to dance out of reach, to taunt from deceptively short distances just across hidden quicksand, to float just one bridge away. Flashes turned the black to yellow and blue, but he refused to be fooled by these retinal will-o'-the-wisps into opening his eyes and letting her escape him again.

IX.

FLEETING, OF COURSE, THOSE SENSATIONS OF CLARITY AND ARRIVAL.
Despite her physical generosity, Nicky was in her own way as unattainable as
Emily: He felt, in her spattered apartment, like a much cherished witness to her
life, even a key supporting character, while again suspecting that his own real
life was locked up at the top of a Buda hill, in Emily's bungalow. Infuriating: all
this time wasted in unquenchable unrequital. He stared at his reflection in the
bar's long mirror. This was too much, the worst sort of foolishness, and not
even confined to romance: His evenings with Nicky imagining Emily, meetings
with Imre longing for Scott's unsolicited forgiveness, nights with Nádja wishing her younger, and here now yet one more drink pretending Scott might
someday develop into some other brother entirely. This must end.

Scott was yelling something at John now, even though he sat only two bar
stools to the right. He yelled, but to very little purpose, since the music was far
stronger than even his pink lungs. Only a few scrappy phrases plowed through
the din and found an inlet to John's ringing right ear: . . . *going to . . . harried . . .*
moon . . . Romania. John stared straight ahead, nodded, crunched an ice cube.
He had decided some minutes before not to bother scraping the hell out of his
throat in order to engage in pointless conversation under the sampled sirens,
bass, and keyboards. Behind the bar, behind the bartender, behind the glass
shelves of liquor that rattled in music appreciation, a long tube of purple neon
ran the length of the back wall and was duplicated by the mirror immediately
behind it, so that John could stare at his reflection and see two purple neon
strips stretch just under his nose, a thick, glowing purple mustache as long as
the bar. And while he played these games, the studio-stuttered voice of an Australian dance-pop phenomenon howled, *When ya gonna dance are ya gonna*
gonna dance gonna dance gonna gonna dance dance dance? and in the mirror, the
veins in Scott's reflected neck were now swelling into throbbing cords, and he
plainly (but inaudibly) was yelling at John, "Fuck you, fuck you, fuck you."

Outside—later, drunker—within the shifting crowd and clashing odors,
John found them all in a closed circle, one person thick except at one bump,
where Scott stood immediately behind Mária with his arms around her waist
and his head on her shoulder, her hand arching up to ruffle his hair. The circle:
Mária, Emily, Bryon, Mark, Zsolt, Charles, and a new (temporary) young
woman, four fingers of her right hand comfortably pinched in the right hip

pocket of Charles's jeans, a stranger to John but undeniably branded as Hungarian by her perfume. "Thank you, thank you," Scott was saying. "Thank you, thank you," echoed Mária. Charles smiled lazily, amused. Mark sucked a tooth, his sweat perceptible to John. Bryon had an arm around Emily's shoulder but one around Mark's as well. "Oh, it's so great, it's so neat. Isn't it great?" Emily asked John, the late arrival. "Yes, it is," he answered to please her, without caring to know what "it" was. Only after Scott and Mária had left, arm in arm, did Charles say, "Congratulating that was hardly natural," and described the couple waking up on the first morning of their honeymoon to share "a good, contritious breakfast." *Harried*, John understood only now was, of course, *married*. *It*, so neat and great, was an engagement, the annunciation of which had excited from John merely nods and crunched ice and purple neon mustaches the length of a bar.

He wondered what he would have said had the Australian dance music not turned that one consonant away, and if *harried* had stayed *married*. Hadn't the music, in fact, given John the opportunity to respond sincerely for once? He told himself he had made his last effort.

X.

NICKY ATHLETICALLY DISMOUNTED, AFTER AN IMPRESSIVE DISPLAY OF Latin terms. "I gotta do some work now." John didn't immediately catch her meaning. "You can't assume the package includes overnight hotel every time, friend." She tossed his underwear at his head. She stood in front of one of her dozen mirrors, this one a cracked, dirty full-length mounted on an antique wooden stand, and she adjusted the angle of her tasseled red fez. "Wild nights are fine now and again. But if I don't get enough sleep, then the Muses won't visit me and then I'll be useless." She fine-tuned the fez and examined her profile.

"I'll be no trouble, ma'am. I promise."

"Don't be like that," she said to John's reflection deep in the mirror. "You can stay *sometimes* if we keep at this little project."

John propped himself up on one elbow to watch her remove tarps from unfinished paintings. "Can't you work with me here? It's almost midnight. I'll be mouse-quiet."

"I just told you. House rules: Art first, everything else third. Guests are encouraged to reread those rules before requesting entry."

"But I like your work," he tried feebly.

"Oh, thank you, thank you," she said, as sincerely thrilled as ever to receive praise. She stroked his face and kissed him softly. She whispered in his ear: "But you have three minutes to get the hell out of here so I can work."

"I think you want me to stay."

"Stop it," she snapped. She stood and walked back to her easels. "Please don't say stupid shit to me. Rules are rules, or no more playtime. That's all."

And so, just after midnight, he sat perched at a hotel bar and watched English-language TV news footage cycled perpetually on the half hour. Iraq repeatedly invaded Kuwait and animated arrows unfurled across map borders in sweeping curves. On the second repetition, John laughed quietly at this quickly old news, and a live, unbroadcast voice said, "What's funny? Where's the joke? What's the gag?" John looked to his right. About forty-five, he wore a tan canvas-and-nylon-net vest with a dozen Velcro-fastened and zippered pockets. His brown hair was thin in the standard patterns and combed straight back in damp ridges. "Really. What's the joke? Big trouble in the Mideast, no?"

John shook sticky peanuts into his mouth. "The joke? I don't know. I had the idea for a second that this might be a hoax. Doesn't it seem slightly funny to you? A war between whatever and whoever, and one of them invades, and there's tanks and desert strategy and a world in crisis, and the journalists get to sound more intense . . ." John ran out of words; the man listened and nodded but plainly was not getting it.

"Ted Winston. The *Times*." The man clenched his jaw muscles and offered his hand across his immobile body.

John introduced himself, waiting vainly for the *Times*'s city of origin. "*BudapesToday*, I suppose." He waited for the real journalist to start laughing.

"*BudapesToday?* Oh yes indeed, the local English thing. Envy you. I could tell you were a journo. First post? Getting to understand the country? That's the way." Ted Winston clinked his glass twice with a black plastic stirrer, then clicked his tongue and pointed the stirrer at the thickly mustached, muscular, black-vested, and bow-tied Magyar who was lazily wiping condensation rings off the bar. As his glass was refilled, Winston demanded of John, "Describe this country to me in sixty words or less."

"Sixty words or less?"

"Good training. What you're here for."

John clinked his own glass twice and clicked his tongue, but his magic fizzled. "The girls are pretty. How many is that, *the-girls-are-pretty:* four? So, then another fifty-six words . . ."

"You're joking, okay, I appreciate that. I like a sense of humor. This is good," Ted Winston said. "But here's something I learned when I was about your age, Price. I learned this from Chou En-lai, the Chinese premier. I was green, Price, green green. I'd seen a bit of the 'Nam, but I was still young. Seeing a man die doesn't necessarily make you one. I learned that the hard way. Anyhow, I was in Peking, following Nixon over there, Peking then, you know, very big moment, very serious events." Winston clinked his glass, clicked, and pointed again. "Had a moment alone with Chou himself. Handsome devil. Smelled like jasmine, though—oddest thing, never will forget it. Handsome devil, and I don't swing that way, I should specify at this point in time. Any rate, the premier was answering one of my questions, and he fixed me with his little gaze. You know, when they want to, they can just about pierce you through with a hard look, those people. The strong ones can just look at you. How else do you explain the billion people who *didn't* overthrow Communism last year, huh? Point is, the premier explained to me that the Chinese ideogram for—have you heard this? The Chinese ideogram for *opportunity* is composed of the two ideograms, in progression, for *midget* and *giant,* in that order. The midget becomes a giant. Do you get it? That's an *opportunity.* That's how the Chinese see it, anyhow, and I think they're right on. Fascinating little bastards."

The TV was repeating the headlines from one half hour and one hour earlier, and as the war hadn't proceeded very far, the same journalists filed the same reports from Baghdad, Washington, Kuwait, and elsewhere. "But if one thing is clear from Brussels, we haven't seen the end of this crisis."

"You can say that again," Ted Winston confirmed. "By no means have we. By no damn means the end of this crisis have we yet seen." Clink, clink, click, click, point. "How long you been in-country? You know the soul of this place?"

"I don't, but I generally wouldn't trust a landlocked country for seafood."

Winston nodded as if he had received the answer he expected. "You should be getting under the skin of these people. That's what I'd be doing in your shoes. This country needs explaining right now, right this damn instant, and you're in the catbird seat. Grab this nation. Shake it. Look at it from every goddamn angle. If you write what you know—and *only* that—you can shape this country. People look to us—they'll look to you—to make sense of a senseless world. And what's that mean to you?"

"I'm sorry, what's what mean to me?"

"Midget to giant. Remember that. Midget to giant."

Two peroxide prostitutes sat down to Winston's right and began speaking rapid melodious Hungarian to the bartender. The smell of their perfume was overpowering, and John discreetly hid his nose in his empty glass. "I smell a lot of me in you," Winston said to John. "Make your mark and the big boys are going to come calling. That's how it works. Opportunity."

"As far as the emirate of Dubai is concerned," said a young woman in front of a black metal security gate flanked by palm trees and surveillance cameras, "it's all wait and see. At this point in time, there is conjecture and still more conjecture. For the people of Dubai, there is only waiting. They can only wait . . . and see. And then? It's still too early to say, but the fear is, not for much longer. Back to you, Lou." The bartender delicately licked one index finger and began counting the large stack of cash the two hookers had given him, forming separate piles on the bar with each new national currency he uncovered, tapping occasionally at a pocket calculator and making penciled notes with an awkward left hand, interjecting now and again quiet, menacingly dubious questions. Ted Winston suffered brief solitude.

John left forints on the bar and stood to go. The reporter remained seated to shake his hand. He clenched his jaw muscles and blinked several times. "Outstanding to meet you, Jim. Call me here tomorrow, I'm staying the week."

Still too early to face his wife and child, John found himself on the familiar piano bench. He talked to Nádja almost at random, trapezing from slippery synapse to slippery synapse: his infuriating brother's baffling engagement, an artist friend who worked too hard, pompous journalist drunks, the eternal Emilitic mysteries, the assistance Charles Gábor requested of him, which he was not sure he wanted to—"Imre Horváth?" she interrupted, as John sketched his vague, hesitating hesitations about Charles's affairs. "Really? Your friend is doing a business with Imre Horváth? I knew an Imre Horváth. He was a bit of a rascal, I would have said."

They compared Imre Horváths and tried, without perfect success, to come to a conclusion. It was impossible to merge or distinguish the two with any certainty. Nádja had no memory of her Horváth having any connection to a publishing house, but in those days everyone had been trying to hold down whatever jobs they could, and certainly she would not exclude the possibility. As she played piano to the nearly empty room, she described the man she recalled from forty-some years earlier, the man who had inflated her cousin with child, a notorious lothario, but also something of a clown. At one time he had made money by juggling and doing magic tricks for little children's parties, sometimes performing on street corners for change, even singing and dancing passably when necessary. She had heard someone say, though this was years and years ago, that he had set up shop as a pornographer in Bonn. A monumental figure? Certainly not the man she knew. Tortured and imprisoned by the Communists? Not that she could recall, but that was hardly a distinguishing characteristic in those days. A natty dresser? No, this one had been like everyone else, making material last, inheriting, patching, through wartime then postwar then Communist shortages.

John felt himself straining to make these two Imres one. He wanted very badly for the giant to have been a midget. "Did your Imre have the ability to make you feel your whole life was very, very stupid?" he asked before he could stop himself, and the left half of his mouth climbed high in a strange sort of laughter while she raised an eyebrow at him. "Phew," he said, and rested his head in his hands. Through the cracks between his fingers he watched her wrinkled paws move with surprising quickness over the keys until she grew bored with speed and melody, then her fingers stretched and clawed and crossed over one another into intricate chord positions and she played only harmonies in slow, pulsing rhythm.

"Fire me up a gasper, John Price." He lit two and placed one between her ancient lips. "Your little friend the other evening," she said, rolling the cigarette to one corner of her mouth. "She is not going to fix your very, very stupid life, I do not think. If that is your plan. She is not for you."

"That seems to be the consensus."

"And this makes you unhappy and peculiar? Why? You have other ones, I think. Why a girl with this awful, this very strange, big jaw?"

"It is a big jaw, isn't it?"

"Quite big. Very big indeed. You know, at this hour, I stop playing entire tunes when people are tired like this." She gestured with the cigarette between her teeth at the sleepy faces in the corner. "They will remember this sound even when they forget the tunes." She splayed the wax-covered twigs and produced a dark and distant noise. "I loved a famous American astronomer once, John Price."

He laughed. "You did not. You're a notorious liar. Everyone says so."

"No, no, not everyone. Only fools like your dark brother and your little friend with the giant's jaw would say this. She did, did she not? Don't look surprised and ask me how I know. Of course she had to say this. You can see that, no? No? Oh, then you are not paying the attention I hope from you. And, yes, I did love a celebrated astronomer. Never doubt what I tell you. I will never lie to you."

"I'm sorry," John said quietly.

"Good Lord, you promise to be terribly unamusing tonight. Try to amuse me, please, my dear. Chin up, chappy. I *did* love an astronomer and he was a very boring man. Like your little Miss Oliver, he was admirable but not very interesting, like a joke explained. Do you believe me now?"

"Wait," said John, and shuffled to the bar for his Unicums and her Rob Roy. He greeted the saxophonist from Harvey's office and the black, bald singer, eating their salary for the night. They asked him how he knew Nádja. "She's my grandmother."

"One night, my astronomer and I made love in his observatory on a mountaintop in Chile. For the occasion, he opened the roof of the observatory and spread a mattress on the floor for us." The chords shifted more rapidly, brightened. Loud laughter was punctuated by the clicks of pool balls. "We lay on our backs, nude, looking up through the roof at this night sky, far away from cities. There were, of course, more stars than I have ever seen anywhere other."

"That's why they put observatories there."

"Precisely, clever boy. We lay there, and I ask him why it was that, when you look directly at a star, it disappears. 'What sort of science is this,' I ask him, 'where you cannot look at your subject without it disappearing?' And he said— like a teacher always, him, very boring, 'You must learn to look *obliquely*.' I had never heard this word. He said, 'You cannot look at it directly. You must look near it, not at it, or you will frighten it away. Obliquely.' Of course I knew this already—every little child knows this—but I liked this new word, this *obliquely*. You know this word?" John watched her settle into a chord, then strike it again and again, altering the position of only one finger at a time but each time changing the light in the room. "I think perhaps you might benefit from this skill. You might, for example, look at your friend with the monster's jaw a little more obliquely." John had long since abandoned his efforts to understand things for the evening and was hoping only that she would keep striking the keys. "Oh, you foolish boy. Why do you want to be with one of those? She is not even good at it. She has given up everything one can enjoy from real life, and what has she won in return? Very little, I think, not comprising your sad heart, which, I concede, is not without value. It is neither here nor there how she makes her money, but what do you *want* with her precisely? This is not an interesting person with a life of stories ahead of her. You don't want this type. In a war perhaps I approve, but I don't see a bit of a war right now. And even then, her skills! Horrifying! That is, when said and done, half of their charm, to watch them dance for you, to think and maneuver and smile for the footlights. But she! She would not even defend herself when I toyed with her right in front of you; she just ducked away and pretended not to understand me. Why would you want someone so weak and foolish? Don't look like a sad puppy. She *is* weak. At least do not you lie to me. Confess to her body, you want her body, though I saw her and there are certainly finer bodies to be had. Good Lord, that jaw—there would be three of you in the bed. Do you really want this one's heart, John Price? Do you want her to take yours and make it right? Do you want this one to peer deep into you and see how wondrous you are? You want her to be the one who saves you? I do not think she can do this. This is very unlikely, I think—"

Nádja teased, laughed, while John, draped across a folding chair, blew smoke rings and, with one eye tightly shut, poked his finger through each uneven and trembling nebula, tried to understand what Nádja was saying, the improbable idea that Emily was a . . . that she had lied in everything she had ever said since the day he met her . . . she was amazing . . . she approached the world entirely self-contained, able to project whatever she wished, whenever she wished, hiding everything, needing nothing and no one, in control of every element of herself and her surroundings. No wonder she would not accept him; no wonder he did not measure up to her. At that moment, he loved Emily Oliver more than ever before, but he did not wonder how he could win her, since she was unwinnable. She retreated up and away from him, out of reach, like a smoke ring. He crossed his arms, closed his eyes, propped his feet on the struts of Nádja's splintering piano bench.

"Play it, Grams!" yelled a voice from the bar.

Then there was a male singer crooning—almost croaking—a song John had never heard before:

> You're common, you're beneath me
> You've nothing of value to bequeath me
> I've better choices for my bed
> Yet I can't get you out of my head.

Your crimes no one could defend
I often hope you'll meet a ghastly end
Still, every night I think of better lines I might have said
Because I can't get you out of my head.

I have some sort-of friends who still insist and sing your praises
They scold me and say I've misunderstood you
They shake their heads at all my cool, cruel practiced phrases
Then look away and sigh, "Oh, how could you?"

But I don't bother with them anymore
No friends of mine could defend such a . . . [unintelligible moan]
Surely I can face the future without dread,
If only I could get you out of my head.

John was awoken, shaken, by the bartender, the last one there in the clean and well-lighted club, the man responsible for locking up and shutting off the stereo, the output of which John had just dream-requisitioned as his own composition, and the two of them walked out together into the first gray premonitions of dawn.

XI.

MONTHS LATER, ON A SMOOTH BUT NEVERTHELESS STOMACH-CHURNING flight home, examining a plastic-coated map of Budapest unfolded on her tray table, Emily found two possible, not quite mutually exclusive symbols for that day months before. One: It had been August 20, 1990, the first celebration of Hungary's national day under its proper name (the Feast of Saint István) since 1950, a statement of independence and self-determination. Two: Her path that evening as traced on this map of the city—from 5 P.M. to 3 A.M., seven stops in the shape of a spiral, circling a drain.

Five o'clock, top floor of Liberty Square. In the spacious office, she held three different ties up to the ambassador's jacket selection for the festivities to be held at Parliament that night. "I think we have a winner here, sir."

"Thanks, Em, lost without you. Listen, we've had a lot of late nights in a row here. Why don't you take tonight off, celebrate with friends instead of me.

Watch the fireworks down by the river. You could use a break." A simple act of employer generosity, although of course she could not stop herself from wondering if she had complained or, worse, somehow unknowingly shown by her behavior that she needed his kindness.

"That's very good of you, sir. Let me run that by Ed."

"Ed's not the ambassador, Emily. Take the night off."

"Of course, sir. I'm sorry. Thank you."

Five forty-five, upstairs responsibilities complete, actions logged, down one flight of stairs, other boss's office. "His Excellency told you to take the night off?" Ed asked, loosening his tie and splashing himself a tremendous vodka tonic, beginning his changeover for tonight's events at Parliament. "That's a wee bit peculiar, lassie. And profoundly frustrating to my universe, because I had a particular po-faced Jordanian I wanted you to bat your innocent eyelashes at this evening." He regained his office face. "Did you tell the ambassador that you needed"—and here comes another scolding. I'm probably breathing wrong, callow, no tone color, still somehow not Ken . . . but no, squeezing his lime wedge directly into his mouth, Ed had already moved on: "Well, no matter. Take the night off, then. I'll talk to H.E. m'self. Say—so big day tomorrow! Ken Oliver in the flesh, eh? I know you'll bring him by. Lot of people around the joint want to make the hero's acquaintance."

Two hours later, ashamed of her no longer deniable desire that her father not visit, she walked through the gathering crowds and the chatter of firecrackers until she was hungry enough to eat, and she ended up in a little six-table place just off the Elizabeth Boulevard, mostly because she was curious about what could justify the sign claiming Tex-Mex cuisine. She ate paprikás with red beans and canned jalapeños, drank Bulgarian beer, and tried to concentrate on her evening read, *Tactical and Strategic Elements of the Mujaheddin Victory over the Red Army*, by Col. Keith Finch, U.S. War College. She brushed blue corn chip dust out of the surprisingly impenetrable book's center, ordered a second beer, and began instead to write down all the sights of Budapest to show her father in the coming week. She had thought of three he might enjoy when she realized that he had probably been to Budapest at some point in his opaque career, though he had never said so, probably knew it better than she, would find easy everything she secretly found hard.

At the Gerbeaud, she found the Julies already in hilarious possession of a dusky patio corner, and she joined them for the eightieth reanalysis of Calvin's potential as Julie's soul mate. When the life had finally bled out of that whimpering topic, the other Julie told Emily, "Eric in Consular asked me about you again today. But he really is too creepy-looking, so I told him you were going out with John Price."

"Oh no, no. John's a little out there for me, thanks. My family would think he was a Martian." And they talked about entertaining Mr. Oliver for the coming week. "Does he want to see a lot of, like, farming stuff?" asked a Julie.

Caffeinated and pastried, they wandered to the river to watch the fireworks blossom over the palace. "And it celebrates what, exactly?" asked Julie, and Emily effortlessly rattled off the history of violent, well-loved Saint István.

Eleven o'clock, A Házam. As she took comfort in the overwhelming noise near the bar, she recalled a snippet of last year's required reading: *Crowded nightclubs offer the advantage of both noise—as it is difficult to be overheard or recorded—and excuses, as there are any number of people you might justifiably be there to see.* She danced agreeably with an egotistical dolt from Commercial Section, easily identifiable by his eye movements and mistimed jokes as a would-be fumbler (there: not so callow a Motivation Analysis, thank you very much) and actually (as she looked at him sweating under the steaming spotlights) reminiscent of the JV football player/aspiring drummer who had quickly relieved her of her girlish burden the fall of her sophomore year at Nebraska.

She smoothly declined the dolt's offer to take a walk, babe, citing Julie's blues as her responsibility and excuse to stay upstairs on a sofa. She watched Calvin-less Julie chat up a goateed American P.R. executive while she bore the brunt, all alone, of another hour of Julie's Calvinomics. And then, nearly midnight, nine hours until her father's plane was to land at Ferihegy Airport, she stood to go, dreading the looming Calvin rehash surely still to come back at the bungalow when: "Hey, it's the farmer's daughter at last. You don't come here often enough."

"Don't I?"

"I've been hoping to bump into you since we met."

"You have?"

"What are you drinking?"

"Why bump into me?"

"Because I've been thinking about you. You puzzle me."

"Me? That's hilarious. I don't puzzle anyone."

"Okay, right there. See, this is going to be fun, because I can tell when you're lying. So what are you drinking?"

"My friends were just leaving."

"Great. Do you want to go with them, or do you want to talk to me?"

And the Julies don't mind at all, catch you later, and two hours pass in inexplicably perfect conversation, never veering anywhere near work or anything threatening. Even better than being listened to attentively (which is joy enough at the moment, after weeks of Ed and Calvin-chatter and the attentions of tonight's dolt and his brethren) is savoring her companion's spicy stew of complaints, passions, self-criticism, self-love, self-interest, and the sudden, unstrained compliments for things no one ever noticed about Emily before. That's what a compliment should feel like, she thinks, nearly misty-eyed: completely motiveless.

One in the morning. Off the noisy square (more rat-a-tat firecrackers for Saint István) and suddenly swallowed in the charm of the dark and decrepit Pest streets, Emily would do anything to keep the conversation going, but her effort isn't necessary: The conversation thrums on its own internal power. "But how did you become you?" Emily asks, wants to know this more than anything, hypnotized as she is by the girl's irregularly shaped personality, which seemed to take no notice of any functional requirements but was instead the purely ornamental, unashamed expression of what any right-thinking person could only call selfishness. But in this one case, selfishness was suddenly—no other word would do—attractive. "Everything about you is so . . . I haven't ever known anyone like you, I don't think."

"Well, that's because they don't allow us in Nebraska, as a rule."

"Oh please, but please let's not bring up Nebraska."

"Oh no, let's. Absolutely let's bring up Nebraska. If Nebraska makes you that uncomfortable, we are definitely going to talk about Nebraska. Nebraska, Nebraska, Nebraska."

"My father's coming to visit tomorrow."

"Good or bad thing? Because if it were my father, I'd ask you to steal me a gun from the embassy."

Two in the morning, too tired to stroll in circles anymore. A dark little café-bar only two tables wide. Up three narrow wooden steps to the back section behind the hanging drapes, the tiny room lit with hooded green lamps, the velvet banquettes the only seats, so they had to sit side by side, squeezed close together to reach the pear brandy on the tiny carved table. (*It's best to avoid quiet, intimate eating places, as they are easily surveilled, both visually and audibly, and there is no excuse for your presence there if there is no overt justification for the meet.*)

"When did you know you were an artist?" Emily asked.

"When I was about four. I cried if my mom wouldn't take me to the art museum. I could copy anything there by the time I was nine."

"I'd love to see your paintings."

"Really? I'd love to show them to you. We're pretty near my place right now, if you want." And only just then did she consciously know: floating exhausted in the small hours of the night, having the first undeniable fun she'd had in ages, dead tired, dreading her father's arrival, irritated at the self-imposed restrictions of her work, owed something for—but she stopped creating false justifications. They were, she scolded herself, dishonest. More to the point, they were irrelevant, as she could think of no reason to resist this attraction (managing with almost no effort to ignore the risk to her work, her family, her carefully constructed public persona, even to what she had long considered to be her true private one).

At three in the morning an artist's studio has an overpowering effect on outsiders, even people who don't like art in general or the artist's work in particular: the unfamiliar smells, the physical evidence of frustration, the naked presence of some success but vast amounts of failure, the obvious sacrifice of conventional values (cleanliness, order, luxury) for others (space, ventilation, light), the merely functional furniture splattered and ripped. The unmade, squeaking single bed.

"I've never done this before," said Emily.

"I know. I would've remembered."

"You know what I mean."

"That's not a very interesting story, I have to say."

"You can't tell anyone."

"Oh, *that's* original."

"I am totally unoriginal, aren't I? Why don't you hate me? Don't answer that. I'm sorry. It's just, this isn't me."

"Really? This part here?"

"You know what I mean. I don't even know how I got here . . . What? What did I say? I didn't mean you should stop."

"That's pathetic. Don't be a chicken-shit with me. I didn't drag you here. You're not drunk. You can go home now if you don't like this."

"You're right. I'm sorry."

"Of course I'm right. This is obviously you. It's just no one has ever told you so before."

And only then she allowed herself to recall that this was reckless, a career-ending offense if discovered, but that didn't alarm her. What alarmed her was how little she cared, how much she wanted to be her own creation and judge, how much she wanted to be like Nicky.

And on that awful flight home months later, bumping down into Lincoln Airport, still not sure what she was going to say to her father, not sure herself if she had quit or been fired, feeling the weight of his heart and her mother's death in her hands, she still felt (at least for right now, until she saw his face) that Saint István liberated from Communism was a more apt symbol than a drain.

XII.

ONE HAZY MORNING, NOT LONG AFTER NÁDJA EXPLAINED TO HIM THE woman he loved, John sat in the Forum Hotel lobby. He thought of Emily's secret life, how he would guard the truth for her until, perhaps, such an exercise might teach him something that would make him more like her, more appealing to her. He understood that this was pretty pathetic.

" . . . Because the Jews did that to Hungary." Imre shrugged and mopped his forehead with a silk paisley pocket square. John studied his notebook to see if any of the mandarin jottings there could delicately wrap Imre's icy comment in some warming context. His attention having wandered, large swaths of this interview had been lost, and his notebook offered only the indecipherable scratches of a long dead civilization. *He might have been quoting. He could have scornfully been voicing the opinions of others. He could have been making an ironic point. Charles could have paid him to say it for entertainment's sake.* These possibilities all came at once, one on top of the other, until their sheer tangled mass sufficed, and John—recalling Imre the juggling street performer and pornographer to the good, horny citizens of Bonn, recalling the money at stake for all three of them—blamed his own lapsed concentration and dismissed the comment as not serious.

Imre dabbed his brow again and turned his chair away from the late afternoon glare of the river-view wall of windows. "I've a terrible headache—these vile televisions everywhere in these days," he muttered, and waved his damp handkerchief at the large screens wheeled into the lobby to provide constant coverage of the dogs of war snarling and peeing in the faraway desert. A German tourist was disputing his bill at the front desk, decrying the supplemental phone charges, the cable television surtaxes. His young son began to cry, then scream. The boy's mother seized him around the waist and loudly told him to be quiet. The child screamed with more force. "It is really too much," Imre told his two young companions, and wrestled with the knot of his tie as if it were actually blocking air. "Outlandish."

"*Nein! Nein!*" the tourist was yelling.

"The view: one of uncertainty, but one of readiness," bawled a young woman standing on the pitching deck of an aircraft carrier, trying to make herself audible over the scream of jets and the roar of water somewhere classified in the Mediterranean.

"*Bitte, mein Herr,*" tried the deskbound concierge.

"No! No! No! Let me go!" screamed the little boy in German while his mother attempted to soothe him by striking his bottom with an open hand.

"Károly, perhaps business later," Imre mumbled.

Charles rose from the lobby coffee table, strode to the desk, spoke German to the tourist and Hungarian to the concierge, smiled on the little boy, and within two minutes had the family out the door and the concierge warmly shaking his hand. He tipped a bellboy, who turned down the televisions' volume, and peace completed her reconquest of the Forum lobby. John watched admiration kindle and glow on Imre's face and marveled that it could take so little.

After his interview and their shared meal, Imre held court in the hotel lobby: Over five and a half hours, Charles presented to his partner six tentative investors with lingering questions. The investors—all of whom had read John's ironical but apparently grudgingly admiring profile of Charles in *BudapesToday*—took their turns examining this investment opportunity, talking about themselves while Imre nodded and Charles and John walked around and around the block. They had a drink in the John Bull English Pub, then stood by the sunset-frosted river in front of the hotel, leaned against the railing, and watched their business mutely unfold at the lobby table behind the huge picture window and their own ten-foot shadows, watched Imre charm the salt heiress, impress the sporicidal-efficacy-validation-equipment manufacturer, and listen with evident interest to the discount lawn products magnate.

At the end of these audiences, John took the elevator to the fourth floor and returned with his colleague from the *Times*, whom he introduced to the subject of that journalist's next insightful story, which, echoing John's own column on Imre, would run in the *Times* three days later and be picked up by the *International Herald Tribune* the day after that.

"Am I excused now, please?"

"You are excused, my Hebraic conniver," said Charles. "Exquisite work, by the way. Heroic, really." And as Ted Winston and Imre Horváth leaned toward each other over the glass-topped table behind the glass wall, John left Charles on the Corsó and walked slowly through the gathering evening to a cracked and colorless building on a deliciously charmless, no longer desirable little street not far from A Házam.

"Yes, you can stay," she said at the door, kissing him and wiping turpentine from her hands with a fuzzy multicolored rag. "You're cute, and I even admit to missing you lately. But you're out of here first thing in the morning, because the show goes up the day after and I'm hanging stuff all day tomorrow. No grumbling." He moved from lamp-illuminated brightness to shadows, dropped onto her bed, and watched her clean her brushes, wondered if he might not be in love with her. "But will you come to the show?" she asked in a different tone of voice entirely. "Will you? I really want you to. Please come."

XIII.

VISIBLY OUT OF PLACE AMID THE SUMMER-OF-'90 CROP OF EXPAT HIP-sters at "The New Americans" opening night, John and Mark sidled slowly through the gallery lobby of the old movie theater, past art photos hung from corrugated cardboard partitions, while from stereo speakers on the ashtray floor Stan Getz and Astrud Gilberto's duet fondled the memory of tall, tan, young, lovely, unwinnable women who strolled the beaches of 1960s Brazil. The men gulped sour white wine from plastic cups, smoked, and periodically stepped aside to let Hungarians reach the movie theater's concession stand or ticket booth. (That evening's double feature was selling well: *Battleship Potemkin* and *Battlestar Galactica* with accompanying music composed and played live by a Hungarian rock band.) The photos on display were, for the most part, reasonably accomplished renderings of the accepted artistic subjects of the day, comparable to similar hangings in New York: black-and-white close-ups of genitals, tattoos, old people, factories. Against this stark background, Nicky's two entries outstood sharply.

Her first was of an epic size, easily seven feet tall and four across; the small price tag next to the work quietly requested a buyer of substantial means. Glossy black plastic framed the complex self-portrait. Nicky herself, lifesize, posed as a variety of art professor: a tweed, leather-elbowed jacket over a black, ribbed turtleneck, corduroy slacks, loafers. She wore a thick brown mustache, oval spectacles, dark and rebellious eyebrows, and her own bald scalp. Her expression was pedantic. She stood, unaware of the photographer, in what appeared to be the gallery of a museum. In the midst of giving a lecture, she pointed with a stick at a large painting, opulently framed, hanging from a dark-wood-paneled wall to her left. This painting (Holbein? Dou? Teniers?), which she evidently described for unseen students, portrayed a type of seventeenth-century courtier: a young man in buckled shoes, dark hose, puffed and slashed slops, a jeweled dagger at the belt, jerkin, starched ruff collar, a pointed beard, and thin mustache. He, in turn, stood with one leg turned outward, stiff in the style of the era. The tiny black filament cracks of the painting's age appeared most visibly on his face, collar, and hands. Unlike the professor who described him, he stared directly at the viewer. With his left hand, he made an iconic, stylized gesture of sincerity, his fingers resting on his heart, and, with his right hand and an expression of haughty pride at owning such a valuable object, he invited the viewer to enjoy yet another framed work of art, this third item resting on an ornately carved easel to his right. This small work—equidistant from the professor and the courtier—was framed in dark wood, counterbalancing the gold-painted frame surrounding the courtier himself and the glossy black plastic that framed the entire piece. This second painting—the painting within the painting within the photograph—was in fact plainly a photograph, and unabashedly, unenjoyably pornographic: a couple, photographed head-on, engaged in a variety of posterior interconnection, the man kneeling behind the woman, who rested on all fours. They both faced the camera and the viewer, as if in obedience to their seventeenth-century owner. The man performed open-mouthed with half-closed eyes and a tilted-head, exalted expression of ecstatic enlightenment; the woman stared blankly, anti-titillatedly bored. Her long red hair, parted severely in the middle, framed her supporting arms, which, in turn, framed her exposed breasts. Her mounter—his upper arms and torso behind and above her hips, his legs visible only to the knee behind and between her supporting thighs, his hands on the points where her buttocks melted into her foreshortened back—sported a diabolical beard and mustache identical to that of the proud seventeenth-century "possessor" of the photo, but also a lush head of blow-dried blond hair. Under a toy tiara.

This internal photo—so jarring to the expected retrograde progression (professor to courtier to older portrait still)—usually won the work more attention than a quick walk-by. In his happy examination, Mark realized that the seventeenth-century painted courtier, like the twentieth-century photographed professor, was in fact Nicky. Mark understood this first, but at the same moment that he was asking, "Isn't that your friend, too?" John was saying, "Oh man, that's Nicky, I can't believe it," except John was pointing at the gloomy red-haired woman taking it from behind.

"Oh my," said Mark.

"Hello, handsome," said her voice behind them, and her hand slid into John's hip pocket and squeezed. She kissed him long on the mouth. "Do you like it?" she asked with her eager and unironic appetite for praise, slightly manically heightened by the event-ness of her opening night. John's hand skimmed her scalp, and she looked at both men with unblinking concentration, her wide, round black eyes openly hoping for love.

"Absolutely. Of course," said John. "What's not to like?"

"You are an original," said Mark. "I love it."

"Oh, Johnny, I love your pal! Thank you! It's not really done until it's purchased, of course. To really be finished, you have to imagine a fourth person: some proud owner who stands here, like this, and points to it for his friends with the same pride as Elizabethan guy."

"Yeah, great, great, great," said John. "But oh yeah, say, who is this?" He pointed to the ecstatic, tiara'd man, nestled securely behind his red-wigged girlfriend.

The artist wound her arm around John's waist and smiled conspiratorially at Mark, who was plainly enchanted by her. "Listen to Mr. Prude," she singsonged to the Canadian. "I happen to know he's sleeping with me *and* with Karen, our office airhead, and *he's* jealous of a painting."

Which comment left John several steps behind the conversation. "It's a photograph," he said, for lack of better options.

"Look carefully. Take away the beard and the coiff and it's . . ."

"Oh hey, it's you, isn't it?" Mark clapped his hands.

"The head at least, anyhow."

"And the body?" asked John, unconvincingly offhandedly.

"Gentlemen," she responded in a professorial tone. "Look closely! Exercise your critical faculties. Note"—she pointed at the stud's chest—"the dark, oddly geometric equilateral triangle of chest hair. Note"—she pointed at the two hands, just visible over the rise of her hip—"the fine, almost journalistic fingers clutching my ass."

"Oh," said John.

"Yes, my sweet." And she tugged at John's earlobe with her teeth.

"Those are very fine fingers," Mark agreed.

She happily told Mark of the "delightful little visit" John had made a few weeks earlier. She hadn't finished this one section of the piece, and, to her permanent frustration, she could not fill it with her own form. She wanted the encounter to look natural, though, so she snapped a few shots on a timer, then added new heads to both bodies ("I wasn't *quite* that bored"). John sifted through a handful of thwarted emotions: He couldn't get angry (it wasn't really his face); he couldn't feel complimented (it wasn't really his face); he couldn't be embarrassed (et cetera); surely he saw the humor, artistic statement, whatnot.

"I've heard all about you from our mutual friend," she told Mark, wrapping an arm around each of their waists. "You're the nostalgia queen, right?"

Nicky guided them past others' photographs (at which she emitted murmurs of quiet scorn) until she halted them in front of her second entry in the show. Quite small, this one openly proclaimed itself a photo collage. A woman in a sundress and straw hat reclined in a white wooden gazebo, caressed by the sun and shade of a green and perfect English garden. She and the gazebo had certainly been clipped from a catalog of some sort, some clothing store trading profitably on the ever-viable English country house fantasy. She stretched lazily, lengthily, on the shelter's pillowed banquette and gazed onto the park and garden through the latticed slats of the gazebo's decoratively carved walls. Her expression read as some variety of commercially appealing boredom. A few feet in front of her, there on the emerald grass dappled with the shadows of leaf and branch, she observed two mangy mongrel dogs engaged in a spirited display of copulation. The top dog was curved almost double, and one of his back paws had come off the ground in his avidity. His eyes rolled upward (where they appeared to focus hungrily on the fruit of an apple tree arching over the gazebo's red, conical roof). His black and dripping lips were frenziedly, unevenly pulled back, undressing white-and-yellow fangs, foamy saliva, mottled pink-and-black gums. The female dog, however, looked as bored as had Nicky in her red wig, and seemed to be making eye contact with the British lady in the gazebo. One had the irresistible feeling that the two females were sharing a moment of sympathy and communion. For this small work, Nicky had chosen a carved, gold-painted wooden frame, appropriate for a museum-prized old master. She had purchased it from a Budapest antique store, cutting up for collage scrap the painting it had held.

"I love your work, I love your work," Mark repeated several times to the reward of Nicky's increasing joy.

"I was taking pictures of the Soviet troop withdrawal. They're leaving now, you know, turning over these filthy bases they've sat in for forty years. The Russian guys were whistling and hooting as I was taking pictures of them, and I thought it was for me, but then this one Russian points behind me and I turn and see these two going at it. I just fell in love with these two, humping along as this pathetic parade of old tanks was going by."

She excused herself to greet other people—rival artists, potential buyers lingering in front of her works, friends unknown and unintroduced to John, a whole community and life about which he knew nothing and from which her ever proliferating house rules excluded him. She commented extravagantly on her work with obscure references and provocative, imaginative profanity to some demi-comprehending Hungarian art critics, then said her good-byes to the event's organizers. She returned to the men: "Let's get drunk and screw, boys." Her hand re-entered John's hip pocket, and she massagingly steered him out the door of the cinema, with Mark following close behind. They coasted down Bajcsy-Zsilinszky Boulevard, past the state-owned Cuban restaurant where the goulash came with black beans and rice, past the new discos named, in international-trademark violation, for hip brands of American clothes, and they docked at a sidewalk table of a café-bar. John ordered them six Unicums.

By the end of his second, he had begun to relax again. Nicky was answering Mark's renewed compliments with sisterly tenderness, the same woman who only minutes earlier was having to invent new profanity in order to express her thoughts, and John felt great fondness for her. The sensation of being in Nicky's hands was different than resting in Nádja's, but they were good hands, trustworthy guides, providers of lifelike excitement. "I can see why you didn't want me around for your last-minute preparations," he said. "I may have protested the unlicensed use of my likeness."

"Oh, don't you be worried about your precious little privacy. No one will ever know it's you." Nicky signaled for another three shots, and he wanted her with sudden and rumbling hunger, as soon as possible, for as long as she would keep him.

"You should be honored," Mark said, "modeling for great art. I'd buy loads of it. The more she makes, the more I'll buy. I'll be so modern."

"Mark, the first time I slept with John, he squeaked. Literally. Like a mouse. I thought he was joking. I'd never made a man squeak before, as far as I can recall." Tremendous bilateral gaiety ensued.

"The bed might have creaked. I'm sure I didn't squeak, exactly. I probably moaned, you know."

"You squeaked, Johnny."

"Squeaker," Mark clucked, shaking his head. "Squeaker."

John retreated inside to the bathroom.

"Do you love him?" Mark asked her with childish frankness as John disappeared inside.

"Not quite my life-mate type." She paused and sipped her drink. "A little too mushy. We're just entertaining each other. Honestly? I think my heart is elsewhere. As of late. I think." She laughed, rolled her eyes. "My God, I think that's the most boring thing I've *ever* said. What about you? Do *you* love him? Okay, forget it. I'm going to fall asleep, this conversation is so stupid—us and our little secrets. So answer me this: How does a nice young Canadian become a nostalgia queen?"

"When your parents first caught you smoking, what did they do?"

"I don't remember exactly. Grounded me. Pictures of diseased lungs. How could I be so stupid, et cetera."

"Precisely," said Mark. "*My* parents gave me a cigarette holder. Ivory and ebony. An antique. When I was fourteen, I smoked every night *with* my parents and I wore a red velvet smoking jacket, spats, and a monocle. That's the kind of people they were. They did this to me."

Another tray of Unicum arrived, compliments of an impatient John passing the bar on the way to the bathroom. "You're lying, aren't you?" she said. When John returned, they were laughing so hard that Nicky was crying and Mark was coughing violently.

"Actually, if you want to know, I'll tell you. I don't know how it started, is the short answer. I'd like to blame someone, but I think it's just me, actually. I do remember when I noticed it. Do you really want to hear this? It'll be pathetic."

"Pathetic," said Nicky. "Yes, please." John, not knowing the topic under discussion, knew she was collecting garbage to feed her ravenous, drooling Muse, and loved her for her open use of people, even himself.

"I remember very clearly when I was about four or five, I was riding on my dad's back in our parlor. He was on all fours, a horse. We did this every night when he came home from work. So, okay, one night he said, very nicely, just a throwaway line, laughing and very kind, he said, 'Whew, you're getting so big, eh? Soon you'll be too big for me to do this!' And that was that. I just couldn't believe it: There would be a time—soon—when our nightly horsey ride would be over, a fond memory of better days. And I just knew: Everything good dies. Before it's barely begun, it's already gone. A law of nature."

"That's so pathetic."

"I did warn you, but all right, here's a better story. This is when I knew definitively that I was different from the rest of the world."

"No, please," protested John, "not another sensitive young homo emerging from his cocoon."

"No," agreed Mark. "God, not that. That's nothing. This was much more important. You remember the Maurin Quina posters from the 1930s? No, I don't suppose so. They were advertising posters for this French apéritif. I don't think the drink has been around for decades now, but the posters are sort of legendary. Anyhow, the point is, I saw this poster for the first time when I was eleven or twelve and I fell in love with it. Head over heels. I was looking through a book of old advertising posters and this one just killed me. The poster has this green devil, and he's struggling with a corkscrew to open a bottle of Maurin Quina. He's entirely green except for this long, thin red mouth and bright red eyes. He's got wild, sharp green hair shooting off in all directions and a green tail with an end like a little shovel. And he's grinning and sort of skipping, floating through the air as he tries to open this bottle. And then you notice his feet: He seems to be wearing green ballet slippers. Not like a devil, you'll admit. Then you notice he's a little paunchy. Then you realize, this isn't a real devil. This is a drawing of some plump guy who has *dressed up* as a green devil, probably for a costume party or something, and now he's trying to open the Maurin Quina for the party. I loved this poster. I couldn't sleep sometimes, I loved it so much. I still have to remember not to look at repros of it right before bed. This was a picture of a good time, when you had costume parties and people went all out to dress up as a bizarre green devil, a time of great fun. Yeah, okay, so life was actually just about getting drunk and trying to get sex, but when you went to this kind of effort, it made it seem more important, sophisticated. I know now that none of this exists anymore, that all the good stuff really is in the past. But when I was twelve, I still had hopes I might live to see these good times. So, okay, Halloween 1975. I work very diligently in secret. My parents ask me, 'What are you going to dress up as?' but I keep it sub rosa. I gather my materials, do a lot of painting, sewing, dying, so forth, yeah? So, okay, I start the evening at a kids' party. I go up to the bathroom there, and it actually takes about a half hour to get my green hair and everything in order. I do it perfectly. Green ballet slippers. I've already got this paunch. I have a corkscrew and a cola bottle I painted like the old Maurin. I float, I skip downstairs, and no one has any idea what I am. 'Oh look, Marky Payton is a little monster!' says one mum. 'Mummy, Mark is scary!' says a little girl, and she starts to cry. I try to explain to them, 'I'm not scary, I'm all about good times, great parties, cool old advertising.' No response. 'Hey, look! Conrad Davis is a race-car driver! Jean MacKenzie is an astronaut!' I just kept thinking, An astronaut? Are they joking? But I remembered, hey, they're mostly just kids. I'm going home tonight to my parents and they're having a dinner party, and I'll make a great entrance—"

"And everyone will say, 'Look, it's the fat green devil from those wonderful posters of fifty years ago'?"

"Well, yes," Mark admitted. "I was twelve. I thought grown-ups would understand. I got dropped off at home, and as I walked toward the house, I thought, There will be a sophisticated group here, brilliantly costumed, handsome people, sipping champagne from tall glasses. I'm not actually clear why I thought this; my parents were pretty lame, very conventional suburban Toronto bourge-o's. Anyhow, I came into a table full of people in bad suits and flowered dresses asking, 'What are you supposed to be, dear? What poster is that, dear? Malcolm (my dad), Malcolm, the boy's an incipient alcoholic by the sound of his obsessions, hahahahahaha.' And so forth. My mum asked me what the other children had dressed as, and I said, 'Horrible modern things. A space suit or something.' 'Really?' she said. 'An astronaut! How exciting!' I was so disgusted with all of them. And then I knew. I knew there was something wrong with me, or something wrong with everybody else." Mark drained a glass and reflexively laughed enough to make the other two comfortable again, watched John hold Nicky's hand.

But it was wasted on Nicky; she had spotted something across the street and sat very still, just squinting her eyes and following something a hundred feet away, a newly tickled anger on her face. "Hold on a sec." She pushed back her chair and ran across the boulevard to the far sidewalk, holding up her palm to braking traffic.

"I have to tell you, I just love her. I'm totally in love with her, actually.

Really, John." Mark sighed and rubbed his eyes. "She's who you should be with, I guess."

"Love who?" John answered distractedly. Between rushing and parked cars, he periodically saw Nicky on the far sidewalk, standing in front of a window with a short-circuited neon sign that fritzed and blinked some word in green that would have been illegible even if he knew Hungarian. Nicky talked and gestured excitedly to a young couple. After a few moments, she forcefully shoved the man; he stepped backward with an expression of surprise, anger, some amusement. The girl at his side screamed something John couldn't quite make out, then she pawed at the lapel of Nicky's blazer and slapped the artist hard across the face.

"Whoa," whispered John, and Mark sat up at once. "That's different."

The blow momentarily immobilized Nicky, but then she punched the girl in the stomach, collapsing her in two at the waist, so that from John's seat it looked as if Nicky had deflated her opponent by pulling a plug at her navel. Nicky spat at the astounded man, who had placed one hand on his companion's back, then she turned to walk slowly back across the street, a fireworks display of imaginative profanity again sparkling from her mouth. Standing, she called the waitress over and ordered three more Unicums. Seated, she gently squeezed Mark's cheek and John's crotch. "Sorry about that, boys. Old business."

"Who was that?" asked John.

"As I believe I just said, old business, okay?" Her cheek nearest John bore a very clear impression of four white fingers, a phantom admirer marveling at the softness of her skin, and she drank her share of the next tray quickly. "No good to wallow in the past, right, Marcus?"

Mark blinked hard to focus his eyes, wipe away the summer haze, and fend off the late-night shrivel of his contact lenses. "Can I interview you for my research? You're my new hero."

"No can do," she said, standing and pulling John by the hand. "Because after a fight, Mark, I like to get laid. So I need Johnny here to take me home now. I'd invite you to join us, but a lapsed heterosexual is of no use to me this evening." She began to place forints on the table, but Mark refused them and told her he meant to buy the larger of her two photographs as well, that he would contact the show's organizers tomorrow to arrange it. She literally jumped up and down twice, clapping her hands. She kissed him on the forehead, plainly moved, stroked his cheek, and looked as if she might cry. She thanked him and thanked him again, then took her date in hand toward Andrássy út.

As they walked in silence toward his apartment, where no hidden cameras awaited him, John understood for the first time that Mark came from money, possibly a great deal of money. For months, the Canadian had bought rounds and rounds of drinks, meals and meals for everyone, had bought John weekly gifts, and now he planned to buy a work of art priced at nine months of John's salary, even though the scholar had no visible means of support. "That's kind of terribly sad," John muttered, meaning that he hadn't known this and Mark was probably his closest friend in the city, but in the volatile, variable emotional landscape that liquor—and Unicum in particular—can create, John was soon over that hill of sadness and into new country, a green and pleasant vale, where he was happy to be leading such an interesting life, happy his friend was buying art he had modeled for, happy to be following Nicky, who obviously held some secret for living a full and rich existence, happy to be drunk, happy not to be photographed having sex tonight, happy to be so clearly free of Emily, terribly sad not to be with Emily, though he knew that yet again, after a misdirected struggle, he had been thrown back to hardly knowing her, wondered what she must feel like living entirely in secret, following only her best judgment, but then very happy again to be pinned against this brick wall and feeling this soft and gnawing mouth attached to his, the taste of cigarette smoke and liquor on the lips and then the feeling of her scalp against his face and her face against his neck.

"You know what I like about you, little boy?" She licked his ear. "You miss all kinds of stuff. You just glide right through, totally peaceful."

A lonely drink or two later, Mark left the sidewalk table, returned directly to the gallery, and pledged to purchase the photograph of the couple having sex, who were in fact at that moment having sex (after Nicky had pulled from her backpack a gift for him: a contact sheet where his torquing body still supported its own head, a head displaying, over twelve photographs, a narrow range of alternately bovine and vulpine expressions, which their owner could only try futilely to forget a few minutes later, even as he knew he was duplicating them).

Concluding his transaction at the gallery-cinema-disco (a small label now read SOLD, in two languages), Mark set off through the night for the lobby of the Forum Hotel, where comfortable chairs and broad, glass-topped tables sprouting a garden of bowls flowering salty peanuts awaited him, where Western-polite waiters in black vests would bring him Coke in little bottles, and where, best of all, CNN would be playing the latest news from the Persian Gulf crisis and he could sit until dawn watching the approaching war story unfold and think of nothing else, for once. He was so hungry for it that he once or twice broke into a jog, which quickly ended with out-of-shape gasps and self-mockery, and the happy knowledge that he needn't run after all, because it played twenty-four hours a day, the very, very latest at any hour.

XIV.

FOR MOST OF AUGUST 1990, FOR THE VERY FIRST TIME SINCE HE HAD painted himself green and wondered why his Canadian world did not understand and love him, Mark decided he was living in the present and he was overexcitedly proud of it. He had never even heard of CNN until three weeks earlier, but now not only did he love it, he loved that he loved it, that he sincerely savored something so very, very modern. This infatuation proved he would be okay; it distracted him from his multiplying fears. He quickly learned the names of the American generals and defense officials, all the news network's postulators, the titles and relative influence of the various coalition representatives. In his apartment he hung a four-foot-square map of the Middle East and daily festooned it—consulting the latest *International Herald Tribune* for the appropriate coordinates—with paper cutouts he had spent a morning trimming: little boats for the coalition fleets, little tanks for artillery and armored units, little helmets for infantry, paper flags of the proliferating belligerents, and red, curved, dated arrows to show troop movement.

News, and so literally *new:* a war on TV with real-time play-by-play. What could be more modern than to watch news all the time, coverage of events happening in any corner of the world, what must have once required days, weeks, months to reach you? He was living in the nineties with all his heart—the 1990s. A joyful anticipation he had never felt before: When the headlines came up again on the half hour, would they be mere repetitions of the headlines he had just heard at 3 A.M., or would something new have broken in the interim? The very history of the world formed itself for him, every half hour, a time lapse comfortable enough to render Mark an Olympian spectator, lounging on his cloud while horned, shaggy-shinned goat-men finger-fed him delicacies from gold goblets and silver salvers.

For three weeks his precarious happiness gave him an aggressive, feverish sort of confidence to pursue his research with a semblance of personal detachment and equilibrium, because the high point of his day—for which he longed while in libraries or antique stores or at his desk—balanced undeniably in the *present* tense, when the welcoming Forum Hotel would open its maternal arms to him and he would watch the mortals perform their antics.

Until his night with John and Nicky, when, three hours after they left him at the table, he realized exactly why CNN so pleased him: It reminded him of old newsreel footage. He had just watched four repetitions of American soldiers marching under a journalist's baritone voice-over. Four times, and each half hour the one goofy soldier looked straight at the camera and mouthed the words *Hi, Mom!* And each time the troops walked by the camera, they seemed less and less modern, more and more a future historical document or bouquet of future personal memories—*the time I was in the service, I was on CNN, my son greeted me on CNN, my late son, my son who was killed in the desert war, my buddy said, "Hi, Mom," on CNN, I remember my sergeant chewing our asses because some joker I didn't even know had said, "Hi, Mom," when CNN was filming us looking sharp, your father was a soldier, here's a videotape of him, your grandfather was in the army and fought in the first desert war, you can view the footage on the computer-visualizer unit, the film looks funny, Mom, why do the soldiers look like that?* And on their fifth inspectional march-by of Mark, a film of fine sepia clung to these young men, newsreel marching soldiers off to save the world again, may as well be in jerking, sped-up, black-and-white, and with a shock of discovery, Mark stood up from the hotel lobby table where he sat at 3:37 in the morning, shoveling peanuts into his mouth and drinking the lukewarm Coke right out of the little bottle (out of which glass teat it tasted just like it had in the Toronto tennis club where he had sat once a week—ages six to nine—and watched his father play badly), and he realized miserably that he had been conned. No one ever knew they were old-fashioned; everyone always thought they were up-to-the-minute: Rickety Model T cars weren't rickety when they were invented, scratchy radio wasn't scratchy until television, and silent movies weren't a feeble precursor of talkies until there were talkies. Your two-piece telephone that demanded you hold a cylinder to your ear while you screeched into the wall demanding a particular exchange of a harried, plug-juggling operator was the highest of high-tech. To know it was anything less would have been like acknowledging you were going to die and life was transient and you were already halfway to being a memory or worse. The real and worst tragedy of twentieth-century Eastern Europeans: They had known they were old-fashioned before they could do anything about it. Their politics, their culture, their technology, their lives were out-of-date, no problem as long as they didn't know it, but they knew. They knew that life was faster, sleeker, richer, and in full color just over that vicious Wall, just across that Iron Curtain (the defining feature of their lives built and dubbed in the 1940s, crafted from barbed wire and mines unchanged in design for decades).

He turned away from the screen and looked out the picture window onto the nearly empty (one pimp, one drunk, one sleepy, hostel-less backpacker) Corsó. CNN was the newsreel of his day, he thought. "My day," he said aloud, and the waitress looked up from wiping down the same square foot of cocktail table she had been slowly, vacantly polishing for minutes. My day: That in itself triggered misery. Dying was happening all around him and within him. Faster than he could live and grow, he was dying and shrinking. Could it be—he examined curiously the Forum night staff (the concierge, the bucket-wheeling maid, the waitress)—that some people were still living and growing, that they didn't know everything was already old and dying? Was it right to tell them, or was it right to hold his tongue?

The same poison oozed into his blood two hours later, as the sun was just rising. He was in the midst of Saudi territorial waters, blearily scribbling dates on curving arrows, repositioning paper ships, when he knew the whole act was futile, a vain effort to ignore the noise. He was fooling no one. He angrily tore the map down the middle, leaving two strips of West and East dangling irrelevantly from the wall, and he shredded slowly each lovingly clipped boat and helmet and tank and curving arrow, heaped a little pile, beat his swords into confetti. The ominous feeling thumped stronger still at noon, when the gallery people roused him from sweaty, head-turning sleep to deliver his purchase and accept his huge stack of forints in a shoe box, and he leaned the enormous work wrapped in brown paper and twine against the peeling, faux-wood armoire. Not even worth unwrapping: The art was already old. Nicky was the improbable, eccentric character in someone's future memoirs of fin-de-siècle bohemian Budapest, and the future reader would be shocked to see her as she looked at publication time, age eighty, would prefer to cling to the grainy old photos of her as a bald and beautiful young woman. The same feeling pulsed at twilight, when John came by to pick him up and they walked toward the evening's party (at the home of Charles Gábor's attorney, a dashing Anglo-Hungarian who had hired members of the Budapest Opera to sing in his garden while his guests cut deals, flirted, drank), and the two friends talked about the Persian Gulf, and John laughed when Mark hopelessly said there would be a war.

"A war? Over that stuff?"

"Not a war. *The* war. *Our* war. The very feel of this city is going to change; it's already changing. This is not just the end of August 1990. These are the last months of our peace, the end of the summer before our generation's war. 'What did it feel like the summer before the war? Did you know time was running out? Could you tell it would all be swept away?' The summer before." John turned to gauge his friend as they walked.

Mark felt himself being examined, knew how he sounded, and wanted to say something to put his friend at ease, even though he sounded that way because of how horrible this truth was, but he didn't know what to say, and didn't know how to explain that *he*—Mark himself—was the summer, the dying peace. Though they walked slowly through a quiet and pleasant evening, Mark felt time rushing by his ears like drunken traffic, like supersonic trains, like a herd of salivating, rolling-eyed, dust cloud–stamping beasts. He had let his guard down. CNN! For some reason he had stopped watching time carefully, and now he was being made to pay for his inattention. Now he was forced to sit, brutally strapped to a stake, with his eyelids pried open. One idea soothed him, a new idea: Perhaps time rushed by less painfully in a place that didn't look old, that had no history. Toronto, for example.

"Are you hungover still?" John asked.

As they passed the Gellért Hotel (uniformly hailed in every guidebook for its "faded glory," making it, for a couple of weeks way back in mid-May, Mark's favorite haunt on the Buda side) in the first clear touch of evening, when the humidity vanished before a cool sigh of breeze, Mark bit at his lip and said he wasn't feeling well, and before John could say much at all, the Canadian had turned around and sweatily puttered back up Gellért Hill toward his apartment.

XV.

IMRE SELECTED FOR THEIR MEETING A SMALL AND DINGY COFFEE SHOP wafting bleach and wet cat, a mystifying, willfully weird choice of locale as far as Charles was concerned. "I signed comparable papers just there, in that building," Imre explained. He pointed across the one-way street to the pocked offices he had entered the afternoon of his father's funeral to receive the rusty keys to his crumbling kingdom.

"Did you? Well, I don't expect you'll sign anything today." Charles withdrew from his leather case the deck of papers his lawyer had delivered at the garden gala the night before. He laid them on the ringed and burned simulated marble. "Why don't you look these over at your leisure and then initial at all these little yellow tags: here, here, and here, and sign there. You date that and then another initial there and then sign the bid application there and there. Krisztina can run them over to Neville's office."

"My father's attorney became my attorney this day, you understand. It was a very strange moment." Imre sipped his coffee and, surprising Charles, thoughtfully removed his cigaresque fountain pen from an interior pocket. "I had known this moment would come, of course. I must have waited for years for this day to come. Still, one is always a bit surprised when it happens."

Charles blindly agreed. "But wouldn't you want some more time to look these over?"

"Yes, yes." The older man tapped his capped pen on the pages, but still he looked through the sun-sparkled dusty window and across the street. He poked his pastry with his fork and a crack appeared across its fitted top sheet of amber caramel. "You are in a similar position today as I was then; it is remarkable."

"Of course." Charles composed his face in accord with Imre's melodrama.

"How I could have been happy on such a day, I cannot now say. But I certainly was. And this city, this wreck of a ship that once was proud—I was happy to be a help rebuilding this ship. It was a wonderful time to live here, to tell the truth. Today is not so different. To rebuild. To know your role."

Through the window, Imre considered the building that had once housed his family's fortunes, and the shade of that July morning, altered from its years of wandering, appeared to him. He remembered the obvious significance that had filled the room. His father's lawyer had hesitated: Would this young man rise to the occasion? Imre had been tangibly transformed by the very act of signing; his signature itself was a voyage across an invisible frontier—the trip from the left side of the empty line to the right, leaving a curving black trail behind him. A swirl of black ink and the conclusive stabbing slash of the accent mark on *Horváth*—´—made him a symbol of something important and large. Everyone in the room had understood.

Charles chafed, not for the first time, at the similarity of his and Imre's suits, both a light tan twill this morning, though Imre's was double-breasted. It irritated Charles to be dressed similarly to anyone else in a room. It implied a slipping market value for his uniqueness and made him feel as if he were talking to a child who had just learned to annoy through mimicry.

Imre rose from the table and walked to the window, where backward letters and old webs and clots of dust cast shadows on his face. He absently carried his fork and left his pen on the table with the partnership agreement and the privatization application. "The weather comes back to me, very distinct. Sun, some clouds, terribly hot. I smelled something bad in the courtyard of the office building, old rubbish in the heat. My father's lawyer wore trousers sewed together from scraps. We all did in these days, though some of us wore them better than others, I may say to you of all people. The most important day of your life, a wonderful moment, but to know it as it happens, you feel like God Himself is holding you up in His hand. I knew the importance, that Imre the man was now secondary to the future of this . . . You are the same. You are learning this." He spoke with his back to the younger man, stared at the large, dark brown bricks across the street. "Each of us together—ohhh, listen to me. Show me where to sign and we will get on with it." He did not turn from the window, though.

"Good Christ, it took some strange twists and turns, but it's done," Charles told John later that day as he handed him a light blue check, the flimsy, thin equivalent of seven months' salary at *BudapesToday*. "After all that, he barely read what he signed. Just challenged sections at random. But he kept misting over with memory while I told him where to initial. How the hell he managed to run anything for forty years is beyond me. Hey, did I tell you that two of my investors *quoted* your profile of me back to me when they signed on?"

John squinted and held the check up to the shower of glaring gold arrows shooting off the river and streaming into Charles's office. The paper cast a light blue rectangular shadow across John's eyes and nose. Its watermark—two sirens kissing the cheeks of a surprised sailor, his mouth and eyes perfect O's of astonishment—vanished and reappeared as John passed the slip back and forth between himself and the light.

"I'm going to miss this view." Charles slapped his palms against the giant window. He had succeeded, and would soon resign, revealing to his flummoxed, flabby firm that he had accomplished in his spare time what they couldn't manage during business hours. He had tricked sufficient funds from the pockets of various missionaries of money, and, with Imre's unexpected initials that morning, that consortium had become the 49 percent shareholder (with the entire 49 percent of the voting rights held by Charles) of a new Hungarian company comprising Horváth Verlag (Vienna), Charles's sizable infusion of other people's investment, and Imre's privatization vouchers (hardly a windfall, just the gesture of a proud but impoverished government). Gábor had, at the last moment, instructed his attorney to augment the company's wealth with the nearly worthless vouchers issued to his own parents for their childhood apartments. He was now the highly influential junior partner of something very real.

For two days, however, John did not cash his check—payment for "press relations consulting"—or send it to his bank in the States. Something about depositing it put him off; it was too abrupt, a farewell to the watermark, he joked to himself, that he was not yet prepared to make. Two nights the sirens kissed their sailor and John considered. Two days, he kept the paper in his wallet, and at odd times—while typing at the office, tippling at the Gerbeaud, tupping at Nicky's—he imagined the watermark—two-dimensional, pale, fluid—come to life in his pocket: the sirens' streaming hair, the soft lips on the cheeks of the startled mariner, the sailor's desire to seize them both in aqua-carnal embrace battling with his knowledge of their power, his inevitable surrender. "Kiss me, my siren," John murmured to the bald and naked woman painting by 3 A.M. lamplight on the third night. She had thought he was asleep. Trembling slightly at his voice, she coldly told him to leave and sleep at home. He liquidated his tormented sailor the next morning.

XVI.

MARK'S ABSENCE, AFTER TEN DAYS AND SIX UNRETURNED PHONE MESsages, John diagnosed as unmistakable stage-two Visiting Family Syndrome. The symptoms were now easily recognizable in the plague-ravaged community. Stage one: murmured references to "a busy week ahead," increasing quietness, sporadic personality aberrations (irritability, childishness, hysteria, isolation). Stage two: total disappearance for five to fourteen days, except (possibly) for hurried introductions of friends to jet-lagged, shy, elderly people with peculiar or nonexistent senses of humor. Stage three: sudden and boisterous return to society with exaggerated ubiquity and gluttonous appetite for drinking, dancing, and romance; and a twitchy, logorrheic rhapsodizing over the joys of living single in Budapest.

John would have much to report when Mark recuperated. Charles Gábor had quit his job, to the dumb amazement of the Presiding Vice, and now had fifteen days to move out of the bungalow his firm had bought him. In depositing his check, John had added nicely to his annual income, but could not think of anything to acquire except perhaps a rocket pack with which to soar high over Budapest, orange cones of flame propelling him—a legend of the expat-journo scene—on his cometlike way. He would consult with Mark on how best to be rich, since the Canadian carried it off with such aplomb. And Mark would learn Charles had also soared high above the rooftops, courtesy of John, Ted Winston, a squadron of felonious gentlemen on Wall Street, and the insatiable appetite and daffy logic of the American news machine, which in this case John himself had tickled into action with a series of pieces as the deal heated up:

. . . Finally, for those of you following my ongoing coverage of the capitalist who saved Hungarian culture, my sources tell me the Gábor-Horváth bid to reclaim the ancestral institution is in to the government, and the money-famished Maggies find it extremely compelling. Other bidders should think twice or three times before bothering to challenge these zealots. "There are lots of marvelous other properties to be bid at," I was told by one highly placed representative of the State Privatization Agency, sounding very much like an ungrammatical used-car salesman gearing up for a holiday weekend . . .

. . . If such a thing were possible, the news is even more humiliating from some of their overseas ventures. In Budapest, for example, after several months of apparent paralysis, during which time the firm seemed unable to kickstart any projects, a junior associate of the firm has now resigned in unmistakable frustration with his do-nothing employers and is leading his own efforts at rejuvenating an old Hungarian publishing house. This story, carried in the local English-language paper for several weeks, came to international attention in light of recent investigations of the firm's U.S. dealings by the federal prosecutor's office, led by an attorney whose political aspirations are hardly a closely guarded . . .

. . . And, on a lighter note, one of our own young Cleveland men is showing what's possible with a little imagination, some money, some nerve, and a whole bunch of American-style idealism and Lake Erie can-do. Carl Maxwell has the story from the fine old city of Budapest, the capital of the nation of Hungary, located far away in Eastern Europe. Carl? . . .

And, in expectation of continued payments, John strove, inside his column and out, to keep Charles's success churning along. He swallowed hard and played the role of hearty networker on Charles's behalf, harvesting rich people and Hungarian government officials unearthed in the course of interviews and stories. More entertainingly, he prepared descriptions for Mark's amusement of these inane introductions and repetitive conversations, of the faux-macho manner and the coy behavior. "I turn out to be a very gifted pimp," John planned to tell his friend. "It's a noble profession, with a great history."

But Scott's wedding day arrived, and that evening Charles reported to the uninvited John that Mark had been notably absent from the small ceremony. Charles, in an attack of sensitivity John found almost funny, did not mention John's absence but produced instead an amusing edition of the nuptials, highlights selected especially for him: Emily had worn a broad, round straw hat, a sundress, and sandals that crisscrossed her brown ankles. "In other words, she looked like she was auditioning for a douche ad." The church was scarcely occupied: Charles and Emily, a few English teachers, a half dozen of his students, a quartet of Mária's sultry friends, and seven of her relatives. The groom, wearing traditional Hungarian formalwear, stood between Mária's brothers, two fire hydrants wrapped in Hungarian Army dress uniform. "It looked like a capital punishment trial." The Catholic ceremony was aggressively lengthy. Hymns swelled and rolled infinitely on like symphonies, sermons droned like college lectures, blessings passed like merger-and-acquisition negotiations. The congregation rose and stood until Charles's legs ached and shook and he struggled to straighten his spine. The congregation sat immobile until his buttocks melted away against the smooth wooden bench transubstantiated into steaming concrete. Some hours and one kiss later, they were directed just next door, to the Hilton's patio. Under a yellow-striped canopy supported by metal poles flaking white paint and sporting little Hungarian flags on their ends, four tables were set with lunch, slightly to one side of identical tables serving identical lunch to tourists intimidated and exhilarated by the sudden apparition of verifiably nontourist life.

And that was all John ever learned of his brother's wedding. He had not spoken to the groom or seen him since the engagement was announced a month earlier. He certainly hadn't received a written invitation as others had. But he also had failed to congratulate his brother after the purple-mustache fiasco, and perhaps that's all it would have required. But now, after so many years of pursuit, that had been more than he could muster. It didn't matter. Seriousness was certainly elsewhere.

As Mark's absence persisted into the second week of September, John decided the Canadian was probably on a research trip. He should have said something prior to departure, but Mark could do as he pleased. John had stopped by enough times, left enough messages. In the meantime, he had better things to do.

That afternoon, he stopped by Mark's building to see if his friend had returned. With Scott a lost cause once and for all, with Emily still too daunting to approach, with Charles shuttling between Budapest and Vienna, with Nicky oddly unavailable and more than usually off-putting, and with a long two hours before Nádja started playing, he had nothing better to do. In truth, he hungered for company. He was flinging the early autumn rain from his twirling umbrella, knocking on the unresponsive door, rattling the resentful knob, peering against the rebelliously reflective windows, when a large, bearded Hungarian emerged from a neighboring apartment. A long stream of foreign words—John caught *az amerikai*—accompanied this ursine arrival. John pointed at Mark's apartment and corrected the beard floating just above his eye level: *"Kanadai."* More foreign chatter ensued. Finally the man rubbed his right thumb and fingers together and banged twice on Mark's door: Rent seemed overdue. "Ahhh," John said. "Okay, okay." With more sign language he convinced the man—a landlord or superintendent, evidently—to unlock Mark's door and the two of them walked inside, each with the other's permission.

The super stopped in front of the enormous photograph leaned against the wall, John's copulating torso at its center. Nibbling his beard and staring at the work with a worried concentration, he slowly nodded. John wandered from room to room, opening cupboards, drawers. Mark's clothes were gone, his luggage was gone, his toiletries were gone. Some laundry had been forgotten, now stiff and stinking in the washer, and his jumbo gramophone stood in the corner. His books and his notes remained, all removed from the shelves and neatly stacked on the kitchen table, under an envelope with Nicky's name on it. A panicked rip, but John found in it no suicide note (and quickly resented being tricked into the momentary panic), only a blurry Polaroid: one half of Mark standing to one side of Nicky's grand work, pointing toward it with the same air of proud ownership as the Elizabethan courtier. Nicky's work was inverted in the photograph (professor on the right, courtier on the left), and the visible half of Mark's face was covered with a Polaroid camera: The photo had been taken, badly, by Mark himself, using a mirror.

Whatever this scene was, it seemed at first to John a bit unreal or just the latest off-kilter display of the peculiar scholar—not so much something he did do as something he *would* do. Mark hadn't killed himself or been kidnapped: He'd just gone away, pointedly saying good-bye to no one, and now John was childishly angry at the affront, then quickly sorry for himself. He phoned Charles: "Did Mark tell you that he was leaving?" He felt relieved not to be the only one. "In that case, I have someone here for you to talk to if you're still looking for an apartment. And tell him to let me stay alone until you get here." He handed the phone to the landlord (unwilling to pull his eyes from Nicky's vast and stimulating work).

Left to himself, John knew he was supposed to take some action, understand something about all of this. He boiled water for the Czech strawberry tea the stingy kitchen had yielded. He listened to and then erased three weeks of his own lonely voice on the otherwise unoccupied answering machine, the pleading tone of his messages both fascinating and repellent. He sat at Mark's small table, underneath the Sarah Bernhardt poster and the hollow map borders. He read Mark's notebooks from beginning to end, ready to understand, expecting explanations with each turn of a page, open to any messages Mark or Fate cared to send him, even as he began to tell himself that, yes, Mark had left without saying good-bye, but it didn't matter, wasn't serious, couldn't have any bearing on anything real . . .

The dated journal entries began in March, six weeks before John's arrival in Budapest, and they comprised, for a couple of months, dense, efficient, formalized records of research: numbers, quotes, references, cross-references, chapter outlines, half-finished essays, descriptions of antique stores spiked with parenthetical library call numbers. Essays on particular episodes of Budapest's history and the effect of these episodes on the city's landscape made John sleepy; he refilled his tea and opened the window. He began to doubt he would find any messages, lost track of what he was expecting to find, imagined himself—sometime in an indeterminate future, in a better place—discovering that some friend had disappeared and intently scouring the friend's abandoned notebooks looking for an explanation.

. . . with neither insight nor interest, the matter dropped by Parliament, and lingering questions of responsibility to the past ignored by population eager to (selectively) forget . . . cross-ref: Pruth on collective nostalgia during transformative eras . . .

. . . percent of pop knowledgeable about and angry at treaty of seventy years earlier remarkable—compare to pivot dates in West. Cross-check betrayal-centric national myths to measurable depth of affection for pre-betrayal habits, etc. . . .

. . . How long until the country, or certain sectors (elderly, e.g.), begin to long for some intangible element of recently discarded Communist past (stability, security, etc.)? Worth measuring the penetration and durability of this "nostalgie de la misère" and comparing it to the penetration and durability of ironic *faux-nostalgia for Communism (i.e., photos in A Házam, V. I. Lenin's Pizza Shack, college-age participation in campy October Revolution parades, etc.) . . .*

. . . Ponder this: a teenager in 1953 Hungary rebels against the fools who teach him and the foolish peers who sheepily go along with the Party line. It turns out, thirty-six years later, that that rebellious teenager was moral, *a hero of conscience. Question: Had he grown up in Canada, would he have rebelled anyhow just because he was a teenager? Survey thought: Is there a higher degree of nostalgia for adolescence among people who, retrospectively, turn out to have been adolescents under a system subsequently acknowledged to be immoral?*

These initial semischolarly efforts soon wandered away from grovey academia. Even as early as late May, essays about Mark's reactions to his research dominated, displacing the research itself. The writing grew introspective, almost adolescent: descriptions of loneliness and desire John found embarrassing, long lists of questions about the meaning of life and work, tirades against family members and acquaintances, odd essays: *Is memory a substance, a fluid secreted from within coiled knots of slick brain jelly, tricked out by smells? Do bumps on the head dislodge this mnemonic ooze? Or is memory an electrical force tickled out by quacky or wise practitioners of alternative medicine who touch mappable mnemo-nodes, and unleash a sudden flow? Or is memory a library, dusty and stuffed beyond all logic, a chaos beyond the skill of any taxonomist to save, book and book are dumped, a thousand thick volumes a day fill the library lobby and climb the stairs, overflow the elevator shafts, clog the toilets and sinks, crush metal shelves like paper, fall from the shattered windows in a schluffy heap onto the sidewalks and a few ancient, torn copies, deposited long ago, are suddenly available again, and old men stop and stoop and marvel to flip through crumbling pages that nearly melt under their touch and their tears as they read of their childhood pets and their mothers' private recipes, of neighbors inexplicably menacing and the smell of father's face after he shaved . . .*

Man's third primal urge. Unlike Thanatos, which drives man to look forward to the end, and Eros, which drives men to look directly down, Retros drives us to look backward.

Mark had done no work at all for several months, perhaps nothing of any significance since the first few weeks after his arrival. The scholar would attempt, in the midst of these outpourings, to focus, and for a day or two would produce the same sort of serious entries he had made at the beginning, but they would not last.

There is an old Canadian school of thought that runs: If you don't talk about it, it will go away, and this is a valid point. Nobody likes trouble. Look in their eyes when I relax—they tense up. Now why is that? Because I am inverted. I am the hanging man. I walk backward and I must stop being proud of it. It is wrong to walk backward in front of other people. Things could be significantly worse. The pain of others worse off than oneself. War dead, of course. They killed a lot of Canadians at Dieppe, lots of little boys with pasts, lots of favorite hand soaps, lots of nights spent with the wireless set, lots of other memories. Every time I ask them to see like me, they smile. And they are right; I must stop. Viruses demand quarantines. I am ready, I tell you, it's all done now, it's tamped and tamped and tamped I am stamping and tamping and stamping, I'm ready, I'll be good, please I'm done being away from everyone I'm so ready, please, please, please, I'll be good.

The journals did not end here, on this unpalatable cocktail of the pathetic and the deranged. Instead—and this bothered John more than all the rest, more than the tedium of the research, the grating angst, or the increasingly credible yet still somewhat unbelievable notion that Mark was literally "ill" or "in danger"—instead, the last of the notebooks ended with Mark realizing how he sounded and then flinching. John saw Mark grow disgusted and drape himself in ironic amusement:

Wait! This is becoming the testament of someone "unwell." How boring. I've gone all unwell. I see I need to remove myself from unhelpful stimuli, go where things are safely bland. You agree? Fair enough. And this is unfortunate, my failure, as it necessarily obscures the point; sickness is boring. The most interesting thing about Einstein was not his lactose intolerance. Just because I'm not tip-top doesn't mean I'm wrong. I could be perfectly healthy and still be right about everything else. There are billions of people who are healthy and who agree with me. I know there are; I can prove it; read my dissertation; I did prove it. Of course, I just can't bear to talk to them, any more than you can bear to talk to me. And why should you? Of course, one must remember this: Unrequited love is not fatal, it's just a temporary digestive disorder that leaves no visible marks, only a newly acquired but permanent inability to ever eat certain specific, unnecessary things again without having terrible digestive distress. Shrimp gives me gas, so I don't eat shrimp. I don't sit up nights crying about shrimp, right? All right then. Have two aspirin and a full glass of water, remember?

Now I really need to shut up. I have grown "!" and a little "yikes" and somewhat "ah, I see . . ." That's fat Canadian fags for you.

Thus ended Mark Payton's efforts to expand his doctoral dissertation into a popular history of nostalgia. And John remembered with sorrow that he had never introduced Mark to Nádja, though Mark had asked several times.

He didn't know where to put his eyes, embarrassed, even ashamed, by everything he looked at: the two strips of disparate geography with soft white torn edges, the poster of Sarah Bernhardt, yellowed where it met the wall and spotted with something orange-brown that had spattered from a frying pan, the stack of spiral notebooks and thick texts: *Shreds of Glory, Remnants of Pride: How Empires Die and Are Remembered. Was Sade a Sadist? Was Christ a Christian?: An Exploration of the Nomenclaturic Issues Surrounding Charismatic Leaders. Budapest 1900. Are You My Sergeant?: Mnemo-Temporal Dysfunction in Combat Veterans.* A fly materialized on the cover of the top text, *A Century's Ends: Cultural Transformations in the '90's, 1290–1899* by Lisa R. Pruth, M.Phil. It strolled a few inches and rested, then promenaded again. It stopped for the second time in the recessed black title stamped on the red cloth. It rubbed its hands together and examined John through its hundred golden eyes. John crushed it into the black *C* of *Cultural* and sat for several minutes examining its new shape in the gray, rain-spotted light pushing through the window. Fractured hairline legs and translucent wings angled from its wet body like modern sculpture. No matter how hard John blew, the wing trembled but did not detach. Less than an hour until Nádja started playing. Everything that was serious, that truly mattered, waited on that piano bench.

Charles arrived untouched by the rain and was intercepted at the door by the rolling Hungarian of the gigantic super and the one-word punctuating assents of his tiny, denim-encased wife. "What's become of Madame Nostalgia?" Charles asked.

"I think Mark had enough of this place."

"He got that right. Did he leave anything to eat? Because I'm starved."

John stuffed the notebooks into a mesh sack the super's wife fetched for him, and he left the three others crowded in the abandoned apartment, preparing to negotiate. The wife stopped short, covered her mouth, and yelped at the indelicate photo collage.

He tried to angle his umbrella to shield himself and the journals from the majority of the rain, but his ankles were quickly soaked; he suddenly was wearing dark, uneven boots. A puckering puddle leaped and embraced him to the groin; he sported the particolored tights of a court jester. Passing cars twice massaged his traffic-side arm and hand with cold brown water. By the time he made it downhill to the river—a chaos of concentric circles in frenzied competition—he was cold through. Soon he was running across the Liberty Bridge and down the Corsó, and he was out of breath and soaked when he sat down next to her in the nearly empty room, bearing his mesh sack and the childish, hopeful bribe of a Rob Roy. "Tell me a story," he demanded quietly.

"Good heavens, John Price. You look—"

"Tell me one of your stories."

"About what?"

"Anything. Please. About anything. Just tell me a good story."

PRAGUE

PART FOUR

NINE CLEAR RECOLLECTIONS OF AUTUMN 1990:

(1) Charles Gábor answering his (formerly Mark Payton's) door wearing underwear on his head, his nose peering unappetizingly from the Y front.

Charles spent so much time in Imre Horváth's company now—redrafting revenue models and management plans, being gently lectured or intensely exhorted on the press's importance to Hungary's history and its future moral development—that the younger man was prone to remarkable childishness when liberated from his partner's magnificent company. Charles answered the door with underwear on his head; he also wore a silk Chinese dressing gown, metallic blue and spangled with golden dragons and pagodas. "I'm beginning to suspect the previous tenant was not practicing the most rigorous hetero-sexuality." Charles flapped the tails of Mark's abandoned robe, rescued from a secluded and hence forgotten bathroom hook, and produced a long cigarette holder from a pocket.

John's world had shrunk to Charles, Nádja, and Nicky, when he could win her attention. He slumped into a chair. "You actually liked that guy, didn't you?" Charles asked, slightly amazed at the possibility. "I could only take so much of him, to be honest. I'd've liked him fine, but I always thought he was pretty judgmental. Like people didn't do business in the past, or something, and I invented it last month."

"Whatever."

Charles finally took the underwear off his head. "Say, ah, did your brother mention anything to you about today?"

"No, I haven't talked to him in a while."

"That's what I figured."

(2) AND, SO, later that afternoon, Charles, explaining that he was "all about better family communication, baby," took John to the Keleti Station, without an explanation, and there presented him to Scott and Mária, about to board their train for a permanent move to Romania—specifically, Hungarian-speaking Transylvania—to teach English and music, respectively.

John's eyes floated irresistibly through the cool air to the station's over-hanging roof: peaked at a right angle, ribbed with rusted metal supports, not quite transparent, dirty white, like the plastic top of an enormous, shabby garden shed. The two brothers slowly walked the platform—lit by sunlight distilled through the dusty translucence—while Charles and Mária went in search of newspapers and chocolate for the journey. "Why didn't you tell me you were leaving?"

"Oh please."

"How was the wedding?"

"It made all the international bridal magazines."

"Listen to me." John stopped walking. "You know what I think? Everybody hates their childhood, and they talk about overcoming it and how their shitty family shaped their personality. But how can that be? If everybody had a shitty family, then why do we all have different personalities? It must not be the relevant thing, you know what I mean? It doesn't have to be . . ."

"*This* is precisely why I didn't tell you I was leaving." Scott laughed, checked his watch. "So okay, bro, now don't follow me this time." Another laugh. "Or I'll have to kill you, which is completely legal in Transylvania." A laugh. "Seriously"—a serious face to match—"I don't ever want to see you again." A pause, then a laugh.

"What did I ever *do* to you?"

"What do you mean?"

"Whatever happened to you, I didn't do it."

"No, of course you didn't. You're perfect. Don't ever change." A pause. "You have to flow a little better, bro. You take things way too heavy." Pause. "But really"—smile—"I never want to see you again." Laugh.

And then the train: a smudged, battered, smoking refugee from an old war movie, the very curve of the serif letters on its rounded, soot-gray flanks a typographic throwback (BUDAPEST–BUCUREȘTI NORD) that Mark would have loved, and Scott leaning from the window as the beast jerked into motion, dragged itself toward the bright blue autumn daylight that was the station's fourth wall. Scott leaned dangerously far out the window, an aggressive display of joie de vivre; his legs were the only part of him not visible. He waved both his arms in an exuberant farewell windmill; his face split into a smile, wide and dental; he held his brother's eye; and then his near hand folded into a standard obscene gesture, only for a moment, then broad smiling waves again, then the obscene gesture, back and forth, until the train receded far enough to make its first curve. A cool fall breeze pushed candy wrappers and cigarette ash along the platform; all that was good about the season wafted in the air around this ambiguous recollection in the making: Mária, quietly appalled not to be headed west, smiling resignedly over Scott's shoulder, and Scott—dressed up in a tweed jacket, a white oxford shirt, and a tie—leaning out from the antique train, waving and smiling, hostilely or mock-hostilely giving his brother the finger as impossibly white clouds met the first chugs of black from the dwindling locomotive and an impossibly blue sky jigsawed itself into the space between the uneven façades of neighboring buildings and the overhanging roof, and Hungarians on the platform waved to other shrinking passengers, and the enormous clock, unwashed in decades but keeping a fair semblance of correct time, advanced in echoing clicks without benefit of the Swiss quartz chronometric technology advertised in the watch billboard beneath it.

And with every passing year, when bright September days outside an open and steamed bathroom window recalled the scene to John, he would examine the slowly but unmistakably aging face squinting above his bathroom sink, and though it had never much resembled Scott's, the boy in the receding train never aged another day; only the occasional scrap of his handwriting—written in moments of sentimental weakness from points ever farther east—showed any evidence of passing time, but his face was always and would forever be blond-framed and smiling, always touched from behind by a lovely Hungarian wife, always possessing some profound and crucial knowledge John could not achieve, always heading off into blue late-summer skies with early-fall temperatures, the kind of weather that exists only in retrospect.

"Now some entertainment, please!" was the battle cry of the season, a phrase flexible in meaning. John muttered it now, Scott and Mária's train having left a strangely quiet station behind it, and Charles understood that John meant "good riddance."

"You slept with her, didn't you?" Charles asked.

"It seemed like the thing to do."

"Oh, that it was, absolutely."

They walked out of the station and into the bright sun of Baross Square just in time to see, at an outdoor café table, a large man in a blue windbreaker stand up in fury and tip the table over, spilling drinks and glassware onto his horrified female companion. They watched him scream at her as she covered her face with her hands and began to weep. They watched him unzip his pants, remove his member, and laughingly spray urine all over her shoes and the upturned table and the scattered dishes. Two slight waiters consulted and chose not to intervene (one decisively retreating inside the café, but only to return with a mop).

"It's going to be a good autumn," Charles said. "The omens are looking very positive."

(3) THE FIRST unarguably fall night (September), when a sweater alone is insufficient after dark.

The tree was shedding its distinctive leaves, almost all at once. In an effort to hold her attention one more minute, and to impress her with whimsy, he said they looked like little Oriental fans. Nicky said no, they looked like a fleet of perfect, motorized half-shells, frothing into shore, off of which a swarm of nude but shy newborn Botticelli Veni had just disembarked, padding onto the sand to check in at an exclusive, goddesses-of-love-only beach resort where they would lounge and sip frosty, fruity cocktails (served by eunuch waiters) while still managing to keep their legs delicately crossed and one arm strategically positioned over their naked breasts. Oriental *fans*!

So, he kissed Nicky, pressed her against the rail and kissed her hard, with all he could muster in his heart and groin for her, tasted onion and smoke, felt the swell of her chest, kissed her with force in the vain hope he could drive away the distant, familiar look he had seen creep over her face an hour earlier during dinner (as they debated whether poor Mark wanted to be found or not): Soon she would say she was feeling particularly inspired and itchy for work, and she would not let him come over, or would not let him stay any longer than was necessary for certain combinations to be executed. He kissed her to argue for time. He held her arms tightly at her sides, then gripped her face in his hands. She moaned; he sighed. "Damn, boy, very hot, but you're gonna have to hold on to that till tomorrow, 'cause I'm feeling itchy to . . ." And he let her walk home alone—"rules are rules, playtime is over"—but after they parted he couldn't help wondering if she was really going home to work, and he toyed with the idea of following her, steadying himself behind cold trees, watching from a safe, dirty distance as her smooth scalp glided down Castle Hill, onto the round-about, over the bridge, down the boulevard toward her decayed little street, and would she work or would she be met?

He didn't watch her descent for long, turned instead and walked back up the hill and side-streeted aimlessly until he thought to walk toward the little basement bar decorated with bullfighting paraphernalia and operated by a teeny old Hungarian couple who, that summer, after John had come regularly over a month or two, introduced themselves shyly and offered him a taste of real absinthe, stowed under the bar in a black bottle blown into the shape of a laughing, crying bear.

(4) THE LINGERING RING of crystal kissing crystal.

"In business school, you know, the phrase had a distinct meaning: 'I'm going into publishing' meant something very specific. Like when you came out of an exam and someone asked you how you did and you knew you blew it, you just said, 'It looks like I'm going into publishing.' Or someone gets nailed with a professor's question on a case study, unprepared, and they fumble it, you can hear other students in the class singsonging: 'Looks like someone's going into publishing.' If they could see me now, I would get so much crap for this deal."

Imre arrived late and accepted a glass of Bordeaux. "Károly was just telling me how the future of publishing was an issue of frequent discussion at his business school," John said.

"This is marvelous, and I tell him that he must bring just this thinking from his education, he must bring home the new thinking, what he has learned abroad." The two men clinked glasses and said something in Hungarian.

And for some reason that exact moment distilled into pure memory and clung to John for many years, drifted throughout him like a dormant virus. They almost looked alike at that moment, the two businessmen, and John believed in the story, in Imre's destiny and life, believed that an ancient institution was hurtling into the future with all the youth and energy of Charles Gábor, mock-embarrassed or not, as its turbine. At that moment the two men formed a mirror image centered on the point where the two wine glasses touched: the bent arm sheathed in a light wool suit sleeve and a pinpoint-stitched shirt closed with a silver cuff link, the shoulder leaning slightly forward like a fencer en garde, the stern and (mildly ironical) focused expression, the mobile wrinkle around the eyes, the sweep of hair, the intense hard faith in the fellow staring back from just across the crystal bridge. John sat to one side, and for the brief time the ringing crystal echo sprinkled through the air and fell to the table, he felt a hot throb of envy at the back of his throat, like a professional matchmaker when she wonders—for the first time in a long, successful career—if she hasn't left her own happiness until too late.

The three of them walked, that cold October evening, through Deák Square, where the pit that would become the underground parking for the Kempinski Hotel had reached its lowest point and the glass hotel was primed to spring upward from this deep crouch. Imre led them down the boulevard to the front door of a gentlemen's club called Leviticus. John politely announced he was heading home to an early bed. He let the business partners disappear under the canopy shaped like the entrance to a desert hut: fake skins (canvas) stitched together and stretched over (artificially) straining wooden (painted metal) staves. He turned onto the boulevard and counted his blessings, laughed aloud at the sycophantic antics Charles still had to perform—having to follow the old man into a strip joint, for God's sake, archetypal haunt of the world's loneliest men and women. Mark would have had a field day with that.

John identified constellations on his way to the Blue Jazz, looked obliquely to bring them into focus. Just as Imre, when seen obliquely, he decided, had no grandeur at all, was, to be honest, a ridiculous, ridiculous man; Charles had condemned himself to a career of indulging the whims and appetites of a very nonserious old fool. Charles, viewed obliquely, was not much more impressive.

(5) (A RECURRING DREAM image in later years, long after he congratulated himself that he had forgotten even to think of her, forgotten even her name: Emily Oliver nude but for a feather boa, floating against a green sky, lofted by plush, luxurious, silver wings and cradling an American football against her body with one arm, her other extended in a running back's locked-elbow blocking position.)

This perennial, gaudy oneiric bloom sprouted from seeds planted Halloween of 1990, when, floating over other guests' heads on a slightly raised platform, Emily really did wear football shoulder pads under a green Philadelphia Eagles jersey, and her tight white pants, although convincingly gridironic, were in fact a pair of her favorite casual slacks. John considered approaching her, using Mark's vanishing act and his own (failed) efforts to track him down as an excuse for their first conversation in months. But the opportunity kept skittering away. Now she was talking to a man whom John did not know but could identify—from his haircut and bulk—as an embassy marine, despite his sparse Tarzanian wardrobe of a fake leopard-skin bikini bottom, loincloth, and shoulder strap. Far across the rented hotel ballroom, unnoticed in the crowd and shadows and his costume, John watched them talk under a banner with greetings written in two languages: English (HAPPY HALLOWEEN) and Hungarian (WELCOME TO THE AMERICAN-STYLE COSTUMED CELEBRATION OF THE EVE OF THE FEAST OF ALL SAINTS). The jungular marine held Emily's football helmet (the painted silver wings on its temples would later sprout into three plush, luxurious dimensions), and he spun it lightly between his two middle fingers; he touched it gently with fingertips that, John thought from his post across the room, proposed something sinister in their dexterous manipulation of the headgear.

The skeletal octet of Franz Liszt conservatory students, unclear which of the elderly songs in their tattered *American Popular Tunes* book were actually familiar to Americans, counted off a Hungarian-language rendition of "After-Breakfast Girl" played with a Latin beat, and the crowd shuffled, and five gigantic, puffy playing cards with pink human faces and skinny limbs in red or black tights and sleeves—an improbable royal flush—danced in a sort of conga line, two steps forward and one step back, one more step back and two steps forward. Finally, the last royal rectangle waddled out of his way and he could see her again. Tarzan had swung off. Her back was to him. Emily floated farther away now, her bright white number 7 proud under the familiar ponytail, and then there slithered a white-gloved hand and black-sleeved arm around her waist, and the hand's twin circled the front of her neck, insinuating itself under her chin, tipped her head back, and then there were lips against her ear, or perhaps a nose against her cheek—John couldn't be sure, because from where he stood there was only a back covered by a cowled cape and a mask of a famous trademarked cartoon mouse, with his signature enormous ears but a smile altered by the costumer: wide open and menacing, with four razor-sharp fangs.

"The journalist! I owe you a big thanks." A sudden intrusion hobbling in from the middle distance: an eye-patched, kerchiefed pirate, a live parrot on a shoulder, Harvey the investor atop a very convincing peg leg, which must have been severely restricting the circulation in the calf he'd tied out of view. John's article on Cap'n Harv had won its subject significant attention, apparently; he'd attracted some investment queries, the story had been picked up in his hometown newspaper and radio back in the States, he'd found himself in the center of some interesting deals and people, he was feeling pretty pleased with the nice coverage, et cetera, et cetera. Even when John could shift his jealous focus onto this unsteady, clunking man, he had difficulty assessing if Harvey wasn't pulling his leg, or even obliquely threatening him; John had, after all, written a profile so aglow with uranium-poisonous irony that it should have sent any normal man's heart ticking up like a Geiger counter. It was inconceivable that it resulted in business investment and respect. To the extent he had expected ever to hear from him again, it would have been in the deliciously un equal combat of the "Letters to the Editor" page, where John could savor some ill-conceived, ungrammatical, unprovable claim to decency, which would of course only present to John the delightful gift of writing *another* column ("Our reporter responds . . .") in which to try out new barbs on this fish's slick silver lips. Or, John half expected for a few weeks that Harvey, failing even the courage to risk a public duel in print, would squeeze out some oily legal correspondence, amusingly suitable for framing. But no, here instead there was nothing but rosy-cheeked Halloween glee and future gain coming off this grinning, chattering pirate, and now Harvey had, if John understood correctly, a tip if John was interested; there had been inquiries—Harvey had made/received some inquiries—and the question of the Horváth Press's privatization was a little more hotly contested than it appeared in the, shall he say, interestingly slanted local coverage to date, and would John be curious to hear about a syndicate— not a syndicate, that's the wrong word—but a sizable interest, a concern, as it were, that may be in a position to throw some thumbtacks on Gábor and the old man's road, or, on the other hand, in the alternative, as lawyers like to say (and here a wink, unnoticed, since his winking eye rested behind a patch), they may be in a position to perhaps bring the end of the rainbow a little closer and make it a happy little leprechaun day for everybody close enough to the deal to drop their hand in the pot o' gold, and perhaps, if John and Gábor would like, this concern, let's call them South Sea islanders (perhaps a pirate joke of some sort), South Sea islanders (repeated with a self-congratulatory laugh), I think I am alone in the unique position to convince them to turn in their thumbtacks for rainbows, if you see my point . . .

Far away, over Harvey's shoulder—over the parrot's shoulder, too—this was more than just a friendly whisper. John could, of course, not hear what was whispered, or see the mouse-obscured face, but he recognized, even at this distance, the substance of intimacy. He could see that much in Emily's smile. Should Harvey arrange for a summit meeting of sorts?

He looked down at the pirate and back up to the far-off stage and now Emily stood in front of Robin Hood, helping adjust the laces of his jerkin, tying them off for him at his chest. The hero of Sherwood, a gawky middle-aged man well over six feet tall, wore too-large tortoiseshell glasses and had gray and thinning hair, no thicker than a baby's, under his cap of Lincoln green. His long bow scraped at his calves, and had begun to cause runs in his bunching green tights. Noticeably unhappy, he fingered his quiver nervously and repeatedly scratched at his temple under the bow of his glasses. Emily stopped him; she took his hands away from their bad habits and smiled at him. Something she said made him shed one layer of worry and enjoy himself slightly more.

In an effort to protect Charles's bid (and his own share in it), John told the buccaneer to hold off his South Sea islanders a little longer, not even knowing precisely what he meant by that. John spoke at some length, trusting in the power of speaking with, and in, confidence. "I think it will be worth everyone's while if you can keep your South Sea islanders content a few more weeks and then bring them to meet the appropriate people under circumstances that by then can be, ahh, amenable. There won't be any shortage of . . . opportunity when these mousy governmental details are put to one side. The government can still slow things down to a Communist-era crawl if it gets a whiff of hungry foreigners like you or your islanders. Let Imre talk the government off the property, then who can say what is or isn't or may or may not be possible." John promised everything and nothing, and the pirate nodded significantly.

The mouse passed him and he didn't see the rodent until it was almost too late, and his previously half-formed plan—tear the mouse head away and confront the rat beneath—was already too delayed to put into operation. He hadn't time to see if the scurrying mouse looked guilty or not; impossible to see which way its beady little eyes were looking. As the mouse wore boots, he found it difficult even to gauge its height, and as its cowled cape and ringed, sparsely furred tail slithered off into the crowd, John's imagination choked into action: Nearly anyone could have been Emily's secret verminous lover. He struggled to guess who was sweating and festering under the black mask of the mouse: Was Bryon back in town? Where was Charles tonight? Is there some other marine in there, and does she take them both at once, Tarzan and the rodent? Some unknown, some visiting athletic alumnus of Nebraska who had debauched the girl years earlier and had now come to Budapest to spread his viral affections even here? Or, unlike the marines, was she licensed to fraternize with Hungarian nationals, engage in illicit congress with some Magyar Romeo-Zsolt who cooed sexy Hungarian gibberish from under those circular ears?

And so he abandoned Harvey in midsentence and stalked out of the ballroom, out of the hotel and onto the dark street, where a caped, vampiric mouse had just turned left at the end of the taxi rank. The smoking cabbies leaned against their Mercedeses, made little zigging circles with the orange tips of their cigs, and muttered, "Taxi, taxi, taxi, taxi, taxi, taxi," until John had made the same left turn, but his prey had already vanished. He broke into a jog and made the first turn he could, but there were neither doorways nor exits from the dead end he had penetrated. John stood stupidly in an alley, next to overflowing trash barrels surrounded at their bases by garbage, under a few flickering yellow lights, while scrambling and squeaking at his feet, very real, very hungry (but nonvampiric) rats were startled from their evening routine by a man in full-dress marine uniform, a rattling plastic saber at his side.

(6) "CHIEF, AM I INTERRUPTING?"

"No worries, mate. What's on your barbie?"

John halfheartedly pitched his idea: a series of profiles to run throughout the rest of November—introductions, one at a time, of the Hungarian government officials Westerners would most likely meet in the course of their work, beginning with, probably, someone from the State Privatization Agency or something like that.

And through the horizontal slats of Editor's unfurled venetian blinds, on the other side of his soundproof glass, Nicky and Karen leaned over Karen's desk and flipped through one of Nicky's portfolios. John couldn't see which photos they were so enjoying together, and when he had entered Editor's office,

Nicky had delighted in his unsatisfied curiosity. Now striped a half-dozen times by those venetian slats, the women laughed and pointed, looked thoughtful, and tapped their fingers on favorite shots. From time to time Nicky looked up through the glass to confirm and savor John's surveillance. She discreetly pursed her lips into a kiss for him, then threw her arm around the other woman's shoulder and theatrically pointed out for her a particular aspect of composition, which John of course could not see, even though he walked to Editor's window and, with his high-school-basketball-broken, permanently half-healed, crooked finger bent down a venetian slat with a metallic snap just as intrigued Editor assented to his half-baked, crooked proposal, the brainchild of Charles Gábor.

(7) **THE MIDDLE-OF-THE-NIGHT** sensation of awakening in a room where the heat doesn't work well: the drafts that whip themselves into existence in the middle of the room like desert jinn; the 2 A.M. sounds and smells of rapidly approaching winter; the metallic snap of the floor against bare feet; the tickling, cold aromas of drying oil paint and photo fixative and of diesel fuel rising from the street through a cracked window, and the faint whiff of familiar perfume embedded in the rasp of a woolen blanket that warmed him enough to make his legs sweat, though his exposed chest and arms prickled with silvery, slivery cold; and the moment when, checking his watch on the scavenged bedside table, he caught the second hand unawares and it sat immobile for a long breath, until it finally knew it was being watched and jerked into a nonchalant rhythm, playing it innocent.

"Are you asleep?" he asked.

"No."

"The frost on your window is beautiful."

"Hm. It looks like snowy branches."

"I suppose so."

"As seen through a windshield."

"I guess so, yeah."

"Over that little curved quarter-pie wedge that windshield wipers make."

"That's true. Do those have a name?"

"And the heat doesn't work in the car."

"Just like here."

"No, different. In the car, it's because of an electrical malfunction. Sabotage."

"Sabotage?"

"Yes. We're driving along this dark road when our heat stops working, then the headlights start to flicker, then they shut off entirely. Then the car just dies and it's very quiet outside. You ask if we're out of gas."

" 'Are we out of gas, Nicky?' "

" 'Why, no, I don't think so, John, the needle is on three-quarters full.' But the car just sits dead on the road and it makes that sick wheezy sound when I turn the key and then it won't even do that. We're miles from anywhere. Sabotaged. And we're dressed in nothing but feather boas and stiletto heels."

"We are? Both of us?"

"Yes. Now you have to get out and go for help."

"In nothing but a boa?"

"And stiletto heels; don't whine. And very long eyelashes. And a jet-black wig."

" 'But, Nicky, I'll freeze if I go out in the snow dressed like that.' "

" 'We'll both freeze if we don't get help, damnit, and no one is going to just walk by this isolated road.' But you have a point, so I sacrifice my boa for you. So now you have both boas on. You get out of the car and look back longingly as your stiletto heels squeak into the fresh snow. You wrap the two boas around your naked body as best you can, adjust your wig, and you see me through your long eyelashes and my breath is misting up the windows already, so it's already difficult to make me out, but you know I am counting on you entirely, a woman wearing nothing but stiletto heels, shivering inside a car on a deserted and snowy forest road in the midst of the coldest night on record. I'm relying on you for my life. In a tiny convertible from the 1960s heyday of Italian design. Black. Sssssabotaged."

"Nicky?"

"Yes?"

"Are you sending me home?"

"You catch on fast, little man."

"I see you put Mark's picture back up. It's a little daunting to do it when I'm looking at a blowup of us doing it."

"You seem to be doing it just fine. If he ever comes back, he can have it and I'll keep the Polaroid. Hey, I want to meet your old piano friend someday."

"Did I tell you about her?"

"Of course you did. Or someone did, Mark, maybe, whatever. It doesn't matter. I want to meet her, okay?"

"Do you ever think about where we're headed, Nick? You know? I some-times feel like, I don't know, like, maybe we could be—"

"Stop right there. Now I'm really sending you home."

"I just mean—"

"Really. I have to paint."

"I know, but—"

"Hey. Hey. Really."

He dressed. She kissed him on the threshold of the open door, handed him his backpack with Mark's journals in it. She had the thick plaid blanket wrapped around her torso, her bare arms and shoulders blanched silver-white by the humped moon that washed the courtyard and the doorway. She had also put on a fake-feather headdress, the key element of a Bulgarian-made "Ameri-can Red Indian Chief" costume she had found in a scavenging trip to a pecu-liarly Hungarian toy store. It was hard to take anything too seriously with a bald, seminude American Red Indian Chief girl. Still, he wanted to say some-thing, she could see that, and so she stroked his cheek and smiled, then turned her back, stepped into the apartment, let her blanket fall and her trailing head-dress brush its lowest fake feathers against the rounding of her naked hips, and closed the door behind her.

(8) JOHN SUBMITTED TO EDITOR his first installment of the series "Hungarians You Need to Know but Should Not Try to (Blatantly) Bribe." To cover his tracks, he began with someone unrelated to Charles Gábor's business: the elderly guard who worked the front door of the U.S. embassy, the man responsible for waving a handheld metal detector over a Danube of visa seekers, businessmen, visiting government officials. John's profile of Old Péter ran in the company of an extreme close-up of the guard (PHOTO: N. MANKIEWILICZKI-POBUDZIEJ), stressing the deep canyons in his face, the softness of his squashed-lip, squinting smile, the furry wattles that flapped from his chin and fell into the open collar of his Romanian polo shirt. The caption: WELCOME TO THE EMBASSY OF THE LEADER OF THE FREE WORLD, THANK YOU VERY MUCH.

Their simultaneously translated interview (Old Péter knew only employee names, titles, and floor numbers in English) took place after hours at the em-bassy (vibrating with the constant and constantly disappointed promise of an approaching Emily) while an obese, whiskered Hungarian woman scrubbed the lobby steps on her hands and knees. John learned from Old Péter that three of the marines he had met in July (including "the giant Negro boy") had traded in embassy blues for desert khaki and were now somewhere in the Persian Gulf, preparing to fight the Arab Hitler. "Hussein Saddam boom!" slurped Old Péter. "U.S. marines!" He sprayed the room with machine-gun sound effects. The cleaning lady paid him no attention, only churned her rags again into the bucket of steam at her side and sloshed the floor with both hands.

Two days later, John submitted the series' second installment: "Psst, Buddy, You Wanna Buy a Paprika Factory?" The prodigiously complimentary column profiled a subdirector in charge of midsize enterprise denationalization for the State Privatization Agency. John described the bureaucrat as "a key architect of a new world" but also "a defender of Hungary's entrepreneurial past." John hailed the man's answers to repeated questions about the importance of restoring Hungarian commerce into Hungarian hands as hallmarks of "twenty-first-century brilliance" and "one of the many reasons this man's name is constantly bubbling to the top of conversations about candidates for ministry portfolios."

"And exactly which conversations are those?" Charles asked John the evening of the piece's publication.

"Well, this one right now, for example."

John listened proudly as Charles read the entire piece over the phone to Imre, laughed from time to time, and answered the old man's questions in liquid Hungarian. "We're closing in, Imre," he said in English. "Closing in."

"It seems a scandal," John had mentioned in the course of the interview, "that foreigners look upon the privatization process as a discount sale and not, as it of course should be, the restoration of justice and logic to an economy battered by injustice and illogic. Why should an American or a Frenchman or a, a, a South Sea islander buy a Hungarian business when there are Hungarians eager and qualified to run them? Why is a foreigner—a carpetbagger—any better than keeping it in the state's hands?"

The bureaucrat's answer, though balanced, grappling with the complexities he felt the young reporter's question had missed, nevertheless won him yet more praise: *an understanding that his job is more than simply that of an estate auctioneer but is closer to that of a wise overseer of an enormous garden, entrusting the appropriate natives with the tools and knowledge to make this country blossom again.*

"You think he meant Gábor has won the bid?" Harvey asked the next morning.

"I don't know. I didn't want to push. But he was clear that there was a desire, at the very highest levels of the government, to keep the nation's historic legacy in the proper hands—at least in the initial stage of unloading the heavily symbolic stuff to the private sector. After that, let the market do what it will, but the government certainly isn't missing the public relations issues at stake."

Now Harvey read the article over the phone to an unknown auditor, answered questions curtly, then replied, in a tone that implied special access (which John appreciated), "Because the reporter's right here in the room with me, *that's* how."

"So who's got the best bid for the Horváth Press?" John couldn't resist asking the shy man behind the metal desk at the tail end of the interview. The quiet economist, only twenty-nine, had all through college studied the official Marxist economics he knew were absurd and written term papers extolling (or only delicately cajoling) the latest five-year plan. Then every afternoon he read Adam Smith and Milton Friedman in the library of the U.S. embassy, took copious notes on the secret religion he knew explained the universe.

"Mr. Price," he answered. "You are aware, I hope, that I cannot tell you of this. You are a journalist, no? This bidding process is completely ominous. You ask ominous information." And John remembered for years the unpleasant sensation in his stomach that he had pushed too far, until he realized the man had only meant to say *anonymous*.

(9) FRIDAY THE THIRTIETH, the last hours of November, some American kid vomiting against the base of an apartment block across the street, and from the large window of the new Thai restaurant next to the bar, a wedge of yellow light fell on the dark road. Charles pulled open the bar's heavy wooden door, under the dull orange nautical lanterns. "Now some entertainment, please," one of them said ("Ten minutes maximum here if it sucks"). John, Charles, and Harvey (a tenacious social barnacle since John had introduced him to Charles, who later declared him "possibly a gold mine, possibly full of shit") all descended into the old bar, shaped like a frigate. Everything about the place whispered to these experienced customers that only a few more weeks remained before the end, before the old haunt tipped irreparably and became fully Westernized, unacceptable to any self-respecting expat.

Overhearing two American women, John spoke with a very slight Hungarian accent to the less pretty one. "I am sorry to be interrupting you," he began. "I know you must be told this all of the time. I do not mean to bother you, but I want to tell you very much I like your movies. I am the very big fan of you."

She played along for a bit, but soon set him straight and explained to the poor Hungarian that he had mixed her up with someone else. He pretended to be embarrassed, she was flattered at the error, and a few drinks and a couple of dances later, immediately after she had crunched and swallowed an ice cube coated with the last remnants of her sweet vermouth, they were kissing, and her tongue felt corpsely cold but humanly soft. The ice had raised little bumps on its buds, and she tasted of the sweet-and-spicy apéritif. He was amazed he had succeeded in his ploy, but a few drinks later, as they walked to his apartment (his Hungarian accent forgotten back in the frigate, along with Charles and Harvey's quiet business tête-à-tête), she said something—he couldn't quite remember what—that made him understand she had never believed his line, never believed he was even Hungarian, and, realizing this, as the sofa bed voiced its first creaking complaint, he wished he had not aimed so low but had complimented the prettier of the two women instead. The next morning, a cursory, throbbing investigation revealed that the now-anonymous girl had stolen not money but his dental floss, his only belt, and the backpack filled with Mark Payton's notebooks, a loss he took very, very hard.

II.

ADVANCED KNOWLEDGE OF THE NEWS MURMURED INTO CHARLES'S LAWyer's office late in the afternoon of the sixth of December: The State Privatization Agency had accepted Horváth Holdings' bid (combined cash and restitution vouchers) and the company was now the owner of both Horváth Verlag (Vienna) and the salable remnants (some improved, some dilapidated) of the Horváth Kiadó (Budapest): reasonably modern printing facilities; decrepit trucks and tolerable warehouses; a staff of forty-eight (fully 50 percent superfluous); a catalog of textbooks and old, Party-approved writers; partnerships with two newspapers and two magazines; and two floors of a grimly unashamed, squattingly ugly office block in the Pesti suburban wastelands. For Imre, the right to profit from his own name in his native country, unopposed. And for Charles, 49/51 splits aside, the chance to run something real.

The next day, Charles spent his morning organizing a celebration of their victory, and that evening the tribute opened with the last guest's arrival inside the warm Gerbeaud. Before John had finished brushing snow from his shoulders, Charles stood up and recapped for his audience the relevant details of Imre Horváth's story: heir to tradition, victim and survivor of Communism, indefatigable protector of a people's memory, visionary, hero. Krisztina smiled ceaselessly while Imre himself pursed his lips in majestic calm and lowered his eyes, but not his head, to examine the tiny glass of golden liqueur on the table in front of him. Charles lifted his own cordial to "my mentor, my second father, my conscience, a hero of Hungary." The old man, never more imposing, more etched and girded by history, rose to embrace his partner, and the other five applauded and touched drinks.

Around the corner from the Gerbeaud, on the soft, fresh snow, they found two fuming, humming limousines, patiently waiting and commissioned to ferry the party from past to future. In each of their womby interiors, two backseats faced each other and, next to each, a collection of half-filled crystal decanters sat snugly clinched in formed black velvet holders. In the lead car, Charles solemnly poured short drinks for Imre, Krisztina, and himself, while in the trailing limo, Harvey, his sax-playing assistant, the English lawyer, and John started giggling like schoolboys as they topped up tall, textured tumblers with a little of this, a little of that, a bit of the clear one, and—*voilà*—that's called a Long Island Iced Tea, Neville. Oh, is it?

At their next stop, as the two groups reconvened, two distinct moods met and bounced away, like two weather fronts crunching into each other: "My God, this is . . . good Lord, you have the key," Imre was murmuring in quiet Hungarian as Harvey emerged from the other car asserting that the best place to learn a foreign language is in bed.

"I do. We *are* the owners, after all. It was simply a very kind gesture on a friend's part to advance me a copy for tonight." Charles put the key in the lock but did not turn it. Instead, he waited until his audience had quieted itself on the snow-dusty loading dock, and then he recited in English. "This is, of course, a warehouse now, and it is one of the properties that Horváth Holdings acquired yesterday. It was, more relevantly, the stage for a piece of history of which this nation should be aware and proud. A little more than thirty-four years ago, when our country fought futilely for its freedom, our friend Imre stood in the middle of the storm, standing for truth. From this dock where we now stand, he fired broadsides of truth against tyranny, and for thirteen days he reclaimed his Horváth Kiadó from its captors." Charles turned the key, heaved up and open the rolling metal door, and, inside, pushed a button on a rectangular box dangling from the invisible ceiling on a thick black cable. After two fluorescent stutters of surprise, all the pieces of a sparsely stocked, high-ceilinged hall with cracked concrete floors showered into order.

"My God, how did you know?" Imre asked his partner, his voice thickening and moistening.

"I said to him only what my father said to me," replied Krisztina Toldy.

"Welcome home, Imre," Charles whispered in Hungarian, shaking his partner's hand.

Krisztina and Imre walked far into the starkly lit, nearly bare warehouse, out of earshot, and the old man lightly touched spiral metal staircases and corrugated walls, turned small lights on and off, gently picked up and replaced a leaning mop, gazed at the ceiling as if it were an unlikelihood. The rest of the group lingered by the door.

"My God, it is the most beautiful warehouse I have ever seen," John said to Charles. "Can we see a sewage treatment facility next?"

"Old boy does seem to like warehouses," agreed Neville, swirling the remnants of his Long Island Iced Tea.

Harvey sat on a crate, his mute musical assistant shuffling at his side. "All right, Charles, spill the beans. Is the old-timer banging the Toldy woman, huh? What do you think?"

For the warehouse-to-dinner leg, Charles and John changed cars, and John spent a teetotal trip watching Imre and Krisztina speak nearly inaudible Hungarian across from him. After several minutes, the pair fell silent and they looked out their respective windows, through the smoked glass that filtered exterior life to little more than nervous headlights, Impressionist river lights, and haloed, pale streetlights hovering over perfectly circular banks of silver snow. John watched the old man's eyes shift in back-and-forth twitches as they followed first one light, then the next. After a bit they closed, and Imre folded his hands in his lap.

"What happened in that warehouse?" John asked the woman softly.

"Unimaginable courage. Principle. A rare moral clarity." She said each word slowly, her eyes on the brown and gray and white world outside.

They arrived sedately outside the Restaurant Szent Lajos, where the four others smiled easily and laughed loudly as they descended from their vehicle. "How was your guilt trip?" Charles asked John, the two of them holding the restaurant's doors, waiting until last to enter the fin-de-siècle Hungarian institution.

"Don't put me in their car again."

"Believe me, I know the feeling. Welcome to my job."

Where Charles had opted for fine cuisine on previous occasions, tonight he painted with other colors, and the old man's conversation justified the choice: "I dined here for the first time with my father, my mother, and my two brothers on my name day when I was, ohhh, ten years. In these days, there was so many waiters, and they moved like nothing you have ever seen. It was a very great thing to come here. Like a dream—the waiters and the dishes and the music, the smoke from cigars, the women. A magic place, even if you were not a little boy."

A tired, elderly man in a baggy vest and drooping clip-on bow tie slapped a stack of sticky laminated menus on the table without stopping to speak. A younger waiter unwillingly watered their glasses and shouted something to his older colleague, who was now already halfway down the length of the room. The older man did not look back, just raised his hands and dropped them in a gesture of exhausted disgust, while the unsupervised waiter filled two glasses to overflowing and never touched two others.

"To be at the Szent Lajos. At ten years, anything can be very beautiful because everything is new. You don't wait for something better. What is in front of you can still amaze you. A room of stylish people is only amazing. You feel beauty very strongly. It shocks you. I had never seen a place so alive as this night here. I know my brothers were trying to look as they belonged here, but I knew they were not old enough yet. This room was full of people who were living lives of great importance, I thought. Yes, *this* room was full of music and chandeliers cut from the sun. The chairs were dark wood and had the softest cushions. The tables were golden and marble, and the silver shined. The ceiling was a fresco of angels and clouds."

The vast dining hall was almost empty. Dozens of dissimilar tables, placed intimately close to one another, held only a few widely spaced parties: American businessmen, loud and laughingly happy, making fun of this crap restaurant that their concierge had recommended; visiting Hungarian exiles, quietly stunned after ten to forty years, trying to distinguish what was visibly in this room from what was in their insistent, contrarian memories; local bureaucrats, hunched over the same meal they had ingested for decades, accustomed to the setting as to old shoes; and at one table, like a corrupted, feeble echo of Imre's recollection, a family self-consciously and unhappily celebrating some milestone of one of the children. The room's odd, nauseating light seeped from large 1960s space-age plastic globes hanging from orange vinyl-coated wires. Stained steel cutlery swaddled tightly in paper napkins formed an uneven, trembling pyramid in a plastic tub on a wheeled cart. A boy rolled the cart slowly up and down the aisles, pushed a wet rag across empty tables, leaving a damp *V*, then scattered a few of the cutlery rolls behind him.

"Ohhh, and there was a zinc bar just there, the whole length of that wall. The bartenders were strong men and handsome, and they tossed glasses and the steel shakers to one another. They spun off each other as they passed in this little space there, under the windows. And outside the windows there was the first snow of the year, and lights outside so the snow falled like pieces of silver against black and yellow, and it looked very quiet outside and was very loud inside, and the two separated by only a window seemed very beautiful."

Two inevitable Gypsy musicians were moving now from unwelcoming table to table in sequined vests and tight, spottily shiny trousers. One stretched and bear-hugged his accordion, looking only at his fingers or the floor, while the violinist bobbed and grimaced.

"Mr. Price, I see you laugh when the Gypsies play now, and you are correct. They are a joke now, for tourists, like so many things after state control, a little dead, a little more shabby product. But then! Ohhh, people were different. Hearing live music was different. We did not have stereo cassettes in our ears all day and your compact discs to capture any kind of music in the history of the world. When music was difficult to find, it was very powerful. And the Gypsies themselves were men of fire, rustic gods who could enchant you and make you dizzy. People throwed money—not just coins, but *paper*—at the musicians, and late at night the dancing was extravagant, and furs were draped around women more beautiful than you can imagine, with necks all like swans, and they danced until dawn appeared in the window up there."

Through that window they could now see their waiter outside, laughing with a colleague, lighting one cigarette on the butt of the last, untroubled by any sense of pressing responsibility elsewhere. Sometime later he returned and, with yellow fingers, scraped a pencil stub across a torn slip of pink paper. He said nothing and did not look at the person whose order he was taking, but three times he just shook his head when someone requested a particular dish, and he wrote nothing. No explanation: His eyes stared far off until Harvey's assistant, Krisztina, and Neville all changed their orders and the waiter, still looking elsewhere, made a few marks on his paper. Charles ordered two bottles of wine even as the man walked off, shouting at the kitchen doors.

"Tonight is my third time here, thanks to our friend Károly. Later, I was with a woman, and I was twenty years old. I knew I was watching a theater, but that was no less beautiful. We were all the actors in this amazing theater. I felt something else as well that second time. Budapest was still fortunate, but there was a war. In the beauty and the excitement and the sound of an orchestra that night—they sat just there—there was a taste of something like desperateness. Everyone knew perhaps tomorrow there will be no Szent Lajos, no party. You taste it in everything. The women were still beautiful and laughed, but they laughed one little piece too loud. One felt we were rushing to the end, to the limit of beauty, and also we were trying to hold it back, and to show everyone else we were not afraid. It did not all end the next day, but it did end soon. And, ohhh, very suddenly."

Seven plates of congealed chicken paprikás, seven limp side salads heaped and wet with cold canned corn, three bottles of surly wine, and five half-filled glasses of tepid, suspension-filled water straggled to the table in lazy groups. John laughed and Neville laughed and Harvey laughed, and soon all seven of them were laughing loudly as one after another identical, unappetizing dish was tossed to the table with a clatter.

No one dared dessert or coffee. Charles paid for the untouched food. But when they stepped into a biting wind and the drivers stamped their feet and swung open limo doors, John and Neville and even Harvey shook Imre's hand and sincerely thanked him for the meal.

The caravan set off for the Hilton casino on top of Castle Hill. The front car held only Charles and Imre, as the rowdier elements had kidnapped the only available female, vowing, with Neville as their cultured spokesman, to render her "really quite embarrassingly intoxicated," a plan as chillingly daunting as an interplanetary voyage. The front car crossed the Margaret Bridge to Buda, but instead of climbing to the hotel, it followed the quay and crossed the Danube again, back to Pest, this time over the Chain Bridge. It wove through the Belváros, then crossed back again over the Elizabeth Bridge. The second car's driver placidly followed his colleague, but his male passengers grew louder in their protests as they continued their zigzagging route, back and forth over the river.

"There are two people I really must find soon," Imre told Charles in the silence of the leading vehicle. Through the slightly open window, Imre watched the river, which he had impulsively requested to see over every bridge, and Charles gathered his coat around himself. "I have—I do not think I have told you this—two children somewhere in Budapest. They do not know me. But I would like them to know now, now I have something to show them. Now that our project is coming to success."

Charles sat quietly, hugged himself against the cold, heard this odd confession with his black overcoat buttoned tight at his throat, and felt his heart beat fast at the thought that he had very badly miscalculated. "I'm sure they'll be very proud of you."

"Ohhh, let us not overstate the case, my friend."

"Why the hell do they keep crossing the river up there?"

"I am sure there is a very good reason Mr. Horváth and Mr. Gábor have."

"Does he make you call him Mr. Gábor? You really shouldn't encourage that."

"I have not seen either of them since they were fourteen."

"Twins?"

"No, not precisely."

"So, counsel, all you guys get raped in boarding school, right?"

"That's right, Harvey. Rather a rite of passage for our people. Won't hear a word against it, old boy."

"I do not know even if their mothers still live."

"Would you like me to look into it for you, try to track them down for you?"

"Don't your parents mind, for Christ's sake? All their sons are being sodomized for, what—like, six years? Will you let your son go through that?"

"As I said, a rite of passage."

"Ohhh, I do not know yet. Now that I say it aloud, I am less sure. Let it be for now, I suppose. But thank you, friend."

At the Hilton, the slightly neurotic excitement trembling on the perimeters of the gambling tables repeatedly shook the group apart and reorganized it into different combinations. John had the impression that all around him bubbled matters of great importance while he was left with chats about nothing at all. Imre and Charles bet and won side by side, and, though facing the same direction (their eyes rising in tandem from the spinning wheel to the croupier), they slightly tilted their heads toward each other and spoke out of the sides of their mouths. Harvey took Charles aside twice and explained something with broad gestures while Charles looked him in the eye and nodded very slightly. Krisztina, whom her captors had utterly failed to intoxicate, seemed at times to beam with happiness and at others to wear an expression of darkest suspicion, usually whenever Charles and Imre were alone together. Charles and Neville had a very serious-looking drink at the bar, but when John stepped up to join them, the conversation turned out to be entirely about cricket. Later, John watched Harvey in barely controlled anger issuing inaudible scolding to his assistant until they were blocked from view by three wide Hungarian gangster types, who rolled up to a blackjack table in one massive, sextuple-breasted row.

"What were you getting chewed out for?" John asked as they watched Harvey and Imre bet on roulette and Harvey shouted at the unsympathetic ball bearing.

"It doesn't matter," saxman replied expressionlessly (not much for eye contact outside of the jazz club). "It really doesn't fucking matter one fucking bit."

Back in the lobby, they compared winnings and Charles offered to drop people at their homes. "Oh, but we are staying here in the hotel," Krisztina reminded him.

"Of course. I'm sorry, I forgot completely. So then we'll say good evening to you. But, Imre, will you help me see the gentlemen home before I return you here?" And the men kissed Krisztina's cheek, then cycled through the revolving door into the snow, crowded into the same limo, and heard Charles give the driver the address for Leviticus as the empty second car trailed obediently behind.

Just inside the desert hut, the six men passed under the assessing eye of two muscled bouncers, gigantic Hungarians in short skirts, sandals, headpieces with sculpted snakes and vultures at the forehead, tubular beards wound with spiraling golden thread, and guns tastefully tucked in tunic waistbands. "Oh isn't this *sexy*," John said. "I'm already *muy* aroused." The palm trees swayed under the disco ball, and the tables were laid with plastic dishes of figs. No chairs, only rugs and throw pillows: The gentlemen sat cross-legged on the floor, and their shoes were removed by women in golden bras and translucent silk trousers, which flared then gathered into slender golden anklets shaped like serpents devouring their own fake-jeweled tails. On either side of the sand-strewn stage, imposing video screens played a loop of climactic moments from classics of the world's intimate cinema, and after fifty minutes, one's sense of déjà-vu could no longer be explained merely by the limited ways those climactic moments could be performed.

"Wow, what's best is the authenticity. Because this is how people lived in biblical times. I mean, of course, you know, really *swinging* people." John's voice was muffled by hand-fed figs.

Vaguely Middle Eastern music yowled over loudspeakers while, on the stage, a pantomime began. Two harem members—bound together and under guard by a shirtless, none too Arabic man with a plastic scimitar—mimed anguish, pleaded silently for pity from their merciless guard. Soon an idea dawned on one of the two women, and very little time was lost before the scimitar was tossed aside, the guard was stripped, and the two harem members began negotiating their freedom with an unsurprising (and oddly uninspiring) form of ransom, while the audience smoked, drank eighteen-dollar fingers of Scotch, munched gritty figs, and had their shoulders rubbed and their hair tousled by staff in golden bras. This drama was performed nine times daily by the same company of commedia—two married couples, all childhood friends.

Here the service was aggressively competent. Charles was gold-carding the drinks, and refills came quickly, sometimes without even being ordered. "We have lots of new people we can fire starting next Monday, so don't worry," Charles said when people thanked him for drinklet after pricey drinklet. Harvey was unable to pull his eyes from the stage, trying to not even blink, but out of the side of his mouth he said to his assistant, "Didn't I tell you I'd show you amazing things if you came to work for me?" Two women flanked Imre, and he placed forint notes in the garment pouches designed to receive gratuities. Neville watched the stage with an expression of tremendously serious discernment, a litigator searching for the fatal flaw in a complex cross-examination.

"Jesus, what am I going to do with you people?" But John got no response, whispers swished from Imre to his partner, and a gesture was made to the maître d', and then a woman was straddling John's lap. Imre raised a silent toast to John, and John smiled back with a head shake of strained amusement. Soon she evaporated.

A fake camel trotted across the little stage, and it bowed to the sand to allow another actor—an emir? the harem's owner? a brigand?—to descend and approach the writhing trio. With no physical evidence of arousal other than the flaccid expression of passion on his face, this new addition was soon nude and writhing too, to no apparent surprise on the part of the earlier entries. John pointed out to his colleagues that under a close reading, one could discern a certain lack of penetration in the performances and a certain softness in the definition of the male characters; they seemed unable to achieve the firm *bonheur* that the merry tone of the scene demanded. Scotch appeared in front of him and quickly disappeared like the smoke its flavor resembled. More whispered orders crackled from Imre to Charles to a waiter, and Charles apologized to Imre for something unclear. Across the room, a bouncer irresistibly asked a drunken German to leave the club while a bikinied waitress stood by in a cocked-hip, pursed-lip attitude of violated dignity. The people of the desert formed a caravan. The German tourist tried to join it on his way to the exit. He was lifted by the hair and invited to the door. Behind the bar, a bottle broke and Hungarian obscenities spilled out. The people of the sands whirled like two clumsy quadruped dervishes.

"Your friends make you Christmas present," steamed into his ear in a vaguely Russian accent.

Charles laughed at the expression on John's face, but Imre nodded solemnly at John, accepting gratitude that had not yet been born. "You kids be home by ten," Charles said. "With the grateful compliments of Horváth Holdings."

The girl in the overcoat held his arm, but John turned back at the door for a last look at this sclerotic erotica. Everyone seemed at their ease in that palace of secondhand lust and thirdhand furnishings. One of the women sat on the table's edge, suspending herself over Horváth's lap with arachnid grace, her long bottle-and-booth-tanned legs arched angularly to form most of a hexagon and her toes pointed on the floor far to each side of the publisher. Her hands gripped the back of the old man's head; she bunched his silver hair between her fingers and moaned. She hunched her shoulders, threw back her own head, and pulled Horváth's face into her chest.

The limo left the two of them in front of John's Andrássy út apartment, and John was still chuckling to himself as he turned the massive skeleton key in his building's front door lock. The hero of antityranny—the memory of the people—had bought him a Kyrgyz hooker named Claudia, with feline eyes and a little Euro B.O. under a fruity perfume. They would have a cup of coffee and call it a night, and the next day he would show that he could take a joke, be one of the boys, do business the way it was done around here, evidently, and still maintain both self-respect and good genital health.

But then the girl removed her clothing with such velocity and facility that John realized how much more practiced strippers are at undressing than the average person, and his priorities shifted.

Later, the girl said, "Now I fake the finish for you, okay?" At first John thought she must have stumbled on a knotty vocabulary problem or that perhaps she was offering a special service of Scandinavian origin, but no: She stared up at him with the expression of a tired end-of-shift waitress. "Now, mister? Okay? Now? Okay?"

"Yes, fine, Jesus Christ, go ahead and—" But already her shouts and moans were rattling John's picture frames, and a stream of Kyrgyz words filled his ear, conveniently foreign, translatable however he wished.

Unfortunately, a noticeable amount of time passed after her tour de force before John understood she was awaiting a similar finale from him; she was waiting to punch out. "Some other thing, mister? Some other thing?" John closed his eyes. In this new darkness, he imagined, as he thrashed himself against the girl, that he was thrashing himself against . . . this very same girl, the sole difference being that he was enjoying it. He pictured himself roaring with masculine, earthy pleasure, clawing at the very parts of her that he was in fact clawing at, but with a tactile shock and intensity he had never achieved in reality. The imagined girl watched him with eyes widening in growing excitement, and behind his closed eyes, John pictured his own eyes wide open and widening further as heat and electricity washed over him, poured fire from his spine and coccyx. He saw these two happy people enjoying each other with neither doubt nor second thought, living nowhere but in this nuclear embrace. He imagined their hands gripping each other until blood seeped crimson around the perforation her nails would make in his knuckles. He imagined the two bodies squeezing together tighter and tighter until all distance was erased.

To no avail. He opened his eyes and saw hers were impatiently open, too. His hands clutched the pillow behind her. "Some other thing, mister? Some other thing?"

"Shut the fuck up. I fucking told you no," he spat. He closed his eyes again and buried his head between her breasts, arched his back, and, with a groan, returned her favor and faked the Finnish, too.

III.

THE LAST EVENING OF JOHN'S 1990: JOHN AND NICKY SHARED A STREET-corner, lamp-lit kiss under sticky, fast-falling snow (turning from white to yellow then to white again as it crossed diagonally into and out of the lamplight). They descended into the crowded Blue Jazz as the American singer was dedicating the last song of his band's set—"Georgia on My Mind"—to the memory of Stalin. By the time John returned from the bar with three drinks, Nicky had already sat down and introduced herself to Nádja, and the two women were leaning across the table toward each other, overenunciating to make themselves heard over the slightly too loud music and chatter. "My darling boy, I already like her so very much more than the filly with the jaw. May I touch your head, my girl?"

"The jaw?" Nicky asked her escort while bowing her head and allowing the ancient fingers to skim the texture of her scalp. "The jaw?"

"Never mind. Long story."

"I've heard so much about you," he heard Nicky saying. He was a little surprised to hear the self-proclaimed princess of candor produce something so tritely polite and lightly a lie, as he had never told her anything at all about Nádja.

To go back: John's New Year's expedition had begun a few hours earlier in the *BudapesToday* newsroom, where people wandered around their own desks, shy among co-workers they had seen every day for months and months. With Charles and Harvey off skiing in Switzerland ("Swiss misses give frosty kisses," Harvey had said unprovoked while Charles, out of view, rolled his eyes), John felt a real ache, hoping Nicky would turn up. He could not stomach setting off into 1991 with any of the others, not even Karen Whitley, who had lately donned a transparent attitude of jaded, sophisticated, take-it-or-leave-it disappointment, laced with a golden thread of ironic guilt-mongering, dusted all over with a heady vanilla body-spray scent of still-availability.

Passing a dull hour at this office party—listening to four co-workers' similar movie plots and Karen's alternating insinuations and scorn—he finally saw Nicky. He gave her the chance to smell for herself how fetid the overgrown earth of this gathering had become, then took her aside, asked her to travel with him across a liquorish sea to the sunny, welcoming coast of 1991— a green and promising country rich with sweet, orange, fibrous fruits and red berries shaped like tiny nipples, an island of unsurpassed happiness, where in fact (here he bit her ear) he quite seriously expected to be named king, a happy, naked king beloved for his munificence and slightly feared for his unpredictable appetites. He confessed to her what her nose had already reported: He had already set sail on his boozy crossing. She would have to swim a ways to catch up, but he was willing to wait.

Before they could escape, Editor stood on a desk chair holding a plastic cup of cheap Hungarian white and painted a picture of "prahspruss toims ahett," while the two seafarers grabbed each other's groins behind a screen of computer monitors but in view maintained profound, wrinkle-browed interest in the remarks of their chief. She agreed to voyage with him; she tickled his

Adam's apple with her nails and whispered her assent in his ear. He smiled at her. She was probably, he realized, his closest friend on the entire continent. In persistently asking nothing of him, in repeatedly rejecting his offers of anything resembling emotion or affection, she had become (he saw in the fluorescent light of these cramped offices) overpoweringly important to him. (He was far enough into his evening's cruise to grow sentimental—but not so far that he could not recognize it and excuse it as the inevitable and acceptable response to the shimmering, whispering, accelerating rush of 1990s dwindling hourglass sand.)

Despite her laughing assent, Nicky did not cast off with him. As John wobbled and wavered and threw up from seasickness on his little wooden raft, she easily crossed the narrow, shallow straits to 1991 on the flat stepping-stones of exposure after exposure, click after shutter click: John outside the offices of *BudapesToday* painting his name in the white snow; John standing on the Chain Bridge, his hands in his coat pockets, his shoulders high against the wind, an unlit cigarette on the very edge of his chapped lips, a beefy and mustachioed Hungarian policeman gamely frozen with a ferocious expression, pretending to strike John on the head with a truncheon; Nádja and John on the piano bench talking; a very round-faced woman at the bar gently crying, half her lower lip twisted and bulged between her teeth; the skinny Hungarian bartender leaning his elbows on the bar and listening dubiously to a customer (back only); a peevish couple at a small table, arguing in front of their embarrassed third friend, and Nicky capturing the instant when the angry woman's drink flew horizontally out of its glass toward her boyfriend; the black singer holding the microphone by its stand with one hand, looking at his watch on the other, and beginning to say the hard-won Hungarian words announcing the New Year; kissing couples wrapped in spirals of backlit smoke; a digital clock posting a red 2:22 just over the head of the round-faced girl, now happy again and talking eagerly and gesturing, a little wide-eyed and manic, to three men: the saxophonist, a young goateed American P.R. executive with a copy of József Attila's poetry held at his chest behind crossed arms, and the singer, at the maximum dilation of a gaping, leonine yawn . . .

To go back: 11:42 on the piano bench: "Now what does that remind one of, shaven heads and New Year parties? Oh yes. May I bore you with a memory?"

"Please."

"Then here we are in 1938. New Year's Eve again. Berlin was a very entertaining city in those days, a certain electricity in the air, assuming you were, well, you know, of course. Not everything was clear yet, you understand. I was a little tight, most likely. I believed I played better the piano when I was a little tight. So I am playing. What would the tunes be, I wonder? Mostly German things, no jazz that year for them, best to know your audience. We are in a private party. Thanks to a friend of a friend, I am gathering some very handsome money at parties. A lovely season; 1938 is becoming 1939. I do not know how much longer I will stay in the city. Perhaps I will leave the next month. I am young, anything is possible—friends, romance, adventure. You know this feeling, I am sure. And now a soldier—a party guest—has made a suggestion, very loud, to me. He suggests he and I should celebrate the New Year, which is only a few minutes away, in a particular fashion. I am not sure I can even tell you the English translation for what he proposed; it was one of those German words that simply stretches on forever and in one word manages to convey what in English would be a very long paragraph. So let us leave it to your imagination, Mr. Price. I think with your beautiful and provocative friend there busy with her camera, there is very little you cannot imagine. Berlin: My crude tormentor is wearing jodhpurs. He is young, but he is an officer. And the scars: He has one little ridge across his cheek and another longer one on his scalp. This second would not be obvious, but he has a shaven head, like your new friend. I say nothing, I play a little louder, I am hoping he will go away. But he says his notion again, louder now, quite loud. I am very young; I do not know what to do. So I lie and I say, 'Thank you, but I am married.' 'Ach, the little fräulein iss married? Vvvere iss diss hussband who sends you to sell yourself as a piano playing whore?' I have no friends at this party, it is late, I am staying in an hotel across town. I am beginning to imagine horrible endings to this evening. I am still playing, I make believe that I need to look at the keys, even though this is a little humiliating for me, to pretend this, and then, before I can frighten myself too much or say something witty but foolish, which was also a possibility, I am rescued. Another officer appears on the other side of the piano. 'The lady iss a friend of mine,' the new one lies. 'If she vvvishes to be left alone, then I advice you leave her alone.' This new one is the same rank, I think, or higher perhaps. Jodhpurs also. Shaven head. The scar on the cheek the same. Like a man scolding his mirror. I smile at my savior and move my eyelashes like a lady and continue to play. Of course, the first soldier is a little tight as well and is not about to finish with me so easy. Fear goes fast, and now I confess to pride; I am worth the attention of two young military lads. I am safe now, so I can enjoy this. And I confess also to amusement as the first soldier insults the second, the second insults him back. Their voices are very quiet as they threaten each other. The first one leans across the piano and slaps my hero. I continue to play, but now I am not going to miss anything by foolishly looking at the keys. And I confess, I smiled. It was delicious, John Price."

The best photograph from nearly an entire roll that Nicky exposed within the three surrounding minutes: the two of them sit side by side on the piano bench, Nádja closer to the wall, John nearer the audience. Lit from above by spots designed for bands, their faces are brightest at the top, more shadowed toward their necks and bodies. Nádja's left hand dips into the keys while the other floats just above them, poised to snag with a deft swoop the next melodic idea. She wears the red gown she wore the night they met, which she wore often. He has angled his head to present his left ear to her story and still aim the stream of his exiting smoke up and off to the right, away from her. Above them both, painted on the wall, the tenor saxophonist Dexter Gordon—winged and haloed and a little droopily bored—angles his head in just the same way and emits a stream of lightly painted smoke parallel to John's.

"With that, they very slowly walk away from me. The first soldier shows me a very serious look, a little dangerous, a little vvvolfy. If he should return alone from whatever combat is about to happen, then I should certainly not expect the kid-glove treatment. My hero, though, smiles quite gently, almost laughs, to tell me this is only a silly game and no harm will come. He is taking off his gray jacket. And, John, I am very pleased. I know that women must not confess to things like this anymore. We are not, of course, your gewgaws to scrapple over, you terrible men. But I confess! Find me guilty of thought crimes against my sisters! It was a pure sense of new power, like they tell me I am crowned queen at midnight. I feel at this moment I can have any man I wish in this room, or in all Berlin, and in fact I did meet my husband not long after this. But to go back: They are about to disappear out of the apartment's doors, but first they have become very polite to each other. Each tries to hold the door for the other; it takes them some long time even to go outside. The bowing and the clicking of their boot heels becomes a little music-hall farce. They do not look at me during this, but it is for my benefit. At last they manage to leave the room: My hero has finally agreed to accept his enemy's courtesy, and he exits first. The door closes quietly behind them. The crowds of guests, many drunk, many dancing, fill the space. I continue to play, and the hostess approaches me to make some musical request."

Months later, spring of 1991 was making its initial assault on winter's ramparts, and the white March rain made acidic hissing noises as it drilled little silver-gray holes halfway into the depths of the crusty, brown-spotted banks of old snow, leaving behind a landscape of lunar craters, and in the evening, as the indecisive temperature dipped again below the critical figure it had so recently overtaken, the snow that had been winning its release toward waterhood reverted again to filthy, bumpy ice and sand and a whole season of frozen, time-suspended traffic and dog odors. The photograph of John and Nádja and Dexter Gordon lay flat on a worktable in the photographer's underheated studio. Her adjustable razor blade moved slowly around John's ear, hair, nose, and his stream of smoke, which was now as integral a part of his circled, chapped lips as a comet is unthinkable, is something else entirely without its tapering tail. His tilted profile and smoke stream were destined to top a composite of his naked torso (imperceptibly younger) on the galloping back legs of a goat (courtesy of a photographic field trip to the Moravian countryside). Running hard and exhaling that cool, gray, now-sourceless smoke, John the satyr would soon stride with caprine surefootedness on cloven feet and hairy, naked thighs over the hexagonal bricks of Vörösmarty Square. A week later, when pasting, rephotographing, and developing were done, he would chase—around the front of the metal crowd gathered at Vörösmarty's feet—a maiden, nude, laughing mockingly over her shoulder at her mythical, smoke-breathing pursuer. Her long, blond, windblown tresses would be just insufficient to disguise Nicky's face and slightly insincere laughter. Her arms would reach forward away from the goat, her fingers tensed into a clawing grasp of unmistakable avidity for the other female haunches just disappearing behind the rear of the poet's post, all three of the photo collage's participants chasing in a permanent circle around the crowded monument.

But to go back: On this March night (which felt colder than the depths of January, because of one's overripe longing for spring), the razor successfully cut away the last component, removing John's hands from Nicky's hips and John's vertical torso from both its grimacing head and its invisible nether regions. Nicky spread flat the various curling pieces of her future work, began to assess differences in scale and shadow, when a sarcastic, complaining voice called out from the shadows that blanketed the bed, "I think it's a little much, you doing that with pictures of him while I'm here."

Nicky did not look up; she even let enough time pass in uninterrupted concentration that the complaint was about to be reissued, when at last she allowed herself a response, mellowed from the delay: "I don't remember asking you. It's an absolute miracle I even *can* work with you here." The urge to burst into tears—tedious, the root of too many headaches that spring—announced itself but was not permitted to mature. Yelling was tedious, too, the cause of too many wasted hours while ideas for art simmered away until only stale residue remained. Something easy and amusing had transformed into something stupid and sticky. Emily's initial appeal—her innocence, her total transparency, her ready malleability—had somehow lured Nicky into this, this middle-aged marriage, a cycle of strife and forgiveness where work was endangered and Nicky was growing accustomed to being scolded. "Oh look, I'm sorry," Nicky finally said, but could not look at her. "Please don't do that. Please just lay off tonight. I am so tired of fighting. Just lie there. Just sleep and let me watch you. I love that I can work with you drifting in and out of sleep. Just let me work. Please."

"You saw him this week. You promised you wouldn't see him anymore, and I know you saw him."

"You *know* I did?" The brittle, tapered end of her attenuated tenderness snapped. Nicky put down the razor blade and rested her forehead on the heels of her hands. The bright lamp screwed to her worktable cast dark and peculiar shadows of her head and fingers against the wall. "Goddamnit, his friend died. Please. Just not tonight, okay?"

"Not tonight? Well, how about never then? Would that suit you?"

"Oh my God, until this very instant, I never saw what my dad liked so much about hitting girls, but right now—yeah, never would suit me just fine. I am so sick of you both. You're just the same. You're weaklings. You *should* be together. Just get out so I can get some fucking work done for once." But the last sentence was bluster; Emily had already left.

To go back: the first instant of 1991. The singer's Hunglish announcement of midnight brought kisses and cheers, pursed lips and raised eyebrows, a round of drinks on the house and mock combat with pool cues, handshakes and sudden generosity with tobacco in all its forms, truces in ongoing arguments and the strange, sudden calendar-triggered emergence into consciousness of long-growing, subterranean tendrils of feeling. John lightly kissed the pianist on her cheek. "That's far enough, Price." Nicky's voice came from behind them. "I can't have him laying his hands on yet another woman in Budapest, Nádja." The photographer kissed his boozy lips, then sat on Nádja's other side, the three of them crowded onto the piano bench. Nicky loaded new film, and Nádja playfully exaggerated the squeeze for space, pretended she could only move her forearms to play.

"So my Germans, John Price. They return after perhaps one quarter hour. The New Year instant has come and gone, like here, and we are now in 1939. They left to fight for me last year, and when they return, much has changed. They have fought, this is clear. My enemy and my hero both have bloodied shirts and marks on their faces. The jodhpurs of my hero are torn at the knee. The villain has an eye that is blackening in gradual shades, but it is like trying to see a clock's hour hand move. My hero also has a cut on his cheek, just above his scar. But, believe me, these are things you do *not* notice at first. How can this be? Because at first you notice they are *happy*; you see they are great friends now, this year. Much has changed in a year. At first, I see that in 1939 neither one cares enough about me even to look at me. They walk into the room with their arms around each other's shoulders. They call for kirsch. They toast each other and shake hands and embrace. Again the kirsch, again the embrace. It is disgusting. This has nothing to do with me at all. Perhaps combat has made them *respect* each other, or some cock-and-bull like this that men sometimes worship when they spend too long away from women. Perhaps they were friends before, perhaps they do this often at parties, they find a girl to play on and frighten and then they humiliate her. Perhaps they are of some intimate friendship that demands this ritual."

Years later, pick an age for John, pick a city somewhere, and another New Year's Eve begins with acquaintances and drinks at his new apartment. They ask about the pictures hung on his walls, carefully framed and transported memorabilia of his world travels, the first thing he unpacks and places in each new home. And when the strangers stop in front of the moody black-and-white of the piano in the smoky room with the old woman and the boy side by side, someone asks who took it and someone else asks who is it, and John (answering both or neither) says, "An old friend." Polite curiosity touches on the antique photo of the crying baby, and then another guest (an acquaintance's newly introduced husband, whose name has still not adhered to John's memory; a jazz fan and a trivia buff and something of an incorrigible know-it-all, he and John will grow to dislike each other irreparably before the night is over) says, "Well, if you ask me, I'd say that's Dexter Gordon," and the conversation swings into jazz stars of the mid-twentieth century.

To go back, John was far into his ocean crossing now, with no sight of—and no interest in—landfall. He was very drunk and therefore alternately sullen, sappy, disoriented, chatty. "I don't even know her last name," he was complaining to Nádja when Nicky was far across the room photographing something. "Can you believe that? I mean, I've seen it, but I've never heard her say it. I can't even pronounce it. Symbol there somewhere, if you can find it, because I can't . . ." The next instant, both women were sitting in front of him laughing. When Nicky had arrived, he had no idea; she had just been far across the room, and what was so funny anyhow?

"That's the fucker hit me with a rock." John squinted at a man sitting at the bar, plainly an American, talking with a plain American girl. "That's the fucker, Nic, hit me with a rock." The man sneezed often, and the bar in front of him was bumpy with bunched-up cocktail napkins. "Whom hit me. Let's you and me go kick the shit out of him." Nicky laughed as John advanced, blinking and talking before his enemy had even noticed him. Nicky's shutter clicked and clicked. "You want to hit me with a rock? You can't just hit me with a rock. I'll show you how to hit me with a rock."

The man turned his head toward the angry drunk wobbling in front of his traveling companion, a childhood friend reeling off a messy divorce ending a very short marriage. "I'm sorry?" the tourist said in response to the little he had heard ("himmy wihuh rah"). His voice was soft, stuffed from his cold, slightly apologetic.

"Not good enough, chum. Too late to be 'I'm sorry.' Not good enough at all."

"Do we know you?"

"Oh there are lots of us I suppose hard to keep us clear, all us rock catchers." John lunged at his sworn foe but could not maintain his balance, and he fell to one knee, grabbing the man's arm as he descended. When that arm was instantly shaken free ("Hey, guy, get your hands off me"), John continued his fall and struck his lip—with sharp, incisive teeth perfectly angled behind it—against the woman's foot and then was led off in another direction by Nicky.

"Save it for me, darling," she consoled him. "My feet need ferocious biting, too."

Nicky sat him in a booth, tipped a glass of ice against his mouth from time to time, and watched it slowly turn cloudy red. "I'm in no condition to fight, to be honest," John admitted, and the glass fell over and ice and pink water turned black on the table's surface. "Hey, listen." He could not open his eyes, but something in him compensated; his eyebrows, his lips, the muscles of his cheeks all became enormously expressive so that he resembled a very agitated, blind vampire as the blood dribbled from the corners of his mouth. "Hey, listen. I think I gotta say this now. I really, I love you, Emily. I know you don't want to hear that right now, but I do."

"That's very sweet. Thank you," she said, and John passed out for a while. Later, Emily must have left because, slumped against the booth, no different in posture from when he slept but for his half-open eyes, he saw Nádja speaking to Nicky. They laughed and smoked a few tables away, their heads together, and John knew he must be dreaming because those two had never met. He watched them touch each other's hands when they spoke, watched Nicky snap close photos of the old woman's face and hands and shoulders, watched them point to him in his booth and make unhelpful, pitying faces—a moment so clichéd and cinematic that part of him wondered about the paucity of imagination such a dreary dream must imply. Later, that concern was allayed by a long and feverishly hot round of REM that seemed to go on forever, at ever decelerating speeds, and he woke alone to 1991 in the turpentine steam of Nicky's apartment, dressed and sticky on her bed with unrecollected resolutions and low-resolution recollections and a wheeling, circling desire to feel that this year might, in some unspecifiable way, be *his* year.

IV.

EARLY IN JANUARY JOHN NOTICED, WITH A SURPRISINGLY SHARP SADNESS, a certain fleeting science-fictiony feel to the dates at the top of newspapers. He thought of Mark simply leaving, just knowing this place was not good for him and somewhere else would be better and so decisively departing in a certainly temporary moment of strength. John considered, staring at the improbable, odd date stuttering its way across the hotel's newspaper display table, whether this place was good for him, whether he shouldn't go away. But he had too much to do here, too many ties.

Outside, large-flaked snow materialized just above his head from out of the monochrome gray, as though the low sky were being rubbed against a cheese grater. He stood on the Chain Bridge and remembered kissing Emily Oliver here, months ago. It was *months* old now, that cherished memory, though of course a split second later it provoked a wince of shame, since that cherished memory was atomically fused to the stinging memory of the awful moments that followed it, and the stupidity he had displayed to her for months, and her secret that he still proudly, dumbly guarded. (And the kiss hadn't even been on this bridge, he only then recalled.) Months had passed since then; he hadn't even seen her since Halloween. What right did her ghost have to enter him as she pleased? And if that doomed bridge kiss had not been the last? If tonight he held her asleep against his chest, so close that the stream of breath from his nose brushed her eyelashes. Or if she stood here now and he leaned in to kiss her, but again she said no and so he simply pushed her hard over the rail and she cried slightly as she fell, vanished into the comforting mist long before he heard the delightful, distant splash.

He needed a change, just like Mark, a break from the same old people, though his circle had been shrinking month by month since the social high point of his arrival last May. He needed to go where he would be encircled by friends of the right sort. He belonged in Prague; he had known this for almost a year. Life waited for him there, waited with some goal achievable yet elegant and thrilling.

Instead, that afternoon Editor assigned him a story that took him to an outlying suburb at the crack of a bright and freezing dawn. He shivered until his jaw ached and his spine spasmed between his knotted shoulder blades. He waited and watched at an outdoor training facility surrounded by frozen, crunching flatland and garbage piled behind fences.

"I saw you cold this morning with your little pen and your little notebook—unh—and you were wishing to be inside the dressing building. You could not suffer cold."

"True."

"And—unh—I watch you ask questions of coach very cold and you were very unhappy. I knowed exactly then your problem. Do you know what your problem?"

"My problem?"

"Listen—unh—I tell you a story."

"Now?"

"Yes, yes—unh—now."

He was safely back in his apartment now, warmer, since on top of him crouched a nude speed skater, displaying Olympic stamina and competitive verve. Her hands (and most of her weight) pressed down on John's shoulders, effectively pinning both his torso and his arms; he could only lift his head an inch or two. Her thighs pivoted forward and back from the knees at a fierce, metronomic clip.

"Listen, boy, when I go to training in winter morning and we are outside in the ice, it is bloody cold. You only do'd it once and you know." She breathed easily despite her athletic pace. "To warm us, the coach say, 'You do two-thousandfivehundred meter fast as can.' We do this, we skate a long way. And then—unh—we do it again. After the seventh time of twothousandfive-hundred meter, it really is hurting, and I think my legs never hurt so bad, I got to stop."

John lifted his head as far as was possible and looked at those legs now. The triangular (nearly pyramidal) sculpted calves lay parallel to his thighs, and her own thighs were folding up and down at an extraordinary rate. At the apex of her action, the thighs emerged from the knees at nearly a ninety-degree angle and, from his viewpoint, seemed like enormous pulsing pistons, engineering achieved on some brightly lit, 99.999-percent-dust-particle-free, laser- and robotics-equipped conveyor belt in Hamburg.

"But I go on through pain—unh. It is how you get great and go to the Games and win gold. I know this. So I just not think of pain and skate. Finally, after two more twothousandfivehundred meter, I say, 'Coach, my legs burn too much now.' He looks at me—unh—like I make fart, you know? And he say, 'Yes of course they burn. This is good. Sprint another twothousandfivehundred meter. Do not stop, because you know what comes after the burning?' Do you know this answer, John? Do—unh—you know what comes after the burning?"

"No, I don't think I do."

"I said no also. 'Coach, what comes after the burning?'—unh." She released his left shoulder just long enough to brush a few straggling, sweaty bangs off her forehead. Her hand returned to its position; her fingers fell naturally onto the white marks they had left behind. "He said, 'After the burning comes agony, okay? Now, skate.' And he shoots his gun. He has a gun always at the training to start races and also inspire. He uses always the—unh—the real bullets."

"What? How do you know that?"

"He—unh, unh—one time trying to make us skate faster and he point up in the air and shooted and a bird fall on the ice—unh. That is for you, too—unh—John. After burning comes the agony. You must—unh, unh—you must reach all the way to the agony, because who knows—unh, unh, unh—what waiting for the brave on the other side!" The rocking accelerated further, to inspirational speeds. "Now, boy! Now!"

As she rolls off, she suddenly becomes almost human: Her lips are a little parched; there is a white something at the corner of her eye that he wants to wipe away for her. When she turns away, puts her legs over the side of the bed, sits up, and switches on the bedside lamp, the yellow light filters through her dangling hair. She pulls the damp strands together and wraps a rubber band around them, and the movement of her hands reminds John of someone, he can't quite think whom. Her hands are, after all, not hyperdeveloped but like a girl's. The curve of her back as she sits on the edge of the bed just out of reach, and her head, turned now to the lamp and her shoulder, the corner of one eye just visible over that shoulder and her arms locked and her palms pressing hard and flat against the mattress: He knows she is waiting for him. He can almost think of the right word now to bring her to him and they can begin, but then John has fallen asleep.

Later she was talking again. "I mean this. What I said. You are like me, I think, but you need to drive harder forward. I see this when you standed cold with your little notebook. And later, too, when you say some things. You know, he is the best trainer in the world. Do you understand I talk not only about skating now?"

He watched her dress, one elbow shoring him up on the too-acquiescent sofa bed. Across the room, she seemed convincingly human but too far away to take very seriously. She wore jeans, rolled several times at the ankle and also folded over the top of her wide, black leather belt, tightened to a handmade hole well past the final factory-punched option. Too long and too big at the waist, the jeans still threatened to burst at the thighs. (That morning in her silver leggings they had resembled two pieces of ridged, hard-shell carry-on luggage.) She put on her bra, a gauze of pink purchased during an hour's break from training, racing, sleeping, and carefully quantified but voracious eating on a three-day trip in eastern France.

He hoped she wouldn't quiz him on what she had said, as he couldn't remember any of it, not two words except for the part about the unlucky bird, but he did feel a last flicker, a snuffed-wick fondness for this girl as she daubed some makeup and gathered her coat and bag; he quarter-wished she'd stay the night instead of going home to drink protein shakes and critique slow-motion videos of old races and fall asleep early and alone.

MTV played a pop tune—that song, the one that seemed to be every-where that season, the song that got under John's skin so that even though he couldn't quite hum it, each time he heard it, he recognized it with the keen sen-sation of bumping into a well-loved old friend. A lush, romantic composition, its lyrics were hard to understand, but something about loss and rescue caught and stuck in John's head. The music seemed to have been written and recorded solely to reach John in moments of happiness or sadness, camaraderie or soli-tude, until anything at all memorable about the whole season was accompa-nied by these sounds crooned by a sultry, six-foot-tall Greenlander, reminding him that rescue was possible, imminent.

And it played the next morning on a radio in the newsroom as he was battling the boredom of an uninspired first paragraph and a snottily blinking cursor—

As the old joke goes, "Who was that woman I saw you with last night?" "That was no woman; that was a member of the East German women's swim team." The chunky, steroidal mystique of those East Bloc Amazons who have whupped the be-hinds of our dainty little-girl athletes for the last forty years of international com-petition is now open to closer investigation, and after being granted unprecedented access | | | |

—when Charles called from the hospital.

V.

25(Q)(III). IF DURING THE TERM OF THIS AGREEMENT, EITHER PARTNER should become disabled so that he is unable to carry out or conduct normal ac-tivities and, in consequence, to fulfill the duties or to communicate to others his wishes for the fulfillment of the duties required of him under this agreement, then in such an event ("Incapacity"), the non-disabled Partner or any such other representative as the disabled Partner has previously delegated in writing shall be entitled to have complete authority in the management and opera-tion of the Partnership's affairs, to make all operational decisions in connection with the business of the Partnership without consulting the disabled partner if such consultation is impossible due to Incapacity. Incapacity must be con-firmed in writing by an attending or examining physician in the presence of both the non-disabled Partner and the undersigned designated attorney for the

Partnership. Third parties dealing with the Partnership during either Partner's Incapacity are entitled to rely on the signature of the non-disabled Partner, or expressly delegated representative.

VI.

JANUARY DIED AND FEBRUARY WAS BORN IN A HOSPITAL THAT FOR ALL ITS sprawl may as well have been nothing more than a single, echoing, nearly windowless corridor and a semi-private, steamy, entirely windowless room, both tiled in dirty white, both smelling strongly then weakly then strongly again of chilling antiseptics and, under that, something persistently, irredeemably, gleefully septic.

"It's a terrible time for this to happen."

"There is a good time, Mr. Gábor?" Krisztina Toldy did not look at the junior partner.

"Obviously, I don't mean to say—"

"We rely on your confidence and knowledge to sustain us for a time. Yes."

"Of course, I merely meant—" In the hallway's erratic fluorescence, her skin was the color of moonlight and the whites of her eyes a bacterial yellow. Charles wished she wore some makeup, even a single flesh-tone smear across the forehead.

Neville interrupted. "I understand his closest family is a distant cousin in Canada. Is that correct, Károly?"

"Ms. Toldy would know better than I."

Plainly uninterested in the question, she made impatient gestures with her head and feet, eager to return to the invalid's room. "He has no direct family member at all. His will is with the lawyer in Vienna. He has no contacts of the Canadian cousin."

"No heirs," Charles confirmed. "He always spoke to me of Krisztina here as his closest family."

"*Speaks*, Mr. Gábor. He is not died yet."

"I didn't mean to imply—"

She re-entered Imre's room.

The hospital was set back from the street, a ring of decrepit brick wards huddled together for warmth around a snowy courtyard with slushy shoveled paths over which bulky male nurses in short-sleeved shirts wheeled stretchers and chairs from building to building. The compound resembled a nineteenth-century model reformatory that, a century later, had long since grown up and abandoned the ideals of its designers, now reforming none but imprisoning plenty. When John had wandered far enough and asked enough semi-bilingual people and misunderstood enough answers that he finally arrived in the right building, he found Charles seated handsomely on a wooden folding chair in the long corridor immediately outside Horváth's room. The junior partner was examining a sheaf of financial tables supported on a leather portfolio. He touched the capped tip of his pen to the papers with a rhythmic bounce, and his lips moved slightly in silent review of the numerical battalions parading under his command. To his side, between his shoulder and the door frame of Imre's room, a mop sprouted out of a stained white plastic bucket and rested against the tiles, peering nonchalantly over Charles's shoulder, occasionally sliding coquettishly along the wall into him.

John, knowing it was a foolish question, pronounced it like the foolish question it was: "So, are you *okay?*"

"What? Yeah, whatever. I mean, obviously, you know, it's a terrible thing."

"True."

"And the quality of care here, my God. I think animal-rights people negotiate better hygiene for lab rats. I wouldn't get my hair cut in these conditions. I feel like I might catch a stroke just sitting here. Honest to God, these people."

Halfway down the long, straight corridor (resembling an art student's exercise in Renaissance perspective), a nurse behind a desk quietly sang that song—John's song—and the Hungarian-accented lyrics trickled all the way to him in sporadic whispers: *canchoo see . . . therr iss no ans-ser buhchoo . . . we coot be in heh-venn . . . so losst forr so lung, too menny . . .* She had misheard "I walk all night long, and think only of being us," however, and the words reached John with a key consonant vertically inverted: *I wohk oll night lung, end tink only uff peen-uss.*

"What's funny?" Charles squinted at him. "Whatever. They are funny, I suppose, the little things your life hangs from, you know?" Charles ran his hands through his hair, an exotic gesture of tiredness John had never seen Charles allow himself.

"I do," said John. "These things make you realize it. *Are* you okay?" He put his hand on the seated man's shoulder.

"I mean, my God. A little, tiny blood vessel bursts and suddenly my young working days are spent bored to tears here in the scummy, tiled bowels of Boris Karloff Memorial." He fluttered his lips. "Just kidding." John bounced the mop handle from hand to hand.

The stroke had raped and rampaged unnoticed, or at least unreported, for perhaps two days before Horváth had been found. Tests showed it had probably set to work in earnest the previous Friday. Krisztina had been visiting family in Győr; Charles had been in Vienna on press business; Imre, alone in Budapest, had most likely suffered all weekend from symptoms he chose not to take seriously. By the time he was tripped over by Charles on Monday morning, at least some of the opportunities to forestall neurological damage had been lost. The doctors were vague; Charles grumbled that their artful evasions would have gotten them booed out of a first-year case study discussion section. In hurried, hushed conferences, the physicians warmed one another with a spirited discussion on the likelihood of potential "damage to speech" as opposed to "damage to language," a distinction Charles would have found obscure even if Imre were not now comatose for the third consecutive day. "He'll wake up when he is ready, we think," offered one of the doctors, gently placing a reassuring hand on Charles's biceps. "Yes, of course," Charles had cooed, patting the pale and furry paw on his arm. "Growing boys need lots of sleep."

"The poor old guy," he sighed to John. "Honest to God, what a mess for him. I almost feel like I should have known. Do you think I should've known? He was telling me a story the other night in the office and he didn't remember he'd already told it to me, like, the day before." Charles drafted John to fill his hall seat for a few afternoons while he steered the press on his own. John was to call Gábor's mobile phone if anything at all should change. Over the following days, when bored, John did phone in reports on lightbulbs being replaced and the disappointing progress of the abandoned mop. Once Harvey answered the phone, and though he put John right through to Charles, John forgot his joke and didn't call again.

Attempting to balance on the back legs of the folding chair, John slowly realized he was expected to maintain his respectful orbit and not stray too close to the flickering sun. As a Károly proxy, he was allowed to sit on Károly's wooden chair in the hall and listen helplessly to doctors conferring in Hungarian. Krisztina Toldy, however, sat inside the room by Imre's bed, consulted actively with the doctors, and said little or (more often) nothing to John as she entered and exited the patient's room and very delicately closed the door behind her.

He read. He jotted notes for columns. He wandered to the very end of the telescoping hall to look out the single dirty window, through the chain-link barrier just beyond its glass, onto the courtyard and the shuttered, smoke-stacked factory across the street. Every day when he turned the corner and approached the hospital, he tried to calculate from the ground where this window was. The building did not seem long enough to contain the hall; the walk from wooden chair to window required a conscious mustering of boredom-inspired energy. When he returned from these cheerless treks, he would look at his watch, then close his eyes and try to guess when thirty seconds or a minute had passed. He was rarely even close; his internal time mechanism seemed to be made of rusty springs and sticky, rickety joints turning gelatinous cogs. *How many golf balls could you fit in this hall?* And Krisztina Toldy would come out of Imre's room and John would raise his eyebrows to ask, *What news?* And she would pass down the hall without making eye contact, and he would suddenly feel accused of dark misdeeds, would imagine she thought all he wanted was the news of Imre's death at last, as if he were there for nothing else and Charles wanted nothing more than the old man's demise reported quick-quick over the mobile phone.

After five afternoons the mop still had not changed position, and John wondered whether its operator had quit or if the families of post-Communist patients were expected to pitch in and mop the halls a bit for the length of their loved ones' visits. It finally occurred to John, looking at the bucket water, which had darkened in his days of surveillance, that he could write a column on this little outpost of authentic Hungariana where no comfortable expat would ever have cause to visit. It would be a burning exposé of a scandalous situation, and better yet, it would be an impassioned plea for Western help in resuscitating the once strapping medical establishment of plucky, unlucky Hungary. This would debut a startling new direction in his work. Purified in the white flame of protest and sizzling with emotion, he would join his generation in improving the world. He opened his notebook and tapped his pen against his teeth. Sometime later, Krisztina emerged and mutely glided down the hall toward the elevator; it was not a bathroom or telephone trip. She would be gone awhile.

Smocked Imre lay on top of the covers; a smoothly folded blanket draped across his feet and lower legs. Fluids traveled at different speeds along a network of predictable tubes. No television chattered, only elderly machines that blinked and beeped unobtrusively. John was surprised to sit on just another folding wooden chair; he had assumed a better place back here. From the other side of a stained white curtain floated other beeps, half a heartbeat slower than Imre's. The two machines—Imre's and the shrouded unknown's—beeped twice in unison, then the hidden one fell slightly behind, a little more each time (beep-p . . . beep-eep . . . beep-beep . . . beep—beep . . . beep——beep . . . beep————bee-beep) until it had fallen so far behind that it collided into Imre's oncoming beep and merged slowly again into temporary unison.

John stared at Imre's slow-breathing belly on the convex mattress under the blinking screens and tangled tubes. He looked briefly at the twisted lips and newly dimpled cheeks, and then away again in haste.

He looked at his own hands and recalled a made-for-TV movie he'd once seen where the loving family of a comatose old woman had spoken to her unresponsive ears, determined in their fierce love that somehow "she can hear us, darn it, I know she can, and I'll do anything, do you hear me? Anything for her, I won't give up on her, so don't you dare give up on her . . ." And so, not wishing to be heard by whomever lay beyond the curtain, John shifted his chair toward the head of the bed, rested his elbows on his knees, and began to speak haltingly to his friend's boss's chest.

"Well, I certainly hope you get better, Imre. You're very impressive when you're not, you know, like this. I don't like to think about what happened. It seems wrong that this can, and that's it for somebody who has done and seen everything you've done and, and seen . . . That whole thing about your life as a work of art. I wonder, was it worth it? I wonder that often about you. Was it worth it? Fighting tyrants? Everything you gave up to be on the right side when it seemed like the losing side? I sometimes imagine making an incredible sacrifice for someone or something: Oh, I lose a limb or I'm paralyzed or I even lose my mind under some extreme duress . . . and then if somebody asks me—and I'm limbless or paralyzed or only semi-lucid—they ask me if it was worth it. And I always wonder what I would say. I would so want to know that I would say, 'Oh yes. It was worth it. Of course it was worth it,' even as I'm sitting there with some horrible mutilation. I think about you often, actually. It occurs to me that you know something very, ah, very . . . It would be a shame, obviously, if, you know, I would feel very bad . . . I actually, ah, feel very bad, huh, about the whole—"

John was ashamed to feel his throat tighten. He rubbed his eyes until the tickling sensation passed. His absurdity seemed to have no limits anymore, and so he thought immediately of that kitschy television show when Krisztina Toldy tapped him firmly on the shoulder. She scoldingly smoothed Imre's blankets and pillowcase, though John had touched nothing.

"Oh hello," he said.

"Yes."

Time circulated strangely in the hospital. In the hallway, it sloshed into standing pools, still and stagnant, so that the clock could barely muster the energy to register a change commensurate with the discomfort John felt in the hard little chair outside Imre's forbidden room as he sat and waited, perhaps forever, for the daily arrival of Charles or the specialist. Then, in a rush, the calendar would drop dates like a palm tree in season, and John would realize with amazement it had been a week, ten days, two weeks, nearly three weeks already since the stroke, and still Imre did not move, did not acknowledge, and still Charles paid John to sit guard for him while managing the press's affairs kept the junior partner "just incredibly busy."

Two days later, some excitement: One of the patient's eyes opened when blown on as the specialist had blown on it every day for three weeks. It shut again, and brain readings showed little difference.

The next day, Charles and Krisztina arranged to have Imre moved to a private clinic in Buda run by Swiss doctors. "For all I know the Hungarian doctors are great geniuses," Charles admitted, "but we have to do all we can for him, you know? It sure seems like this is a better place." John sat now on an ergonomic steel chair molded with a little ridge so that his buttocks were separately cupped. He leaned against the robin's egg–blue corridor wall while, hourly, at five after the hour, doctors nodded at him and entered the shiny chrome-and-marble room, then emerged to make a note or two on the translucent robin's egg–blue clipboard nestled in a translucent Plexiglas rack mounted on the sighing hydraulic door, which bore a brass doorplate engraved and screwed in the very day of the patient's registration, as if he were a new executive: ZIMMER 4—HERR IMRE HORVÁTH. Softly down the carpeted hall, from a doctor's receding back, floated the whistled melody of John's song.

"I can't put it off any longer, is the thing. I know this isn't the most tender thing I can say at the moment," Charles said two days later as Neville spoke in hushed and halting German to one of the consulting physicians, "but he's not exactly leaping out of bed to run his company, and this is not the optimal time for that kind of laziness."

"Sheer sloth," John agreed.

"I'm all for catching up on sleep, but something rather significant that's been simmering for a while is now positively boiling over, and so you can do me a great favor. I've got a group that you in fact helped put together, and I need a warm body in a dinner chair next Monday, and frankly, Imre ain't it. Can you manage not to have a stroke between now and Monday?"

Neville shook the Swiss doctor's hand and rejoined the two Americans. "Under the circumstances," he said in his professional BBC voice, "the incapacity determination's a relatively simple matter. I've arranged for the doc."

That night, the lines to get into A Házam offended the old hands. Velvet ropes unironically held potential guests at bay. Inside the front door, press and guidebook mentions of the club were framed and mounted under the Hungarian words for *As Seen In.* An artfully shabby poster prophesied the arrival of A Házam 2 and A Házam 3, to appear in other districts of Budapest, and Praházam, expected to sprout in Prague even sooner. This imminent pollination (the clubs would all sport the same autographed dictators' photos, the same hooded spotlights, the same random furniture) was the flagship Hungarian investment of Charles's old firm. Forever barring the club from their agenda, John and Charles instead sampled the pleasures of the Baal Room, recently opened by three young Irish entrepreneurs and decorated in an infernal theme. At the long bar shaped like a craggy shelf of molten rock, John and Gábor sat on red velvet stools while horned shirtless barmen in red tights brought them Unicum in fake human skulls and, new to the job, seemed nervously aware of the threat to bottles posed by their pointed, coiled-Styrofoam tails. Cages suspended from the cavernous ceiling housed men and women in carefully torn leather bikinis, dancing/writhing over plastic cauldrons containing red flickering spotlights, while massive bouncers with stylized pitchforks and primitively painted faces roamed the floor looking for trouble. On a large stage, under swiveling and flashing strobes, people danced to British pop music mixed with a looped recording of human screaming.

Emboldened by a few sloshing skulls, John executed the opening maneuvers of the mistaken-movie-girl technique on the woman to his left, when, from the bar stool to his right, Charles spoke in confessional tones: "It was good to talk with you at the hospital that morning. It helped. Really. You know?" Oddly, he felt Charles meant it, but couldn't think what talk he was referring to. A good talk in the hospital one morning?

"Hey, whatever. No problem."

He turned back to his left, but the targeted mistaken movie star had disappeared. He had to admit it was not a heart-wrenching loss.

The high-tempo music ended and was replaced by the long, ear-piercing shriek of a man in excruciating torment. Demonic laughter followed as the man sobbed chokingly. Then came the soft, romantic drums and opening synthesizer chords of John's favorite song; it had taken the DJ nearly an hour to get to his request.

VII.

"THE THING IS, KÁROLY, YOU'RE SITTING ON TOP OF THE WORLD AND YOU don't—"

"Charles."

"—even seem to know what to do about it. What?"

"*Charles.*"

"Oh. Right . . ."

Monday night, the promised South Sea islanders were late, and so from a vast distance, from faraway across the little round table set for five, from over the top of his own trembling black disc of Unicum, John watched Charles and Harvey massage their cocktails and converse past each other. He noticed this slight evidence of Charles's nervousness: Charles's smooth, interlocking surfaces were buckling and his distaste for Harvey emerged from under its protective cover (though Harvey, insulated in his own nervousness, did not notice). "They'll be here. They'll be here," Harvey assured them, unprompted, and sought to bring dead air to life with electrical wit: "So, honestly now, tell me straight—you think he's banging that Toldy woman?"

"Well aren't you a naughty sly boots." Charles looked at his watch and snapped two cuffs back over its face. "If he *was,* he's in no condition to do it now."

"Oh you never know, Károly—"

"*Charles. Charles.* It's English. It's your native tongue."

"Yeah, but she keeps a pretty close watch over him in a private room, you were saying, yeah? It might have been one of those strokes that stirs the blood, if you know what I mean. Heard of things like that."

"Charles, can't you shut this moron up?" Harvey and Charles looked up in surprise, and John realized with a flush of embarrassment that he hadn't just thought it. The tone of Charles's laughter, however, was expertly pitched; Harvey recognized at once John's good joke, not to be taken seriously.

The private dining room's thick maroon curtains, surrounding the table on three sides, parted silently and a tuxedoed waiter held the dark velvet at bay for two South Sea islanders. The winter-pale man in front was the younger, only a few years older than Charles but prematurely gray in every way in his faux-antique accountant's spectacles. Plastically handsome and weekly coiffed, he stepped aside, weakly coughed, and allowed his boss to enter the cramped luxury enclave first. Here was John's promised surprise and a momentary bubble of stopped time in which to examine it: a three-dimensional simulation of a famous TV and newspaper face, a Down Under accent familiar from talk shows and news programs, the stern or slightly smug expression (two options only) that decorated a dozen business magazine covers each year. Harvey welcomed and introduced him with heavy respect. Before sitting or acknowledging the introductions, however, the vision turned to the waiter and ordered an obscurantist, antipodal cocktail as if he were the real man—the televised man—and so John could not really feel any credible doubt. The trademark cowboy hat, the clay of the prominent mole-island off the southeast coast of the nose, the eyebrows like primeval forests that TV makeup ladies must have had to toil long hours to glue into the semblance of smooth human features: The props were all familiar. Stranger, though, were the discrepancies: Just inside the curtained enclosure, the Australian had twitchy bad habits evidently suppressible only for the length of a news profile and no longer. Where the television face always locked onto its off-camera interviewers with executive intensity, 3-D Melchior never made direct eye contact, and so again John could almost convince himself that an impostor had joined them at this private table at the King of the Huns. Under the dim light, under the one solid wall's ornately framed reproduction engravings of royal hunting parties, John felt a strange but physically perceptible relief to find here another larger-than-life man who wasn't much, actually much less than the world had been led to believe.

Hubert Melchior did not own the largest media empire in the world. There was a man in Atlanta and another Australian, and there were, presumably, powers in Hollywood and Frankfurt and the glassed-in aeries of Manhattan, whose names had not bubbled to the surface of world consciousness, all of whom had longer tentacles, more influence, more televisions and books and newspapers expressing their branded opinions. But with enough to go around,

Hubert Melchior's was one of those names that—even if one never followed business and finance—always seemed familiar. ("Is he the one who did that stunt, the thing with the flaming kangaroos?")

"These are the blokes scared you so bad, Kyle?" Melchior muttered as he sat down with a little grunt. His gray assistant laughed slightly and nodded on cue. The jibe was delivered in a weirdly humorless monotone, almost a mumble, not the boisterous corporate faux-cheer John expected. Melchior didn't look at his assistant, had hardly looked enough at John or Charles to determine whether they were, in fact, sufficiently intimidating or not to have scared Kyle so bad. He watched instead his own hands, which, palms down, glided over the wooden table in random, slow-moving patterns.

"Scared me? No, no, gave me pause is all, Mr. Melchior," said the younger man, with the semi-human intonations of browbeaten, hopeless executive assistants the world over, aging at twice the speed of their employers. He smiled at the three Americans, on Melchior's behalf as well as his own, offering extra eye contact with the compliments of the corporation.

Melchior was felinically fastidious. He scraped at a tiny, bulbous starfish of candle wax that had beached on the table. His left thumbnail scratched six or seven times in quick succession, then he brushed the wax crumbs away with speedy sweeps of his right pinkie. He alternated—scraping thumbnail, sweeping pinkie, scraping thumbnail, sweeping pinkie—long after anyone else could see any wax dripping at all, long after his eyes and attention were elsewhere, and still his hands polished of their own accord.

"Mistah G'bore," he murmured, unfolding his napkin and smoothing its individual creases with care. "Saw your face everywhere one week. Journo in the pocket here and there doesn't hurt a young fellow. Know your way around that game nicely, I must say."

Charles laughed politely at the autistic speech emitted in the same voice of barely repressed boredom.

"And with you and your chief there, this Mr. Horváth bloke, in the papers every time he turned around, poor Kyle's nappies were always wet. He just kept saying, 'Not the right time, not the right time, Mr. Melchior.' Didn't you there, Kyle boy? 'Not the right time—' "

"Mr. Horváth, though senior, has—I hope I've made it clear that Károly here is here as the fully entitled representative of—"

"—'not the right time, not the right time,' just because of some nonsense about—" Melchior had heard Harvey's interruption, but he hadn't looked up from the invisible patterns he was drawing on the table with a stiff index finger, didn't waste time scolding Harvey, simply kept talking, and no utterable noise on earth could have made him stop. "Couple of news articles and Kyle here is crying like a girl that it's 'inopportune' for us to bid on Hungarian privatization deals. 'Inopportune,' after everything I've built." Melchior's toneless but candid admission that his multibillion-dollar media empire had been temporarily stymied by Charles and John, of all people, triggered in John a rush of pride. "King Jesus—had to listen to tripe about how we shouldn't tamper with the privatization process, should let the Hungos deal with their own government first. Utter nonsense. And now there you sit, and you're just a little boy, and no more Hungo than I am." He gestured at but did not look up at Charles. "Look here. Truth be told, we were a little late to realize the media needs in this neck of the woods. But now no fooling. I'm in town for three days, and I got six papers, six publishers, two TV stations, and a cable start-up to talk to, so let's not spend a lot of time courtin' the sheep, right? Either she bleats for us or we move on." Even this colorful Austral-corporate vulgarity emerged in the same vaguely bored, mildly sociopathic voice, and Melchior took a bite of his salad, found something distasteful in it, pushed it aside. "Your little house is nice and I want it, but I don't have forever to do this. There are another dozen and a half I want if Hungo and Czecho and the Polacks are going to mean anything for Median. Let's get on with it. Harvey here tells us we don't need your chief for this talk. How's that, then?"

"He's, unfortunately—" Harvey began.

"Yeah. Sorry to hear it," Melchior said.

"I think a key point, a possible sticking point, which is what I see myself being able to help here with, what I'm on the lookout for, preventative, preventatively, to be discussed would be, Does it become the Median Press?" Harvey asked, brokering as fast as he could, before events brokered themselves.

At last Melchior looked at someone: Charles, who had hardly said a word since the Australians' landing. "It certainly becomes a proud new member of the Median family, and is given proper brand support as a result, much more support than you're going to be able to muster with what's left of your little private fund there, Mistah G'bore." Vast personal knowledge implied, he returned to the work of realigning his unused silverware. "You any relation to those sisters, by the way? The actresses? So you tell me: Does the name of the house matter to anyone in this country?"

It had happened so quickly, John hardly realized what was going on: As the last salad plate left the table on disembodied hands, John finally understood the Horváth Press was not only for sale but that the fates had already proceeded to the details of what it would be called when it was swallowed, still breathing, into the snaky belly of the Multinational Median Corporation, where it would quickly be broken down into its irreducible components.

Charles slowly puffed out his cheeks and swayed his head from side to side. "Only very distantly," he confessed. "Through my great-great-grandfather, I've been told, cousins of some sort. I've never met them, of course. It's a relatively common name in Hungary."

"I think Károly's in a, a, a kind of a spot, or like a spot," Harvey offered. "We should be sensitive to the needs, that is, to the needs of both sides, or not sides but interests, the natural needs of those interests."

"*Charles*," Charles corrected him sharply.

"Right." Harvey looked at him blankly. "What?"

Charles ignored Melchior's general question and offered instead a buffet of specifics. He began listing individual Horváth Holdings publications and prospective projects, descriptions of the firm's published catalogs and backlist. He juggled titles, authors, and publications like a Las Vegas card trickster fanning a deck through the air. "*Our Forint*," he was saying, "—and I pause here only as a possible example of some issues we might face—*Our Forint* is branded content with generations of tradition and consumer feeling behind—"

"That's your business sheet." Melchior's voice registered slight interest, but it was not a question, and he did not look away from the engraving over Charles's shoulder, and John saw how the Australian simulated his look of keen intensity during TV interviews: over-the-shoulder focus points filmed from the side. "*Our Forint*, huh?" He reached out his hand and caught with an echoing slap the entire deck as it arched through the air. "No. Maybe for a while it stays under that name, but you know what we have. You're no fool, Mistah G'bore. You picked that title for a reason, and I appreciate your openness to a deal. You know we've put enormous resources into the launch of *Mmmmmoney*. We want *Mmmmmoney* to be a worldwide publication, uniform globally, but with localized insert sections, seamlessly tailored to each market. Those inserts could, presumably, have localized names. Me and Kyle see no reason not to call the Hungo one *Our Forint*, if you can convince me you care."

"I think that's probably a reasonable starting point." Harvey looked back and forth between the table's two interesting people.

Melchior looked Charles in the eye and smiled, almost humanly. He had offered Charles the public impression of a concession, had addressed one small element of the whole, and expected his response to be extrapolated outward, and so the Australian pushed back his chair and stood; he did not need to stay for another course. He concentrated on sliding his spotted hands into plush gloves, even as his dishwasher's dog–destined entrée was arriving at the table. His assistant stood in readiness, napkin in hand, but Melchior would leave alone; Kyle was to finish eating with the three Americans. Melchior smoothed the fleecy interior of his cowboy hat with a practiced action, alternating the palm and the back of the hand. "Based on what Harvey here's told us, the amount of your bid, and the value of the Vienna outfit, Kyle here has an envelope with a number in it. It should be sufficient for you. It's not a negotiating position. It's final. I can't go any higher than that number, so either your little item joins the Median family or it sits alone in Median country and we spend our first months here engaged in getting you out of our way. Kyle will wait one day at the Hilton for you to say you're interested. Pleasure to meet you gentlemen." No eye contact. No handshakes. And the cowboy hat and the mole and the abnormal, asocial drawl were swallowed by the maroon curtains.

There was a certain ice-blue pleasure in Melchior's company, John realized only as the velvet stopped billowing and settled into a vertical red sea. He didn't seem to enjoy his work in the slightest, but he also seemed entirely free of artifice in its performance. He said "I want this" and "I'll pay this amount for it" and "No, I won't name it after your comatose boss" and that was that.

"Lovely venison," said Kyle with real feeling, a sadly eager glimmer on his face. Left for a few minutes to his own devices among people more or less his own age, he rushed to make the most of it. "Are there entertaining places to go around here after supper? Clubs or dancing and the like?"

"Let's see the envelope, Kyle."

"Right."

Charles held the sealed envelope to his temple. "Enjoy your venison, Kyle." He placed the letter, unopened, in his pocket, and everyone spent the rest of the evening wondering when he would finally peek. Kyle, always sensitive to being dismissed, said not another word. He and Harvey graciously paid for the meal.

On the street outside the restaurant, Charles pointed pointedly to two cabs, and Harvey tried to steal a confidential word with him as he could see that the encroaching forced separation was for a good strategic reason and that Charles obviously wanted him to execute certain intricate, advanced negotiatory maneuvers once he had Kyle alone. "Charles, Charles, listen," he said, his arm sliding around Gábor's shoulder, chummily walking him away from the others. Charles bent over to tie his shoe, arose facing the other direction, strode to the cab, pushed John in, and shook two hands. "*Károly*," he corrected Harvey.

Charles didn't open the envelope, didn't even seem to recall he had it, until he and John had escaped, had left the other two standing together in the cold, final February night, the young Australian plainly crestfallen to be left in the company of another middle-aged bore, to watch again, as in so many cities where so many deals were done, anyone remotely fun heading off in the other direction, in a different cab.

The cab had lurched several blocks before Charles, without losing his place in a practiced but still fresh discourse on the Gulf War, retrieved the envelope from his jacket pocket. He fondled the Hilton-crested packet without looking at it and spoke of the ambiguous charms of Saddam Hussein, then finally, slowly, opened the envelope with measured uninterest: He tore the edge off its short end, describing the cold economic truths belying the hot political justifications for the desert combat. With a nonchalant puff, he blew the envelope into a cylinder and slowly slid out a sheet, which he could not be bothered to unfold. A good audience, John was suitably amazed by Charles's languor and repose, or at least by his unquenchable desire to amaze. War motives analyzed ("You *can* be humanitarian and greedy at the same time; it's just harder"), Charles unfolded the typewritten paper but did not look at it ("I really *do* believe you *can* shoot, starve, bury alive, burn, and bomb people, even innocent people, for humanitarian reasons, but it takes a great deal of emotional maturity"). The glow of passing streetlights illuminated his face in regular, sliding washes of pale yellow, each identically speckled with the gray transparencies of the taxi window's smudges.

"Okay, I'm duly impressed. Look at the thing already."

Charles bowed his head in gratitude and at last read the typed sheet. "Huh," he allowed. "That's about what I thought." He started to laugh and shook his head. "If I'd been *high*."

John redirected the cabdriver, and took Charles to the Blue Jazz for the first time. His friend's growing, irrepressible excitement and his admission that Melchior's offer had surprised him induced in John a warm feeling toward Charles that he rarely experienced, and this justified sharing his favorite place with the celebratory partner.

That comradely warmth lasted until just before they had taken their coats off and sat down: Nádja wasn't there, to John's disappointment, and instead the room was smeared with the pea-green sounds of a sextet of avant-garde free-jazz types. "I *love* this song!" Charles exclaimed, and John immediately regretted not sticking with the Baal Room. "Jazz is just *so* great. All the cats poppin' their thumbs to the rat-a-tat-tat of the drums."

The conversation was enlightening, at least. For John, listening to Charles explain the meal they had just eaten was like going out for an entirely new evening, since apparently a whole eveningful of events had transpired without John even noticing. Charles described his frank admiration of, and pure enjoyment in, Melchior's "gamesmanship." The freakish little tics, the candid admission of being fooled, the casual, artless abuse of Kyle, the gruff yes-no/now-or-never/no-negotiating/no-bull manner tickled Charles, and he respected "the work that went into its preparation." John's assertion that it had been Melchior's natural personality amused Charles nearly to choking. "All of it was very well done," Charles contradicted him, "but it would be meaningless if Melchior couldn't turn it on and off at will. If that's all just him," he lectured patiently, "then the man is nothing but a psycho in a cowboy hat. Worse than that, just a lucky businessman rather than a skilled one. No, he's a serious man, our Hubert. It's very well done, so don't feel bad. But—and I say this with professional certainty—it's all a put-on, even if he never stops doing it anymore, even if he does it in his sleep and will die doing it."

Charles had been curious to meet the man, of course, but certainly hadn't expected an offer he could take seriously—maybe a minority investment offer, maybe a slightly marked-up buyout of his 49 percent, he had half hoped back in December, when Harv first started seeming credible about an introduction. But this . . . this was "gloriously, gorgeously high, high beyond dreams."

John longed for Nádja's presence; he felt he would be able to pay better attention to Charles if only it were her on the stage, if only he knew the evening would end with just the two of them, him walking her home. He had never walked her home before, and that seemed a pity. He savored an image of a new nightly tradition: At the gray, quiet close of her working nights, he would see her home and they would have tea or sherry and good conversation in her firelit parlor before he headed off to . . . wherever. Nádja's apartment would be a treasury of her amazing life so beautifully, so fully lived: that unlikely scribbled catalog of books and records—creased, yellowed, but there in the pulp; photographs of all her people and places; letters in remarkable handwriting, from eras when the mail came thrice daily; drawings of her, which she would handle with care but not worship, considering they had been sketched by hands of greatness, hands for whose other, more finished works museums fought one another like enraged children. On a shelf, mysterious souvenirs: a bullet casing; an ancient and curling identity card issued by some long since disbanded organization to some young man long since gray or gone; a rolled and tied citation from a government vanished from the earth. "Good night, John Price," she would say in her leathery foreign-movie-star voice, "or good morning, as the case may be," and they would kiss each other's cheeks at the door, and he would walk out into the dawn air and feel like he was in the right place, ready to go meet . . . whomever.

"But the size of the bid sort of retrospectively gives new meaning to everything that happened at dinner. You can see they're in a hurry, right? We've kept them waiting, thanks to Imre. So now bid high, absorb whatever loss is necessary, because it's a landgrab, that's the order of the day." John noted his friend's wide-eyed excitement, all of his coolness steamed away by the warm liquor, and maybe even by the wailing squeals ricocheting off the stage. "Don't they have strippers here? Why do you come here so much?"

Of course, bully-buying media was a dangerous game. Buying newspapers wasn't like buying a cannery. Newspapers talk: Force one to sell (". . . getting you out of our way . . .") and you might get two weeks of nasty abuse from the very object of your desire before you are able to consummate the deal and shut her up. And thus, Charles motored on tirelessly, here was an interesting detail: Median had started with Horváth before talking to all those other outlets Melchior had listed. "And why does he want Horváth first?" Melchior had complimented Charles on getting good press and understanding its importance. "You get it yet? He wants Horváth first because of . . ."

"Yes, yes, because of you."

"No, child. Melchior wants Horváth first because"—Charles pinched John's cheek hard enough for John to make a noise—"of you, you little darling." Median would come one way or the other, but it was worth Melchior's time and money to try to do things in the right order. Median had chosen not to make a privatization bid for the Horváth Kiadó because John had convinced Harvey had convinced Kyle had convinced Melchior that no foreigners could win a bid for something as highly symbolic as the press. And now Melchior respected the men who had held him at bay. And he wanted their assistance: Median's first acquisition in Hungary—and Austria—would occur under the soft, flattering light of favorable news courtesy of Team Charles, rather than the uselessly hysterical strobe that greeted Melchior's first acquisition in Czecho-slovakia, where a few self-righteous, apocalyptic editorials had led to actual protests, "a bunch of truly silly people lying on the ground in front of the offices of some punky underground newspaper, the sentimental editors of which didn't even realize they had just won life's lottery." *If we are going to sell our-selves, sell our history to faceless moneyed men, why have we gone to all the trouble of rebelling, and of teaching ourselves to tell the truth no matter what the conse-quences? What can it mean when this organ chooses to surrender itself to the first brainless millionaire who offers us a little hard currency? Now that we are a free coun-try and a poor country, what are we not willing to sell? I only hope that my Czech brethren are wiser than the men who employ me and who . . .*

Across the room, the bandleader, his giant hands cradling a tiny trumpet, mumbled some grateful farewell Magyar into the microphone, and Thelonious Monk's recording of "April in Paris" rained from the speakers. The two friends stumbled through a very clumsy game of pool, and John was keenly aware of the snickers of better players waiting for the table. "Guys at this level"—Charles leaned on his cue and spoke while John shot—"don't waste their time over asset-by-asset valuation drudgery. They leave that for sparkling personalities like Kyle to deal with. Guys at the top just have the right instincts, and what doesn't work at first, they make work out of sheer force of will. You have to love that. He'll make Horváth profitable, faster than I can, just because of how big Median is. To make people feel they're *asking* you to act. So beautiful." Charles sat on the edge of the table. His feet dangled and he held the cue under his chin; a little blue chalk circled the tip of his nose. He had the face of a little boy look-ing forward to a baseball game. "Honestly, John, I'm not a sentimental guy, right? But it's rare, isn't it? To see something so beautiful. It's elegant." The point Charles had taken two hours to come to was that he needed John again, both for his typewriter and for talking to some of his press pals he'd made back when the Horváth deal had started. "Hubie was late to come here because he believed you. You're a talent of rare ability. This is the start of a serious career for you. You have the ability to make things *happen*. That puts you up above the mass of people. You can see things as they really are. People think the world and the newspapers are just full of all kinds of acts of God. But you understand the true meaning of events. You've proven you can control the mechanics of what other people think are forces of nature."

It took John nearly three hours and several drinks to remember to ask, back at the bar, "What about Imre?" but by then Charles had already taken a cab back up Gellért Hill.

He sat alone at the far right end of the bar, Charles's words still singing ("like the Gulf War boys keep saying, Don't get in if you don't know how you're going to get out"), and he gazed at the antiquated pay phone wreathed in black-ink garlands of graffiti in three languages. His thoughts moved with liquorish fluidity: *That's the phone Emily used once introduced her to Nádja wish Nádja never told me what she saw in her.* And he asked the bartender where the pianist was.

"She died, man. Too bad—she was a good lady."

John sat still, waited for the stupid joke to give way to a serious answer, croaked, "Really?" heard the confirmation, nodded, chewed his slippery, rebellious lip, walked slowly away from the bar. He meant to walk to the bathroom, but before he was halfway across the room, he started to run.

VIII.

SHE WAS BREATHING A LITTLE HEAVILY; THIS DID NOT ESCAPE THE SWISS doctor's notice. She insisted: He had squeezed her hand when she said his name.

"It is extraordinary unlikely, fräulein, at this moment of the progression, for such a turning and, while I know difficult as this is to be hearing, those who are not physicians are so often fooled by . . ." Krisztina Toldy closed her eyes tight, shook her head, very slightly shuddered as if to shake from her neck and shoulders this doctor's snowy alpine manner, absolutely refused to listen to another word. She had no time for perverse disbelief. She had said Imre's name and at last Imre had responded; it was a simple truth.

But the doctor's uniform smile unfurled, tautly immobile over his closely trimmed, triangular black beard. From his great height, he looked down on the frenetic little woman as at a small girl with Father Christmas fantasies, and he tolerated himself to be led into the patient's room, to cradle the patient's limp hand, and to be hushed by an increasingly intense Krisztina while—each minute slower than the last—she chanted Imre's name. He stood across the bed from her, slightly hunched, his translucent clipboard under one arm, keenly aware of the ticking clock, his hand damp in that of the comatose man, and a measured dose of anger diluted his patience, drop by drop, repetition by repetition of *Imre* . . . *Imre* . . . "Now please to listen to me, fräulein. I must insist. I have in every way my sympathy for you, but Herr Horváth faces—*mein Gott.*" And then, with sharpened attention, he waited in silence for several more minutes (now flitting by, where previously they had slouched), until he scribbled in German on his clipboard the observable facts: *22:20–22:35: patient responded to verbalization by producing hand pressure, feebly, 3x/.25 hour, each occasion immediately after enunciation of patient's name, right hand only.* Krisztina bent over and gently kissed the sleeping forehead, caressed the contorted, silver-bearded face.

"IT'S WONDERFUL, THAT'S WONDERFUL, Krisztina. I'm absolutely thrilled. Please call me as soon as there's anything else to report. I'll be in this evening. And by all means I'll tell everyone here the happy news." He hung up. Her enthusiasm was not uninfectious. "These spreads here," he said to the young Australian, both of them working late, with their neckties pulled into loose Y's, "are foreign-language sales of the Hungarian-classics catalog, by country. Obviously not a gold mine, but a low-cost and reliably renewable—"

"STILL, ONE MUST MAINTAIN a realist view of the roll of events," the physician said, injecting a health-giving dose of Swissimism. He was able to perceive, with the clear-sightedness for which his colleagues had long esteemed him, that this unbalanced young lady could easily fall victim to hyperemotional responses if the patient did not immediately leap from the bed and dance for her. This image amused him, and he hoisted his smile both for his own pleasure and to soothe her overexcitement.

"WATCH OUT, WORLD EVIL, 'Cause Here Comes Hungary!"—John's two-part consideration of the Hungarian contribution to the Gulf War coalition—had him traveling steadily for several days. He had not quite exhausted his dwindling reserves of irony; he noticed the incongruity of his surroundings to the internal monologues he could only turn off temporarily and with great difficulty. "I'm a Pathetic, Sentimental Idiot," for example, blared so loudly as he sat in the waiting room of the newly minted press relations officer of the Hungarian Army headquarters that it may as well have been on a public address system. "She Was One of the Rare People Who Know How to Live" belted out its kitschy libretto a day later in a military camp as a press aide guided him from underheated building to underheated building. "What Kind of Freak Bawls for an Hour in a Hungarian Toilet Stall?" gave the first of its several performances to the rhythmic shoop-pop-bang accompaniment of mortar practice on a snow-dusted, wind-blasted plain halfway between Pápa and Sopron. Typing up the first installment of "Watch Out, World Evil . . ." back in the *BudapesToday* office was delayed by a particularly insistent, richly appointed revival of "I'm a Pathetic, Etc." At noon the next day, he impatiently, quasi-bilingually interrogated three Blue Jazz employees before he found one who could give him Nádja's home address. "She Was One of the, Etc." murmured a subdued reprise as he walked back and forth past her apartment building that afternoon, the next morning, and the afternoon after that, ridiculously unable to enter or knock on the flaking paint of the little door cut into the gigantic old carriage entry. Astonished at his gaping absence of nerve, he retreated to Nicky's. She was the only person he could imagine accompanying him, no matter how many weeks since last they saw each other.

A CURVED PLASTIC RAKE scraped along the sole of his foot and then returned to its special felt case in the doctor's jacket pocket. There were controlled experiments involving series of loud noises and voices saying different words at different volumes. Long gusts of paprikás-scented breath swept his face. Pins prodded his toes, gently at first, then ferociously after the doctor had left the room, and Krisztina drove the pins with enough force to bring little beads of red blood to the thick, textured surfaces of his pale yellow feet. When left alone, she held his hand and chanted his name, with little more inflection than a regular churchgoer for whom the meaning of it all has begun to slip away. A special machine propped open his eyelids, then allowed them, with an almost soothing hum, to descend into repose. A specialist shared the news that recent research had suggested, in certain cases not entirely dissimilar to that of Herr . . . Herr (embarrassed clipboard examination) . . . Herr Hortha here, that it would seem perhaps there is some thinking that a well-positioned and very mild electrical stimulus could perhaps have a salutary effect. Krisztina declined to electrocute her hero on such lukewarm testimony. A very kind English nurse suggested that music to which the gentleman had been partial whilst awake might very well be the thing to hurry events along a bit; she had seen it work jolly well before. And so a small compact disc player and a CD of some traditional Gypsy music (both gladly paid for by Charles) were duly summoned and did indeed produce, to Krisztina's careful eye, a sporadic and tiny contraction of the right cheek as well as at least two grade-2 squeezes of the right hand, but then nothing. And then late—very late—one evening, with the television playing loudly (a proudly vague explanation of what U.S. Special Forces had accomplished behind the Iraqi lines), Krisztina struck Imre across the face. She had been virtually living in two hospital rooms since the end of January, and now, after the short-lived exhilaration of the hand squeeze, no matter how loudly, sweetly, seductively she said it, his name was no longer producing any results at all. She had drunk a little that night, and some small measure of self-pity had seeped into her blood with the alcohol. Her usually homogenized feelings had curdled slightly and, to her confusion, she was angry at Imre. She slapped him that night, twice, while pleading with him a little nonsensically. She struck him out of anger and frustration and also because it might be the desperate, unconventional, but successful tactic guided by feelings surer and deeper than complacent Swiss medicine. Either way, he did not open his eyes, and, having turned up the volume of the television ("these boys each carried what we call a 'hot ball,' and the less said about that, the better"), she sat heavily in the contoured chair next to the bed and allowed herself to weep, slightly and with great control.

"I'M SORRY TO HEAR IT. I had high hopes for the music myself. Please keep me informed. No, no, of course not, it's quite all right. By all means stay there. Operations here will suffer on without you. Oh, not at all, you're quite welcome." Charles hung up. "The thing is, Krisztina really is an asset to the organization. You should keep her on—not to tell you your game. I'm sure you have plenty of your own people like this, but she's a local, and that can really help." He turned down an Australian cigarette.

I KNOW I'M JUST one of the parasites, but sometimes we have the best view of our host body. Frankly, from where I've latched on, the thought of Hungary and its post-Communist chums suddenly becoming quasi-NATO members has the feel of being introduced to your dad's new wife's kids, your new crap stepsiblings, who move in and start playing with your stuff and call your dad "Dad." Yet whose heart doesn't go out to the Maggies, the new kid in a big school? Like the last tyke to be picked when choosing sides for a game of kickball, Hungary stood sheepishly on the sidelines until President Bush finally said, "Aw heck, come on, Zsolt! We sure could use your spunk!" Or, as Lieutenant Pál, my host at mortar practice, so eloquently explained, "I am not altogether entirely certain that our mortars would be very effective in a desert situation. So we were happier and also more confident in being help by sending the medical personnel." Well, water flows under the bridge faster than it used to, and this particular

epochal war seems to have become a memory before we even got the chance to ration,
or do middle-of-the-night civil guard duty, or sleep with soldiers' left-behind wives.
It's hard to keep track of the passing epochs nowadays, as a friend of mine once
pointed out. It's early March, so that puts us in the delirium and exuberance of the
postwar period. Of course, a war that starts with Churchillian calls for blood, sweat,
and tears, victory at any cost, the salvation of the free world but then ends with the
military equivalent of a violent retarded child suddenly forgetting why he is in the
middle of throttling this particular gerbil and then tossing it aside while it's still able
to catch its breath . . .

"YO, CALL ME when you get in. I just had my islanders in again. These guys
move. I love watching efficient people in action. I'd forgotten what they looked
like, I've lived here so long. Loved your Gulf War thing, by the way. Call when
you have a minute to talk about real work, okay?"

"HEY HO, IT'S THE KING of 1991! Long time no screw, your majesty. How's
the Price of Love?" She pecked his cheek and led him by the hand to the clothesline loosely stretched outside the black curtains that formed her darkroom.
Clothespin-supported, there hung, still slightly damp, ten enlargements she
had just spawned—goats in a field, the statue of Vörösmarty, classical French
paintings of nude goddesses in varied poses, each ham-hock thigh more generous than the last. There were also pictures, still streaked with reflective and
evaporating liquid, of events in which he was a star but that had never even
made the short trip to his short-term memory. He gazed at them in amazement,
wondered if perhaps they were collages, but they seemed too normal for Nicky
to have bothered, and they did tickle, ever so delicately, if not memory, exactly,
at least a sense of personal plausibility: a piano bench supporting him and
Nádja, Dexter Gordon smoking on the wall just behind them; a bar stool he
seemed to be kissing on its leg, two puzzled faces above him; his face sharply
top-lit, on the Blue Jazz stage, holding the microphone, his eyes sleepily half
shut, his lips curled into a rascally, lascivious semi-smile; his top half in a booth
at the Blue Jazz, his head propped sloppily in both hands, a little line of drool
catching a blue light, the only filament of color in the black-and-white composition. "Will you come with me?" he finally managed to ask, and even wheedled
a little, to erode her unexpected, nonspecific resistance. "For art's sake. You
might find it, you know, artsy. I could use the company. I've walked by it for the
last three days. I think you'd just, you know, for curiosity's sake." Some very

small part of him wondered quietly if this might not be the long-approaching moment when she would just come to him.

KRISZTINA HAD FALLEN ASLEEP, at three in the afternoon of all times, on the contoured chair, her arms crossed, her heels hooked underneath her on the chair's crossbar, and her head hanging heavily, nearly to her lap. Even through sleep the soreness of her neck persisted, and in her semi-slumber she could feel the sickly space between each vertebra, clotted and hot and almost audibly starchy. She tossed her head from side to side in search of the pillow that for weeks she'd known only in dreams, and her eyes opened for a moment, and she saw Imre staring at her. Before the thought had registered, her eyes had shut again, and it took her several seconds to fight upward, to break the surprisingly thick surface and emerge into full wakefulness. Even then, she lost another second or two trying to focus her gaze. His eyes were shut. It might have been a dream. She took his hand and stroked his brow and chanted, chastened.

"HE'S MUCH THE SAME," Charles responded. "Thank you for asking. We're always hoping for news of progress."

"And so his position in regards to this agreement?"

"Unchanged," Neville answered.

HER BUILDING'S CONCIERGE—a mustachioed, athletic-looking man in a shiny red tracksuit—smiled broadly as soon as he peered at John and Nicky through the lace curtains of his apartment door, just inside the archway leading to the courtyard. He had known with a glance that they were foreigners, and he opened his door already apologizing, "*Nem English, nem Deutsch.*"

John said simply, "Nádja," and made a face to express that he wasn't expecting to be led to a live woman's door. His ignorance of her family name struck him only then.

"*Igen.*" The man nodded sympathetically.

John mimed turning a key. "*Igen?*" he asked. The man shrugged broadly and looked down to the floor as his eyebrows rose in a bilingual display of hesitation. "My grandmother," John said in English, then managed in Hungarian, "My mother on my mother." The Hungarian touched his slicked-back hair in confusion, and so John held his two hands flat, one above the other, to simulate a family tree. "My mother," he said, and moved the bottom hand. "And my mother," he said, and moved the top hand: "Nádja." The superintendent shrugged, locked his door behind him, and walked them up four flights of stairs, his athletic sandals slapping rhythmically. John imagined his poor elderly friend trudging up and down all these stairs, every day.

"*Amerikai?*" the man asked them as they stopped for breath at the top. "*Yoowessay?*"

"*Igen.*"

The super nodded with admiring significance, lofty-browed. "*Igen, igen, yoowessay, yoowessay, nagyon jó.*" He led them to a short, dark hallway off the main corridor. He paused in front of the last door at the hall's underlit terminus, and he absently jangled the keys. "*Jó.* New York City," he offered conversationally.

"Yes, New York City," agreed John.

"Ah! California," suggested the man, nodding.

"Yes, yes," John concurred. "California."

At last he unlocked it and held it open for the Americans. "Okay," he said, almost sadly, perhaps hoping to be invited in. "Okay." Finally he retreated, leaving the deceased woman's family alone in the apartment. The sound of a sliding deadbolt gave him a moment's pause.

"PLEASE PLEASE, IMRE. Please, Imre. Please, Imre. I saw you before, didn't I, Imre? Now please again, Imre."

NEVILLE DISTRIBUTED FOUR COPIES of the document and opened his own to page 6. "We do have two points still to discuss. I'm terribly sorry to bring them up now, but perhaps we can reach a quick accord and initial the agreements as necessary. I think we can still have everyone out by four. Your flight is when?"

TWO ROOMS—A NARROW rectangle entering one side of a small square— suggested the very first, teasing chambers of a pharaonic tomb, though not as well lit. John fumbled for lamps. Nicky reached the far side of the square room and swept from the single window the stained, thin, pea-green curtain. John walked the perimeter of the rooms slowly; he could smell the unmistakable aroma of unoccupancy. A pivoting, warped, discolored metal rod jutted from the wall just over the foot of the tiny bed, and from it dangled Nádja's red dress on a hanger. The bed was unmade; the sheets were thin in places. On the bedside table lay a paperback romance novel, facedown, opened a little past halfway. On its upside-down cover, under the title in English and the author's name, a muscled, shirtless man with a rapier squeezed the arms of a woman, who tossed back her head and lifted up her leg. Next to the book sat a battered, unidirectional English–Hungarian dictionary and a notebook filled with closely written Hungarian, the romance novel's in-progress translation. A small cassette player sat on the floor, two unlabeled tapes on top of it. On a hook over the tiny stove hung a garland of pointy dried red peppers, a diabolic lei. In Nádja's tiny bathroom (a closet off the entryway rectangle), John found a teeming garden of perfume bottles, a collection without any logic for either daily use or obscure investment, dozens of bottles, balanced on the sink and on a rickety, wickery table and on the sporadically tiled floor, most of the bottles with just a final few spittly bubbles of scent remaining in their bellies, golden and clear and light blue liquids just deep enough to envelop the tips of their spray-hose stamens. Underwear—painfully old, old, old—molded itself to the edge of the cracked and caulk-flailing tub.

He found Nicky still standing by the window, holding a small framed picture to the light. "Look what she kept," she said happily. "I can't say I approve of the frame." She showed him the New Year's photo at the piano, under the muralized, smoking Dexter Gordon, the only picture in the apartment. There were no posters on the walls, no letters, no scraps of this or that, no medals, no proofs. He slumped on the bed. "There's nothing here. Nothing," he muttered, amazed to unearth no evidence in the dwarfish chest of drawers, nothing beyond the few clothes and forint coins, the comb and brush. "This isn't her life," he said sadly. Perhaps someone had already come by and taken personal items away while John dithered on the street in the March wind and fickle sun. "It's a good picture," Nicky said, "if I do say. She was so happy when I brought her a batch to choose from. It was very flattering. And sweet. She was very funny about you." John noticed, as the surviving sunlight licked them, how delicate and beautiful were Nicky's hands. Despite the paint stains, despite the bitten nails and the raggedy, ridged cuticles, her long fingers curved gracefully and she held the photo to the window's light with a gentleness he found touching, even if it was an act of self-love. She, too, could be a pianist with those fingers. He pulled the flimsy, stained curtain off the battered peg; it swept in front of the little window again. He imagined the two of them in this small apartment, in the enforced darkness of a wartime blackout, in the menacingly unpredictable electrical power of a crisis, a coup, a counterattack. Tanks rolled down the street, his street, where he had lived all these years in peace with her. He laid the photo on the little table, covered the romance novel with it, took her hands.

"NOW LOOK HERE, Mr. Howard. I'm sure Mr. Melchior hasn't come all this way to be told you have any significant changes to the agreement at this point in time."

"Let it be, Kyle." The monotone again, the eyes anywhere but on another human face.

"As I mentioned, they aren't major changes, but I cannot in good conscience advise Charles to—"

"Maybe let's not sweat the small stuff, Nev. Hubert's come a long way to get this done."

"OH, MY IMRE, thank you, thank you. Can you hear me? Can you let me know you hear me? You have such beautiful eyes, you are so good to show them to me! Thank you. Can you squeeze my hand? Can you? Oh, very good! Don't make yourself tired, of course. You are so good, you are so good. I want to get the doctor now. Oh, you don't know where you are, you poor man, you are so good. I will be back in only a moment. Don't be frightened. I am here, I have never left your side. You don't understand me, do you? Oh, you look so lost, please just believe me, you will understand, you will be yourself soon, Horváth úr."

AND IF THEY COME for him, then this is how he wishes to be taken, from her arms, from this narrow little bed, which can scarcely bear the weight of the two of them. Let them all climb out of their tanks to sit and gawk and applaud as she and John ignore them. Her hands are everywhere, her mouth is everywhere, their clothes, emptied, collapsed in a useless pile—let the Russians have them. Though they never left their beloved little apartment, they have made their successful escape, he and his wife with the beautiful pianist's hands and the hoarse voice and the soft day-old stubble on the top of her shaven head and the acquired taste of that tremendous jaw. His beautiful, brave wife: She would not choose to be anywhere else but here making love with him; she would choose a city under attack with him over any safe paradise that lacked him. And the list they have spent so many hours making, let it go, let the Russians burn it or eat it or give it to shrugging, stymied cryptologists. There is no frontier to cross that they cannot cross right here and now as their bodies merge—his and his wife's—as they close so tightly that there is no longer a clear distinction where one begins and the other ends; a fusion has occurred, as it does every time they are together; parts are exchanged, and no one finishes quite the same as they began. So let them have her piano, her easels and canvases and darkroom, all her secret papers from the embassy—the hell with all that.

"CAN YOU BLINK? You can? Did he, Doctor? That was a blink for us, wasn't it? Oh, Imre—Horváth úr, excuse me if I call you Imre. You have been asleep for a very long—"

"Fräulein, perhaps we should allow him to adjust slowly. We do not wish to shock—"

"Yes, fine, but let go of me. Horváth úr, if you can hear me, just blink twice quickly. Can you do that for—hey! Yes! You are so brave! You Swiss, did you see? You saw? You would not believe me, but you saw! He hears, and he can say yes. Two blinks is yes from now, okay, Imre? And one is no. Until you talk we will do this . . . Oh, there is so much to tell you, yes. Let go of me, Swiss! Okay, I will leave with you, but, Horváth úr, I will be back. You rest now, Imre, and I will tell you everything when you are feeling more energy. Please, Swiss, let me be."

"AMAZING. I BOUGHT the damn thing in Tokyo a week ago and now it's stone-dead. Won't make a bloody mark. Paid five hundred dollars to have the damn thing in monogrammed gold."

"Please take mine."

A KNOCKING ON THE DOOR, quiet at first, then quickly louder. "*Amerikai?* Hey! *Amerikai! Mit csinálnak? Nyissák ki az ajtót!*" The sound of troops—John held on for one more moment—the sound of troops who knew he was here. Let them splinter the deadbolt and beat down the door and storm in, poor imbeciles, stunted cruel children; let them shoot me dead just as I am right now, I will fall forward, exhausted, onto her body and into her arms one last time.

THE SENSATION WAS a new one, something vibrating through rubbery muscles. He was amazed to feel his thoughts moving far more quickly than the corresponding events. A peculiar and wonderful feeling, like coming to himself after an incredibly long and deep sleep. The sight of the pens moving across the documents was remarkable: They moved so slowly that Charles could see the ink pouring out in black rivers around the tiny balls in the pen tips; he could hear the scratch of those balls carving canals in the paper, could hear the rustle of the ink rushing into those canals and then crackling as it froze. In the space of a single signature, he had time enough to think of poor old Mark Payton, not (amazingly!) a total fool after all: There *are* moments that matter a great deal, moments that draw onto and into themselves all three time zones—past, present, future—and forge of them strange hybrids: future-past, present-future, past-present. As his own pen carved and poured and froze the beautiful lines and swinging curves of his signature, he knew the feelings he would have about this moment forty years in the future, the growing love he would have for this precise instant. He heard the beauty not only in the sound of his pen scraping along the paper right now but the growing beauty of that same sound with each passing year, as if a noise could grow louder with each echo, ringing out perhaps most loudly at an anniversary (March 12, 1992; March 12, 1999; March 12, 2031), but loud as well on dates wholly unrelated to this one, triggered by little things: a broken golden pen, a man with a substantial subnasal mole, a metallic cologne like poor Kyle's, a tie like Neville's (an odd taste the Brits all seem to have—where did he find such a pattern?). But most of all there was this present—the sight of that signature and the tremendous testimony of it: He had sold for much more than he had bought. He had definitively proven his alchemy. What was financial genius but an ability to see the future more quickly than anyone else? This signature—right now spilling out from around that tiny metal ball—proved that he could grasp the very soul of assets, could assess their essential worth before anyone else, could then mix with those assets his own magical, potent seed. Payton had been right, and for a moment it was *true:* He sincerely *did* envy the researcher his impassioned scholarship (. . . *one of the game's most beautiful aspects* . . .). His heart beat in his ears, and he suddenly feared he might blush or giggle or otherwise give himself away to these other men.

"YOUR COLLEAGUE IS very loyal to you and was with you for every of these days for a very long time now." Imre did not have the muscle control to smile or to cry, but the news, in this cold doctor's poor Hungarian, that his partner had not left his side (throughout whatever this experience had been) penetrated the clouds of his cyclical semi-wakefulness, and he hoped Krisztina or the doctor would bring his colleague in as soon as possible. He understood he was in a hospital, and that he was very tired and that his eyes moved but nothing else and that his throat was terribly dry. But that Károly had not left his side, had been here every day for a very long time now during this . . . Imre's eyes closed again, and the doctor wiped the pool of moisture away from the corner of his patient's mouth.

"HEY, *AMERIKAI!* New York! California! Hey, hey! *Tor! Porte!*"

"Oh for Christ's sake, get a fucking *clue!*" Nicky climbed off, stomped nude down the narrow rectangle, and unbolted the rattling door. Faced with this naked baldness, with this self-explanatory, disgusted fury, the red tracksuit retreated, launching a defensive, lame sort of lascivious leer at the nude vision, then turned away, threatening something unintelligibly Hungarian. When Nicky returned, ready to pick up where she had left off, she found her partner in tears. "What is *this?*" she asked, still angry at the interruption, and now horrified at this gross violation of house rules. But she wasn't cruel; she could make herself semi-lean against the chalky white and yellow wall, and hold the sobbing boy's head on her lap and stroke his damp, curly hair and mutter the embarrassing little nonsensibilities that people seemed to like muttered in these cases, even as she scolded herself for all the work she could have gotten done this afternoon.

IX.

MARCH. A SERIES OF NEWSPAPER ARTICLES AND TELEVISION STORIES, A dozen concentric circles radiating from an epicenter in Budapest (John's desk, to be seismically specific) and trembling all the way across oceans: *I promise this is my last column on this deal, but its twists and turns are worth keeping an eye on as your legs dangle off your comfy chair in the Forum lobby and you irritably ask your indifferent waitress why she can't make proper coffee. Because now, with Median, the new Democratic-Capitalist Hungary™ has earned the noisy, vulgar trust of a real, live multinational, and there can be no better endorsement for an orphaned, ex-Red nation hoping to join the family of nations than the cold-eyed blessing of men whose money matters to them . . .*

. . . If you recall our story a few months ago about our own hometown boy, that young Clevelander far away in Eastern Europe whose spunk and determination . . .

———

AT LAST, WINDOWS could be opened a few inches at the height of day. Krisztina opened one now. "We should celebrate with some fresh air," she said softly, for with fumbling and spillage in equal measure, Imre had used a straw: A small trickle of orange juice had bubbled between his lips and, sated, he blinked only once when asked if he wanted more. Did he want some air? Did he need another pillow? Would he like to listen to some Gypsy music? She still could not quite bring herself to talk press business to his blinks. She decided he needn't worry himself with it yet, though she knew she simply could not bear to be the one to tell him or, perhaps worse, to be the last to learn that he had known all along and had simply never bothered to tell *her*, had approved it all long before he was ill. Still, she could hardly look at him, sick and dizzy as she was from the syrup of guilt and fury that boiled in her. Unable to scream or sob, instead she tried to force herself to enjoy her role as a full-time nurse of sorts, a tedious cheerful voice with an artificial smile and exhausted eyes who allowed herself to go home once a day for a shower-bath and a change of clothes, and, she noticed lately with overwhelming sadness, that she wasn't even enjoying the usual pleasures of early spring weather. She had noticed recently that Budapest was in what her mother used to call "the impatient time," when children demanded winter's end, and they hated the dark spaces between buildings that protected the last of the last season's snow, stubborn and horrible little leftovers precisely the shape of their patron-shadows.

NEVILLE HOWARD'S LAW FIRM occupied the second story of an Italianate villa high up Andrássy út, the first floor of which was still a faint and fading pink remnant of other times, red times when the villa had been on the Avenue of the People's Republic, of even brighter red times when it had sat at the top of Stalin Avenue. To the firm's chuckling irritation, the villa's first floor was still occupied by the Society to Promote Soviet-Hungarian Friendship, which had recently watched its ideals and purpose vanish in one befuddling event after another, until the Soviet ambassador himself was looking for other work, never to give his old Friends another thought. The members of the society clung to the inside of their villa like confused ivy, and swallowed their bile and their doubts, heard the supercilious greetings of their new neighbors—specialists in stock market deals—and today looked through the windows that remained to them, at the ornate wooden benches on Andrássy út. There, under the newly warm sun and over the quickly surrendering snow, young client (a newly minted financial genius) and young counsel (his star rising fast in the firm) consulted post-lunch, both leaning back and stretching out their legs, both allowing the sun to warm them through their closed eyelids and open topcoats. "He's slightly better," said young client. "He seemed glad to see me, as much as you can tell with him. Pity. I explained the deal, the value of his shares, the arrangements for his care. I think he was relieved I had taken care of everything, to the extent he followed me. Ohhh, mixed feelings probably inevitable, of course. So look. You'll be in charge of executing all those odds and ends for him, since my plans are pretty well set." "Of course, naturally," said counsel.

SPRING DOESN'T IMPLY WARMTH in this part of Canada, but the plump, red-haired young man, slightly dulled by pills, was satisfied to wait for his ride outside in the eye-stinging chill. He had grown to like the outdoors these past months; after Budapest, the rural surroundings here had an inoffensive timelessness to them (except for one view, through the game-room picture window at dawn, uncomfortably reminiscent of the Thomas Cole painting *The Last of the Mohicans*). He sat on his luggage, said nothing to the mild psychologist who waited with him. When his parents' station wagon arrived to collect him, he accepted another of the doctor's business cards and was reminded of the helpful mnemonic for daily peace, and he shook his well-wisher's hand. He absorbed gentle hugs from his parents, now in their second decade of finding him saddening and obscure, and he sank into the backseat with the elderly chocolate Lab he had named for one of Charles I's dogs years earlier. He watched the collegiate hospital recede through the car window, noticed that he did not yet achingly miss his time there, and he would have been hard-pressed to say that the pills were not basically an improvement, more or less.

ON THE LAST EVENING of March, it would be another week before you'd be tempted to take your evening drink on the patio and another two before you could indulge that temptation without quickly regretting it and retreating, fumbling with cups and saucers, back inside. But on this last evening of March, sitting warm inside the Gerbeaud, near the window's reminiscent views but far from the door's drafts, with the sound of clinking dishes and the scent and rattle of coffee beans pouring in or out of brass bins, relaxing under the lighted mirrors and mirrored lights, well-accustomed to the by now endearing sight of grouchy waitresses in fringed vinyl boots, taking as long as necessary on your way back from a job that didn't matter to you on your way to wherever you were going next where it wouldn't matter if you were late or not, you could find very few places more pleasant to sit alone and have a coffee than the Gerbeaud, unless you were bothered by the unmistakable prevalence of noisy Americans having conversations like this one:

"Now, *this* is funny. Guess who turned up at my apartment last night. Slightly drunk. No? Krisztina Toldy. She *threw* herself at me. Threw herself. As in, 'Hey there, good evening, let's skip the drinks, just take me.' The classical model of throwing oneself. Wait, it gets significantly funnier. So I say, 'No, I'm sorry, old evil sorceress lady, I'll pass,' and she gets violent. Extremely. Like she threatens to *kill* me. 'Kill' me. She has a gun, she tells me, and she's going to shoot me. 'Shoot me? For not having sex with you?' Which, you know, is not unfunny. And what does she do? No? No guesses, Mr. Price? Fine: She starts to kiss my neck. Little nibbly things with dry lips. Like a rodent taking little bites to see if I was salty enough to store for winter. So, fighting down my red-blooded manly urge to throw up, I say, 'No, really, gunshots aside, I'm not going to have sex with you.' But what did our mothers teach us to say, John? 'Please,' she says. 'Please, please.' Which is what I like to hear from all my nympho-violent admirers. So I said, 'I appreciate the offer, and your politeness, your manners are impeccable, but really, I'm not going to—' and hey, presto! The gun is *real*. They can be quite daunting, guns, you know, even little ones, which, to be fair, I think I have to admit might be the right description for this one. 'What I said about your manners, Miss Toldy? You recall that comment? Well, under the new circumstances, I have to say—' but she tells me—and I am translating loosely, directly into English vernacular here—to 'shut my fucking mouth or I'—she—'will kill you.'"

"Kill me? What did *I* do?"

"No, I'm sorry, John, that was a poor translation. *Me.* The point being, my mouth was now shut, so I can't ask what my other options are, what her negotiating target is, as we used to say in b-school, couldn't plot out a road map for getting to yes, and so I swallow hard. I know what I have to do. I nod philosophically, under the circs, and I start to unbutton my shirt like, 'Okay, okay, we'll have sex and nobody needs to get shot,' and I admit the thought is going through my head a) things could be worse; it's conceivable she could be uglier, b) being this desirable is a cross I have to bear, and c) it's not completely out of the question that in the throes of passion, I may be able to disarm her. So I start to unbutton my shirt and give her a sort of basic, 'Okay, even though I'm doing it at gunpoint I'm not a complete spoilsport, so come hither' look. And she does what?"

"She shoots you dead."

"No, but a good guess. She lowers her gun hand and starts to *cry*."

"You're lying."

"I'm not. I swear to the filthy God of your afflicted, unpleasant people. She starts to just bawl. Which to me is a little much, because, hey, I was willing to go through with it. Sobbing now. Sah-Bean. So I button my shirt and, real delicate-like, try to take the gun, as in, 'Hey, you're obviously pretty shook up, babe, let's put this away while you just have a good cry and we'll wait till you feel better before we call your country's corrupt and muddled law enforcement officials and see who can afford to bribe them the most.' But, amazingly, she doesn't go for this and sort of feebly points the gun at me again. Feebly works as well as anything else, so I sat down on the couch and waited for her verdict on which way the evening was headed. As I said, I'm the sort of man who is willing to have sex with an ugly, middle-aged hag rather than being shot with bullets. One of those things that sets me apart."

"Everybody knows this about you. We admire this."

"I'm willing to believe that my grip on time was a little weak at this point. So I think I sat on the couch and watched this woman sob and occasionally wave her gun at me for, I'm thinking, let's say, twelve minutes. Sob, sob, sniffle, shake and point shaky gun at me, drop arm, sob, sob, sob, repeat. Like, fifteen minutes. And for what? Did she shoot me? No. Did she make me have sex with her? No. She cried and pointed and started to say she had a demand to make and then I'd start unbuttoning my shirt again and she'd say, 'No, not that, not that,' and start crying again and then after a while she just leaves. I look out the window, and she's had the cab waiting the whole time. That was my Saturday night. That and then German porn on cable."

"But why?"

"Because they all look like the St. Pauli girl."

"Let me rephrase: But why?"

"Oh golly, John. Gee, I have no idea. Let's ponder the possibilities. She'd had a really bad day? I remind her of the guy who killed her dog? She was raised in soul-crushing, loveless poverty? Hmm, it's an overwhelming mystery that will puzzle us to the grave. Oh, by the way, can you drive me to the airport in a couple weeks? I'll borrow a van for my stuff. I got some funny news this week."

"Well, had you ever gotten around to telling her?"

"Me? No. I think you did, in your articles. I told *him*."

"Did you call the police?"

"Oh, but of course! That's *exactly* how I want to spend my last weeks in this shit hole. Oh come on, don't look so put upon. She didn't shoot me, after all—focus on the positive! It was meant to be a funny story. You are a vindictive race, you people. Poor woman was blowing off a little steam. In the end, no one got hurt and no one had to have sex with anyone old and haggy. I had already made sure to get her some money, too, you know. I went out of my way. Put a bonus for her in the agreement. She deserves it. Like you, by the way. Neville'll be in touch."

The stuttering, half-formed, badly pointed questions that Charles would have mocked and left unanswered anyhow were spared their humiliating fate when a knock spattered against the window behind their own reflections and a bald head and portfolio were waved in. In the time it took Nicky to walk right to the door and then left to their table, John and Charles were unable to come up with a convincing lie or plan. "Hello, little boy." She kissed John on the mouth, and he smelled liquor. "Hey, I'm Nicky," she said to the man in the suit.

"I met you this summer, if I remember right," Charles replied.

"Oh hey, yeah, at A Házam, that's right." She took Charles's hand and curtsied, dropped her stuff on an empty chair between them, and borrowed a coin to pay her toll to the dragon guarding the bathroom. "You speak Hun, right? Order me something good."

"Well, little boy," said Charles when the white saucer clinked and the aged waitress atop the velvet stool nodded Nicky sternly past, "this is not a promising start to an evening of tender courtship. You want to run and I'll cover for you?"

"Too late. Let the tender courtship begin." And a few seconds later John was rising and Emily was descending into the other empty chair between the two men.

"Hello, gentlemen. I'm very glad to see you maintaining fine old traditions."

He had smelled diesel fumes mixed with spring scents one recent morning and decided that he and Emily were equals at last; having guarded her secret during the long, eventful winter proved something. Before his confidence faded, he had called her with an out-of-the-blue invitation *à trois* (on an unassuming Sunday, for heaven's sake). And in fact she had responded so eagerly that he had been briefly heartened, had put the phone down, lain back, and received some refreshed and nearly convincing visions of future Emilial bliss. And yet the sight of her now slumping into a chair and rebinding her ponytail was undeniably underwhelming. Her winter and spring appearances in his dream-life had been glowing, throbbing; she had been multiples, exponents of herself, a boiling, universal female essence barely containable, practically Hindu. In person, however, she was unable to change forms, did not glow, was plainly tired. She was as pale as every other nonstripper after a winter on the Central European plain. Her white oxford hung limp, defeated and unironed.

Nicky returned and kissed him again on the mouth, an entirely gratuitous gesture: He hadn't, after all, seen her since Nádja's apartment three weeks earlier, and besides, she had already kissed him a few minutes earlier. And so he thought for a moment that Nicky felt threatened by this unknown girl's arrival and was immediately making all relationships clear for the stranger, but he had to admit to himself that such things didn't really happen. He introduced the two women. Charles's face projected a favorite expression.

"Nice to meet you," said Emily, and John noticed a coldness in her voice, or (he corrected himself at once) merely hoped he had. He toyed with the corollary idea that perhaps *she* was jealous, and this time a different and better story might unfold.

"Yeah well, to be strictly accurate, we met this summer, at A Házam." Nicky set her straight with a certain subdued irritability.

"Did we?" John saw Emily's momentary confusion. "Yes of course. I remember." He appreciated Emily's desire to make things easy for people.

Silence followed until Charles asked to see Nicky's portfolio and she withdrew from between the black cardboard flats a photo collage. "It's called *Peace*," she said, passing the picture to Emily, who held it for the two in-leaning men:

A family of four enjoying a picnic in a park. Arranged around a sky blue blanket, under a blanket blue sky, circling a wicker basket of shiny food, a smiling mother and father, a smiling young girl, and a smiling younger boy. Everyone smiled. The mother was in the process of smilingly unpacking the meal. The little boy smiled hungrily at the spread. The father, smiling, rested his hand on the mother's shoulder. The little girl in a little girl's dress lay on her stomach, resting her smiling head in her palms and kicking her bare legs and feet up behind her. The mother was missing a tooth. The little boy was drooling from the far corner of his mouth, and bleeding slightly from his near ear; his tan trousers were grotesquely soiled. The father was not looking hungrily at the food; follow his eyes: He was looking hungrily elsewhere. The little girl had three parallel bandages adhering to both of her bare soles. Partially obscured by a tree, a man—naked under a raincoat, fedora, and sunglasses—was squatting and defecating while photographing the family from his hidden vantage point. "That's supposed to be you, Johnny," Nicky explained, quickly and quietly, not wishing to belabor the obvious. In the upper left, bugs—"locust season," Nicky clarified—were just entering the scene; their densely spaced limited number implied a vast swarm croaking to appear from just out of frame. Finally, in the far-distant background, on a pond in the park, a rowboat with a figure standing unsteadily in it. The figure—too distant for its gender to be clear—held an oar over its head, caught in the backswing before clubbing something or someone either in the boat or in the water.

"It's basically a big fuck-you to my dad," Nicky offered offhandedly before adding, "or really anyone who tries to own me."

"It's very disturbing, as I'm sure you intended," Emily said a little priggishly. She passed the photo to John. "You obviously have a very active imagination," she backhanded.

John was disoriented. As usual, he hadn't the faintest idea what to say about one of Nicky's mysterious works, and suspected she had been trying to tell him something with the mention of people owning her, but Emily was undeniably hostile. He had never seen two women detest each other so quickly, and he did not dare allow himself to believe what he so desperately wanted to believe. He had to bite his lips not to speak; he held power over her at last.

"So why does your father deserve a big . . . you know?" Emily asked, a society matron thrown into unavoidable conversation with a gate-crashing hooker.

"That's very sweet," Nicky purred. "You won't say 'fuck you.' That's very fucking sweet. That's the most fucking endearing thing I've heard in who the fuck knows how fucking long. I'm growing fucking misty-eyed, for fuck's sake."

"I'm sorry. I guess I'm funny to you. I just wasn't raised to cuss all the time."

"*Cuss?* You weren't raised to *cuss?* Oh my fucking Christ, that's delicious. Johnny, where did you find this angel? Whatever. My dad deserves a big *you know* because of the usual boring shit: booze, emotional 'n' physical abuse, incest, blah, blah, blah."

"Well, you've had a very difficult life, obviously," Emily said in her sweetest tone. "That's terribly sad." John and Charles, head-pivoting tennis fans, glanced at each other to be reassured they still existed. "On the other hand," Emily said, striding boldly but quietly forward despite the red tint to Nicky's bald head, "maybe he made you strong."

"Made me *strong?* What are you, some kind of Nietzsche freak?"

"I just mean maybe your special gifts, your artistic talents, your evidently very flamboyant personality, all come from your ambiguous experience with him, and he made you who you are."

"*What?*" Nicky began to stand, but John grabbed her arm. "Get your hands off me," she spat at him, pulling her hand away in a fist. But she did sit, although a little fleck of saliva jumped from her lips onto Emily's shirt. "So he made me? Fuck you, farm girl. I made me. Can you even understand what that means, sweetie? I made me. I. MADE. ME. Ladislau didn't make shit. His participation ended with the sperm, thank you very fucking much."

The angrier Nicky grew, the calmer Emily became, and John thought he saw a gleam of pleasure in her sudden taunting mastery of the enraged artist.

"Well, who's up for dinner, then?" Charles asked.

"No, I was heading home. Fuck this." Nicky stood and gathered her things. "You know where to find me when the itch comes," she said to John, standing directly behind him. She bent over the top of his head and kissed him upside down, deeply if necessarily awkwardly. She pulled away, a line of saliva connecting their mouths like an echo of the kiss. She whispered something acid and sticky in his window-side ear, then spoke to the others: "See you around, Charlie. Bye-bye now, Sister Mary Cathcrine." She left them in a silence punctuated by Charles's laughter.

John's intended trio walked into the cool darkness of Vörösmarty Square, cut past the Kempinski scaffolding into Deák Square, up Andrássy in search of food. His thoughts knotted, tousled in the wind: Emily's cold and pointed provocations, Nicky's whispered venomous send-off: "Lose the farm dyke and come to me tonight." He had savored the spectacle of the two women fighting over him, and enjoyed watching Charles watching. But in her combat calm, Emily seemed to accuse him of insincerity, for how could he be with Nicky, someone so unlike Emily in every way? Emily walked in this oppressive, accusatory silence (but for her conversation with Charles). They read a menu on a rusty metal stand in front of a restaurant and Charles vetoed the establishment. Emily obviously thought Nicky had attacked out of jealousy or because John had instructed her to, had invited Emily there precisely for this sort of infantile ambush. (And here they were trying to pick a restaurant on Andrássy as if nothing had happened.) But Emily *had* fought; she *was* jealous. And side by side, how marvelous she had seemed: energized, calm, serene, essential, while Nicky was a mess, a spiky ball of jagged, ingrown fears and uncontrolled appetites.

And tonight Emily had risked candor by fighting for him, tipped her heart just far enough for the light to reflect off it. She had said as much as she could say to let John know she was ready for him. (She and Charles laughed at something in a doomed and dusty shop window display.)

An overture of a few raindrops drummed the pavement, and then the entire untuned orchestra crashed its clumsy way through the clouds. Charles shouted something about the sanctity of his creases and ran into the first restaurant he could. Emily moved to join him, but John took her hand as Charles disappeared into the dimly glowing doorway, and the two of them were left half under a streetlight and fully under the falling cold. "What are you doing?" she yelled over the downpour, and he saw one half of her face in shadow, one half in dripping light, and he understood why this was so. He put his hands on her cold wet cheeks and he kissed her. "What are you doing?" she repeated (the same volume but with different accents), and pushed him away, the second woman in fifteen minutes.

"You baffle me," he granted.

"Evidently."

"But it doesn't have to be like this anymore. I think you've been trapped—"

She nodded. "Let's go inside and get something to eat," she concluded for him.

"Come home with me," he said, and took her hand. "Come home with me. I know you—"

"What? John. Enough. Please." But her hand still lay in his, and that was not nothing.

"No," he said. "This is me talking. Listen to me. I've never been more serious about anything. You have to believe this."

She took her hand away and, saying something inaudible under the spill of rain against the shining pavement, turned toward the restaurant, and he knew that now was such a moment as men wait all their lives to face. "Emily, wait. I'll tell you. What if I told you I knew? I've known for ages. I'm a journalist. I could've told the world what you really are, but I haven't. I understand you."

"What I really am? What did that idiot tell you? Why would you listen to her? She's plainly a pervert, she's a lunatic." She pushed wet bangs off her forehead, breathed deeply, even smiled slightly. "But fine, go ahead. I'm very curious to hear what she said."

"Do I have to spell it out? Fine. I'll speak for both of us. Hide if you want, just know that you don't have to hide from me. You *can't* hide from me. I care about *you*. I don't care that you're a spy."

Emily stood entirely still for a moment, seemed to stare past John, and John saw that he had reached her at last. Another moment passed, and she spoke so quietly he had to lean toward her to hear: "Fuck you, John, you little prick."

X.

A CASE COULD BE MADE THAT THE WHOLE EVENT HAD BEEN A VALUABLE icebreaker, a steam valve. One more push and they would be past it all, beginning at last. The next morning: the rain symbolically past, blue sky, yellow stone bridge, birdsong above carsong, perpetual motion river, cloud wisps like eyelashes just parting after sweet conjugal sleep. (Yet some shapeless doubt tickled the inner ear, hummed just out of view, made rude faces when he was not quite looking away.) He composed his speech to her, and the Danube's rumble and splash were audible from this best of all possible bridges, providing a tympani roll to the avian oboes and the automotive strings. Just ahead of him, elderly orange-vested municipal sanitation workers stooped and swept the sidewalks with stiff bound-twig brooms, fairy tale props. As John passed, one sweeper leaned against his staff and caught his eye, expressionless. John wished him a Hungarian good day. The old sweeper hmph'd an ambiguous response and returned to sweeping into a heap tiny pieces of blue and white sky—bits of mirror smashed and sprinkled over the walkway.

Ahead of him on the sidewalk, in the shadow of the Parliament, knelt a young woman, her back to him, her head hanging low. Walking by her, looking over his shoulder without slowing, he saw she was petting a cat, who lay on the sidewalk with its head in her lap. The young woman wept quietly, and the cat's innards slumped damply out onto the pavement. The cat's half-open orange eyes sluggishly followed John as he passed, but the poor creature had no energy left to move its head or paws. The woman stroked the animal's still, soft head. She seemed to John unafraid, even though in tears, though she had no options, could not call on a flying squad of crack mobile cat surgeons. She wept and stroked the animal, and John did not have the words to ask what had happened, to be of any help or comfort at all. He walked on, shaken, and tried to concentrate on the written message to Emily (a fallback if she could not be lured down to the lobby to hear his principal address).

He reconsidered his prepared remarks (*I would never do anything to . . .*). He rehearsed and made slight changes as an unknown marine called upstairs (*I only said what I said to show you I . . .*). "She's on leave," the Alabama-accented, microphone-muffled voice filtered through the bulletproof Plexiglas. "Yep, as of today. Naw, didn't say how long. 'Scheduled leave' is all they said. Wanna leave a message, sir?" On the walk back toward the river, he edited the appeal that had now been redocketed for her bungalow (*I just need you to see how . . .*). On the way he stopped into the newsroom and graciously rehearsed her responses on her behalf (*Of course I'm not mad at you, come here, these things happen, mmm, you are terrible . . .*).

"Excellent. A surprise visit from Proyce. A moment of your time, sah." Editor's manner had lately been modeled on that of a Dickensian headmaster, and John laughed at this summons—the stern eyebrow, the crooked beckoning index finger slowly curling and uncurling as if Editor were studiously tickling the chin of an invisible and frightened child. Editor shut the door, sat down lightly, and began marking pages heavily. "Very good. Price. You're fired. Everything off your desk and out of here in—let's be fair—fifteen minutes. And no: no references."

John dropped into the extra chair and rubbed his eyes, still dry and itchy after a relatively sleepless night (*Would you have really wanted me to be an aching virgin?*). "Man, I'm beat. I haven't slept right in ages. Oh, before I forget, the stripper piece is going to take one more day, I think. It's almost done."

"Won't be necessary," Editor mumbled, and violently scratched out a line.

"Oh, don't pull it. Really, just one day. I have an appointment this afternoon with this quartet who do a desert orgy thing. I promise—finished tomorrow."

Editor looked up from his scribbling. "Are you still here? Were you listening? Fifteen minutes started when I said fifteen minutes."

"Also, I had another idea. What do you think about a series of ambassador profiles, very social-like. Tennis with the U.S. Hopeless restaurant-hunting with the French. Sex clubs with the Danish. Sad, impoverished window-shopping with the Bulgarian and North Korean."

"Have you gone barking mad? It's a very simple transaction. Take your belongings. Leave mine. Go away. Don't enter my line of sight again."

"Are you angry about something?"

"Mr. Price. If this is how you want to spend your"—dramatic displacement of cuff, inspection of black plastic watch face, mental calculation, replacement of cuff, interlacing of fingers on desk—"thirteen minutes, so be it.

Did you think the embassy would not complain? Did you think I'd defend you? Or that you'd pass for a symbol of the free press? It's a crime to print the names of embassy employees and say they're spies, even to threaten to do it. The embassy gets angry if you get it right or not. And I would be liable."

"They said I said I'd—I didn't say I'd . . ." For a long moment, John stared at the unblinking man. The very dim possibility that she had massively misunderstood, had then told someone above her, that they had called Editor . . .

"Are you still here? You're not going to bore me with a free-press lecture, are you, my young moron? You've more sense than that. Just go."

John sat very still and tried to think. "You want me to call somebody to explain or whatever?"

"No. I want you to leave. Now."

"You're going to fire me for this? This is ridiculous. I had a fight with my girlfriend and you're firing me for treason? That's absurd."

"Are you still here? Fine, Mr. Price. Apparently you think I'm a monkey. I admit this is not the bloody *Times* or the *Prague Post,* but we are not, you know, absolutely corrupt, you little twat. Have you or have you not written profiles for this organ in exchange for payment from your subject?"

"That is completely out of context. You're getting this wrong, whoever your source is. The tone of it—this was not this serious thing you seem to think."

Editor picked up speed, and his nostrils took on an animated life of their own. "Are you still here? Very well. Mr. Reilly, the undereducated, oververbose embassy security person who woke me from a dead sleep last night also informed me that this is *not* your girlfriend, Mr. Price, but that you have been, and I quote the unfortunate man, 'predatorily stalking the young lady in question up to this point in time.' So you have to excuse me, Mr. Price, if I ask you again, *are you still fucking here?*"

"That is one hundred percent nonsense. Categorical lies."

"Delicious. A stirring denial at last. Felonious sexual blackmail? Sort of. Violation of this paper's trust? Yes, but it wasn't serious, more a matter of tone. Stalking? Definite no. Mistah Proyce, are you still here?"

Finally, no. John wasn't. The large clock that hung in the newsroom comfortably settled its minute hand, with a booming click, on the number three, fifteen minutes after his arrival, and John walked out the front door with the three items he could rightfully claim as his own. Just outside the door, Karen

Whitley stopped him, kissed him, whispered, "If there's anything I can do . . ." and hurried back into the office.

Despite several efforts over several hours, no one answered at her strangely empty bungalow, and so, with dreamy speed and sudden nightfall, the set changes and John is now knocking on a door back across the river, in Pest. (He took a different route on the return; he couldn't risk seeing the cat.) He realized—with that evanescent clarity which could be forgotten an instant later—that he had made a mistake of categorization: Emily was not serious but a little off balance. He knocked at the door of the only serious person he knew. She would provide unemotional, even-keel straight talk, shower cold reality on the gooey unreality of the day.

She opened the door and left it open. Without a word, she walked back across the room to her work. She perched atop a paint-stained wooden stool, picked up a brush but immediately put it down again. With a twist of her hips, she spun the stool to face him. "So what happened last night? Did you fuck the farm girl? Did you?"

"Why are *you* mad?"

"You did. I can't believe this."

"Stop it. I came here because I, I just need to talk. I just got fired, I'm a little—"

"*Please*. Stop. Just stop. Steady that little waver I hear, okay? Explain something to me: How did *I* become the person you come crying to? Once, okay, but that was a weird little exception. I'm the least qualified person in the world for the job. I don't think there could possibly be anyone less interested in it, okay? This is exactly why we have house rules." She spun from her hips again and picked up her brush.

"Are you *jealous?*"

She threw the brush end over end across the room, where it struck a dirty full-length mirror with a feeble tick-click-tick and two smears of blue on the glass. "Oh my God. You people kill me. You people fucking kill me. If I'm jealous, believe me it's nothing to be proud of, stud. I couldn't be more disgusted with all of us."

"Please talk to me. I feel like—"

"Really, John, whatever you *feel*, well, that's life, and not even nearly the most interesting part. So spare me."

He fell backward onto her bed and tossed a crusty, paint-splattered tennis ball at the ceiling, catching it just above his face. "Since you ask, no, I didn't 'fuck the farm girl,' though why you of all people would care, I'm at a loss to figure. I've known her longer than I've known you. I've always felt about her, I don't know, like—"

"Christ almotherfuckingmighty." With a clatter, the easel dove to the floor and slid along its back into its fast-approaching reflection. John caught the falling tennis ball and remained paralyzed, one hand clutching the yellow fuzz as if he were a yarn-batting cat turned to stone. "Listen, dumb-ass, we're all in love with someone else, okay? Everybody is. Every last idiot I know. It's a bit of a bore. If we all talked about our secret little aches, they wouldn't be secret anymore and we'd all be so similar, we'd probably kill ourselves." She stared at him and took a deep breath. Her tone changed to something quieter and forcibly kinder: "Please, please, *please* get out of here and let me work."

He lay in his own bed. Emily's bungalow had persistently proclaimed its emptiness, and her telephone its unreceptive solitude. His own answering machine played no less than fifteen clicking hang-ups and one long, menacing message from "Lee Reilly, want to converse with you about some complaints from a numerous number of the female-gendered members of the embassy staff, had several complaints, in fact, sir, filed by many of our ladies regarding what can only be termed—" He shut off his machine. He lay in his own bed, and the words of that favorite song ran through his head, albeit with a Hungarian-accented voice he didn't recognize. He dipped in and out of sleep, like a child negotiating cold seawater. Nádja entered through the French window from his balcony, and she carried moonlight with her. "It's a matter of willpower, John Price," she said in her leathery movie-star voice. "Because strong people just don't." "Which?" he asked her. "Don't feel it or don't talk about it?" "Exactly," she said, and sat on his chest with a faint but distinctive cracking noise. Slowly, caressingly, she ran her young, transparent, moonlit finger over his closed lips. Slowly, gently, she worked the finger into his mouth, using first her transparent, moonlit nail, then her ancient fleshless knuckle—at first a gently sexual probing. John suddenly began to grow fearful, but he did not know how to manipulate the muscles in his jaw to prevent her intrusion. She sliced her fingernail through his tongue with a ripping noise, then, with the lightest of glancing touches, caused his teeth to crumble. With his punctured, twitching tongue held in place, the teeth tumbled down his gagging throat, except for one outsize molar atop two arching walrus-tusk roots, which she pulled from his mouth and held between thumb and forefinger for his wide-open, weeping eyes. "Something to include in the report," she whispered, and brushed an elderly hand over his groin, walked out the way she came, through the closed French window, taking the moonlight with her.

He slept a great deal, often but not exclusively at night. Lee Reilly left him several messages, as did Karen Whitley. From Lee Reilly's gravelly Deep South voice and ornate G.I. phraseology he tried to reconstruct the man himself; he crafted a bald, portly, squinting, mustachioed ex-marine (who resembled a television private detective now in dubbed syndication on German cable). He saw several different flesh approximations of this composite sketch on the streets of Budapest, and tried, always too late, not to make eye contact. It would be difficult to find her without running into Reilly or his men. How would he bear up under a beating? Would his assailants whisper hot threats or merely rely on the irresistible force of unincriminating wordlessness? Would they declare themselves or pose as Hungarian toughs, hopped-up club kids, Gypsies? Black eyes. Broken nose. Kicks in the ribs or the crotch. And then into Boris Karloff Memorial for some recycled stitches from a smelly, smoking nurse.

Still she did not come home. When her bungalow door opened after a painfully long closure and he vaulted up from the wooden bench across the street, he only came upon an exiting Julie. "Hey, you! We haven't seen you in ages," she cooed, so entirely normal. "How've you been? No, she's on a leave. Like, two weeks is standard, but I don't really know. She didn't say. But, hey, I'll tell her you came by. But you should come out with us sometime soon, even though *she* won't be there, hmm? Oh, I'm sorry, honey, that was mean, wasn't it? Between you and me, I think you guys would be really great together. Well of *course* we talk about it, silly. But there's no telling Emmy anything, you know? I'm sure you know. She's like, well, whatever. Anyhow you should come. Julie and I are going out tonight, to the new . . ."

He sat in the Gerbeaud—if not that same day, then a day very much like it. He had time to kill, and it was obediently lining up for execution. The days lazily refused to differentiate themselves. She might come to the Gerbeaud, maintaining fine old traditions.

Reilly had stopped leaving messages and so, his collar high, John braved the embassy lobby again. A different marine (or the same marine with a different mask) said, "MissOliver'sonleavesiry'allwannaleaveamessage?" John shook his head at the metal speaker. He left the building as a discreet limousine was discarding its passenger onto the sidewalk. John recognized the ambassador, Robin Hood from Halloween, remembered her hands tightening the laces of his Lincoln-green jerkin. "Sh-sh-sh-she's on leave, son," he stuttered at John's sudden sidewalk question as machine-gun-toting Hungarian police circled them, facing outward for potential attackers, a cocoon of blue-vinyl backs providing sudden and disorienting outdoor privacy for their impromptu interview. "Where did she go?" John demanded. "Y-y-you sound like the French am-am-ambassador's wife. 'Whe-whe-where is zee lovely Emilie, *hein?* We are weeshing to make a deen-air of 'er?' But, son, as I t-t-told Madame Le-Le-Le-Le, leaves are pri-private matters." Cued by signals too subtle for John to notice, the shell of policemen opened at one end and the ambassador was absorbed into his building. John watched the black wrought-iron trellis shut as the diplomat graciously acknowledged Old Péter's creaky but formal bow. The police melted away into slim booths and around corners. The Andean band was somewhere close by, guitars and pipes, mountains and condors, love and vengeance, cassettes for sale.

The doorbell rang, was ringing, had been ringing, would soon stop ringing—a spray of verb tenses showered his sleep until he stumbled blearily to the door. "Dummy, don't you have an alarm clock?" Charles was dressed in sneakers, torn jeans, and a T-shirt of a rock band long out of fashion. "Wake up, dude. You can sleep in the van and smash it on your way home. Not my problem at that point."

The orange van, MEDIAN HUNGARIA painted in black on its flanks, held Charles's possessions in its belly. Charles drove, hunched forward, his chin on his knuckles on the wheel as the radio crackled in and out of AM range. "You seem triumphant," John said as they merged onto a highway indistinguishable from the highways of Ohio, California, Ontario, Nebraska.

"I only seem that way because I'm triumphant."

Charles was the first person whose elevation to minor celebrity John had ever witnessed (or helped effect). The young powerhouse who made his name in the Wild East was going home to a plum job with some New York VC firm or investment bank or hedge fund or something, some financial nonsense the details of which John could not trouble himself to bring into focus. Charles was hailed as the only hero-survivor of his old firm's fast and self-inflicted decline, even in articles John hadn't written, planted, or inspired. And now he was returning to his world, via Zurich, like a Crusader (a white crucifix on a tail fin gules) back from a conquered Holy Land, coming to reassure his people that their Gospel is true and powerful, the Red devils convert with ease. "Did you see Imre to say good-bye?"

"Yes, Mom, I said good-bye. You know, his vaunted 'communication skills' "—Charles released the wheel to provide visual quotation marks, and the van veered into the slow lane—"are greatly overstated. I mean, I asked him, 'Imre, is it not true that, barring great fluctuations in the value of the forint— and interrupt me if that seems more or less likely to you than I'm assuming— then the value of the press's Viennese holdings in relation to its Hungarian holdings will only steadily rise over time, even assuming Hungary were accepted into the European Union in the next ten years, or not?' And, John, he blinked twice, which I'm told means yes."

The last of Pest's buildings approached, passed, ceded the field to the steady hum of power lines and fences interrupted by eager emerald signs, each correcting its predecessor as to how far away the airport lurked.

"Will you miss Budapest, considering your big triumph here?"

"No."

"No, really. Will you?"

"Really? No."

"Charles, please. Aren't you sad to leave? You must have some feelings about, about . . ." John trailed off, and Charles honked and eloquently condemned another driver's crimes.

"I have to admit to being a little disappointed in you, JP. When I met you, I had high hopes for you, but listen to you now. You've allowed yourself to become one of those boring little beggars who goes around pleading with people to share their feelings. You're a horrible little feeling-beggar, rattling your can. The world does not need more discussion of our feelings. That's not a good route; it doesn't work. Trust me. I've looked into this. I've given this some *very* concerted thought. The people who talk about their feelings are miserable. I'm not for repression, but really, you can't possibly take feelings seriously. Trust me, this is the best advice I can offer you as your friend." He tapped the wheel pensively in rhythm with the British pop pushing through the AM static. "You're very much like me, you know, as much like me as anyone I've met in Hun country. Just without the focus and, and the willingness to pay certain prices. And the charisma, obviously. The fact is—and this is *science*, John—the *less* you talk about them, the less you even notice them, until finally, you can become a real human being and not some ball of *feelings* bouncing up and down all day staring at your own ass." He looked over to John, and the van veered to the right. "But fine, my little beggar, fine, here they are then, my handsome feelings: I hates it here, I hates this filthy li'l town, I hates the Hungarians, chum, and all their shitty little half-baked corruptions and lazinesses and this attitude they teach their kids from birth that the world owes them salvation, because history has beat up on them so bad and they are always betrayed and all the rest of it. The whininess of these people just kills me. Hungarians are—to the last man—a pack of—"

"*You're* Hungarian. You. Are. Hungarian."

"That's not very nice, John. After I just tried to help you."

John remained strapped to the van when they pulled into the Swiss-air cargo area, and Charles bounded out to begin his special brand of labor negotiations: He placed ten-dollar bill after ten-dollar bill into one of the aproned handlers' open palms, sternly instructing as he paid. After a sufficient amount of cash filled the worker's hand (the man even moved it up and down as if gauging the weight), all other work in the area was temporarily abandoned; the full team of four beefy luggage men (in scarlet aprons with white crosses on their chests) cracked open the van and gently cradled Charles's possessions onto a wheeled cart. Labels were lovingly affixed and paperwork quickly processed. Handshakes all around. A few more Hamiltons.

"You know what I *will* look back on fondly?" Charles asked as the orange van, much lighter now, squealed a U-turn and galloped down the frontage road to the passenger terminal. "Because you're right. I *will* have one lasting memory of my time here. A memory that encompasses, oh, everything for me—my personal experiences, but also a symbolic meaning, what this country was going through while I was here. Even more, a picture of a whole era for my generation. The moment that summed up all of this"—his hands gestured grandly, vaguely—"what I will tell my children about, if I can do it justice. I mean, I know I'm not a great communicator. I'm just a businessman. But do you know what that moment was for me, John? It's funny—to see it happen and to know that this is *the* moment you will hold dear, in your heart, forever. Do you know what it was for me? It was when those two incredibly ugly girls were catfighting over you. I'd never seen ugly women fight before. It was refreshing."

John twisted the radio knob in a vain hunt for a clear signal. An Austrian DJ's voice cut through the fog, talking over a song. Charles tapped the steering wheel in rhythm as the van slowed and took its purring place in line. "I was considering not telling my parents I was moving back to New York. I was thinking about paying you to write them letters from me here, telling them how much I love it. That I'd decided to apply for citizenship. Marry a nice Hun girl.

Settle into my dad's childhood apartment up in the First. Send them fake pictures your bald friend could do of me and my Hun children picnicking on Margaret Island. All the while I'd really be home, lined up at Zabar's like a normal person. Unfortunately, you made me famous and so now they're going to sit on my couch and go on about all the glories of 1938 Budapest." He drove a few feet, took the parking ticket, stuffed it behind the sun visor. He laughed oddly, sadly. "Did I ever tell you I was their second child? I was born after they had a boy who died. Mátyás. He was four when he died of leukemia, which is a long and hideous thing. There are still pictures of him all over the house. I grew up with that. I always felt like, I don't know . . . like I was expected to . . ." Charles sucked his lip and pulled into the short-term parking lot, between two Trabants. He sat still, stared out the windshield.

"You're lying," John said.

"Yeah well, true. But still." They walked toward the terminal. "I was a twin, though, and the other one, a boy, was stillborn—that *is* true."

"No, it's not."

"No, I guess it's not."

Advertising posters papered the terminal walls: for consulting firms, accounting firms, public relations firms, computer networking firms, bilingual temporary placement firms, German condoms. The public address poured Hungarian onto comprehending and uncomprehending heads alike. The two Americans slouched in plastic seats. Charles's boarding card flapped like a feathered tail from the back pouch of an extravagantly made black leather monogrammed briefcase (a sly sign that one shouldn't judge the passenger in his T-shirt and jeans too soon). They swirled their espresso in Styrofoam cups, and Charles offered pensively, "You know, a case could be made that Imre got the best of this deal."

"Naturally. In that he's almost entirely paralyzed."

"Funny, but no. There are those who would say he got more than he deserved."

"What does that mean?"

"Oh nothing. Forget it. I don't agree with that old implication—slur—anyhow, so I shouldn't spread it. He's a good man, our Imre. He is. And he gave me a great opportunity. I'm glad I was able to make something of it, for both of us. And for my investors."

"Is this what he wanted?" John asked quietly, only slightly embarrassed.

"To have a stroke? Yeah, I think so."

"Is this what he wanted?"

"You *do* understand he was the biggest shareholder, don't you? I made him more money than he'd ever imagined. I made Imre Horváth a multimillionaire after he couldn't even run his own company. You do understand that, don't you?"

Out of earshot, Charles said something that made the Swissair hostess laugh before taking his ticket. He turned and sort of waved to John, a gesture that pointed out the silliness of waving farewell at airports. He stepped into the little wooden tunnel that led to New York. And he was gone. There were no windows to watch the plane taxi or take off. The whole thing could have been a hastily constructed soundstage. John shuffled outside, past the surly taxi ranks, paid for parking with the cash Charles had stuffed in his hand prior to boarding. *Is that all? Is that how an era ends?*

He pulled off the frontage road and saw Charles walk again to the boarding tunnel, again offer his pass to the pretty Swiss stewardess at the gate, but this time John adds sense and proper closure: There is a noise, a booming rupture in the firmament, the frustration of a deity who will not tolerate events to fizzle out without meaning. And Krisztina Toldy—a glowing, pulsing, sexless archangel of retribution—screams his name, just his family name, as if she invokes with it all his ancestors, his nation, his Danube tribe: *Gábor!* He turns in the midst of priority boarding. His left hand holds his monogrammed black briefcase; his right hand holds one end of his boarding envelope. Out of its other end the stewardess is withdrawing his boarding pass, but now that stewardess is propelled backward against the dirty wooden door of the boarding gate, and her white, ruffled blouse is rapidly blossoming red, like the outline of a cartoon rose deftly filled in by an animator. As her head strikes the door, her pillbox hat falls over her eyes. The hat props comically against her nose as her convulsing form slumps to the floor, and the breasts that John was just admiring heave with a strange and shallow stuttering. Again the cracking, ripping blast of an angry God, again the smashing-glass sound of his name shrieked by the blood-gargling harpy, and now Charles's T-shirt spreads red at the shoulder, the phallic tip of a guitar obliterated in the process, and at last a pure and unironic emotion flashes on the face of Charles Gábor, witnessed by dozens. People scream and hide under plastic seats, will remember forever the internal-organ look of the dried old gum they saw in that moment when reality burst through the artifice and irrelevance of every day and everything. The remains of Charles Gábor have no time to plead, to maneuver for position: The next shot tears the cheek from his face. He falls, and his last view in this life is of her standing above him. She fires twice into his neck, then, sobbing, turns the gun upon herself.

John pulled into the lot behind the Median warehouse, where Imre Horváth had swept the floor the evening of October 23, 1956. He waited for his song to finish playing on the radio, which he had finally coaxed into FM. He asked at the rolling door for Ferenc, an office assistant, and tossed him the keys. He took the subway home. He was strangely exhausted. Sleep would not wait another minute. His head bounced against the plastic seat back.

XI.

HE LAY ON HIS SOFA BED. A BREEZE DANCED WITH THE ILLUMINATED leaves outside, then with his thin curtain. Motors rattled the air. The remote control fit perfectly, ergonomically, into the line of his forearm and wrist, an extension of his will.

If he could explain to her in real time everything that had happened to him—every single feeling and misunderstood action and distorted, grotesquely misconstrued intention—then in the passion and tears and apologies that must certainly follow there would come at last their connection, and she would be his and there would be a we. *I walk all night long and think only of being us.* She would fall asleep in his arms after, and he would stroke the soft skin under her chin and the curving line of bone that made her jaw such a splendor. He would spread her hair out behind her on the blinding white and convex pillow. He would slowly parachute a billowing, cool sheet over her body, each of her limbs relaxed but perfectly straight, and her body would press against the shroud, outline itself in the merest hints. Rolled onto her side now: The line from the bottom of her rib cage to the top of her hip would curve through three dimensions like a living force, the dream line that haunted the troubled, unsatisfying sleeps of animators, automotive engineers, kitchen appliance designers, desperately lonely cellists.

Young American males, dressed in the style of five years earlier, spoke German to one another through awkward lips and were rewarded with overwhelming laughter. He recognized the American sitcom, popular when he had been in high school and college, now dubbed and redelivered to German cable.

He remembered with ease the characters' names: Mitch, Chuck, Jake, and Clam. The four men—now Fritz, Klaus, Jakob, and Klamm—wisecracked *auf Hochdeutsch* in a TriBeCa loft apartment, in a SoHo bar, in Kafkaesque offices in midtown Manhattan, in Brooklyn parks, until John recognized this very episode. He dimly remembered a couch in his freshman dormitory, remembered slouching with three slouching friends (one whose name escaped him entirely). They had watched this very episode. The four characters had made a bet, he recalled: The first of them to meet a girl and manipulate events so that she invited him to her apartment to prepare him a "good home-cooked meal" would win one hundred dollars from each of the other three.

Five years later, in German, John could hardly believe how dated the men's outfits and hairstyles appeared. Nineteen eighty-six had not been so long ago, but there—with their lips forming words entirely different from the ones coming from the television's speaker—they seemed as antique as hippies, greasers, G.I.s, flappers, doughboys, Edwardians, Elizabethans. He remembered the episode's last scene several minutes before it came on, remembered sitting on the couch with his three friends, enumerating and berating the show's absurdities and insults to their intelligence: The four defeated characters sat on their own sagging couch, watching their television, glumly but wittily mocking an overdrawn romantic film from the 1930s in which a woman prepares her average-Joe beau a good home-cooked meal.

John held his thumb to the appropriate rubber pimple and the channels each flashed a frame or two for him in desperate pleas for attention—a race car changing la, a billiards ball ricocheting off the near bumpe, an occluded front moving in from the Atla, Hungar, ungari, Ger, erma, erman, Germa, Fren, in the execution of unconventional warf—until a series of electrical stimuli moving faster than thought pulled his thumb off the rubber pimple and four buxom, beautiful, blond German women moaned and pleasured a very fat middle-aged man with a shaggy horseshoe of greasy, gray hair and no clothes but a monocle.

The remote control escaped to the floor and he grew too occupied to retrieve it. His eyes narrowed and his thoughts disconnected as the blood evacuated his brain. A car stopped outside and honked to summon a passenger, and as its door opened, its stereo was so loud that even up three stories floated the sounds of that one song. The four women courteously and efficiently took turns and John imagined himself in their midst, imagined their faces under their blond hair, the faces of Emily Oliver and Nicky M, of Karen Whitley and the speed skater and the two girls who had thought he was a movie star, and—his thoughts slithered free of all censorship—even old Nádja and Krisztina Toldy; and synapses buzzed and even Charles Gábor's face appeared for a moment before it was replaced by another Emily Oliver and another, four times over, from every direction, equipped with extra arms and hands, four heads and faces, a hydra of Emily, who smiled and snarled upon him from every direction and serviced him in ways that no earth gravity would ever allow.

Breathing slowed, and the photographs of his wife and child sat in their accustomed places . . . *gotta remember to bring those.* He fell asleep as the car and its radio faded down Andrássy, and (one last feeble thumb exertion) the television murmured weather reports from around the world, as he had lately found it difficult to sleep without the sound of subdued broadcasting in the room. He dreamed, he woke and flipped channels and dozed again and woke again and dozed again and back and forth. Charles Gábor was on TV, submitting suavely to interrogation. He and the interviewer sat in revolving leather chairs under a dangling, illuminated sign: MONEY TALKS. The interviewer asked easy questions disguised as aggressive questions: "For a fellow who seems to *me* young enough to still be fascinated with *shaving,* how did you *accomplish* this feat, Charlie?"

XII.

HIS LIMITED LUGGAGE STOWS WITH SATISFYING SYMMETRY AND FLUSH edges, like toy baggage built especially for the form-fitting overhead bin of a toy train. He sits at the open window and gazes at the platform, that very word redolent of possibility, potential.

The station platform, where arrivals and departures change everything and . . . Who might come to see me off? Oh . . . Still, something thrilling about . . . The giant skeleton key will be a great conversation piece there, if they don't use the same sort. On the cobbled streets, with my group, or my head on a pillow with just the right face facing . . . Is that her come to, did she find out, relent, track me— Well, the same hair, sort of. *Look at this, this was the key to my* . . . Platform. Like the beginning of some movie: the young man at the train station, about to head off for who knows what, places unknown, leaving just in time . . .

The train stutters forward, and his heart with it. His heart lunges far out along the kilometers of track, far faster than the train itself, over borders, to new lives, reaches nearly to its goal, but is snapped elastically back. Just clear of the station's roof, the buildings that flank the tracks on either side, like canal-front properties, glide by, accelerate in uneven bumps of speed. Through May-first fog, he leaves the city behind him; he faces the way he is going—not what he's leaving—ready for whatever, whoever, might come.

Countryside of green and the occasional factory, farmhouse, hut, eviscerated hillside (green frosting on gray cake) with immobile cranes and abandoned trucks, the magic seductress dance of undulating black lines in the window.

That poor old man, a work of art, to live a work of . . . It's all a game, remember, and the winners are those who can tell serious from not. It isn't, after all, war, tyranny, poverty, torture, Nazis, or Soviets. Not really fatal, after all, just a digestive disorder, avoid certain foods, not as if he didn't become a multi-millionaire, I do understand that. Just keep clear on what's serious and . . . These things that happened are not really . . . they're just . . .

The outskirts are the worst. For hours seated in one position, you feel—deliciously—nothing. You are free of past and future, you float in amniotic potential, but then the outskirts and the last twenty minutes stretch out forever, grow immense, relentlessly block your increasingly urgent arrival.

Life will start there, at the end of this ride. I will step off the train onto the platform. But there it will be Europe for real, untouched by war; no reconstructed "old towns" for the benefit of self-deluding tourists. Honesty in everything. And that honesty attracts a different type. There I'll find the people who . . . I spent a birthday in Budapest. No, can that be right? Did I not notice? I arrived last year in May, today is May, so what did I do for it? Doesn't matter. This year will be different, surrounded by seriousness. Real life awaits, birthdays, a redem . . .

The train circles and circles. After crossing all this globe in a speeding straight line, suddenly the train slows and spirals in imperceptibly smaller circles around his destination, and he imagines being condemned to wander forever the interminable outskirts, a gray limbo of almost-thereness. The train continues its bank through dismal suburbs, the destination still invisible; it hides somehow just inside the endless spiral, postpones the moment. He dozes.

The temperature of the window against his cheek changes, turns suddenly hot. He awakens, and there she is at last, with one half of his own transparent, wet face faintly superimposed upon her like a watermark. There she is, though still far away, strangely far for all the agonizing minutes burned in approach. She is entirely contained, a single image exposed in a moment's glance: a land of spires and toy palaces and golden painted gates and bridges with sad-eyed statues peering out over misty black water, a village of cobblestones and stained glass unlicked by cannon, and that fairy-tale castle floating above it, hovering unanchored by anything at all, a city where surely anything will be possible.

ACKNOWLEDGMENTS

Prague would be significantly less coherent (and probably not even bound) without the good work or good works of superstar editor Lee Boudreaux, Tony Denninger, Phebe Hanson, Erwin Kelen, Peter Magyar, Mike Mattison, ASP, DSP, FMP, MMP, incomparable agent Marly Rusoff, Toby Tompkins, *Budapest 1900,* by John Lukacs, and, of course, Jan.

ABOUT THE AUTHOR

ARTHUR PHILLIPS was born in Minneapolis and educated at Harvard. He has been a child actor, a jazz musician, a speech-writer, a dismally failed entrepreneur, and a five-time *Jeopardy!* champion. He lived in Budapest from 1990 to 1992, and now lives in Paris with his wife and son.

ABOUT THE TYPE

This book was set in Photina, a typeface designed by José Mendoza in 1971. It is a very elegant design with high legibility, and its close character fit has made it a popular choice for use in quality magazines and art gallery publications.